# THE AMBER CROW

## A Pacific Northwest
## MURDER MYSTERY

## by L. C. Mcgee

TwoNewfs Publishing
Values in fiction from Pacific Northwest Authors
Seattle, WA

The Amber Crow is a work of fiction. Names, characters, places, and incidents are the products of the author's imagination or are used fictitiously. Any resemblance to actual events, locales, or persons, living or dead, is entirely coincidental.

Copyright © 2014 by L. C. Mcgee
eBook Copyright © 2013 by L. C. Mcgee

Library of Congress Control Number: 2014942097
ISBN 9781499134209

About the crow:
It is a black crow. His name is Zondi. He represents the father of the amber crow;
diving down to save his crow-mate, Flick, and their fledgling sons from two hungry coyotes.
Our crow is adapted from an illustration by Boris Artzybasheff, Crow & Canary. Published by
E.P. Dutton, NY, 1922 (Verotchka's Tales) [Public domain], via Wikimedia Commons.

Cover design by Kate and Charles Thompson
Book design by Charles Thompson
Cover photo: Goose Rock Trail by Ricardo Martins via Wikimedia Commons

TwoNewfs Publishing, Seattle, WA
www.TwoNewfs.com

# *Dedication*

*This book was written*

*to honor the memories of*

**Thom and Edgar**

*blazers of indelible trails*

*through this firmament of absurdity*

*called life.*

HAVE A good life

*[signature]*

# *Acknowledgements*

These scribblings would not be the least intelligible if it weren't for the following wonderful people.

1. To my wife Roberta who read the first draft and ran screaming into the night.

2. To my daughter-in-law Gayle, a brilliant and lovely woman, who can wield an editing pen as if it were the scalpel of a skilled surgeon.

3. To my tolerant and indulgent friends Chuck, David, and Vern who did serious editing too, and were actually rather pleasant about the entire ordeal.

4. To members of the writers group, 5 Northwest Authors, Charlie, Kate, Gwen and Cathy who help me to become a better writer; amazingly, they're still my friends.

5. And lastly to Cathy Ruiz, teacher extraordinaire, writer, poet and seeker of the light. She is the creative core around which the 5NW Authors grew and spun their ideas and stories. Punctuation, word usage, sentence structure, ARGH! She kept me on my feet with encouragement and perceptive suggestions regarding the elements involved in writing short stories and the novel. I am grateful and indebted to her.

For me, encumbered with dandruff, dyslexia, ADD and whatever else, it has become a marvelous journey. Luckily, this assemblage of fiction writers has opened up a deep world of fascinating friends, ideas and great fun.

All mistakes are my own, who else's would they be?

L. C. Mcgee

# *Warning*

**Eric Templeton's shoes were soaked.** Though the heavy fog lifted an hour earlier the path up to the cliff was lined with wet underbrush. He paused to savor the aroma of fir boughs and the faint mossy-scent of the forest floor. Far below, the morning sun flashed off the waters of Scoon Bay. On the opposite shore, called Heron's Hook, drifts of water vapor twisted through the trees; ghosts reluctant to let go of the night.

He looked at his watch. Curious, Janet was late. Not like her. He shrugged. Her cell-phone message had sounded peculiar. "We should meet early. I've got lots to tell you. Come to our special place. I'll be there at 8:00 a.m." She sounded weary, not herself. Possibly, it was the bad connection, but it was a good idea. They could relax alone, and she'd no doubt bring a thermos of her excellent coffee. Too, at this early hour, the view from the bluff was unsurpassable.

He shook beads of water from his pant legs, placed his field jacket to cover a spot on their favorite log then stretched and sat down. He plucked the top out of a young sword fern and chewed it. The fuzzy almond flavor burst on his tongue.

Across the narrow bay, the sun outlined the forest that clung to the dragon back ridge of Heron's Hook. From his perch on the high cliff, one could make out the spreading shapes of ancient broadleaf maples, madrone and alder. During hikes, Eric discovered it wasn't entirely leafy trees that grew there. Large Western hemlocks, Douglas fir and cedars intermingled with the deciduous. Logging companies were salivating to 'harvest' this valuable second growth. After the first cutting, over one hundred years ago, the Hook had gone largely untouched. Eric smiled. Now, if Janet and he had their way...

Something dark moved at the edge of his vision. Eric turned. A large bird settled quietly on a branch to his left. He shaded his eyes. The bird was remarkable, not only in its size, but in the dark amber feathers of its body. Three pure white ones accentuated the tips of each wing. He kept very still. There were many birds on Bradestone Island, but nothing like this. Mustn't startle the creature, he thought. But, as if it sensed his presence, the bird squawked a sound of alarm. Urgently beating its wings it flew over his head and plummeted down the side of the cliff; its frantic caws echoed over the bay below.

Eric was astonished. It was an amber-feathered crow! He couldn't wait to tell her. It must be a genetic fluke; she would be as excited as he was. Maybe the strange creature would return before she got here. He rubbed his hands and again glanced at his watch. Shouldn't worry; obviously something important delayed her. He took a deep breath. Recently they'd been meeting here, at his sanctuary, his place to reflect and meditate. She should have been here to see the magnificent bird with him.

Shaking his head he reflected on her message. It was damn peculiar. She said she'd found something, something in the changes that they'd made to the La Grange plans.

What changes? They couldn't be too significant. Over a month ago she'd assured him that everything was complete and in order. And he had checked the documents thoroughly. It had been an arduous task, and she needed a vacation. He smiled, it was mutual. The intricacy of their work and the consequent romantic involvement had become intense. He'd thought it prudent that he remain on the Island and she go off to New York to stay with her friends. It was evident from postcards and the few phone calls, that she was having a marvelous time. To his surprise, and delight she extended her stay one more week. And then, on a whim, decided to go off to France to visit close friends who had moved there recently. It would be just for another week she'd assured him and then she would be back on the island. He chuckled. He admired her spontaneity and quick decision making. She was clever and that's what first attracted him to her.

The island rumor that she'd run off to marry her close friend Martin, was laughable. Well, maybe not too laughable. After all Martin was only five years older than Janet. Eric, being fifteen years older in comparison, felt a little stodgy at times. He'd wished her the best, and fortunately lost himself in his work.

Janet's postcards updated him on where she was going and what she was doing. But the call last night was still vaguely disturbing. Before she'd hastily rung off he managed to find out she was staying at the Sheraton in Seattle. He expressed anxiety about her health, as she sounded hoarse and confused. She reassured him it was a combination of jet lag and a nasty virus she'd picked up in Paris.

Briefly she had mentioned that a few minor difficulties remained in finalizing the land trust agreement and the related Indian Heritage Center. Oddly she had said it was 'the only right thing to do'. He frowned. Difficulties he could understand, but the right thing to do? What did she mean? Most of the contractual safeguards were in place. True, the water rights were still pending, but Bradestone Island's Nature Conservation Committee had already okayed the sewer lines. And Caen and Justice had shown him that any problems that remained were insignificant and could easily be resolved. Ah progress, he could hear the backhoe rumbling in the distance.

He placed his hands behind him on the log, leaned back slightly and shook his head. Why had she sounded so upset? Where was her self-assurance? It surprised him that she'd been working on the plans;

their mutual agreement was to take a complete break from the project. Oh well, a little tidying around the edges was always needed. It would soon be over.

A branch snapped, there was a whooshing sound and something heavy slammed into the back of Eric's head.

A flock of gulls screamed from the rocky beach below then wheeled into the sky. Stillness reigned in the forest. Only the sounds from the distant backhoe marred the silence.

CHAPTER 1

# *Beginnings*

**Rose Bracken's shoulders drooped** as she squinted from her office window. Business was terrible and it was another dripping, gray day in the Northwest. She reached over and flipped on the switch to the outdoor sign: "William's & Bracken Realtors, a Step Up to the best Homes on Bradestone Island". The feeble, reddish message was reflected in the parking lot lake. For Rose, a congenital optimist, the sign was a bait-beacon adrift in the mist. It beckoned during the long wet months of winter twilight. Soon a tourist or visitor from the mainland would strike. They had to.

But the weather wasn't cooperating. Any glimmer of spring shyly fled back into winter. TV weather forecasts alternated between rain, light rain, showers, heavy showers, intermittent showers and then back to heavy rain.

 Power outages were frequent. Many Islanders, who could, retreated to their fireplaces. They armed themselves with their ever-present emergency lanterns and stacks of books. A lucky few had gas-powered generators and thusly computer usage. Already the wealthy had fled to their condos in Hawaii, the Southwest, or other homes in sunnier climes. The newcomers to the Island gave up hope that spring would ever arrive.

Puget Sound news didn't help either. The papers were rife with panicky reports of roof-ripping storms, two-week blackouts, impassable roads, and canceled ferry service. Nothing of a dire nature went unnoticed; from docks washed away, to houses knocked off foundations by mudslides. Disaster screamed from the front pages.

But yesterday had deceived all: a teasing promise with the first breath of warm zephyrs and glorious sunshine. Rose frowned, today the goddamn waterworks. Why couldn't it be like California? When she'd moved from the sunny south, four years ago, her new friend, Raymond Toda, 'My friends' call me Toady,' warned her, "Northwesterners don't tan, they rust." At the time she'd found it marvelously funny, but not anymore.

Rose rubbed her chilled hands. Damn that small office heater, it hadn't been groaning long enough to drive out the damp. I should have turned it on first thing, she thought then smiled. The warm months would arrive, business would certainly pick up.

"Like right now," Rose muttered as a small red sports car pulled up beneath her Realtor's sign. Her hands fell into prayer position. She'd misplaced her glasses and stared myopically out the window. It appeared to be a woman driver. And was that a man in the passenger's seat? Immediately she turned to fire up the coffee urn. Her spirits improved by the minute. Maybe spring had arrived, finally.

Kay Roberts switched off the ignition, put the gearshift into first and pulled hard on the handbrake. Why do I always put it in first? This parking lot is flat. The car really can't roll anywhere.

"I'm a belts and suspenders person, like my father," she mused aloud then glanced over at Alex. He hadn't heard. Head back, and snoring softly, his rugged facial features relaxed, he was fast asleep in the passenger seat. Poor Alex, no wonder he was exhausted.

After he found an excellent accountant and put in weeks settling his brother's estate he'd called her and said he would be heading for

Seattle on Monday. During some very amorous suggestions over the phone he detected a hesitant and concerned undertone in her voice. He then prized out of her that three days had passed since she'd heard from her Aunt Olive and the kids. She'd left many messages on Olive's answering machine with no returned calls. And it also seemed that everyone had turned their cell phones off.

He quietly listened to her concerns about Aunt Olive's camping trip with Kay's wandering wonders and said 'no problemo.' He'd change his direct flight plans from Chicago to Seattle and reroute to Sedona to check out the territory. After all it would be a pleasant and much needed diversion. She was grateful.

Good old phlegmatic Alex. In the two years she'd known him, major changes in his life were akin to the swiveling of a weather vane. Nothing seemed to upset him. At times it exasperated her, but overall his rational detachment was stabilizing.

Kay pulled off her headscarf, shook loose her auburn hair, and reached for the brush on the dash. She stroked through the long wind-whipped strands. She made several last adjustment pats, critically eyed the results in the rear-view mirror then glanced at Alex.

The other day she hadn't meant to sound anxious on the phone, but they both agreed it was unusual not to hear from Aunt Olive or her kids. The last call was after Teri and Byron had landed at the airport and complained there was no Aunt Olive to pick them up. Her 21-year old Teri, at times the most dramatic, said they were, "stranded." Kay rolled her eyes. How unpleasant could it be, stranded in Sedona? When the phone was passed to Byron, he replied in his cool, 18-year old manner: "Not to worry. We've got time to burn anyway. If Aunt Olive doesn't turn up we'll call a cab…we were just wondering what our old mom is up to." Old mom indeed!

Kay smiled. They teased when she referred to them as kids, but to her they always would be. Her son, Byron had laid an impressive campaign to get out of spring quarter and then Teri, not to be outdone, pleaded: "I need a break too. I'm in the final stretch for my B.A. in Anthro, I only have a few credits to mop up and my advisor assured me that I could easily finish those during summer quarter."

The morning after Alex arrived in Sedona he called Kay and told her it was a tired but happy threesome that greeted him at the door. Of course, Aunt Olive fumed about Kay's concerns and explained that they'd taken a spur of the moment camping trip; with the conditions being, no interruptions from the outside world. And by the way, she would immediately call and inform her nosey niece that they we're taking off again tomorrow to visit the Lowell observatory, including a jaunt to the meteor crater, and yes she was sorry, and avowed to keep in better contact.

Alex squirmed in the small seat. Was this the man she was going to marry? She loved him, but after Frank's death in a climbing accident and the hardships that followed, she wasn't sure she wanted to try the official marriage state again. Alone, she'd raised two children, put one through college and made a success of her livelihood. Sure Aunt Olive offered to help, but Kay never wanted to owe anything to anyone.

"Here already?" Alex asked yawning and reached over and tousled her hair.

"Thanks a lot big fella. I just combed this mess. God, what a fresh air fiend you are, the ferry deck was a Mix-Master." She cupped his unshaven chin, kissed him passionately then drew back. "But I loved it anyway." His tanned face had been warm and sleepy but now, his dark brown eyes were arched in surprise.

"What's that all about?" He asked with a grin and lazily reached for her.

"Oh, for being here and being with you..." Then her eyebrows joined in a frown; her green eyes flashed. "Do you think we're crazy?

Going in on a house together? Isn't it a bit... much, and too soon?" She hated the fact that her voice suddenly sounded panicky.

Alex studied her seriously then pulled her closer. "No, I don't. With our combined finances we can handle whatever comes our way. And the kids need a home, not an apartment. We've churned this over before, but," he sighed resignedly, "we can always do this at another time." Her heart lurched as he gazed into her eyes, his voice soft and husky. "I don't want you to do anything you're not comfortable with. It's your decision."

Kay punched his well-muscled arm. "No. You're right. We've covered all the pros and cons before." She stuck out her chin. "We'll take the Minotaur by the horns, as Teri would say. Besides, look." She nodded as a woman peered intently from the Realtor's office window. "I'd say we're expected; if not being drooled over." Kay pushed open the car door. "My, my, it's stopped raining. That's a good omen and there's another one, look." Kay pointed to a thinly veiled sun. "A strange object is suffering in the sky."

Rose Bracken, an eager smile on her lips, managed the Queen's wave.

## CHAPTER 2

# *Hooked*

**The auburn haired woman** put her arm through the man's and nodded to Rose in the window. She moves as graceful as a ballet dancer, Rose noted glumly. And the man was quite tall. Rose stretched the corner of her eye to adjust her nearsightedness; definitely handsome in a rugged sort of way. Both were laughing, enjoying some private joke. The woman seemed to be the liveliest of the pair. "But he looks quite tractable," Rose said aloud and massaged the corner of her eye.

She put on her most charming smile and nodded from the window. Fortunately they hadn't headed toward her competitor, 'Templeton's Superior Island Realty and Development Company'.

Real estate prices had gone through the roof in Seattle. But it hadn't happened yet on Bradestone. Things were slow on the island. The weather didn't help and neither did the long ferry commute. Knowledgeable buyers were not enamored of the sporadic storm-related power outages, erratic ferry service, and perennially rising fares. Tactfully, Rose avoided mentioning those problems to potentials. Mentally, she reviewed her most current listings.

The aroma of fresh-brewed coffee wafted through the office. Rose found it necessary to purchase a latte machine after moving up from California. It boosted her morale, if not her business, and coffee in the Northwest was akin to life's blood. Now if she'd only thought to bring berry squares to warm in the microwave.

Rose returned to her desk, took two more cups down from the shelf then promptly opened a large three-ring binder. She grumbled and shook her head. The computers were on the fritz, again. The heavy book was her backup today. Then she panicked. Oh no, where had she put her purse?

She was still groping for a tube of lipstick when the door opened.

"This is the agency, Beryl suggested," the woman said firmly as the couple entered the office. She nodded at Rose.

"Well, hello there. Can I get either one of you a latte?" Damn! Their faces were still blurred. I've got to find those blasted glasses, Rose thought as she set aside the bulging ring-binder.

"Why yes. Thank you." Kay said with a shiver and rubbed her hands together.

"Make it two, please." The man requested in a deep baritone. "It was colder on the ferry than we expected."

Rose busied herself at the coffee machine. Pleasant hissing sounds issued forth as she prepared the drinks and steamed the milk.

"April is a crazy month in the Northwest; hot one day and cold the next. Sugar anyone?" Rose continued to babble on as she glanced out the window. "It looks like it's trying to clear up. Are you both new to the Island?" She paused in her preparations and extended her hand. "Oh, sorry, by the way my name's Rose Bracken."

"I'm Kay Roberts and this is my fiancé Alex Beahzhi."

Kay's handshake was firm and efficient; his strong and engulfing.

In closer proximity Rose approved of Alex's face. His nose appeared to have been broken at one time, which made him look stubborn, particularly with his prominent chin. But curly gray-black hair and a wide flirting curl to his lips softened the effect. She blinked her eyes and grinned. The day was definitely looking much brighter.

With his free hand Alex made a sweeping gesture toward the window. "You're lucky to live on this beautiful island. After the view from the ferry," he reached over and massaged Kay's shoulder, "we think this might be a great place to pull in our horns, put up our feet, and rest a spell." He winked at Kay who smiled up at him and continued with the ersatz western palaver.

"Sho nuff pardnor, we're itchin to get a fur piece from that there mainland-madness called snivilization." They laughed at some private joke.

Rose chuckled indulgently, obviously a close couple who enjoyed teasing, not to mention irritating asides. Rose countered with a professional and confidential tone.

"Well, this is definitely the island for it. Bradestone, some say, is almost pastoral." Wisely, she neglected to mention the weekend tourists, summer rock concerts, trouble making teen-agers and the Templeton's new and noisy helicopter pad.

Rose gestured toward the window with her coffee cup and assumed the gravitas of a person who had lived on the island for years. "We Islanders keep a pretty tight control on development. We were particularly concerned about the arrival of *that* business across the street. But at the moment it appears that Mr. Eric Templeton, my only competitor by the way, is more of a conservationist than a developer."

Alex nodded at the large reader-board on the opposite side of the road. "Your Mr. Templeton may profess that, but the word 'development' usually implies a more devious and destructive occupation."

Rose shrugged. "At first we all thought that. But Mr. Templeton, the sole owner and a fine gentleman I might add, wasted no time in joining our local planning board. So far the older farms and undeveloped land that his company purchased are set-asides to remain under the auspices of the Bradestone Island Nature Conservation Committee. He's a very active member; it's a local program that we're all quite proud of."

"Aha, maybe he's doing some manipulations behind the scenes and will have to yield to 'external pressures' to sell at a later date. Just a thought," Alex said then asked. "Does he live on the island?"

Rose looked uncomfortable. "He maintains a complete house here, with staff. His other residence is in Seattle." Rose took a long sip of her coffee. "The family commutes by helicopter. His sister is in charge of the island residence," she murmured over her cup.

"Ah, the acute stress of being rich," Kay said, then eyed the book of listings on the desk. "We're actually interested in buying a house." She looked up at Alex. "He would like a place with a view, if it could be worked into our budget."

Alex laughed. "I've changed my mind. The necessity of a view has been dropped from my priority list. There's beautiful scenery everywhere. However, I'd like to find a house with a porch where I can kick back in my rocking chair, trusty Irish setter by my side and pipe at hand. Once settled in, I'll light up and contemplate writing the memoirs of my former life as a wastrel." He took a sip of his latte, and managed an angelic look of innocence.

Kay winked at Rose. "These retired silver-backs are a royal pain. As they mature they become more romantic. The only setter he has is the one he sits on, and it's not Irish it's Italian. He doesn't smoke either." She smiled. "But I do hope you have a derelict fixer-upper, preferably surrounded by a large forest that needs selective logging. You know; something to keep the old man busy and out of trouble in his retirement."

Rose nervously fingered her coffee cup. She wasn't too sure about this couple. "Retired? Why you don't look old enough," she offered brightly. Alex and Kay burst out laughing.

Alex brushed at his eyes. "You're about the four-hundredth person that has said that. I loved my work, but twenty years was enough.

When I started teaching on automatic pilot it was fairer to all concerned that I make tracks, and soon."

Rose opened her ring binder. She said distractedly, "Oh? What did you teach?"

Alex shrugged and smiled apologetically. "Math and Astronomy at Tesla Community College in Portland, Oregon; the subjects aren't exactly a turn-on for most. In fact, the scariest thing to dress up as on Halloween is a math teacher."

Kay chuckled and put an arm around his waist, "I met 'scary' Alex when I had to fulfill required science credits." She looked up at him. "You were a skilled teacher and you made complicated things easy to understand and most of all, interesting. Yep, he made a major change in my life." She winked at Rose. "I like a guy with brains." She appeared to reconsider, "Not too many though."

"Um, yes...let me see." Rose's attention had wandered. "Currently it's a seller's market in Seattle. And Islanders are trying to keep their prices comparable with the mainland. But with the ferries and infrastructure the way it is." Whoops, she held her breath and waited for questions, but there were none so she continued, "So, we have a strong position to negotiate from, and..." Her voice trailed away as Alex leaned over her shoulder. He smelled of sandalwood.

Alex spoke in a stage whisper, "I have an ulterior motive Rose, like finding a place that one could easily turn into a bed and breakfast, and ... Oof!" He exclaimed as Kay punched him gently in the stomach.

"Alex can be such a bore...don't listen to him. He has grand ideas, but they're not very practical." She twirled a finger around her ear, "and an extreme case of hazy logic when it comes to running a B&B."

"I thought you said I had a few brains," he countered, dramatically clutching his stomach.

"Brains don't necessarily imply sense." She looked at him critically. "You know, those abs definitely need a work-out."

"Oh great guru that's easy for you to say," Alex cast Rose a wounded look. "Kay's the athlete of the family. She jogs three miles every other day and teaches Ashtanga Yoga in between."

Rose didn't know how to take these two, much less their teasing. Vaguely, she wondered about their living arrangements. Oh well, working with the public, you run across all types.

"Are there any specific needs, or living accommodations I should consider?" Rose queried.

"Actually there are," Kay paused while Rose visibly held her breath. "I have two children, and they're both in college. Byron is a freshman and Teri's a senior.  They will complain forever if they didn't have adequately sized rooms. I also need space, for an art studio." She gestured at Alex, "And he needs a large workroom for his projects."

"Maybe you should think about building." Rose said hastily. "There are many land parcels for sale." She reflected on those that were buildable, marginal, and downright unsafe. She was appalled when her partner sold the old Luyten's property. It had been slowly grinding its way toward the beach since the last century. What was it called? She remembered now, glacial creep. She rubbed her nose. "Recently, we've acquired several high bank properties. They may meet your needs."

Kay looked at Alex, who appeared to be engrossed in studying a flyspeck on the ceiling.

"I think building would be a little ambitious at this time," Kay said. Evidently Alex had resolved to dump the whole thing in her lap. His B&B idea was ridiculous. Neither one of them would know where to begin. It would be a lot of work, and where would they find time for their own pursuits?

Kay crossed her arms. "We would like the house to be not too large, three, maybe four bedrooms at the most. And if there were a view of the water that would be a plus... oh, and we definitely need land attached. We want to try our hand at organic gardening."

"Please do sit down," Rose said as she flipped open the binder. After they were settled in their chairs she turned the book toward them. "Here's a low bank location, on Clover passage, about an acre. And it has five bedrooms," she smiled, "also it's a great buy."

Alex eyed the photo. "Um, no, too many roof pitches. There are at least five. And look at the entry, what on earth is this...this type of house called?"

Rose sniffed. "I believe it is referred to as Bellevue French, it's quite popular on Seattle's eastside."

"Phony Phrench is more like it," Kay mumbled.

Rose stiffened and turned to another page. "Well...I do have this four acre estate. The house has only three bedrooms, but a lovely territorial view. And it's at the center of the island." She quickly suppressed the thought of the adjacent swamp, and an unpaved access road that became a quagmire in winter.

"Humph, that is aggressively Spanish," Alex commented. The house sported a tile roof, black-iron railings and a plethora of arching features and balconies.

Rose answered defensively. "Well, it has the most up-to-date kitchen features, a large and lavishly furnished entertainment room, with its own wet bar. It also has an eight car garage and an attached auto shop."

"That's fine if you're running a cab company," Kay remarked and slowly leaned forward to cup her chin. With her other hand she pulled the large book closer and slowly flipped through the information. "What's this?" She stabbed her finger at a page and turned the book to face Rose.

Rose squinted at a small grainy picture. Damn, where were her bifocals? She held the photo closer. "I didn't know *that* was still in this book. It's the old Petoskey place, been on and off the market over the years." She took a closer squint. "The Catholic church inherited it in the forties. At one time they were planning to build some kind of nunnery, or retreat there. Ah, now I remember. There was a problem with water rights and sewer line access." She fingered the page. "Someone, I don't remember who, told me it was a fire hazard and should be torn down." Rose's eyes lit up. "But there is potential. According to the property stats there's plenty of room for new construction."

Kay traced her slender fingers along the edge of the page; the old picture fascinated her.

Rose cleared her throat and chuckled. "I haven't been out there for a long time. But, if I remember correctly, you're looking at an ancient farmhouse with a verandah? Can you imagine having a verandah nowadays?"

Kay leaned back in her chair. "Actually I can," she replied absently then tugged at her lower lip. "Alex, take a look. We may have found your porch."

He moved closer. "Hmm, it does look...ah, interesting. How large are the bedrooms?" He glanced at the info. "I notice there are six mentioned here. And bathrooms upstairs and down?"

Rose removed the picture from the binder and handed it to Kay. "I have to confide in you. This is one property I haven't handled personally. My partner knows more about it than I do. As I said, there are problems. He must have stuck it back in the listings within the last week."

Kay cocked an inquiring eye, "How long have you lived on the island?"

Rose busily rearranged several items on her desktop. Crap, one of those nosy parkers. "Oh. I've been here over a good four years."

"Somehow I formed the impression that you've lived here for a long time," Kay said and handed the photo to Alex.

"Oh, it's because I've taken so quickly to island life." Rose blushed. "Why I already feel like I'm one of the natives. My partner purchased this business six years ago." She smiled mysteriously. "But I had to take care of a few personal obligations, so I wasn't able to get here right away." She took the picture of the Petoskey place back from Alex and gave a conspiratorial wink. "Most of my friends and acquaintances are new too. Many arrived only within the last ten years."

"There's some interesting information on the back," Alex said then looked thoughtfully at Kay.

"Oh yes, there's a note." The writing seemed so small Rose's nose almost touched the back of the photo. "It says there's a key taped inside the mailbox." She handed the picture to Kay and frowned. "That certainly isn't very secure."

Rose regarded their questioning faces then glanced at her watch. The sale would probably be a wash anyway, but anything was worth a try. "Look. I've an idea. If you want to see the place now I'll be glad to drive you there. However, I'm the only one in the office this week and I must to be back within the hour."

Kay and Alex stood up. Kay asked for a moment of privacy and pulled Alex aside.

Rose rearranged her desk blotter and the in and out boxes. It wouldn't hurt her to see what the property was like either, she mused as she strained to hear what the couple was saying. She could make out few words, then clearly heard an: "Okay, hope she goes for it..." before Alex turned and approached her.

His large brown eyes were mesmerizing. "Ms. Bracken, er Rose, we have a slight problem and you have a slight problem. But, I think there is a win-win solution here. When we took off from Seattle we weren't sure that we'd want to live on an island, nor purchase a place here. We were just tossing ideas around. But, since we've talked to you, we want to look over this particular house and explore it at leisure. Less than an hour wouldn't give us any time at all." He nodded towards Kay. "And she's really interested in this property." Alex's smile bordered on ingratiation. "What we're wondering, is if you can let us see the house by ourselves? We will bring the key back here, or leave it in the mailbox. That would save you a trip and give us plenty of time to look around." Rose paused, she did have a hair appointment this afternoon and they appeared trustworthy, but it would be quite irregular.

Alex took advantage of her indecision. "Look. We can leave our car rental papers with you as security. I'll even throw in my driver's license if you like." He glowered at Kay and rubbed his stomach. "I wouldn't mind being chauffeured. After that unprovoked attack on my person, I've been feeling considerably weaker."

It was a crazy idea, but they were leaving sufficient collateral. And a possible sale was looking a bit more promising. Why not? Rose smiled.

"I think what you suggest would be satisfactory and I'll put your papers and license in the safe. But be sure to be back before 5:00." She sat down at her desk. "I'll give you directions on how to get there." Rose selected a tattered map from the many in her side drawer. Ah, *there* were her glasses! She hastily put them on, took an orange magic-marker and highlighted a series of roads on the map. She then went back to the beginning of the line and unnecessarily wrote, 'you are here.'

Kay watched her intently and cleared her throat. "There is one more, er little thing. We, or I should say Alex, didn't make any arrangements for staying overnight." She paused. "I'm wondering if you might let us camp out at this place, tonight. We're used to camping and we do have sleeping bags in the car. We brought them, in case we got lost, or…" Her voice trailed off.

Rose blushed deeply. "That's probably not a good idea. There's a liability factor and the closest house is about an eighth of a mile up the road." She reflected. "Now that was a property that would have interested you. But I sold it to a very nice young Asian man last August, a Mr. Raymond Toda. If you buy the place he would be your next-door neighbor. "

Alex was not to be deterred, he leaned forward. "Rose, we're experienced campers and environmentally conscious. We know how to clean up after ourselves. This house could be just what we want. But, I'll need time to inspect the foundation, the roof and the surrounding grounds, essentially the integrity of the structure. And I'd like to do this without making an extra trip back to this island."

Rose considered their intense interest and their considerable security offer. She tapped the side of her glasses, reread the back of the photo, debated with herself, and took a deep breath.

"Well. I guess I could do what you ask. I'll call Mr. Raymond Toda and let him know you'll be at the house." She peered over the top of her glasses. "He graciously offered to be a sort of caretaker for us. He told my partner that having an abandoned house nearby can attract all kinds of problems. I'll explain your situation to him. He'll keep an extra eye on things." She looked at them sternly. "But I'll expect you back here at nine o'clock sharp tomorrow, that's when we open." She sniffed and wondered whether or not she wanted to get up that early on a Sunday morning.

"Great," Kay exclaimed and clapped her hands. "And here's my attorney's card." She placed it on Rose's desk. "He'll take care of any legal arrangements, when and if we come to a decision. And you could give his office a call to vet us."

Alex carefully folded the map. "Actually I'd like to spend a week here." He put his driver's license on Rose's desk then headed toward the door. "Maybe you'll have suggestions on places to stay, like a hotel or dare I say it, a B&B. And while I'm getting the papers out of the glove box, you should call Kay's attorney, the notorious Max Maltin. He'll vouch for us." Alex winked and was out the door.

Negotiations concluded, they shook Rose's hand and waved goodbye. She could still hear their laughing chatter as they descended the steps. Using a soft cloth, Rose sat down and wiped her glasses. My, so much energy, they reminded her of two big kids on holiday. She pushed herself away from the desk. She wouldn't be surprised if they peeled out of the parking lot.

Standing at the window she happened to glance down at her feet and was horrified. She was wearing her work moccasins. Maybe they hadn't noticed. After all, she was behind the desk most of the time. She looked over at her new shoes she'd kicked under the coat stand. They were fancy Italian leathers, with stiletto heels. She smiled then grimaced. They weren't very comfortable. Sabra assured her that all new imports must be broken in. Well, it was worth the torture. Raymond would think they were sexy and that was all that counted.

Rose picked up the attorney's card. It identified a Mr. Herbert Maxwell Maltin and associates.

Mr. Maxwell had a deep sexy voice. Rose imagined what he might look like. His offices were located in the luxurious Metropolitan business building in downtown Seattle. He assured her of their bonafides and said he would handle any legal factors when necessary. She shook her head and smiled as she slipped the card under her desk blotter. Humph, she thought. They must be not hurting for money; they hadn't even discussed a price.

*CHAPTER 3*

# *Competition*

**Edward Caen glanced out of the large bay window** of Templeton's Realty. An attractive couple, talking and waving their arms, walked down the steps from Rose's office. The auburn haired woman was a stunner. Edward studied her intently. The man, gesticulated excitedly as they got into a wine-red convertible. He was attractive, too, and dressed in casual but expensive looking clothes. After the car made a right onto Main Street, Edward focused on his own mirror image in the window. Adjusting his cuff links he nodded. Satisfied with his tanned good looks and clean jaw line he took in the reflection of the blond man fuming at the desk behind him.

Edward cleared his throat. "It would seem that La Rose has snared the first two birds of the season." There was no response. "They appear to be pretty well-heeled." He smiled then strolled over to the other man's desk.

Mark Justice snorted as he hunched over his computer, jacket off, sleeves rolled up. He couldn't be less interested. "I still can't find the papers to the new land-grant deal," he said glumly. "I specifically told Anne to leave the folder on my desk. The papers were in the envelope marked 'La Grange'." He ran long fingers through his thick blond hair then gestured with a free hand at the extensive bank of metal cabinets behind him. "They're not there. I've checked. She's put them somewhere and they are not in the computer files either." His Nordic eyes, usually a calm blue, were angry. He punched at his keyboard then looked up.

"Edward, if you've finished gazing at the scenery, I would appreciate some help here."

Edward ducked his head then arranged himself carefully in the chair next to Mark's desk. He ran a hand across his fresh shaven chin and reflected on whether or not he had used the right cologne for the morning. He looked at his well-groomed nails, polished them on his jacket lapel and crossed his legs.

"Take a break, Mark. I'm sure Anne entered them in a different location. No doubt she's made a backup file too." He smiled.

Mark flared. "Hiring a temp like Anne was a mistake. We should've replaced Janet with a full-time secretary. Templeton always cuts corners at the most ridiculous times." He stabbed at the keyboard. "Besides, I don't think Janet is coming back. It's been about a month since she and that Martin character ran off. Anyway, if the rumor mill is right, and they are married, she'll work at Martin's new dock studio in Burn. Not here." Mark leered. "She wouldn't want Templeton panting down her neck once she's snagged the right guy."

"Templeton didn't hire her strictly for her physical attributes," Edward said as he blew something off his nails, "she also has a brain."

"Yeah," Mark rolled his eyes. "Maybe so, I've always thought you had more than a superficial knowledge of her outer and inner workings."

"Ha! Edward pointed a thumb to his chest. "I'm not the only one. She told me about your amazing sailing skills. And how you reminded her of 'Leif Erickson' or was it Erickson without the Leif?"

All six foot three inches of Mark bristled; he stood up and leaned forward. His clenched fists rested heavily on the desk. "Now isn't that interesting. She said pretty much the same things about you." The electric whirring of the office clock became quite loud.

Edward stood up and straightened his cuffs. He looked Mark Justice in the eye.

"Well. It would appear that she's taken both our measure," he said and went over to an adjacent desk that held two more computer terminals. He glanced back. The muscles still twitched in Mark's jaw. "I wouldn't let it bother you. She's sized up Templeton as well," Edward said, sat down and began bringing files up on the screen. Mark stretched, as if he were stiff and moved over beside him. Edward's fingers expertly scrolled through the information.

"So she fluffed the old man's duff too?" he mumbled. Edward looked up and cocked his eye, nodded, then quickly went back to searching.

"I wasn't supposed to know. But I thought it was obvious to everyone. They're always inseparable. She's continually dragging him out to see what she terms the wanton destruction of the Island's environment. And she's always bending his ear about one or another threatened species. I wouldn't be surprised if she's an undercover agent for Greenpeace or Washpirg. Before she ran off with Martin, she was trying to make me a convert."

Mark snorted. "Yeah, Martin was touchy feely with her too. When I said he was the horny environmental hot-dog from back east she slapped my face. Martin Gray, what a name. But I gotta say his miniatures of the owls and those other animals are pretty damn good."

"Ah yes. Our sniveling Martin Gray, the only thing authentic about his hippie charade is his continually runny nose. He's actually quite the weasel. You remember? He came to the Island about the same time I did. It amazed me. He took no time in worming his way into Rose's circle. Then he conned her into selling him that historical boathouse in Burn. I thought Rose wanted that place for herself.

Martin must have offered her a lot. It was all on the 'Q.T.' and I don't understand how Martin..."

They jumped when the automatic buzzer sounded and the front door opened. To their amazement, Rose tottered into the room.

"Looks like she's had a few," Edward whispered.

"Rose? This early, never," Mark whispered back. Placing a hand over his smile he casually walked toward her then paused beside the window.

It looked like some sort of futuristic tableau, Rose thought. Aluminum and plastic modules were tiny burrows, painted a bland office white. The glare of fluorescent fixtures furthered the surreal background. Feeble relief came from the natural light that filtered through the windows at the front of the office. It was a battle of contrasts. Mark standing relaxed in the gold reflection of morning light. Edward sitting like a pilot at the computers, his rigid figure bathed in the ice-blue illumination of the overheads.

Not a wonder that they were peering at her so strangely. Rose grimaced; she no doubt looked like a corpse in this light. And thanks to her damn shoes, she walked like a demented robot.

Sabra had insisted that 'Lil Devils' high heels were the latest fashion. Curses to her; the shoes were coals from hell. Sabra swore on a stack of 'Elles' that Seattle's finest stores simply couldn't keep them in stock. She was full of crap. The shoes would be excellent accessories in a De Sade torture chamber!

Rose crossed her arms, bravely jutted her chin at the two men and put a cat-that-ate-the-canary grin on her face.

"Well, well. While you two are being very G.Q. and playing computer games, I snared two babes-in-the-woods!" She smiled triumphantly then noticed the paper-strewn desks.

"Where's Anne?" She carefully toddled over to the first desk. She was appalled. "Did you give her a day off so you could thoroughly destroy her files?" She picked up several folders and handfuls of loose papers. "You're going to have one very hysterical secretary on your hands. That's if she doesn't commit herself first."

Edward leaned back in his chair, hands behind his head, and sighed. "Rose, dear Rose, we most certainly aren't playing computer games, quite the opposite." His voice lowered. "We're in the midst of closing a multi-million dollar land deal while you're crowing about sending some poor souls off to drool over a patch of miserable swampland, or worse."

Mark smirked then chimed in: "Yea man, like sliding bluff-acres, with a terminal view."

Rose gingerly walked over to Mark. Her uneven progress had one advantage; it made her skirt sway seductively. Putting her hand on Mark's shoulder she steadied herself. Heavy magnolia scented perfume wafted through the room. She smiled coquettishly. "You boys are such wheeler-dealers; I don't dare share any of my little trade secrets."

"You never do," Edward said dryly as he flipped through menus on the screen. "But, you gave those two something to be thrilled about. Their enthusiasm was quite obvious and, he's quite the handsome dude." He whirled around in his chair and gave Rose a lecherous wink.

Rose, who was tapping on Mark's shoulder, stiffened and raised her chin. "I really hadn't noticed. But to change the subject, I came over to personally invite you to my annual spring party at the houseboat. Anne's invited too. Templeton and his sister will receive a formal one." Rose glowed with pride. "Raymond and I have decided to give it a 'Fiesta in old Monterey' theme this year."

Mark guffawed and rolled his eyes. Edward tapped the computer keys loudly then said, "You mean tutti-frutti Toady has decided to sway in a La Mexicana way? I'm sure you had very little to do with *that* decision." Both men laughed.

Angrily, Rose stepped back. "I don't see why Raymond insists on that ridiculous nickname." She thought of his strong and handsome Asian features. "It doesn't fit him at all." Her eyes flashed as she gathered momentum. "And he's far from effeminate. He has more testosterone in his little finger than you two put together."

Edward had the sense to back off. "Sorry, sorry, just having a little fun." He winked at Mark.

"We wouldn't miss your party," Mark said, still amused. "Last year's was pretty cool, particularly when the local studs and studettes dove off the upper deck, naked. Should we wear a bathing suit, or would sombreros be sufficient?"

"Don't be silly." Rose tittered as her imagination composed an all too vivid picture. Unfortunately she'd missed the au-naturel interlude in the midst of helping Toady at the bar. By that time, swimsuits were back on.

"It's very casual, just come as you are. We're going to serve slammers, sangria, have an enchilada contest and hot salsa dancing." She clapped her hands. "Doesn't that sound exciting?"

"What the hell's an enchilada contest?" Mark asked, his imagination running rampant.

Rose smirked. "Well, you never cook so you don't have to worry." She paused, "Oh...don't forget, Anne is invited too. I haven't been able to get a hold of her. You'll probably see her before I do, so please extend her an invitation." Soberly she glanced with a somber eye around the room. "She'll need a party, particularly after tackling *this* disaster."

Rose crossed her arms and tottered over to the window. "I'm thinking of having it next Friday. Things will begin around sevenish. Raymond's asked that charming young man from last year to help out again. You remember. I didn't approve of his lack of attire. But he really knows how to work the discs and get people dancing."

Mark snorted and moved over near the computer. "Oh yeah I remember, the one with tattooed pecs and short leather vest. Toady couldn't take his eyes off him."

Rose bristled. "Oh get over it, his female assistant was getting Raymond's attention. How could any man forget her? She called herself Bambi."

Mark licked his lips. "Oh yes, I remember her. She left two very lasting impressions. And you didn't have to dance close either." He shook his finger. "But I have to give her credit; she got all the wallflowers on their feet. She even wangled Thommy Jay into doing a conga line. That's amazing in itself."

Rose tsk-tsked. "I know. I couldn't believe it either. She was quite outré, Raymond said she couldn't keep her hands off him all evening, the poor boy." She shook her head. "You two are so jealous. Raymond's very attractive because he's also kind and considerate. Women see him a real gentleman and you resent it. I have further news." She smiled wickedly. "This will make your macho hearts even more envious. He told me that he and Anne have been dating and it's getting serious. Of course I think she's too young for him."

Edward hooted and shook with laughter. "Ha! And you're *not* jealous? Oh I get it. You expect it to have a very short run." Rose blushed.

Mark was laughing too and flourished a large blue handkerchief to wipe the corner of his eye. "That explains it. Yesterday, I caught the early ferry to Seattle. I saw Toady's..." Rose's eyebrows lifted. "Er, Mr. Toda's car parked right outside the front steps. I guess 'El Tigre' has changed his stripes. He was no doubt having a horizontal conference with Anne before she opened the office." He snickered into his handkerchief.

Edward caught his breath. "Maybe Toady was just balancing his yen and yang, or as we say in the West, having a California quickie." He laughed even louder. "That always gets rid of any toxins in the morning. It's better than jogging." Both men egged each other on.

Rose had it. She turned abruptly and wobbled toward the door, with her hand on the knob she paused then asked in a casual voice, "How do you know it was Raymond's car yesterday?"

Mark recovered himself first and said through gasps, "Couldn't forget it. The parking lot was a swimming pool from the rain last night; then there was this large bird, it looked like a crow, but it was tan and white. The thing was hopping around and pecking up drowning night crawlers. When I stopped to look, it flew on to the top of Raymond's Black Beauty. His car was parked on that raised part under the willow. You can't mistake that flashy Trans-Am. Nor its vanity plate either."

Edward tipped back in his chair. "There aren't any tan and white crows; only black. It was one of those low-life pigeons from Seattle. Those birds fly all the way over from Pioneer Square, just to drop a special calling-card on top of Toady's, er Raymond's Beauty," he said with a chuckle.

Rose's voice became sharp, "It couldn't have been Raymond. He told me he would be in Seattle until Monday. And I was with him last Friday night. I took him to the ferry. He was a walk-on." She was thoughtful for a moment. "Maybe he loaned his car to someone. After all, one of his many qualities is his generosity." She pointed." I see you're even using one of his gifts."

Mark waved the silk handkerchief like a banner. "He gave me a bunch for my birthday; you know how the boy loves blue. That was quite a while back, I might add."

"He gave me a set too," Edward said in a jealous tone and resumed typing then paused, "You think you know our Raymond." He winked at Mark. "He's fickle and likes to take walks on the wild side." Edward stopped and looked at Rose intently. "I'm sure he doesn't tell his Mother Rose everything. Does he?"

Before she could rally to Raymond's defense the door flew open in her face. She tottered backwards in pain, holding her arm.

Elanor Laven swept into the office. "Where's my brother? What have you done with him?" She ignored Rose who was rubbing her injury. "Well?" Elanor continued in a stentorian voice. "Where is Eric?" She stomped over to the two men. Edward and Mark unconsciously drew closer together. Mark's complexion turned a pale red. Edward was oddly calm.

Elanor sniffed as if she detected the odor of something unpleasant. "I suppose you useless poppets haven't talked to him this morning. I rang the house in Seattle and the hanger at the heliport. They say no one's seen him since yesterday. I know he didn't stay on Little Mountain. I was there two hours ago." She looked disgusted. "The decorators are still dawdling. I've told them and told them that Eric's allergic to paint smell. But the idiots don't listen; they just shrug." She sniffed loudly, snapped open her purse, and took out a tissue.

"Eric said he was taking me to that new art gallery opening, in Seattle." She wiped her nose. "We're going to land on the roof," she said grandly, then thrust her face forward. "The owner of the 'Chrysalis Gallery' expects us to meet her, *there*; and at the right time; Eric's not being considerate at all," she whined. "We were to leave the heliport within the hour." Elanor raised her voice. "And Anne, she calls herself a secretary, she's absolutely useless, she was supposed to see to all the arrangements and hasn't had the courtesy to return any of my messages." Elanor walked over to Anne's desk. "When I finally reach her, I'll tell her we no longer need her incompetent services. This time Eric will hire a real temp, and from Seattle." Her angry eyes swept the room. "What a mess! What's happening? Where are they?"

Edward swallowed slowly. "We're doing the best we can Ms. Templeton. You are aware, as per our agreement, we're not and never have been Anne's, nor your brother's keeper. Eric has told us time and again that he resented our efforts at creating some sort of schedule. And that was when we were just encouraging him to keep an appointment book." Edward straightened his tie. He expertly avoided Elanor's livid face and turned slowly back to the computer screen.

He sighed and coughed delicately. "If I remember correctly, this is the same scenario that played out several months ago, when he was wining and dining that Greenpeacer, Martin Gray. But, as we all know, when it comes to the female gender it's even more difficult to pin down your brother's whereabouts; and with Anne not available at the same time..." he winked and grinned at her boldly. "At this very moment they might be skiing Baker or maybe Crystal. Who knows, surely not us."

Elanor opened her mouth, but surprisingly, nothing came out.

"However, I'll pull up the company itinerary. He might have deigned to make entries there." He worked the mouse smoothly over the pad as he talked. "I continually encourage him to keep a current activities file. There are too many times when his views and expertise are needed immediately and he simply isn't there." Edward eyed Elanor. "Eric is aware of this, and I'm sure you, his loving sister, are too." His smile was ingratiating. "Of course we should all be allowed our little eccentricities, but it would help us immeasurably if you would discuss this problem with him."

Elanor growled. "Are you implying that my brother, a successful self-made billionaire, doesn't know how to run his own business?"

"No, no. Not at all," Edward said hastily. "But it would help to give him a gentle reminder. Like, when you're on your way to the art gallery today, you can use this very situation as an excellent example." He smiled. "And with a dash of your usual tact you might convince him that this particular eccentricity of his can, and does, have serious consequences." He glanced sideways at Mark.

Taking his cue, Mark intently studied the screen over Edward's shoulder. "Tsk, tsk. Look at these dates. The most recent entry is last Tuesday." He straightened up with an air of puzzlement and looked down at Elanor. "I'll have to agree with Edward, Ms. Templeton. You're the only one who can convince him. You really do have a great rapport with your brother."

"I don't like it when people pander to me," Elanor said through thin lips.

Mark's voice became weary. "I regret to tell you this, but the files on the 'La Grange' matter are missing too." He stared directly at Elanor. "Which I must have in order to initiate the first phase of the closures related to the land grant. Eric, er Mr. Templeton scheduled the meeting for next Tuesday. The Bradestone Nature Conservation Committee opted to hold it at the library and they're expecting the paperwork completed and on the table."

Elanor looked away. "You two are hopeless," she sneered. "Without Janet or Anne you couldn't find your flies let alone your files."

Edward smirked, but Mark became angry, his arm gestures encompassed the entire office. "That's not fair. Edward and I have looked over everything and the paperwork is simply not here." His hands were shaking. "And as far as we can tell, Anne hasn't left one note or a shred of information on the computer."

Elanor turned a death's head grimace on Edward. "I thought my brother hired a super-power lawyer." She cast a fiery glance at Mark, "and a whiz-kid of an office manager to handle these mundane things." She slammed her fist against Anne's desk and growled, "I'm only interested in getting to that gallery, on time and in style. I refuse to use the tacky state ferry system." Her voice became almost a howl. "That's why we built the helipad in the first place."

Elanor strode to the door. "Christ! I'll find him myself. A two-bit lawyer and a four flushing lackey, what a great team; my brother was insane when he hired you drones." She yanked open the door. "And when dear little Anne returns, give her a final notice." Elanor hesitated at the door, and for the first time acknowledged Rose's presence.

Rose seemed to tremble with fear. But in actuality she'd been holding on to every word. Trying to contain her laughter and maintain her balance at the same time had been difficult.

Elanor shook her elegantly coifed head. "What in hell are you doing here? Taking refuge in the enemy's camp? Or spying for your Toady again?" She tossed the last question over her shoulder as she stomped down the steps.

"That frightful bitch," Mark said through clenched teeth. "If it wasn't for Templeton's largess I'd have been out of here months ago." His last remark was lost in the roar of Elanor's giant car as it shot out of the parking lot.

Edward looked seriously at him, "Don't let her get to you. She's got a great bark, but she's a pussycat… and she prefers young men with balls and G.Q. attire. But it appears she likes her dramatic moments even more." He peered into the computer screen. "However, she's right, Anne will have to go."

Mark regarded Edward through half-closed eyes. "How do you know that about Elanor?" he asked softly.

"You mean about liking us?" Edward flexed his fingers. "Well, it's obvious. With all her yelling, she's never pressured Templeton to fire anyone. You should really take time to talk to her. Wait till she's had a few drinks at Rose's party. You'll find out."

"No thanks. I stay away from her as far as possible. Raymond says she turns men to stone. Now I know it couldn't be truer." He chuckled. "And her hair doesn't have to be made of snakes either."

"I'm not going to invite her this time," Rose said and shook her head with determination. "She's always so rude and she constantly puts me and Raymond down."

Edward smiled nastily. "Excuse me; you said the same thing last year. And since Templeton brought his sister out here, she's cornered the moneyed crowd and the social elite on this island. You couldn't afford the faux pas of *not* inviting her. She'll be there, and with her adoring retinue in tow. And so shall we. I wouldn't miss it; even if I were to win the lottery."

Rose ignored his last comment and cautiously headed toward the door then paused and turned around. "I think I'll invite those two Lookie-lou's, they said they might stay through the week. Mainlanders always set the Islander's chins wagging. It'll make for a great mix and I can do a little hard sell at the same time."

Edward quickly got up and opened the door for Rose. He watched her as she gingerly negotiated the steps. "What did Elanor mean about you spying for Toady?" he called down to her.

Rose looked up at him oddly, "Nothing, nothing at all. But you see what I have to put up with. She spreads rumors like that."

## CHAPTER 4

# *Verandahs*

**Alex crumpled up Rose's map** and stuffed it in the glove compartment. Her flamboyant road marks and guessing what they meant had led them into many a dead end. On the last stop they put the top down. The air was patchy with mist and the growing sunlight lifted their spirits.

As Kay drove down a twisting tree-lined lane, named Miller Creek Road, Alex pointed to a board. It was shot full of holes and tacked to a piece of rotted fence. Kay stopped the car. Faintly, the sign read: 'Petoskey Farm. No solicitors'. Backing the car up, she turned onto the entry of a weedy dirt road.

A rusty livestock gate blocked their way. On an adjacent side post, a mailbox, smashed on top and also sporting bullet holes, tilted at an angle.

Alex sprung out of the car, turned and bowed deeply by the gate. "Madame, here at last; welcome to Manderley. I trust you won't find Mrs. Danvers too bothersome."

"But Alex the gate's padlocked. Rose didn't give us another key," Kay said and stepped out of the car.

He carefully inspected the lock and raised a finger. "Not to worry." Lifting the chain and grunting with exaggerated difficulty, he pushed the long gate into a green wall of blackberry bushes.

"Notice the condition of aforesaid lock. It's rusted open. Someone draped the chain, to make it look secure." He looped the chain over the fence and hooked the rusted lock through one of the links. "Now, let's see if the house key has survived being taped to the bottom of the mailbox." It was.

Alex jumped into the passenger's seat and grinned at Kay's obvious excitement. "Lead on Mac duff. Let's see what lies ahead."

Kay shifted gears and the car crunched and mashed its way up the steep, weed-strewn drive. Aromas of fir boughs mixed with salt air wafted up through the tall grass that swayed on the right side of the road. The day was getting hotter.

Stinging nettles, interlaced with foxglove, edged the steeper left side of the bank. No vehicle had been this way for a long time. After a few sharp turns, the car topped the grade and there was the house.

It nestled below their vantage point and to the left. Rose's picture had been accurate. The house was two-story and long. The first story appeared to be surrounded on all sides by a weathered verandah whose top then became a continuous railed balcony. On this second story, several dormers with French doors opened onto the back part of the balcony. A lone chimney thrust up through the middle of the house and two larger chimneys flanked both ends.

Rampant wisteria wrapped its way around the west side and onto the roof. Left unchecked, the vine had invaded several of the dormers. The verandah had breaks in the railings and porch sections sagged in places. Besides the tumbled condition of the house Kay felt it was strange that Rose hadn't mentioned the spectacular view beckoning through the trees.

Far in the distance Kay noticed the glint of Puget Sound, and further, a glimpse of West Seattle on the mainland. Patches of what looked like a small bay sparkled below the house. Kay pointed to the tree-lined peninsula on the other side of the bay.

"That must be Heron's Hook. It's on this map. "Alex nodded enthusiastically. "You know Kay, that verandah will provide great protection against winter storms off the Sound.

"But serious rot," he exclaimed. "Look at the condition of the roof. It must leak like a sieve. Shingles are missing everywhere." He made a quick mental calculation. "The roofing alone is easily a ten thousand repair job. I don't know Kay; look at those chimneys, bricks are missing at the top. Probably the cement has gone in the original mortar. It's typical of these old houses. And there are no flue liners." He shrugged helplessly. "Those broken windows mean beaucoup water damage. It's not what I'd classify as a winner. Looks like a money pit."

"Oh stop whining," Kay said as she slammed the car door, "those things will help us bring the price down." She wasn't going to listen to Alex's complaints anymore. She ran down a brick side-path and around to the front of the house where the verandah faced the bay. Alex was close behind.

"Oh Alex, the view," she exclaimed, took a full deep breath, closed her eyes and exhaled slowly. "I smell only the sea and trees. Ah, clean unpolluted air!"

He laughed and walked up the steps behind her. "Be careful honey. The porch is rotted through in places. Test the boards first."

Kay nodded then stood with her hands on the railing. "Alex. This is it. I can sense it. This is our place."

Alex wrapped his arms around her and said huskily, "Whoa. Don't get transported, just yet." He nibbled her ear. "We've got to suss everything out. Don't forget Max. He'll have to search the title, and who knows what else." He pulled her tighter.

Kay covered her ears then squirmed around and pushed against his chest. She was excited and it was hard for her to breathe. Alex raised his voice and touched a finger to her nose. "And remember what Rose said. Sewer problems, water problems..."

"Oh, don't be a complainer," Kay muttered as she kneaded his arms. "Look at me. Look at us. You know when I get these feelings I'm right. It will happen. And this place will be beautiful. It's magical"

Alex pulled her closer. He was aroused, and so was she. It was a long kiss. Eventually he quietly gasped. "I do respect your feelings," he paused, "and that sixth sense of yours. It's brought us luck in the past." He grazed her lips with his. "But, at times it's gotten us into a helluva lot of deep trouble too." His voice became ragged. "Now, how about getting into a little of that trouble, right now?"

CHAPTER 5

# *Le Camping*

**A day later** the skies had rained themselves out. Below the Petoskey farmhouse the small salt-water inlet, named Scoon Bay, thrust like a beckoning skeleton finger into the island. It was hidden from the first rays of the morning sun by the ridge called Heron's Hook. It was slack tide.

A blue heron stood sentinel still in the shallows. It eyed the fish swimming beneath the limpid waters. There was a sudden thrust, a flash of silver, then again the quiet and a patient stance.

The blue heron was not alone in the tranquil morning. A faint sound echoed over the water.

At the mouth of the bay, a sailboat, its motor thunking quietly, set up a gentle wake. The heron, used to such intrusions, never looked up. Nor did it move when a lumpy bundle tumbled from the stern of the boat and sank quickly into deeper waters.

The rope securing the heavy bag was inexpertly tied and several of the rocks meant to weight it down, spilled out. The bundle became caught in the changing tide. Slowly, inexorably, the current carried it back into Scoon Bay. The boat chugged on.

Kay stretched and yawned. Next to her, Alex slept deeply. She slipped carefully out of the sleeping bag. Stood up, stretched and mentally thanked Rose again. With a little smooth talking, Alex had swayed her into letting them stay for another five days.

She looked at Alex's contented face then shivered as she remembered the dilapidated wooden bureau they'd found last night. It was upstairs, in one of the bedrooms that faced the inlet. Alex opened the top drawer, chewed paper exploded in all directions as a pair of wood rats shot out. They were very efficient and quiet in their departure. Kay was not. Her throat still scratched from yelling. She wanted to kick Alex, all he did was laugh.

Massaging her neck she walked naked across the large empty living room to one of the bay windows. Warm sunlight streamed in. It cast an aura of copper-colored light around her hair that tumbled to her shoulders. Standing up on tiptoe, she stretched her arms toward the ceiling, reveling in the first rays of the day.

Below Kay, the waters of Scoon Bay rippled. That was strange. It had been still a moment before. As she watched for a tide change she noticed a movement to her left. Ah, that explains it; a lone sailboat chugged out of the mouth of the Bay. Not a great day for sailing, she reasoned. No wind, but maybe it would come up later. Then, embracing the solitude and peacefulness of the morning, she closed her eyes, cleared her mind, and smoothly moved into a morning 'Salute to the Sun'.

When she'd finished her yoga meditation, she again took in the view from the window. Scoon Bay, what a fitting name, she thought. The other evening, Rose said the bay once served as a haven for the schooners of lumber barons. She pointed out the worm-riddled pilings that could be seen from the verandah. They were all that remained of a once gigantic dock. Shaking her head Rose said they were grim reminders of the denuding of the island near the end of the century, and "Yes", Rose answered Alex's question; Heron's hook did provide a natural shelter from weather out of the east and the south. But the north winds were another matter. She also told them that over the years the bay had become useless to deep draft vessels as it slowly silted up from the Miller and Swamp Creek's runoff. But at the mouth of the bay it was quite deep.

Kay studied the shoreline. Too cold for a morning swim, she thought, unless the water was warmer in the shallower parts of the bay. She'd have to find out. A walk around would be exhilarating before breakfast, she thought, and she and Alex would take their time exploring.

Below Kay the gravelly beach changed into a stretch of sand that ran like a gray ribbon toward the swampy area to the south. From their first tentative explorations they'd crossed a border of low bank clay, strewn with last winter's storm debris. Long swords of beach grass and last year's cattail thrust through the tumble of logs and limbs. Most of the debris would drift away, or be cut up for firewood; at least that's what Rose had said. She also said that the beach and its surroundings remained one of the few natural wetlands in Puget Sound. Most tidelands had been filled in. Along with the stress of pollution and man's predation, breeding habitats had basically disappeared. The results were dwindling salmon, birds and accompanying wildlife.

A solitary heron suddenly rose from the inlet. Its silhouette reminded her of the pterodactyls she'd seen in one of Byron's textbooks. Everything was so perfect, she thought. They had to be part of the morning, and at once. Her eyes were alive with excitement, she turned toward Alex.

She smiled, cupped her chin and reflected. Alex had not been the typical boring Professor. Kay audited one class and was hooked. He taught his students with clarity and punctuated his lectures with outbursts on philosophy, anthropology and the puzzling nature of mankind. He intrigued his classes with current theories about black holes, dark matter and space-time.

With his unbridled enthusiasm for scholarship and lust for living, he had no trouble in charming male and female students alike. A few husband hunters made no bones about being hot on his trail. Kay was amused, then pleasantly surprised when she, a widow with two teen-age children, had turned his head. They had fun times together and then there was their unquenchable enthusiasm for viewing and critiquing old-time movies.

Gentle snores came from the large body wrapped in the double sleeping bag. A mass of thick curly salt and pepper hair covered his muscular chest.

Kay grinned. The first time Alex said he wanted to make love to her was when she raised a tentative hand in class, and asked him about the rabbit in the moon. Then, after romantic meetings in a village café and longer, more passionate meetings in his apartment, he'd asked her to marry him. She'd countered with, "Give me time to think". Okay he replied, but his life would never be complete if she weren't part of it. Typical cliché, she thought at the time, but soon found he was a caring and serious person, and when he suggested they continue in life, married or not, she'd thought: 'Well hell, why not? Time was slipping beneath their feet.

Teri and Byron were fond of him too. They appreciated being dealt with as young adults. He made a great dad they said and shook their heads at Kay's foot-dragging. "Go for it mom," was their succinct advice.

"Alex, time to get up, let's hit the beach," she shouted.

"Go away." He groaned into the bag then turned over, further entangling himself.

Kay ran over and pushed his exposed butt with her heel. He sat up, rubbed his eyes, then stretched leisurely and yawned. He focused on Kay. She balanced on the balls of her feet; taking punching jabs at him. "Rise and shine on the Admiral Line," she sang out.

"What's the matter, house on fire?" He paused. "Come to think of it you'd make one hell of a dancing fireman," he said with a slow grin, "or is it fireperson?"

"I'm going to light a fire under *you*. It's a great day out yonder and we should be part of it."

"Hmm, you have inadvertently started a fire. Part of me has decidedly risen to the occasion, but the rest of me is still warm and sleepy." He patted the top of the sleeping bag. "Come here."

"I thought, after last night, you'd be simply exhausted," she drawled, and then leapt back as Alex jumped out of the bag.

Seeming to change his mind he sat down, elbows resting on his knees. A worried look came over his face. "Well, I'm not exactly exhausted, maybe a tad concerned." He looked up at Kay. "I thought the kids would think this was a pretty neat idea. But when I called Teri from Madrona, she seemed down about the whole idea. She said that the place sounded, 'really isolated'."

"Isolated? We're only fifty minutes from Seattle. Alex, stop fussing. I've told you that Teri takes after her father Frank. He was super-cautious when it came to any type of major change. When she and Byron see this place and the island, they'll love it."

Kay crossed her arms. "I had a hunch we were making the right move long before you opened the gate. And, I also know that you and Teri psyche each other out. "Tsk-tsk, with you two everything has to be carefully looked over, and that includes *both* ends of the horse."

He smiled patiently then lunged and expertly grabbed her slender ankle.

Kay tried to twist away, but Alex was strong. She continued chattering as he slowly pulled her toward him. "Teri will hike to her heart's content and Byron will probably paint the bay from every angle but up." When he had moved his hands up her leg she punched him in the shoulder.

"Come on, let's get going. We can explore the entire beach today."

He stood up and pulled her to him. "Hey kid." He said affectionately, "without our morning workout?" His chin nuzzled the top of her hair and she began kissing his chest. "After all, we can take that walk later. Much later," he growled. "Meanwhile back at the ranch..." he didn't finish as they slowly wrestled down onto the sleeping bag.

## CHAPTER 6

# *Tennis Anyone?*

**Kay and Alex were on the part of the verandah** that faced the bay. Ravenously they ate their breakfast as they perched on a pair of wooden sawhorses. In snooping around, Kay had found some usable pieces of china in a kitchen pantry and Alex had uncovered the horses in a dilapidated shed attached to the house. He was delighted with their antiquity and wooden peg construction. He told Kay that though they were very old they would be indispensable when it came to remodeling. But, he was adamant; they had to be handled with care.

Breakfast consisted of a thermos of hot coffee, a jug of cold milk, a box of cold cereal, and two large cheese Danish. They found all their survival necessities at a local country store, Fred's Market. There was a tad too much local crafts clutter for Alex's taste, but he liked the fact that it had an excellent bakery and was located only three miles back on the north road.

They gazed at the vista before them. The only object that marred their view was a tangle of vines and brambles. The vegetation covered what looked like a large garage. Kay pointed at the mound. "When we tear that monster down, we'll have a lovely view."

"Oh I don't know, I might want to keep it as a woodshed and workshop," Alex mumbled through his Danish. Then he put his arm around her. "I see your taking quickly to the role of mistress of the manor."

Kay put on a solemn air. "As soon as Max takes care of the rest of the details, we're in. Actually we're in now. And I'm not budging."

"That's my gal," Alex said as he hugged her. "It's still hard for me to believe Rose had any difficulty selling this place." Alex scooped into his cereal. "You'd think some corporation would have scarfed it up long ago."

Kay laughed, "If you'd been paying attention, you'd have heard what Rose said yesterday after her search. The water rights access is a mess, the septic system has to be brought up to county code. Then there was litigation. Remember? She said the church had been left the farm by one of the Petoskey's children. But a relative contested it. Then there were back taxes. Max will be an angel if he can clear it all up. Are you listening?"

Alex took a sip of his coffee and winked. "Hmm yes, well by now I should think we have squatter's rights. Ha, I bet the Petoskey kids felt like Teri, thought this place was at the edge of the known world." He took another spoonful of cereal and looked up. "And you're right. I wasn't listening. Why didn't the Church get it?"

"Well, they did. They've had it for quite some time and let it sit. Rose said they had plans to make it a seminary. But there wasn't enough backing or parishioners to maintain, much less run the operation. Then there was some sort of local opposition, something about zoning."

"What happened?"

"I had Max look into things and he said the church turned it over to William's & Bracken Realtor's only recently and we were there or here, just at the right time. By the way, where were you when Rose was rattling on? I thought she was going to grind my ear to the nubs."

"I believe nature called. Anyway, I'm still wondering why no one grabbed it before us. Corporations have teams of sharks working while we're sleeping. I can't imagine Superior Island Development Company letting this fish get away."

"Corporations make mistakes too."

Alex shrugged. "Actually plenty of mistakes. At least we have Max to straighten out any legality, but he's not the most..." his voice trailed off as he looked up and saw Kay's raised eyebrows.

"He's been there at every turn in the road for us. Thanks to him, you sorted out some of the finer details of your brother Tony's messy estate." Kay put her coffee cup down firmly. "And thanks to Tony's largess and Max's skills you were able to take early retirement," she paused and spread her hands, "and we're able to go into this venture as equal partners."

"Ah yes. My financial expectations have indeed been realized thanks to Tony." He paused and looked up slowly. "So, does that mean we can finally get married?"

Kay leaned back. She avoided Alex's serious look. "You are a stinker; you would bring that up this morning." She reached over and took his hand. "You know it's not a question of money. Yes, you've been very patient. I'll make a decision soon. Really I will." She shook her head. "This last year has been a train out of control; your sudden retirement, our decision to put down roots. Then to actually say this is it." She squeezed his hand harder. "I just need more time to get used to everything and settling down in one place."

"It's okay." Alex cupped her hands in his. It's been twelve years since Frank's accident. Twelve long years of turmoil for you and the children." He shook his head. "The circumstances involving his death, and your struggle to get the kids through high school and Teri through college, test the limits. You and I have not even had three years together. I'm the new guy on the block. But I love you…you and the kids. It's funny; I feel sort of the same way you do. With this place we finally have the chance to pull our lives together, let things settle." Alex looked away. "Kay, you don't have to justify anything. I just want you to know I understand how difficult it's been for you, and the family."

"I love you even more for saying that." She sighed deeply. "And it's true. This is our year to get everything on track. It's something we can focus on together. And it is *our* family." She looked up. "I'm not the only one that's bonded to you." Her eyes were moist as she leaned over and rubbed his shoulder.

Alex put his bowl of cereal down. For a sunny day things were getting a little too heavy. He kissed her forehead, stood up, rubbed his temples vigorously and looked back into the large, weathered house.

"I'll make a wager that this place is haunted. It's old enough." He took a last bite of his Danish and peered sidelong at Kay.

"Hey, a resident ghost," she said and clapped her hands. "I can hear the rattling of chains on the stairs and the groaning of something nasty in your woodshed over there."

He laughed then looked at her through excited but wary eyes. "It would be a great draw for a bed and breakfast."

Kay frowned. "Oh murder. Alex, don't spoil everything. I, for one, don't want to be cooking, cleaning and fetching for strangers. And you didn't retire to start a new career that would require *real* work," she said with emphasis as, she bit into her Danish.

"Ouch." Alex flinched. "I think someone just jabbed me verbally in the stomach. I was only teasing, a joke, a joke." He held his hands high above his head. "I surrender to your superior logic. And..." He stopped. Something moved behind them.

"I'm sorry. I, I don't wish to interrupt anything," said a deep, but tremulous voice. "But..."

Kay and Alex jumped. They grabbed their coffee and cereal bowls, but the rest of the breakfast fell to the porch.

"Whoa." Kay yelled. "Who are you?"

A tall man stood on the porch step. His athletic body was poured into a white polo shirt and shorts. A dark tan complemented his youthful Asian features

"Gosh. I'm terribly sorry." His left hand quickly covered a beguiling smile of ivory teeth. "Here. Let me help you with this stuff." He easily crouched down and began picking up the Danish container, crumpled napkins and plastic forks.

Finished, he wiped his hands on a tissue taken from his pocket, smiled and introduced himself. "I'm your watchdog from next door," he bowed, "Raymond Toda at your services." He smiled again. "But my friends call me Toady, for short." He carefully looked around. "I'll be very thankful when someone finally lives here. I'm getting tired of being the local 'I Spy' man for Rose. Looking out for vandals and squatters sounds exciting at first, but it becomes a hassle, particularly when things go wrong."

Kay smiled at him lopsidedly. "Well. You're not much of a watchdog. We've been running in and out of here for the last three days."

Raymond blushed and shrugged his broad shoulders. "Everything's cool. Rose's message about you two was on my e-mail the day you arrived. She said you were interested in this place. I called her last night, I was in Seattle; told her I couldn't get back as soon as she wanted me too." He contemplated his expensive sports shoes then looked up.

"It was Rose that sold me the Bremmer's old farmhouse next door. See that rooster weathervane peeking over the tree tops? It's on top of my barn. Rose is a terrific salesperson and a good friend." He nodded toward the fir trees then thrust his hands into his pockets. "It's a little difficult to always watch this house from my place, especially in the summer when all the leaves on the maples and alders come out." An awkward silence ensued.

Alex moved quickly forward and held out his hand. "It's good to meet you. My name's Alex Beahzhi and this is my fiancée Kay

Roberts." Alex grinned broadly. "You must play tennis; you've a grip of steel."

Raymond beamed. "How astute of you. I play tennis and wrestle for the Southbay Marauder's. We creamed the Normandy Mainlanders last year," he said with pride. "I also teach tennis at the Madrona Country Club. You should turn out. It really keeps you in shape. Er, not that you look like you need it," he added hastily.

Kay laughed. "Alex feels that most sports, with the exception of soccer, are as interesting as watching paint dry. But I wouldn't mind taking you up on that offer. I need to get the old tennis arm back," she said and swung her left arm in a graceful but powerful arc.

Raymond's eyes flashed a brief disappointment. "Why, I'd be glad to." He sized up Alex's large and well-distributed frame with a gleam of appreciation. "Not a sports fan? Well, how do you keep fit?"

Alex made a rueful smile at Kay. "She works the crap out of me. I've always got some 'honey do' project." He massaged his chin reflectively, "Of course I like messing about in boats and I do a bit of fencing now and then."

"He also likes to refinish or remodel anything he doesn't feel looks right." Kay gestured at the house behind them. "This will be his next big project."

Alex hooted. "See. I knew it. Kay only wants this place to keep me busy. I'll have no time to play."

"So you've made a decision to buy?" Raymond asked eagerly.

Kay glanced up at Alex. "I was sure the moment I saw the picture at the Realtors. But, Alex has pointed out some existing problems."

Alex nodded his head. "Lots of work here, but Kay's a good campaigner and the surroundings and fresh air are converting me. It has a way of recharging the old bod." He winked at her. Then a sailboat in Scoon Bay caught his eye. With only its motor running it made large lazy circles below them. He half listened to the conversation as he watched the boat below.

"That's great," Toady said enthusiastically, "Rose wouldn't give me any answers on the phone. She enjoys teasing me. All she said was that you weren't exactly sure." Raymond's eyes darted in all directions. "I've got an idea. You can make your announcement at Rose's party. It would be great PR for her." Raymond stood even taller. Kay expected his chest to explode out of his shirt at any moment.

"I'm not so sure about that," Kay said. "We're still waiting for the closure go-ahead from our lawyer. However, Max did say that it shouldn't take too much time to become a done deal."

"What's this about a party?" Alex asked.

"Er, Rose's. I thought you knew. That's one of the reasons I came over. We're all invited to dinner at Rose's houseboat this Friday. It's a once a year bash, but very casual. Everybody who is anybody on the island will be there. And she said I could be your guide... sort of."

Kay winked at Alex. "Sounds like a must. Otherwise we won't be able to meet everybody who is anybody. Will we?" She hesitated then studied the back of her hand. "Actually Raymond, I'd like to bow out. I think we've planned a quiet evening here."

Alex interrupted. "What Kay is telling you is that, in the real world, she's a hermit. And she finds most social gathering an anathema. To her, four is an oppressive group and anything over six is a mob. It's a typical only-child syndrome." He closed his eyes and pursed his lips as Kay stuck out her tongue.

Raymond was taken aback for a second then recovered. "Oh gosh, there will be a lot of people. And it really was my idea. I thought if there was even the slightest possibility we might be neighbors and all." He blushed and looked down; his voice trailed off.

Kay shook her head and chuckled. "Alex is exaggerating, but only slightly. I find crowds an anathema. However, if Rose and you have planned something, well, we would be delighted to come."

"Ah. The Queen of Isolation has decided to grace your presence," Alex said and bowed in her direction. Out of the corner of his eye he cast a quick glance back toward the inlet. Curiously the boat was making even wider circles. Something lost overboard? He asked himself.

Kay decisively stepped forward, her hands on her hips. "We'll be there with camel bells on." Kay and Alex grinned at their private joke. "Anyway, if we're going to be neighbors you may as well know some of my little foibles. It is small doses of people for me, so I'll just have to grit my teeth." She took Raymond's arm, "and I can't think of a handsomer escort."

She walked him over to the porch rail and lowered her voice. Alex seemed to be distracted so this would be as good a time as any, she thought.

"Since you seem to know...er almost everybody; are there any second-hand furniture dealers on the island? Alex and I must find some things to make this place livable. In the last few years we've become minimalists. Although I've kept a few of my mother's good pieces," she sighed. "And mad Alex would never part with his collection of vintage apple boxes," she said in a stage whisper.

Alex looked hurt. "Hey! My family always traveled light. It was my Grandmother Minnie's claim to a 'drop of gypsy blood'. And that drop came from my father's side of the tribe. She swore we were descendants of Tuscanos mixed with a drop of gypsy Basque for good measure. As a little girl she remembered the fires taken from the homeland hearths. She told me they placed the burning coals in cast iron pots at the side of their covered wagon. The fire pots swung back and forth sending out puffs of smoke as they traveled the Oregon Trail, and...."

Kay yawned. "Oh my aching arse, it's family history time again," she glanced at her watch, "And only 11:00 A.M. I'm sure neither I nor Raymond need this."

Raymond looked expectant. "Oh no, please, go on. It sounds absolutely fascinating."

Kay rolled her eyes. "The truth must be told. Alex's sister assured me that this is a lot of Italian baloney. These ethnic events happened after Minnie read about them in the local newspaper. I think you would have to classify Alex's grandmother as a romantic, and an old world wannabe."

Alex looked chagrined. "A guy can't even spin a great yarn around here."

"I think a 'great yawn' is more like it," Kay said airily.

"Okay. What Sis says may or may not be true. But I still don't see anything wrong with apple boxes. They're easily portable and lend a certain ambiance to the decor," he shook his finger at Kay, "and at present hold a lot of your stuff."

Raymond nodded his head enthusiastically. "And the wooden ones with the original labels are becoming very collectable." He removed his arm gently from Kay's. "But if you're looking for furniture, I'm the man. I happen to own the best second-hand furniture store on the island. It's called 'Toad Hall', you know, from 'The Wind in the Willows'."

Alex wasn't listening. The sailboat had stopped circling. Someone, a man or woman, was poking at the water with a boat hook. Kay moved to his side and shook his arm gently. "Yeah?" Alex responded absently.

Kay turned to Raymond. "On occasion Alex suffers from acute attention deficit disorder." She shook Alex's arm again. "What on earth are you looking at?"

Alex pointed in the direction of the inlet. "There's a boat out there. I've noticed it going in circles for the last twenty minutes. It looks like someone is searching for something, or possibly someone. Damn, the binoculars are back in the car. But, I don't see any frantic arms waving for help." Reluctantly, Alex rejoined the conversation. "What were you two going on about?"

Raymond peered in the direction that Alex had pointed, but trees blocked the view from where he stood. "There's always someone poking about." He shrugged. "Probably gathering oysters; they drift off the beds and into the inlet occasionally."

"We were talking furniture," Kay replied as she leaned back on the rail, arms crossed and surveyed the verandah. "There are a few things that would look pretty spiffy on these old boards. Take, for instance, my Grandmother's rocking chair and that pair of Bwana chairs from Byron's room."

"You take them." Alex retorted then visibly brightened. "Hey, how about that old porch swing we've stored at your Aunts?" Alex glanced at Raymond's tolerant smile. "Oh right. I happened to catch that you're the owner of 'Toad Hall'. And I'm sure you're not interested in an inventory of what we aren't going to buy."

Raymond spread his hands. "Oh. It doesn't matter either way. But do check me out. If I don't have it, I'll locate it for you." Raymond's expensive sports watch suddenly beeped at him. "Speaking of furniture, I've got to be back at the store in fifteen minutes; the ferry's docking in about a half an hour and tourists will be tromping en masse up Main Street." He winked at Alex. "It's bread and butter time. Look forward to seeing you both at the party." He waved, nodded in Kay's direction then hastily went down the side stairs that led to the brick path.

Kay shouted after him. "Alex may forget, but I won't. Is there anything we can bring?"

"No. Just your dazzling selves," he said, then waved again and disappeared around the corner of the house.

Alex leered at Kay. "Speaking of dazzle, he sure had his eyes on you." He pulled at his lower lip reflectively. "And Teri will have romantic fits when she meets him. Cripes, I don't think we can weather another infatuation so soon." He made a face as he swallowed what remained of his cold coffee then looked back at the inlet. The sailboat had disappeared.

"Hmm," Kay scratched her jaw and contemplated the last portion of her saved Danish. "Darling, somehow I don't think you have to worry your pretty little head." She batted her eyes, and flashed Alex a toothy grin. "Raymond, alias Toady, seems far more interested in you."

CHAPTER 7

# *Shaman*

**They jogged down the trail** to the beach. Kay carefully watched every turn in the path, but her mind was on the dreaded party. For heaven's sake, they had just met Rose. But she was being a kindly soul and it would be a helpful introduction into island life, Kay reasoned. But, the idea of throngs of people put butterflies in her stomach.

"I'm glad we're heading to the beach before any more visitors turn up," she shouted to Alex.

Alex didn't reply. He was looking for the sailboat, but when they arrived at the bottom of the trail it was nowhere in sight.

He shrugged and turned to Kay. "Yesterday, beyond this point I found a small stream that comes down the bank, a plank spans it. There is a dock near it and there's a path, just visible above the dock. I bet it leads up to Toady's house." He lobbed a rock far out into the inlet. "Well, at least my throwing arm's still good," he said smugly.

Behind him, Kay had picked up a stick and was busily poking around in the sand and gravel. "He said he had a barn too, can't see it from here though." She turned over a rock. "Wow, look at the baby crabs and sea life."

Alex's focus on the sailboat had not gone unnoticed. "It probably sank," Kay said as she stood up. "Alex. Look at all these mussel shells." She pointed her stick at a few old pilings. "Tomorrow, let's find a boat and row out there. How do steamed clams, mussels and garlic in a white wine sauce sound?"

"Great," he said, taking a deep breath of salt air. "A loaf of bread, a flask of wine, a book of verse and thou –." He winked at her. "And to go with that wine I'll make a few loaves of my Tuscan bread. Looked over the wooden stove last night and the flue is clear. It may be a dinosaur, but we can at least cook on the top. I found an old Dutch oven too. And, if the stove's shot, there's always the Island bakery."

"You're on with the bread, and I'll bring a dash of Khayyam to spice it up."

Alex made a sour face and groaned. "That's my pun."

Laughing, Kay stretched her arms. "The air's so fresh. I feel ten years younger."

"So do I. See if you can catch the old man," Alex yelled as he ran across the wide plank and past Toady's dock.

With a whoop, Kay bolted by him then hopped up onto a large piece of drift and did a little dance.

"See if you can keep up with the youngster. The loser touches the sand." Jumping from log to log they raced down the beach.

Alex, waving his arms wildly, signaled a quick stop and pointed.

"Whoa, water hazard dead ahead." A sizable stream cut through the low beach bank and flowed lazily into the salt water of the bay. After much splashing and testing, they could see that it was too deep to cross on foot. "This has got to be the outlet from the swamp we saw on Rose's map." He paused, "Doesn't look like there's any way to cross it. Might be a crossing ahead though, let's follow the stream inland."

A brush-covered bank bordered the clear water. Although overgrown, and sometimes muddy, the trail along the edge was easy to follow. The creek took a sharp turn then wandered through a wild, marshy meadow. A few minutes later they discovered that the stream was an outflow from a small freshwater lake.

"Alex!" Kay exclaimed as she pointed at the lily pad and cattail-lined stretch of water. "What an enchanting place." Her voice surprised a catbird. It scolded as it darted into the reeds. In a sudden flash of blue and white, a kingfisher skimmed over the pond. Chattering at them he flew into the top of a dead cottonwood tree.

"I'm afraid we're disturbing tenants in the Garden of Eden," Alex whispered as a flock of ducks quacked loudly and paddled away. "I'll say it again. It's amazing that a developer hasn't edged this pond with cheek by jowl condos. You know. Something called 'Canterbury Close' or 'Daunting Dunes' or..."

"You do go on and on. What a crepe hanger. See, that's what comes of reading Edward Abbey late into the night. Take one of Aunt Olive's advice gems seriously. Remember? 'Hang loose, enjoy breathing in the present.'"

Suddenly Kay gasped and grabbed Alex's arm. "What's that?" She pointed to a large amber-colored bird with white tipped wings. It eyed them suspiciously from the branch of a large alder.

Alex squinted. "Hmm, don't have a clue. Definitely rare, though. Can't be a duck, the ducks I'm familiar with don't spy on you from trees," he chortled. "They'd find themselves a bit out of water."

Kay elbowed him. "It's lousy form, laughing at your own joke." At that moment, a raucous cawing came from the meadow beyond them. Within seconds two large crows swooped over the treetops and settled beside the amber-marked bird.

They greeted each other with their beaks, then satisfied, preened their wings. The amber one chose to scrape its bill back and forth on the tree limb.

"I'll be damned!" Alex exclaimed. "It's actually a crow, a big one at that."

A polite cough came from behind them. "Welcome to Walsh Lake, folks, Bradestone's unofficial bird sanctuary. I'd wager you're the newcomers I've heard about," the old man chuckled.

He was of an indeterminate age; elderly but not ancient, his clothes shabby, but clean. Thick gray hair surrounded his deeply tanned face. A red headband controlled the flowing ponytail behind his neck.

Reaching forward with gnarled brown hands he clasped theirs. His handshake was strong and vigorous. It was as if he were encompassing them and their surroundings at the same time.

"Name's Willie Cloudmaker," he said smiling. Deep lines creased his kindly, weathered face. "You're the folks who're gonna buy the old Petoskey place. Nice view of the hook from there." He paused and held them with his appraising stare. "I sensed it when I first saw you young'ns, yup, strong staying power, can feel it in my bones. You're gonna be here a long, long time…yup, a very long time."

The moment was frozen. An aura of distant pasts and wisdom eternal emanated from this man. Kay was the first to become aware of their open-mouthed stares as he gently released their hands.

"I'm sorry Mr. Cloudmaker. We're…just caught by surprise. This is my fiancé, Alex Beahzhi and I'm Kay Roberts. We're the newcomers all right. At least the only ones I'm aware of," she paused and laughed nervously, "but there will be two more. My son and daughter, Byron and Teri," she looked at Alex, "fortunately, they aren't here at present."

There was an awkward silence. "Gosh, I didn't mean that the way it came out. It's only fortunate in that their curiosity is insatiable, not to mention their energy. They are able to get into dire situations in a flash. And we need down-time to make decisions right now. But we really are looking forward to them being here." She looked up. Alex seemed in a daze. "Aren't we dear?"

Willie smiled. "I dabbled a bit in mischief myself when I was a kid." His eyes twinkled. "And I didn't stop there either."

Alex shook his head and laughed. "They aren't really kids, they're young adults, but we're going to take a cue from their Aunt Olive and keep them busy. I'll wrangle them into helping square the house away before the winds of winter." Alex paused. "Everyone refers to the farm as the old Petoskey's place? Did you ever meet them?"

Yes, Willie's inner voice whispered. This was the couple. The couple that had been only shadows in his recent dreams. They were here. And they would be the ones to help him. Willie rubbed his hands together. But first, island history, this was his specialty.

"My father told me the family came from Poland. They got here sometime in the eighteen hundreds. They were among the original homesteaders on Bradestone. The Petoskeys sold fruits and vegetables. That's what people today call organic." His eyes crinkled. "Old Mrs. Petoskey use to give us ginger cookies, now they were a wonder."

Willie grinned. "They also raised the most vicious geese on the island. Why I remember one day when we kids were helping ourselves to some apples. Those hissy geese darn near took the seat out of my overalls. Heh, heh, the younger Miss Petoskey warned us that they'd just as soon bite off a finger as look at ya. But she was really protectin' their loganberry crop, from us."

His voice became conspiratorial. "But we kids figured out a way to sneak as much berries as we'd want through the wire fence near the edge of the bank." He spread his hands. "I still got all ten," he grinned. "Well, after the parents passed on, their only son just up and disappeared during the war. The sister went sort of crazy and couldn't handle the place. So one of the relatives stepped in, sold what he could and left the rest to the church...course that was long before your time."

Kay nodded. "The Realtor mentioned something about the church owning it for a while. And weren't there also some problems with back taxes? Max, our legal advisor, assures us that he can straighten out most of it."

"Mmm... There're just a few little details that I'm aware of...nothing too critical. Sides, if your lawyer is a sharpie, he shouldn't have trouble settin' it straight."

Alex frowned. "We're anxious to get in there and make some necessary repairs before the snow flies."

Willie stroked his chin. "Don't worry too much, son. Just listen to old Willie's chin wagging." He winked. "I knows a few things that you can't even guess at," he said mysteriously then laughed at their puzzled looks. "And it's more'n likely the rains will flood us afore any snow flies. But the weather can wait. I'd like you to come up to my shack for a visit."

Alex raised his eyebrows at Kay. She nodded enthusiastically. They followed Willie through a meadow and up the path to a stand of tall Pines and Douglas fir. Partially hidden at the base of the trees was Willie's 'shack'. Alex critically eyed the house. It appeared that planks and logs had been brought up from the beach for the main structure. The front door and windows were salvaged from a variety of buildings. The roof was thickly tar-papered. Even though the dwelling was patchwork, it looked sturdy and neat. Attached to the left side, at the corner of the house was a large sloping shed. It was stacked to the roof with neat piles of split wood.

Willie was still talking. "At one time this land was also part of the Petoskey farm. The oldest son sold it to my father sometime in the thirties. Besides Gravenstein apples they grew Bartlett pears, peaches, and as I mentioned before, dee-licious berries." He pointed back down the path. "Over the years the meadow's gone back to wild. But, it was orchard once. The rest, further up, was all vegetable gardens. I cut down the scrub fruit trees years ago. The wood made for excellent carve'n."

Willie looked back at Walsh pond. "Now, what were you two so interested in back there? Are you dedicated bird watchers?"

Kay laughed. "Not particularly, but we noticed an unusual crow. It was amber colored!"

"Ah. That would be my buddy, Edgar. Showed up last spring squawking his head off, cute little fella. I watched him and his siblings being raised. The parents twere a strange match; his father a raven, black as night. I named him Zondi. His mother was the sleekest, prettiest crow you ever laid eyes on. I named her Flick. They had a nest, top of that old fir tree there. One mornin, after I heard a terrible ruckus, I found them both dead. They'd been trying to protect the yong'uns from two foxes. Guess the kids decided to test their wings. The parents had put up a fierce fight, but 'twas Edgar that had scuttled off into the brush. He laid very quiet like. Yep, I got to know him. He for sure leads a charmed life."

Kay shook her head, "Sorry. It must have been horrible for you."

"It's life Ms Roberts, neither bad nor good, it just is. When you live close to nature things are a little clearer."

Alex squinted back at the tree with the crow's nest. "Living out here, I'd bet a lot of different birds come through. But, I'd sure like to get a closer look at that crow."

Willie turned to Alex. "Well son, if you and your lady are real quiet I just might introduce you to Edgar. Of course he can be a tad touchy at times. Acts like an idjit when you least expect him to. But, we'll give it a shot."

Willie cupped his hands around his mouth and cawed three times. He paused, listened carefully, and then called: "Come on Edgar, get yourself outta them trees. We got some visitors here; they'd like to make your 'quaintance."

There were three loud answering caws. Then, gliding out of the trees in larger and larger circles, came Edgar. The sun backlit his body, his feathers shimmered with an amber and white glow.

"He's magical," Kay whispered.

Edgar flew cautiously. He spiraled once around them. Cawed and landed abruptly on Willie's shoulder. Then he tilted forward almost losing his balance.

"I'll be damned," Alex muttered with a chuckle.

"These are nice people, Edgar. They stopped by to say 'hello'. Don't forget to mind your manners."

Edgar looked sideways at Alex, dipped his head then pecked at the edge of Willie's glasses.

"Okay, okay," Willie said softly and pulled out brown pellets from a bag in his shirt pocket; Edgar beaked them greedily from his weathered hand. "He likes the dried cat food best. Edgar will worry a cat till he can pirate their dish." The bird nodded his head, as if in agreement, then promptly gulped more of the proffered pellets.

"Will he let me touch him?" Kay asked excitedly.

"Maybe, maybe not," Willie said then grinned. "You can try. Just remember, he likes to have the back of his head feathers stroked, in particular. And his bill's plenty sharp."

Softly talking to Edgar, Kay raised her hand. He regarded her warily then let her gently stroke his feathers.

Alex moved forward and whispered in Kay's ear: "That's enough. I'd like to give it a whirl."

Slowly Kay removed her hand. Alex raised his.

"Ouch! That damned beast," Alex exclaimed as Edgar took a peck, squawked and shot around the side of the house.

Flexing his finger, Alex swore under his breath. It bled well. He sucked it and cursed between spats of blood and saliva on the ground. Willie and Kay laughed uncontrollably.

"He's more partial to pretty women," Willie said and winked at Kay.

She was still laughing. "Poor, poor Alex, did the itty-bitty bird draw blood from the big man's hairy hand?"

Alex glared at his smarting finger. "He's not an itty-bitty bird. And this will most likely swell up to the size of a bratwurst. That crow packs a mean peck. And I've read somewhere they can peck clear to the bone." They laughed again as Alex, frowning and sucking his finger, walked toward Willie's house.

"I hope he doesn't decide to attack again," Alex said, peering over his shoulder. They were standing on the small porch of Willie's house.

"Don't worry son," Willie chuckled. "He's got an open cage on the other side of the wood shed, probably worked up an appetite though...heh, heh."

Alex glanced around. "How did he become so tame? I've always thought crows don't like people."

"You're right there. Most other living things give man a wide birth. You can't blame them, the way they're treated. But, it was Edgar's idea. He decided to stick around and become part of the family. He's real fine company, but sometimes he gets too nosy for his own good."

"Anyway, I took him to the shack. Taught him my ways and he taught me his. Then I showed him the door. But he kept comin' back. We're a team now." Willie lowered his voice. "Course he likes to play tricks." He shook his head. "And the crafty bugger has one really bad habit."

"I'm trying to imagine what that could be," Alex said quickly, scanning the sky.

Willie chuckled. "Don't worry about Edgar. It's the wily seagulls at the beach you have to be wary of. If you irritate them, they'll bomb ya. Why I've seen them drop a clam on a body's head when you're just sittin' innocently, enjoying the sun. Course, the gulls are only trying to break the shell open for dinner. It would flatten most people. But you gotta watch 'em all the time, their philosophy usually is: if we miss you from one end, we'll hit you from t'other."

With images of lethal, dive-bombing seagulls, Alex rolled his eyes.

"A crow must make less of a mess than a seagull," Kay said with a giggle.

"Well, that's not Edgar's problem. He's very neat about that." Willie looked around then said in sotto voce, "You see Edgar's problem is that he's a thief. Course you don't want to let him hear you say that. He's sensitive."

"A thief?" Kay exclaimed then whispered, "What do you mean?" Willie squinted. "Anythin's fair game, if he can take off with it. He's particularly partial to things that glitter. You should take a gander at the shelf in his cage sometime. It's littered with pieces of glass, foil, and buttons. Why there's even a gent's cufflink and a pair of cheaters!"

"Cheaters! What's that?" Alex asked.

"Read'n glasses to you, sonny." Willie shook his head. "It can be real embarrassing. He even stole one of my guest's sandwich, once."

Kay and Alex smiled at the look of consternation on Willie's face.

"Well, I could stand here and palaver all day about that crazy crow. But come on in. I'll show you my digs, and I got some iodine that'll fix up Edgar's love bite pretty quick."

## CHAPTER 8

# *Treasures*

**The door opened** into a single large room. A handmade workbench, covered with wood chips, stood against the back wall. Above, woodworking tools hung neatly from a section of peg-board.

Cripes, I'm hungry again, Alex thought, as the aroma of fresh split cedar and smoked salmon made his stomach growl.

Willie cleared a pile of magazines and books from the top of a large kitchen table. The surface was protected by a lively, checker-patterned oilcloth.

"Morning poison?" he asked, pouring a ruby-red liquid out of a Jack Daniel's bottle into a small glass.

"Too early for me," Alex replied. "A glass of water would be nice though."

Kay nodded in agreement then wandered past a wood-fired cook stove over to the workbench. A carving, resting on a rectangular wooden clamping vice, had caught her eye.

"Water will rust your pipes. This here's blackberry cordial. Put it up last year," Willie said then suggested hopefully, "only fruit juice, and it tastes pretty good."

"Well. That does sound delicious." Kay mumbled absently as she picked up the wood carving from the table. It was a crow-like bird, with a long handle for a tail. A fragile man-like creature lay carved in raised relief on the bird's back. The man appeared to be, with a long tongue, performing an unusual act upon himself. It was erotic, remarkable and beautiful.

"That's one of my doodads," Willie said over his shoulder as he poured generous amounts of cordial into three jelly glasses.

"It's amazing. What is it?" Kay asked as she gently handed the object to Alex. He traced the intricate details with his fingers. Something rattled inside. Kay noticed a similar carving hanging above the bench. It was painted red and black.

"That's a Kwakiutl Raven rattle. My great uncle George, on my mother's side, carved 'em, then he taught me how to work the wood."

"Willie, this is unbelievable. What else do you carve?" asked Alex.

Willie set his glass down, walked over and pulled aside a long burlap curtain. It hid five generous, wooden shelves. Items were stacked haphazardly. There were carved bowls, rattles, trays and small boxes of all shapes and sizes. Some of the cedar boxes on the lowest shelf were inlaid with polished white seashells.

Alex picked up a burnished bowl in the shape of a fish. He turned it over in his hand. "This is beautiful! I thought clear grain cedar was almost impossible to get."

"Oh there's plenty around when you've got some special sources." He grinned then handed them both a brimming glass. "You'd be surprised. There are still a few old growth stumps left from the time the white man first logged this island. And at times I still can find chunks of cedar drift on the beach. But alder is good too," Willie said as he tossed his drink back.

Kay and Alex gingerly sipped theirs.

"Mmm Willie, this is wonderful. It gives such a warm feeling… down the throat," Kay said with a gasp.

"Goes right for the toes too," Alex added as he gulped the rest of his.

Willie's eyes twinkled. "Like another? It's real medicinal, particularly if you need a wake up, or got the trots."

Without waiting for a reply he poured and topped his off with a grand flourish of the Daniel's bottle. "Yep, carve'ns kept me in business. I've even done a few things to 'up my income' as the Suits say," he winked. "A few years ago, I buried five of my first masks in the backyard," he winked, "sorta helps them age. People thought they were real old artifacts, heh, heh. Take those whippersnappers from the local museum. They spotted two of them at a friend of mine's. They thought for sure I'd taken them from a burial cache, somewheres. Anyhow, they were going round in circles. In the end I leveled with them. But it was sure fun at the time."

"I can see why they were confused. This rattle looks like the real thing," Alex shook it. "Years ago, when I was in grad school, I had a chance to visit the Indian museum in Victoria, BC. I was with a buddy of mine, Roland Shakleford. You remember, Kay. Role's working on that dig in Mauritania."

"Oh yes. How could I forget Roland? He's the character that always got you into trouble, in your 'traveling-round-the-world-days'," Kay said as she arched her eyebrows at Alex. "I remember when I ran across those photos of indigenous women, au naturel. I'm sure that he'd documented the pictures with detailed field notes. But curiously the notes didn't survive," she said dryly.

Alex blushed then stuck his chin out. "Well, yes. Besides his scientific pursuits he does have a very healthy interest in the ladies." He turned to Willie. "Anyway, one of Roland's hobbies is researching Northwest Coast Indian cultures. He's particularly interested in their artwork. And from what he showed me at a museum one time, it would take an expert to tell your carvings apart from the originals."

Willie stroked his chin. "Probably right there, and let you in on a little secret. Several of my Uncle George's carvings are in Museums. And some look a couple of hundred years old. He was real proud of them carvings. He was pretty clever about aging things too. After all, he was just making things look like they were in the old times." He paused for a moment. "George was full-blood Tlingit, just like my mother."

"Was your dad full-blood too?" Alex asked.

"My dad? ...nope, totally different kettle of fish, he was an Oregon cowpoke, didn't like cow wrangling. Told me Uncle George had a real skill and encouraged me to follow in his footsteps." He looked at the floor with a sad expression. "Course they're all gone now."

Kay glanced at Alex. "Willie. I bet these would bring a hefty price at any native art gallery in Seattle."

"Oh, as I said, I've sold some all right, but Toad Hall's my best outlet." Willie looked up with a grin. "You guys know Toady?"

Alex nodded vigorously. "We met him this morning. Understand he's quite a tennis player."

"Now there you'll find a great neighbor and a real human being. He's always finding me new customers, and the best kind, the ones willing to pay cash. No damn plastic or phony checks and no taxes neither."

Willie waved his arm. "But, as you can see, don't need the money. Got everything I want. Besides fish'n and beach-comb'n, it's carve'n I like best." He ran his hands lovingly over a polished cedar bowl. "I guess art is in my blood."

"Mine too," Kay said softly. "I love working in clay. But my favorite is designing the pottery shapes and also making pine needle baskets."

"And she has the touch," Alex said as he eyed the bottom of his empty jelly glass.

Willie nodded eagerly at Kay. "For you and me, it's the way, the only way, using the blood and flesh of mother Earth. Our lives are too damn short though. We can get our fingers in there, imagine it, create it, and shape it, but only for a little while. I wouldn't want it any other way though. It's our offering of love to the Great Spirit and that spirit within each other. In the end, we and our gift return, return to the earth mother. I think to be born sometime again, don't you reckon?" He didn't wait for an answer. "But, I do figure we artists are the luckiest people alive." His eyes focused on something far away. "Somehow we're able to borrow someth'en beautiful, then allowed to carry it, even if it's just for a little while," he muttered again.

Alex cleared his throat. "Willie thanks for the blackberry cordial. It was really delicious. But we've got to travel on. If we're going to be neighbors, before winter, we can't miss our appointment with Rose. She's supposed to have some news on closing the property deal with Max."

Willie looked around. It was obvious he did not want them to leave.

"I don't see too many people out here. Although, there were a couple of Suits a week or two back. Not too friendly, I offered them some cordial. But they acted like I was goin' to poison 'em. In fact they got down right ornery. Said I didn't have the right to my land. They said I was trespassing. Course, they hadn't done their homework." He looked up and grinned. "It was a good reminder of what my ancestors had to put up with."

Willie held up his glass. He carefully studied the ruby color in a beam of sunlight shafting through the window.

"Thought you otta know. This juice comes from no ordinary blackberry. The canes come from my niece Mary's place in Oregon. She calls them Marion berries. They taste considerable different than the local berries. And make a helluva good pie. She gave me four cuttings six years ago. They took off like Gangbusters."

Kay reluctantly put the rattle back on the table. "Gangbusters? Like in those old movie channels?"

Willie chortled. "Ah you're too young. Twas an old radio program, maybe Alex remembers."

"I heard of it. But, I'm just another child weaned on television. Like Kay." Alex looked around. Willie did not have a television set. Nor were there signs of a toilet.

"Here," Willie said as he took a finished Tlingit rattle hanging on the pegboard and placed it in Kay's hand. "I think you'd like this." He winked at Kay.

"Oh do I, but I just can't take it. I'll buy one from Toady."

"No. I want you to have it. It's a gift. It's from one of Earth's artist's to another." Kay tried to step back, but Willie gently took her arm.

"Look, if'n it makes you feel better, I'll trade it for one of them pine needle baskets. That's when you finally get moved in. You don't want to hurt an old man's feelings, do you?"

"Willie. This is too lovely!" There was silence. She paused then looked at Willie's face. "Okay. It's a deal," she said, turning the rattle over in her hand. "But, I'm getting the better part of it."

Alex could see Kay was moved. He cleared his throat and began croaking good-byes as he steered Kay gently towards the door.

Willie wiped the lip of his decanter with a spotless cloth, poked in a crystal stopper, and placed it back on a shelf. "Don't forget. Edgar and I are never too far away. You know you're welcome, anytime."

When they reached the pond, Alex stopped and exhaled deeply. "Gad it's beautiful scenery. Willie's right. I can see living here 'til the end of our days." He squeezed Kay's fingers then hesitated. "Does he give you sort of an eerie feeling?" he asked, then laughed nervously as he continued, "he reminds me of some ancient 'sayer of sooths'."

Kay shivered then looked up. "Maybe he's not real. Maybe he's some mythological being that guards this pond and the meadow." She looked back. The old house was still nestled in the trees and smoke curled lazily from its chimney. "It hasn't disappeared," she said with a nervous laugh.

Alex shook his head then started to move again. "That must've been 151 proof berry-juice. I don't think my feet are touching the ground. The old fart's an artist with his booze as well as his wood!"

Kay giggled then gently shook the rattle. "Even my toes are numb. But, you're the old fart. We don't have to be back at Rose's until four o'clock."

"The cordial made me realize we haven't had anything to eat since breakfast," Alex said then grabbed Kay's free hand. A salt-scented breeze gently ruffled the tall beach grass.

"You're always thinking about your stomach." Kay said as she punched his arm.

"Hey! It's not just my stomach!" Alex exclaimed then threw her a smoldering glance. "That cordial's had a tremendous effect on me."

"Me too," Kay giggled.

Without a sound, Edgar swooped overhead. He circled unnoticed, as hand in hand they ran down the beach.

## CHAPTER 9

# *House Mosh*

**Rose's party was a last minute decision** for Kay. Alex thought she would likely be miserable so he pointed out all the advantages of attending. New friends, the acceptance by locals, become part of the Island network…etc, etc, but still she had resisted.

As they pulled onto a gravel shoulder, their headlights swept over the houseboat in the distance. The party was in full frenzy.

Alex quickly enlisted Kay's help in scoping out a parking place. She pointed to a vacant lot, dominated by a tug boat on its own dry-dock and well behind the cars that lined the road down to Rose's houseboat.

"Fish and whiskers," Kay exclaimed. "It's a floating pink gift-box."

Awnings, on the first and second stories, furthered the impression by giving the appearance of white and green striped ribbons decorating a giant package. Flexing shapes danced by the windows and laughter, mixed with the beat of reggae, drifted across the water and echoed from the opposite shore. Alex glanced at Kay's grim face. "Kind of reminds me of our intimate courting days."

Kay smiled weakly. "Ha, yeah sure…I'm taking a deep breath before we enter that sardine sauna."

Once out of the car, Kay, in an effort to relax, began to move with the music. Snapping her fingers, she swayed seductively, bumping Alex's hip several times. "We should dance right here. It'll be hopeless inside."

Alex molded her body to his. "You know, we can always use hand signals. Or, if you prefer, there's such a thing as extreme-body-contact."

Kay laughed. "The Magna Cum Laude graduate of Body Glove U swings into action."

Carefully he maneuvered her down the bumpy road to the dock. Once there, they danced with ease.

Kay pointed behind him. "Look! Guess whose muscle car? The Hall must be doing quite well financially." Alex swung Kay around. The first parked car, next to the houseboat's gangplank, was a sleek, black, Trans-Am. The vanity plate boldly proclaimed, 'TOADHAL'.

He swung her back. "Not bad. It pays to advertise. Um, it appears the welcoming committee has spotted us."

Silhouetted in the light of the open door was Raymond. Rose peered around his large frame.

"Hola muchachos!", she yelled as she shaded her eyes. "Is that the very late Kay and Alex? We thought you two might have taken the 'Love Boat' to Vashon." She hooted, hooked her arm through Toady's, and raised a glass of what appeared to be an extremely large Margarita. "Welcome to La Casa Rosa."

Alex twirled Kay around and muttered in her ear, "I would hypothesize that the theme is Mexicana and all hands are three serapes to the win." He yelled back, "We mucho tarde hombres plead the Senora's pardon!"

"De nada!" Rose shouted, raising her drink in a grand gesture. "Prepare yourshelves for an authentic Bradestone fiesta. Toady's tending bar." She clutched his steadying arm. "You can name your desire. But his Margaritas are magnifico!" She gazed passionately up at Toady. "Aren't they dear?"

He put his hands on her shoulders and kissed her hair affectionately. "Whatever the Senora says," he replied softly as he waved at Kay and Alex. "We're having a great time. Come aboard and I'll rustle up some drinks. There's salsa, chips and goodies on the table near the kitchen, that's if you can fight your way there."

With Raymond and Rose as shields, Kay and Alex plunged inside. The houseboat throbbed.

"Name your poison!" Raymond yelled back at them.

"Anything. Just so it's quick," Alex shouted as he caught a hint of panic in Kay's eyes.

"Gotcha! Be right back," Raymond shouted. The crowd made way as he headed toward the bar against the far wall.

"He's shuch a sweet boy," Rose said as she slurped on her straw. "He helped me all afternoon, even closed the Hall early." She smiled up at Alex. "He's taken a real shine to you two." She smiled hazily then glanced into her empty goblet. "Hope he doesn't forget mine!"

Shortly, a perspiring Raymond presented a tray of icy drinks with a flourish. Kay was amazed that he was able to negotiate the crowd without disaster and said so.

"My chief insurance is everyone knows I'm thee bartender, and not to be messed with. A Margarita for you dear Rose and my famous Pina Coladas for my new neighbor; cheers amigos." Alex took a healthy swig, gasped then caught his breath.

"More like infamous," Alex exclaimed as his eyes watered. They laughed, and raised their glasses in a salute to Raymond.

"Thanks. We started on Slammers with the first guests, you two missed out."

"Oh, I think this is more than adequate," Kay said then took another sip of her drink. Rose excused herself and hurried off. Kay began to count heads. This will calm my nerves, she thought and slowly scanned the room.

Furniture had been pushed against walls, and the large room was filled with at least forty people. From the brouhaha overhead, it sounded to Kay that there were probably as many crowded on the upper story and it's deck. Raymond caught her eye.

"This is Rose's yearly blast, among other smaller ones," he whispered into Kay's ear. "She says it keeps the regulars alive and breathing; but a few of the more conservative Islanders consider our party-life a bit vulgar." He looked around him. "They're probably right. But, if you look around, you'll see some of our loudest critics here; they like to boogie too."

The pressure of gyrating dancers slowly moved the trio toward the center of the room. Those who wished to avoid the mix of moving bodies talked in tight cliques along the wall. Hanging from the ceiling above twirled a gigantic goldfish piñata with bulging sequined eye. Kay imagined it was desperately searching for a way to escape through the smoke and the din.

Alex spotted the food table. Mumbling apologies, he excused himself and pushed towards the mounds of edibles. To his surprise, the offerings weren't exclusively Mexican. He stacked two paper plates and loaded the top one with an enchilada, humus dip and a salad, laced with chunks of feta cheese and Greek olives. He also helped himself to a large slice of what looked and tasted like sweet potato pie. Mmm… another small slice wouldn't hurt, he thought, licked his fingers then searched for whipped cream. The container was out. He promised himself a return struggle then grabbed several napkins. Craning his neck, he began radaring for either Kay or Raymond. They should be tall enough to spot.

"Wow, such a hungry man."

With a hot shrimp rolling on the edge of his tongue he looked down into a pair of intense brown eyes, flecked with gold. Curly black hair complemented a rich mahogany skin, and a colorful Caftan complemented her figure.

"Here, your hands are full, let me help you." She reached up with a napkin and brushed crumbs off Alex's chin.

"I see you like the sweet-potato pie…made it myself. Rose always insists that I bring them. Though I'm not sure it goes so well with a shrimp chaser." She offered her hand. "The name is Ujima. Ujima Washington, and to whom do I owe the pleasure?"

She was what his buddy, Role would call, 'thunderingly beautiful'. Like an automaton, he put one plate down and shook her hand.

"I'm Alex, Alex Beahzhi. The pie was … superb. I was taking some to my fiancée, Kay Roberts and her friends. But they are…," he gestured helplessly toward the center of the room.

"Probably un-findable till this shindig takes a breather," she finished for him. "Don't worry. Toady and Rose will protect her," she said and smiled with perfect white teeth. She brushed back her hair, jewels glittered in her multi-pierced ears and bracelets tinkled on her wrists. She took the plate of food from his hand and placed it on the table. "The wrong combinations," she said, shaking her finger.

"Uh, no," Alex said. He didn't even object when the man standing next to them winked and commandeered his abandoned plate of food.

"You're new to the island. I haven't seen you or your fiancée around at all." She waved her slender hand. "What's the story?"

Alex's brain finally engaged his mouth. "Hey! It's okay if you manage my diet. But are you sure you want personal data?"

Ujima looked thoughtful. "Actually I do. You see I'm the local's nosey Sergeant on this small island and newcomers always interest me."

Alex wanted to say, you're way too young. But with a wide smile said: "Really pleased to meet you, er Sergeant Washington."

Ujima smiled broadly up at him and took his hand in a firm grip. "I'm off duty tonight, but I can't shake my snoopy habits," she said with a deep, throaty laugh. "Checking out the newbies has its advantages on a small island like this. But, let's go somewhere else. A 747 could land here and not be noticed. Follow me. And don't worry about the food running out. Rose has plenty left in the kitchen." With a large drink in her hand, she led Alex to a glass sliding door.

He noticed that people easily moved aside for the sergeant even though they weren't necessarily looking in her direction. On the houseboat's deck the air was refreshingly damp. Alex took one last concerned look back for Kay. She was probably miserable, but at least she was miserable with Rose and Toady nearby.

The party sounds eclipsed as Ujima slid the glass door shut. There was still noise from above, but he could hear the lapping of waves on the hull and the echoing bark of a dog across the water. It helped too, that the beat of a slower dance tune had begun.

Ujima shook her head. "Now, isn't that better? Rose does have terrific parties. But they become increasingly louder and sweatier as the evening wears on." She grinned up at him. "I couldn't help noticing, when you came in the door, that your fiancée, Kay Roberts, appeared a tad apprehensive." Ujima raised a questioning eyebrow and took a sip of her drink.

"Yeah, she detests big crowds. But she's a real trooper." He laughed. "She actually wanted to leave before we got here. I halfway convinced her it would be a great opportunity to meet new neighbors, and get the lay of the land, so to speak." He looked back into the crowded room. "Now I'm not so sure."

Ujima made a concerned noise in the back of her throat. "I can empathize with how she feels. I don't like crowds myself, but sometimes it comes with the job." She paused and took a thoughtful sip of her drink. "So you've decided to join the natives?" She looked around. "Bradestone's not a bad place. Not as incestuous as some small communities can become." She took a sip of her drink. "It took some a long time to accept me as their black Sergeant, and a woman at that. Ujima sighed. "Anyway, Rose mentioned that a couple was interested in the new 'Gull' condos on the east shore. Are you them?"

"No. No Yuppie-Ville for us. Rose let us camp out at an old farmhouse called the Petoskey's place and we're hooked."

"Ah, ha, now I'm making connections. You're the couple interested in the farm next to Toady's. He couldn't stop babbling about it. Good ole thinking-out-of-the-box Rose, you're possibly getting a much better deal." She paused. "The Condos were built too fast in my judgment. Superior Island Properties Inc. is the most aggressive developer on the island. There've been complaints, actually many. Fortunately, sub-contractors have gone back and fixed most of the problems. Of course 'Superior' tried to keep it hush-hush, but that's almost impossible on a small island." She shook her head then studied him intently.

Alex laughed. "Yeah, we're the guilty ones. And you're certainly hot-wired into the Island's underground network." His thoughts went to Willie. "Some of the people that we've bumped into seemed to know we were buying the old Petoskey place before we did!" He put his hand to his head. "Assuming you live here too, we already probably know intimate details about each other; we just haven't had the opportunity to attach a name to a face!"

Ujima laughed. "Oh yes. I live here all right," she sighed. "Sergeant Washington by day and some would say, 'Ujima the inquisitor' by night. But I do like to keep my hands on the Island's pulse. I try to acquaint with all newcomers as soon as I can. It's my cop mentality thing. Besides I've such a small department here I've got to know who I can trust to press into service and who I can't."

House lights glittered like jewels on the opposite jet-black shore and a pale moon began to rise behind tall firs. They ceased talking and enjoyed the beauty of the night.

Alex felt that Kay had every right to kill him. Gad, dragging her into this chaos. He wanted her to be with him right now. She'd get a kick out of being grilled and vetted by the local Sergeant. Then his stomach interrupted his conscience with a low growl. He groaned. He should have grabbed an enchilada, or at the very least, another shrimp roll.

Ujima stirred the ice in her drink with her finger. "When I was a kid my father bugged me about asking too many questions. So when I got older it seemed only natural to find a job where I would get paid for asking a lot of questions."

Alex raised his eyebrows and said, "So I guess everyone you meet is in for it?"

"Could be, but first off, I'd like to welcome you and your family to Bradestone. It's a great place," she paused. "The Petoskey farm, I remember, a choice piece of property, with a sweeping view of Heron's Hook and Scoon Bay." She grimaced. "Haven't had reasons to go there ... at least, for a while."

"Yup, that's the one," Alex answered.

She turned around, rested her back against the railing, and faced him. "I know Rose doesn't think this is too significant. But, it seems someone attempted to burn it down last winter. If it hadn't been for Toady hearing prowlers that night, and calling 911, everything would have been toast. We didn't catch them, though. They came up from the beach. We heard a motorboat take off just after we got there. We found a few cans of kerosene and other things were left behind. No damage done and nothing we could trace." She took another sip of her drink.

"Well, an empty and isolated building, what a temptation to kids."

"Funny. Toady thought it was kids too. I didn't. The incident was too well thought out, too coordinated. I think adventure seekers would've gone over the fence or through the gate. They're much nearer to the house. It's quite a bother to drag cans of kerosene up the steep trail from the beach. Most of the teens around here would just flick a lighter and ignite whatever was at hand." Ujima shook her head. "Rose didn't want me to file a report. The whole thing seemed strange to me."

Ujima fiddled with her drink and then looked seriously at Alex. "I don't want you and Kay to get too nerved-out, but I'd keep an eye on things for a while. Toady does an excellent job, but he's not always home. And do call the police if you see anything peculiar. I don't care if it turns out to be a false alarm. Better 'safe than sorry' is the motto I operate under."

"Thanks for the information. I'll catch Kay up on what you said. She'll be concerned at first, but then she'll get curious. And it's better if we're both aware of what's going on."

Ujima looked up at Alex's face. "Here, finish my mai-tai. It's too much for me. I've got two straws and only used this one. It might help you relax. I can tell you're concerned about Kay, but you're not going to be able to get through. The party seems to have slipped into overdrive."

He took a sip of her drink and glanced through the large glass slider. She was right. Bodies hid the bar completely. Where had they all come from? Neither Kay, Rose nor Raymond was in sight.

Alex turned to Ujima, groaned then scratched his head. "I guess we can make use of the time. Frankly, I'd rather listen to your life story and exercise my right to remain silent. If I find Kay then we both can regale you."

Ujima eyed him carefully. "Oh, okay. That's fair enough."

She spoke in a low voice, more to herself than Alex. "I'll go a ways back. Umm… start with my Grandparents on mom's side. They came from Brooklyn. They were real light." She raised her eyebrows. "My dad's parents are darker, and lived in far more interesting places, like Jamaica. You've heard of the island of Curacao in the Caribbean?"

Alex smacked his lips. "It's the origin of that delicious orange liqueur. Isn't it?"

"Yes, it is. Anyway, I've never had the opportunity to meet others of his family that moved there. But I've always wanted to find them, and I intend to take a much needed vacation when I do." She paused, took her drink back from Alex and tugged at it slowly.

There was a glistening in the corner of her eye as she delicately wiped her lips and handed the drink back to him.

"Oh yes. There's always an interesting half to families," he interrupted awkwardly. "With me it's Gypsy-Basque, from my great-grandparents on my Grandmother's side. My Great Grandma Minnie grilled it into us that since we had 'a drop of gypsy blood in our veins' we'd always have an itchy foot." He nodded to himself. "That could be why I've never planted permanent roots; till now that is. Kay says it's because I'm a Gemini… that makes just as much sense." He laughed, his face turned red. "And, I apologize for interrupting your story. So, how did you wind up here?"

Ujima smiled slowly. "I was working for the S.P.D. That's the Seattle Police Department to you. And I simply became tired of big-city politics. Thought I'd try a small rural town. They wanted a token minority here, so I applied, fortunately I have excellent references." She shook her head and took a deep breath. "It's really amusing. The islanders think with a few Blacks in the works they're totally integrated."

Alex nodded. "That's the norm isn't it? Most small communities, including the academic, have a similar view. Though, based on the little experience Kay and I have had here, the town doesn't seem too 'WASPish'. Toady told Kay it's either dull or pleasant, and that depends on whether you run into the 'old guard' or not. Toady says he hasn't noticed any entrenched racists." He made a circle with his hands. "But we know they're always around us."

"Amen to that. But he's right. It's fairly quiet. And I've only caused a few raised eyebrows when I appear in uniform. Before I came here, a black-owned bakery was burned to the ground. It was proved to be arson and the Islanders chorused that it was some shit-disturbers from the mainland." She took a deep breath. "But, I'm not so sure. Some of the 'old guard' actually treats me with civility. Of course, they raise collective howls when we have the occasional problem with visitors. Not in the plans 'don't you know' puts a blot on ye olde Island's escutcheon. But it's usually hyped-up teens, congenital boozers, dopers and burned-out marriages that cause the most trouble." She stretched up on her toes and placed her elbows on the railing.

"So the job, so far, has been pretty routine. And for the first time I've found a place where a person can stretch spiritually as well as emotionally. We're free from most of the inner city hassles." She looked down at her empty left hand. "One has the space and the time to start finding oneself. The locals call it Island time."

Her bracelets clinked melodically as Alex returned her drink. "Sorry, I finished it."

She nodded and laughed suddenly. "Actually, the one major drawback you've already discovered, is that everybody seems to know your business before you do; one learns to take steps to keep one's life private and away from the gossips."

Together they fell silent. Each focusing on the black waters below them and considering the bits from their backgrounds they were willing to share. Finally the moon cleared the trees. Ujima laughed joyously as a light breeze ruffled its silver reflection on the water.

"Well." Alex shrugged his shoulders. "I guess to be fair, it's my turn. You've already heard about the Basque. The rest may be tedious."

"Oh. Not to worry. I've developed a tough hide when it comes to hours of on-droning testimony." She chuckled.

He scratched his chin. "Well. Here's to the new drone. To begin with, there are three special people in my life; Kay, of course, Kay's daughter Teri, and son Byron. Kay and I wanted out from the big city life." He looked amused. "Of course the kids prefer otherwise. But anyway, when I retired from teaching, we figured we could easily leave wall-to-wall freeways, city crime and smog to the young and durable. It's short of a miracle that we found Rose, the farmhouse, and at just the right time."

Ujima looked up at him through her long lashes. "Retired, why you don't look old enough," she said mockingly then chuckled. "Everyone says that don't they?"

Alex snorted. "Truer words were never spake! I've gotten so I tell them I'm a victim of corporate downsizing and I keep a portrait in the attic. It's less involved that way."

Ujima smiled. "Tell me more about your family."

"Let me see. Byron turns eighteen this July. He will be a freshman in college. He's decided to major in Art. Teri will be graduating this year with a degree in Anthropology. Both are spending the first part of their college break with their Aunt Olive. But we hope to drag them up here for the rest of the summer. Teri has reservations about island life though," he remarked darkly.

Ujima looked surprised. "Get her interested in some of the shell middens that are here. And locals have plowed up quite a complement of cannon balls, not to mention a few skulls. This island, according to La Rose, has a history and a colorful past. Amazingly, some local descendants are still involved in squabbles that started when their ancestors pushed the indigenous people out. And there are the land-grabbing disputes of the lumber barons in the last century. From an Anthropologist's point of view, there's plenty to discover, research and document right here on this island. That is if ancient or even pre- modern Northwest history would turn Teri on."

"Oh, she has a wide variety of academic and cultural interests." He smiled. "However, from what Kay and I have been able to gather, they seem to be mainly centered on the puberty rites of young men."

Ujima laughed. "You and Kay do have your hands full." She counted off on her fingers. "Two kids in college. The main man retired, buying a big place on this not so cheap island," she paused, "it doesn't take too much math to figure out you and Kay must have enough loot to make the good life."

"Ah yes, the Nevada millions. It's fairly simple. My father had a rather eccentric cousin. We knew her as aunt Nellie Nevada. Dad said she was incorrigible the minute she shot out of the womb. Anyway, she led quite a life. Five years ago we heard she sailed off the edge of the earth; somewhere in the South China Sea. No one knows what happened. Authorities said that the Boogie Pirates got her. Anyway, she must have had a sixth sense. She left her favorite nephew, my brother, a small legacy." Alex looked sad. "Then he died and it turned out I was his sole beneficiary. Ergo, I could retire early." He shrugged and rolled his eyes. "And then there's Kay's Aunt Olive.

Ujima looked surprised. "Well, well. How does the other Aunt, er Aunt Olive, figure into all this?"

"It does appear that we're at the mercy of caring Aunts. Aunt Olive is Kay's deceased husband's sister. She dotes on the family and always tries to help Kay financially. She's also set aside funds to assist the kids."

Ujima shook her head. "I'm jealous; I'd like to be spoiled by doting relatives."

"The kids could have been, but have limited access to the money. Kay and the family lawyer, the great Max, dole it out, of course under the eyes of Aunt Olive. And Kay makes sure that the kids can only get their money on a documented needs basis." Alex assumed a pedantic air. "It encourages them to create meaningful and reasonable budgets for themselves and it's an invaluable lesson in economics at a tender age."

"Um, I can only dream of what having that kind of financial freedom would have done for me when I was young."

"Me too; I come from a dirt-poor background. So I'm in a pretty amazing place in my life now. But you know kids, even though they've got it all, they still complain. You should hear some of their imaginative reasons for advances. Fortunately, with Kay's wise leadership she helps the kids see reality and hold the line."

"So, what do you and Kay do to keep yourselves entertained? You don't exactly strike me as the dreary world cruise duo."

"For starters, I've a hunch that the farmhouse will be more of an involved remodeling project than either one of us had imagined. Kay is an excellent carpenter, and she has an artist's eye for interior remodeling. Even though she's financially set up better than I am she uses her artwork to supplement her income. So we're doing okay. We won't suffer as long as we keep the house remodeling and our tastes moderate." He nodded. "Yeah, between our incomes we'll do okay."

"An artist, what does Kay do?"

"Pine needle baskets, pottery and she's pretty damned good at jewelry making. Kay plans to convert an outbuilding near the house into her studio. It's a convenient size and close to another dilapidated structure that has possibilities. Unfortunately, the larger one is buried under blackberry vines." He winked. "That's the one I'll appropriate for my workshop."

Alex became more garrulous. "Kay will have a lot of elbow space when we get the two buildings cleaned up." He paused. "Scoon Bay is a great asset too. We'd like to build a boat landing there, and I wouldn't mind someday," his eyes went out of focus, "opening the best damn bed-and-breakfast in the Northwest!"

Ujima downed her drink. "I would say you're going to be a very busy couple. Of course it's none of my business. But wouldn't the state of marriage be a financial advantage to both of you?"

Alex scratched his head. "Now that's a hard one for me to answer. You see, in the beginning, Aunt Olive and Max assumed I was just another gold digger, until my intentions and Kay's deluge of arguments convinced them otherwise. I want to marry her. And I like helping raise those great kids. But Kay's had a few bad patches in the past, and I don't want to get too pushy, right now…" his voice trailed off and he spread his hands. "Max as you know by now is our legal eagle. He had us set up our estate documents so that we're both comfortable with how things work, married or not. And we're both committed to spending the rest of our lives together. The single scene, when you reach a certain age, becomes as the Spanish say, 'muy viejo'."

Ujima seemed bemused. "Say, I just remembered something else about the old Petoskey place. It was an article in our local paper, The Spindrift. Two skulls, brown with age, were found on the beach below the house; nothing else, no related bones. The Bradestone Historical Guild claimed that the skulls were evidence of an old Indian burial ground adjacent to the farm. Later they published a disclaimer. Evidently two very helpful anthropologists from the U-dub determined that the skulls had been lodged in a bank near Miller creek and were washed up on your beach. They could be Indian or

Caucasian. The experts didn't want to commit themselves either way, other than they're old."

"It looks like something Teri would be interested in, and there's sure to be evidence of native inhabitants that once lived on this island."

"Oh yes, several large shell middens and various stone tools have been found by people plowing their fields and exploring the shorelines. The skulls wound up at the University museum along with a few arrowheads and spear points. From the condition of the finds it appears that most of the material was quite old. Interestingly, one skull had what appeared to be a bullet hole in the right parietal area. I thought that was curious. I'm sure there would be more information in the files at the state's Burke museum. It's located on the U-dub campus. That's something that might intrigue Teri."

She paused and twiddled with the straws in her drink. "Also, there was some sort of a legal flap over it, oh about ten years ago. Something regarding a mainland Indian tribe, I don't remember any of the details. But you can ask Willie Cloudmaker, he should know about it." She paused. "You've met him haven't you?"

"Oh yeah," Alex said as he widened his eyes. "Among many of his skills, he's a great cordial maker."

Ujima smiled. "Oh he is indeed that. Anyway, when I first arrived on the island, I remember Willie was pretty excited about the skulls. He got the original town council to placate the tribe and some resident activists by them agreeing to set a portion of the Petoskey land along the creek as a green-belt forever. I'd guess that the possibility of a gravesite or remnants of a village exist somewhere. I think part of Toady's land was included in it too."

"A green-belt, what's that?"

"It's land that can't be developed or built upon. Usually it's set aside due to springs underneath or continual slippage of an area. And according to some of the fragmented island history, if there is a sort of archeological site, that's probably where it would be located, in the shelter of Scoon Bay. Sounds to me like you'll be living right next to a permanent bit of paradise. You look surprised. Didn't Rose tell you any of this?"

Alex shook his head. "Uh, Rose told us some things; like the problems with water rights and back taxes. But, I'm sure she never mentioned any green-belt. Funny, you'd think she'd consider it a great selling factor."

Ujima shrugged. "It may never have been brought to her attention. I know most of this through Willie. Especially when it comes to Indian lands and native rights, the current resident islanders can be a tight-lipped bunch. Like we find in all cultures, promises to the conquered and enslaved are easily forgotten, ignored, or 'legally' changed when it's to the main man's benefit." She snorted. "And the green-belt concept can be used fast and loose. In old Seattle, bribed city officials and wealthy land owners have allowed or chose to ignore the concept. People are continually allowed to build in them, frequently with disastrous results."

Ujima turned from the railing. "Enough palavering, I must be home. Later tonight I'm on call and I work tomorrow. You and Kay should come on down and visit our police station. It's real cozy. I have two cells. One, I use as an office which barely holds me, my computer and a fax machine." She smiled. "I usually let the incarcerated play games on a beat up computer in their cell, keeps them out of my hair. Occasionally they're hosted by the County Sergeant, or let back on the streets with a fine and reprimand. Well. Catch you later." She handed Alex her glass then hiked over the railing.

Only one foot held her on the outer scupper. Automatically Alex grabbed her wrist. "Ujima! I think you've had one too many."

She looked up at him. "Why thank you, I appreciate fast reactions. But everything's good. I live on that sailboat, Talaria, it's over there." She pointed at the opposite shore. "That's my home."

Alex strained his eyes. He could make out the white hull of a sloop outlined against the black of a dock. A small light glowed on the aft end.

"How are you going to get there? Swim!"

"Sir Alex, *you* may have had a tad too much. Notice, there's a rubber dingy just below my dangling foot. Now if you'll refrain from cutting the circulation off in my arm I just might be able to row home." Alex carefully let go.

"That's much better," Ujima said as she settled into her dingy. After rubbing her wrist she unshipped the small oars and placed them in the oarlocks.

"Alex, you have been a true gallant. I'm off across the bounding main. Don't look so concerned. There's a light breeze to starboard, the stars will guide me and," she paused dramatically, "it's only four hundred yards as the crow flies." She chuckled as she rowed into the moonlit night. "See you later, sailor." Her goodbye and the sound of the steady dipping of oars drifted over the water.

Alex grinned, took a deep whiff of the fresh salt breeze and looked up at the sparkling diamond-slash of the Milky Way. He put his hand to his forehead and said quietly into the night: "Willie Cloudmaker, you old rascal, you were right. This is going to be one helluva of an interesting time in our lives."

## CHAPTER 10

# *Murder?*

**Kay was fussed** as she wandered to and fro on the upper deck. Groups and individuals had questioned her, vetted her then left; usually wishing her good luck. I'll never get this freeze-dried smile off my face, she thought, then paused, took several deep yoga breaths and made some subtle stretches. With Rose and Raymond flanking her, as if she were a prize heifer, she felt; they marched her toward another chatting group.

So far, everyone ranged from pleasant, to strange, to uptight. My god where is Alex? Has he fallen overboard? Her last glimpse was when he exited through one of the sliders with an attractive lady clinging to his arm. Mentally she shrugged. This wasn't the first time and it wouldn't be the last. Her friends frequently remarked that Alex reminded them of a tall Brendan Fraser. Kay always offered the rejoinder that if they took a closer look, Alex was swarthy, his eyes brown, and his nose broken in the bargain. Oh, and he was a scruffy dresser. But that never discouraged the ladies from fantasizing.

Rose and Raymond had brought her to a rather abrupt halt. The trio stood in front of a very thin woman wearing a black dress and what looked like real pearls. She made no attempt to hide the fact that she was sizing up Kay with what could only be 'a suspicious grimace'. Oh, oh. One of Toady's 'anybody who is somebody', Kay thought. The woman slowly extended a pale hand and three, limp, bejeweled fingers.

"Kay, thish is Ms. Elanor Laven, Eric Templeton's shister." Rose, on her umpteenth Margarita, pronounced her words very carefully.

As Kay grasped Elanor's flaccid fingers, she recalled that the name, Eric Templeton, had been mentioned in a conversation somewhere. Something about Superior Island Development, something about... Her thoughts were jarringly interrupted as Elanor snatched back her hand as if it had been burned.

"Kay, Kay Roberts! Of course..., I've been trying to place your face." She extended her hand again. Her first handshake had been like a forkful of cooked pasta, but now the fingers closed in a steel-like claw. "What a gifted artist. I've read your articles in the 'Weaver's Journal'. And I was pleasantly surprised by your basket display at the 'Tray Bone' gallery in Pioneer Square. You're one of the few who have vision. And your symbolism is very subtle. I've heard you've currently turned to pottery." She simpered. "Plastic mediums are my favorite. So pliable, so evocative of the artist's skills, don't you agree?" She suddenly dropped Kay's hand, and not waiting for an answer, continued, "We will definitely have a show at *my* gallery, 'The Temple-Laven' in Seattle." Her smile was cold and horse-like.

"I do need several new pieces for my structures garden. Have you already set up a studio here?" Kay shook her head. "Then I must be the first to have a tour when it's finished!"

"Ah, Mrs.," Kay stammered, or was it Ms? Damn, what was this women's name? "I haven't been able to work on any pottery recently. My fiancé and I have only recently decided to settle here. I should have my workshop up and maybe going by next spring, at the earliest." Elanor did not look pleased with the news.

Raymond rose to the call. "Ms. Laven and her brother also own the 'Gull Island's Gallery', in Portland," he said, smiled ingratiatingly. Elanor and Eric are interested exclusively in promoting contemporary artists and their works. I'm sure-"

Kay and Rose followed Toady's intense stare. A handsome, sandy haired man in a blue crewneck and a tan sports jacket had just spilled his drink. His taller, black-haired companion was laughing and slapping him on the back. The darker man wore a blue-stripped open-necked sweater. It closely fit his muscular torso. The men were an extremely attractive duo; in a flashy way, Kay thought. They both had engaging smiles and were surrounded by a loud circle of female admirers.

Raymond gaped. "I, I didn't know Edward was going to be here! He told me he couldn't make it. And he's here with that buffoon, Mark Justice." Raymond quickly excused himself and headed in the direction of the two laughing men.

Rose pursed her lips. "It's so sad for Raymond. He follows Edward around like a losht puppy." She took a sip of her drink and eyed Kay. "Edward is very good at tennish. Raymond really looks up to him." She giggled. "I'm not good at it. Raymond says ish my backhand and my timing is terrible."

Poor Rose, Kay thought then noticed Ms. Laven's face. She was glowering across the room then nodded at Kay.

"Those two men work for my brother, Eric. The blond one is Mark Justice. He's one of Eric's recent hires. The other, Mr. Suave, is our company lawyer, Edward Caen. He has an ego problem, thinks he's better than everyone else. Humph! Doesn't hide it well either. But I know all about that type." She smiled. It reminded Kay of a satisfied crocodile.

"Now Mark has turned out to be the real gentleman; he's been my brother's right-hand man for the last 18 months. Very trustworthy, and does anything for you. Eric needs more men like him. Mark has extensive knowledge of the stock market and the more aggressive type of investments." Her smile was wide and toothy again. "He has very good advice."

As they looked in the direction Raymond had gone, the sounds of voices, raised in accusation and argument began to override the noise of the party.

Ms. Laven's narrowed eyes distracted Kay. "Where do you get your pine needles? I've several pine trees on my grounds. You certainly are welcome to harvest the needles, anytime." Kay was surprised at Elanor's lack of interest in the confrontation. Kay was very interested. But she resolutely held onto her frozen smile.

"That's a very kind offer. But I can only use a particular type of long, pine needle. I special order them from a place in Georgia, and ..." this time further party disruption came in the form of a young woman wearing a hard-hat and coveralls. She swayed as she desperately clung to the banister at the top of the stairs. The room quickly became quiet. Even the three men stopped arguing.

The woman gasped. "Ms. Washington, where's Sergeant Washington? Someone said she was up here." Her eyes rapidly searched the crowd. She spotted Ms. Laven, whose face registered disapproval at the graceless entry. Unaware of Elanor's disdain, the woman stumbled toward her.

"Oh, Ms. Laven, oh, I'm terribly sorry, Ms. Laven."

Kay noticed the young lady's dirt smudged face and the gray mud that clung to her clothes. Tears stained her cheeks. She removed a battered hard-hat; her hands restlessly fingered the rim.

"It's your brother Ma'am. He's had an accident. He's, He's dead Ma'am." She paused. Kay was close enough to smell the sour odor of sweat and shock that emanated from her.

"His head it's... it's been completely crushed."

The announcement was brutal. It wasn't the woman's intent, but unfortunately it seemed tinged with relish rather than horror. Kay quickly turned to Elanor. Ms. Laven swayed on her feet. Kay grabbed her, but Elanor was dead weight, she sagged sideways and folded to the floor.

CHAPTER 11

# *Gauntlet down*

'**Mysterious Death of Eric Templeton Stumps Local Police,**' the Spindrift's headline blared, and below: Sergeant Washington investigates death of local tycoon at local Scoon beach. A group of Manzanita High School student's plans for their annual kegger was gruesomely interrupted while gathering beach drift for their bonfire. The brave teenagers alerted the night caretaker Ms. Jane Williams and she... Alex knew the rest of the story.

He skimmed the article, leafed through the paper then dropped it on the porch floor. Yawning he stretched back in his chair. The closing paper-work on the house was finally going through.

Yesterday they'd agreed to clean up the long unused kitchen garden. They'd worked till sunset. Physical labor and fresh air provided much needed distraction as they again dissected the peculiar events that occurred at Rose's party two days ago.

Kay's muscles had survived the efforts of digging and weeding, but Alex's hadn't. Kay was right, he thought. A little yoga practice every morning would loosen up ye old bod. He took a deep sip of his iced tea and moved his chair further back into the shade of the porch. It was getting hot. A day to just snooze, he'd do his yoga later. And the rest of the vegetable garden they could tackle tomorrow. Maybe it was a tad late to put in peas, but why not? His mind drifted to radishes.

Through half-closed eyes he caught a furtive movement to his right. It was near the porch steps, ah, two men dressed in suits, craning their necks. Alex stretched leisurely, slowly got up and walked toward them.

The blond man, who shot his hand forward, looked familiar.

"My name's Mark Justice." He tipped his head in the direction of his partner. "And this is Edward Caen. We represent the late Mr. Templeton's Superior Island Development Company. You've heard of us no doubt." This was a statement more than a question.

Alex shook the proffered hand. "The name's Alex Beahzhi. I'm Kay Robert's fiancé. Yes, I noticed your reader board and office in Madrona. Please accept our condolences." Alex gestured at the paper on the floor. "I've been reading about Mr. Templeton's unfortunate accident. I watched you guys that night. You did a great job helping Ms. Laven out to her car. Most people don't know how to initiate the 'Firemen's carry' properly."

Mark ran his hand through his thick sandy hair till it stood on end. "Yes, that's true. We do have the knowhow; it's part of our company's mandatory first aid and survival training."

"How is Ms. Laven doing?"

"Better. Edward arranged for a nurse to be with her the last two days. It's a terrible thing to have happened. The accident threw our organization into chaos." Mark was unfocused, his manner distracted. "Uh, I'm sorry, let me introduce Mr. Edward Caen, our firm's legal counselor."

The dark haired man vigorously nodded and turned to look at the view through the trees. "My. You certainly have a lovely location here." He did not offer his hand.

"We like it enough, and currently are closing the deal through our Realtor, Rose Bracken. We think it'll be a good investment. Plus the floor plan is well thought out, particularly for the pipe and slipper set."

"You're hardly of that vintage," Mark said then smiled. "But it is a good investment. Superior Island had its eyes on this parcel too. But the Bradestone Nature Conservation Committee threw a few roadblocks at us a year ago. They have considerable clout on this island and they knew Mr. Templeton was interested in adding this acreage to his accounts. Unfortunately, and it's only on the very rare occasion, we fumbled the ball. We weren't aware it was back on the market. But the gem our corporation is negotiating for is the piece known as Heron's hook." He waved a hand in the direction of Scoon Bay. "It's directly across from you, that ridge on the east."

"I know," Alex smiled. "Kay and I are looking forward to hiking over there."

Mark nodded and continued, "Mr. Templeton hoped this entire area would become one contiguous wild-life preserve." His voice lowered. "At least that was one of his goals before he died."

"Oh yes," Alex replied. "Rose gave us a few back copies of the Spindrift. It helped catch us up on island life in the last six months. However, it appears that not everyone's happy with the late Mr. Templeton's plans. There are heated discussions in the letters to the editor column. On the face of it I think it's a great idea. It certainly would attract more tourists, and in turn increase the profits of local businesses. But on the other hand, the Greenpeacers protest that the islands identification with its rural nature would be threatened and even minor development will break down parts of a fragile ecosystem. Those are the main pros and cons I gleaned. One of the editorials mentioned it could eventually be named the La Grange-Templeton Nature Preserve, I guess La Grange was the first European to explore this island." Mark and Edward nodded their heads in agreement.

"Hmm," Mark muttered as his handsome features changed to a serious frown. "Yes, you've got the main drift of things. But, now there are conflicts of interest that no one was aware of until yesterday. In fact that's why we're here." Both men had beads of perspiration covering their foreheads. Alex, for some perverse reason, did not feel inclined to invite them up into the coolness of the porch. Kay would have said they emanated bad karma.

Alex leisurely stretched his muscles. Thank the gods he was wearing cut-offs and a tank top. They had to be swimming in those shark suits. Oh what the hell. bad karma or not, he relented.

"Won't you come into the shade, gents," he grumbled as he pulled two sagging wicker chairs up to the umbrella table. "And how about some iced tea?"

They dithered for a moment then accepted the invitation.

Edward Caen sat forward on the edge of his chair. "I'll come right to the point Mr. Beahzhi. What 'Superior Island' *is* interested in is your granting a right-of-way from the main road down to the beach, of course with the proviso of a dock. It would be a small corridor between you and Mr. Toda's property and provide a much needed access to the hook. We'll make you a very reasonable offer."

"Have you approached Mr. Toda with this?" Alex asked.

Edward's smile was enigmatic. "He's very amenable to the project, as long as it keeps the integrity of his part of Miller creek. Of course, he understands there are portions, on his side, where we may have to put in underground conduit, particularly along the upper road."

Alex was surprised and looked directly into Caen's eyes. They were cold and challenging. "Access to the hook... I assumed from what you just said that the hook would be designated as a greenbelt. Rose mentioned that Mr. Templeton wanted his new properties to become natural preserves, and not to be developed." Alex looked puzzled. "And Willie Cloudmaker said something about native sites or burial grounds around here too. I think they're located on or near Miller creek and that area can't be disturbed."

Edward sat back and spread his hands. "Mr. Cloudmaker tends to perpetuate island myths. I would never put stock in what he has to say anyway."

Mark cleared his throat. "It's true that Mr. Templeton's original intention was to create an integrated and connected band of wetlands and second growth forests that hopefully would include the Hook. But based on a review of his most recent documents, it would appear that Mr. Templeton changed his mind." He smiled apologetically. "We've found plans for the construction of an elaborate resort. It's much larger than our Gull Condos complex to the south. Included in the new plans are several swimming pools, horse trails and an eighteen-hole golf course, with potential for further expansion, of course."

Alex's eyes narrowed, "Wouldn't the local environmentalists demand an impact study? Many residents regard the Hook as a native bird and wildlife sanctuary."

Edward chuckled. "True. The new plans will put some of the environmentalists and Greenpeacers up in arms. What progressive change hasn't? Their kind has a congenital mandate to beat up on corporations anyway. But let's look at this in the pristine light of reality. We all know that in the long run, it's for the betterment of this community, its future and its children's future."

Mark interrupted. "We were aware that a while back Mr. Templeton had considered a destination development. But, I thought he had dropped the idea." He looked at Caen, "however, the documents I found yesterday, attest to the corporation's renewal and interest in going ahead with the project. I was surprised."

"It won't be too difficult to get the majority of the business community in our camp," Edward remarked smugly, "especially when they see the hundreds of jobs that will be created. Dollar signs have that effect on people."

Alex scowled. "I don't see why we have to be involved in any of this."

Mark squirmed in his chair. "For the project to be a success we must have direct access to the hook, particularly from the less steep embankment on this side.

"A dock or temporary bridge is what's needed," Edward said. "There is a problem with accessing the hook from the side near Swamp creek. At present we have not acquired that land. Eventually, with dredging in Scoon Bay, we can have boat shuttles from Seattle come in and tie up to a dock on the other side. But, that's not until the second phase. A road and a pontoon bridge to the hook are the first and initial steps. We can take advantage of the old logging roads on the Hook side." He looked at the inlet below them. "It's nothing new. Years ago, sawmills lined the shore and lumber schooners tied up to a floating pier that was anchored in Scoon Bay. From old pictures it was right on the beach below this house. At that time the water was over twenty-five feet deep. If it hadn't been silted up by the two creeks, Scoon Bay would be a growing concern at this very moment."

Alex stroked his jaw. "Hmm... The plans for a destination resort don't surprise me. Heron's Hook is a ready-made tourist attraction and it's close to Seattle. However, your internal corporate problems don't concern me. The external ones do." Alex leaned forward in his chair. "One of the reasons Kay and I decided to settle here is to get away from the constant din of traffic; gravel trucks and heavy equipment in particular." He regarded Caen long and coolly. "The environmental terrorization that your corporations produce is always paraded as progress and a boon to the community. I don't see how denuded hills, vapid amusement venues, and pavement from here to the horizon are a benefit to anyone with the exception of the corporate pockets and shareholders... now, or in the future."

Justice glanced quickly at Caen then turned to Alex. "But Mr. Roberts, oh I am sorry, it's Mr. Beahzhi." A tense silence ensued as Mark smiled thinly then continued, "Surely even you realize that you're going to need similar types of equipment to refurbish this place. There's rebuilding your foundation, clearing trees and brush, reclaiming the roads and driveways; not to mention tearing down this...this old building. A correctly built and paved road is what you need. Obviously it would dramatically increase your property value. I'm sure you don't intend to do your construction with hand labor."

Alex arched his eyebrows. "No. Not all by hand. But it will be done on a small scale and have considerably less of an impact on the environment than what you're considering. And, for your information, we intend to keep the house, roads and driveways as they are, gravel and all. It allows for natural drainage."

Kay, who had been eaves-dropping inside the doorway, brought a new pitcher of iced tea to the table. "I couldn't help overhearing. It's a unanimous vote from me too. We want as little intrusion as possible, besides isn't there the not-so-minor necessity of satisfying environmental impact studies? And what about dealing with Bradestone's Nature Conservation committee? Alex and I ran into some of them last week. They seem to have a large power base and are avidly intent on keeping the island as rural as possible."

Alex looked up. "Let me introduce my fiancée, Ms. Kay Roberts. Kay, I'd like you to meet Mark Justice and Edward Caen," he laughed, "our local land-grabbers."

Justice turned quickly, almost upsetting his chair. "Edward, I'm sure we can offer something more attractive than a paved road."

Caen was looking at the view. He appeared to be ignoring them. He shrugged his shoulders as he took out a neat, white handkerchief and dabbed at his brow, then slowly folded it and placed it back in his coat pocket.

"I know Mark is only looking after the corporation's interests. And keeping down expenditures is definitely a large part. But there's a much better idea. A little costly at first perhaps, but in the long run, look Mr. Beahzhi, I, er, the corporation is willing to take this entire acreage off your hands... at a fair price, of course." He smiled complacently. "Entirely in cash, I might add." Justice glared at Caen after this last statement. "And you could find a much better property than this one where you can build exactly what you want. We do have 'Superior' listings." He chuckled. "No pun intended."

Alex looked at the two men and said sweetly, "What did you have in mind?"

Kay put her hands on Alex's shoulder. "Yes fellas. Make us an offer we can refuse." Caen sat forward in his chair. He continued to ignore Kay.

"Well. Half again what you're paying for this, whatever that is of course."

Kay thought to herself. My, my Mr. Caen, you know exactly what this property is selling for. Why the attempt to appear uninformed?

Alex looked pleasantly surprised and winked at Kay. "Have to think about it. We've considerable plans for this place. Developing *our* personal retiree's retreat, adding on a pottery studio," he smiled up at Kay, "Maybe even a bed and breakfast is in our future." She pinched his shoulder.

A dark frown creased Justice's forehead. "Look Mr. Beahzhi and Ms. Roberts, we don't have the time to treat this situation with levity, nor prattle on over a price. There are certain, er, things already in motion. I, we can double what you're paying, and then some. And that's our final offer."

Alex let out a slow whistle. "That's mighty tempting." He noticed that Caen had suddenly lost interest in the distant horizon and Justice had taken an aversion to breathing.

Alex took a long, deliberate sip of his iced tea. "Umm, Kay, this is delicious. Did you put peach juice in it?" She nodded. "Yes, thought so." He slowly turned his attention back to Mark and Edward. "Look. I told you I would think about it. This decision hinges on what Kay thinks. And she's already given her opinion. But there's our family to consult. And..."

Justice had risen quickly out of his chair and was pointing a shaking finger at Alex.

"Stop playing this game. It's not going to work! You'll come around. Everyone has their price." He narrowed his eyes at Alex. "There are certain legal actions we can take in the light of your refusal to aid in something that's in the 'best interests' of the community. I represent a powerful, multi-million dollar corporation and the legal fees in fighting us would be exhaustive. I'm sure you get my drift."

Caen had risen too. He was attempting to calm Mr. Justice, which only excited him further.

"It could all be so simple. I'm sure an Astronomy professor, who has his head in the clouds, not to mention somewhere else, has the need for some cash!" Justice's face was an angry red.

Alex stood up quickly; his voice quiet, his manner measured and calm. "I think it's best you make yourselves scarce, and now. Kindly close the gate behind you...and the answer is a definite no." He forced his face muscles to relax as he took a casual sip of tea.

Kay couldn't leave well enough alone, she had to speak. "And don't try your bullying tactics on Willie. I know he would never consider selling."

Justice narrowed his slate gray eyes. "There are ways of dealing with vagrants and squatters too."

Kay stepped forward. "He's neither a vagrant nor a squatter. He's an artist. And that's his land, he inherited it."

Justice sneered. "With all due respect, Ms. Roberts, don't believe what every drunken Indian tells you. He'll take the money. He needs it to keep liquored up."

Kay winced. "Alex is right. There's no necessity to talk further. We're in complete agreement. We're not interested, period."

Caen tapped nervously on his briefcase. "These kinds of negotiations are a little out of my line. However, when you three cool down and reach a place where we can calmly negotiate, I'll be there." He regarded Justice with a baleful eye.

Justice turned on him. "Yes! Leave, you prim little pansy. As if you haven't soiled your hands before," he snarled.

Caen blanched. He straightened his shoulders and stomped off the porch. Justice joined him. They stalked up the path, a tandem of anger and fuming silence.

Kay sat down hard. "Whew! As Teri would say... 'What a couple of rude racist rubes!'"

Alex slowly sat down. A muscle still jumped on the side of his left jaw as he turned toward Kay.

"I thought I detected a bit of heavy breathing and a nervous tinkle of ice when you brought out the tea."

She stirred her drink with a straw then put her arm around Alex's shoulders. "I'm going to give Sergeant Washington a call. I think those two thugs are way out of line."

Alex smiled and hugged Kay's arm. "I'm sure she already knows how vicious those two corporate dogs can be. And there is really nothing she can do."

"Oh, you're right and I felt that the entire scene was an overacted shtick," Kay said and took another sip.

"Wow, I did too. They were way overboard. But I was angry anyway. That pair is used to shaking people up." He put a hand on

Kay's arm. "Look, don't worry. But it wouldn't hurt to alert Messrs. Dewey, Cheatum and How."

Kay laughed nervously. "Do I hear a victorious 'Alex the Grape' calling on marvelous Max? Somehow I've been under the impression that you thought lawyers were always bad, bad people."

Alex scratched his chin. "Just most of them and some of the time," he replied glumly.

Kay took a sip of her tea. "I felt the entire conversation was a planned shtick."

"That's interesting, I did too. It was way overboard. That pair is used to rattling people's cages."

CHAPTER 12

# *The Fuzz*

**Ujima was apprehensive** as she stood on the porch of the old Petoskey farmhouse. Templeton's death would have to be investigated thoroughly. And it wouldn't go at all well with the county mayor. He resented anything that deviated from his definition of the 'norm'. Murder was definitely not in that category.

But was it murder? She'd examined Templeton's corpse carefully before it was sent to forensics in Seattle. From all appearances his death was the direct result of head injuries due to his fall off the cliff. And the body was in fairly good shape. It had lodged in the rocks and been knocked about by the tide, but fortunately had not washed out into Scoon Bay, or worse, drifted into Puget Sound.

The foreman of the construction team told her that he became uneasy when he noticed Mr. Templeton's car still parked at the trailhead at the end of the day. He remembered Templeton waving to him after parking the car earlier that morning. The three crewmembers accompanied the foreman up the quarter mile trail to the top of the cliff. At first they found nothing. Then one of them, the Cassandra at Rose's party, looked over the cliff in the fading light and spotted the body on the rocks below. By the time the rescue crew found a bank low enough to get to the beach, the tide was coming in and it was dark and they could not reach the body.

The foreman said it was unusual for Mr. Templeton to be so careless. He frequently hiked in the area and knew the paths well. In fact, the day before, he had cautioned the entire survey crew about the danger of getting too close to the edge. He'd said that much of the footpath along the cliff was undercut by winter rains and could easily give way.

Ujima shook her head. It was lamentable that the top of the cliff had been trampled so thoroughly by the work crew. Also the body was moved by the medics before she could look the site over properly. If the foreman was right about Templeton's familiarity with the area, then the accident definitely was suspicious.

I can't stand here all day mulling it over, she thought and rapped on the door.

Kay stood at the threshold, broom in hand. Her long auburn hair was tied back in a kelly green kerchief.

"Why hello, Sergeant Washington," Kay said, nodded with approval and looked at her watch. "My, you are punctual! I haven't even had time to put my broom away." She laughed. "And no, I'm not planning to transform into the wicked witch of the west." Ujima followed Kay through the entry way hall and into the living room.

Kay grimaced, "Although, after working in this mess, I'm seriously thinking about casting a few helping spells."

The main room of the farmhouse was spacious. Personal items were stacked on the floor to the right of the entry arch in apple boxes. Though the room had been cleaned and organized, it was gloomy. Tattered green-papered wainscoting, cracked lath and plaster walls, and a water stained ceiling, did little to cheer things up. The two positive features were oversize bay windows that faced the hook. Ujima congratulated herself. Her boat was a much easier world to maintain.

"We've had to do plenty of work. But, considering how long this place was vacant, it's amazing there was so little damage. The only broken windows are in the basement. It looks like kids have been partying there. Alex repaired three frames this morning."

Ujima smiled. Now here was a gal she could relate to, snappy and fun. "I noticed a lot more than broken glass in those garbage bins by the basement door."

"You did, the rest of the trash is from the vandalism that evidently happened last fall. Alex told me about your concerns. Thanks for alerting us. And thanks for coming over. I'm ready to file a complaint form regarding those two yahoos from Superior Real Estate."

"I'd like to hear your concerns. There's most likely little I can do about those pests, but first I'd like to ask about what happened after I left the party. I understand that you, Rose and Toady were talking to Ms. Laven when she learned of her brother's death. I'm interested in what was said and the reactions of the people around her." She paused. "That's the official reason. The unofficial one is that I make a habit of becoming acquainted with the newcomers to the island. I enjoyed talking with Alex at the party. Now I'd like to get to know you. I figure this would be a good place as any to start."

Kay was surprised. "Let's sit down. I'll bellyache about the bullying duo later." She paused in thought. "You know, it just may tie into Mr. Templeton's death too," she said abstractly as she unfolded an aluminum lawn chair for Ujima. The yellow webbing sagged in its companion. Kay unfolded that one for herself.

Ujima thanked her, sat down and pulled out a small notebook. She licked the end of her pencil with a flourish." I've already talked to the construction worker who made the announcement at the party. She told me she was hired by Superior two weeks ago and desperately needed the work. From the start, she felt Ms. Laven didn't like her. The poor woman panicked the other night, thought she was doing the right thing. She's still rattled, that's understandable, made a real faux pas. Her foreman says she only made things worse for herself."

Kay nodded. "Ms. Laven strikes me as the type who would kill the messenger first and ask questions later. I met her briefly and got the impression she doesn't care for many people. She expressed very acid opinions about those two men who work for Superior. Of course after Alex's and my experience, I wasn't exactly enamored of them either; and her comments struck me as justified."

Ujima was non-committal. "I'm interested in things you may have noticed. Things you may have overheard. I understand that while Alex and I were talking, Toady and Rose were giving you a rapid social tour, covering almost everyone on the island."

"Everybody that was anybody," Kay said with a raised eyebrow. "I'm quoting Mr. Toda. Rose and Raymond were making sure that I started out on the right foot, as opposed to the left. It was all a bit overwhelming."

Ujima laughed. "That sounds like Toady and I can totally empathize. They put me through similar vetting loops at one of Rose's parties when I first arrived here. Really felt awkward at the time, but I have to say some good friendships came from it. And it was a crash course in gathering useful background information on some of the locals."

Kay wasn't listening to Ujima. She was debating how to delicately phrase a question then blurted it out. "Do you think this is a murder investigation?

Ujima looked startled. "No. Not necessarily. Hopefully it isn't. However, the department routinely views deaths of this nature as suspicious."

"I thought you were the department."

"Not exactly, we have a small force here; it includes only me and Deputy Reynolds. If things er, become more involved, we coordinate efforts with the police department in Normandy Park."

"Oh yes. I remember that area. Alex and I drove through it. It's a small village on the mainland; just off the coast road near a settlement called Three Tree Point, very charming."

"That's the one. Their police department is much larger and has access to more sophisticated forensic facilities in Seattle. When things are more involved we coordinate things with them," Ujima said.

Leaning gingerly back in her chair, Kay returned Ujima's smile. "Rose says that life on Bradestone is pretty sedate. If this is murder, I'd say it just became un-sedate."

Ujima paused, made a notation in her notebook then looked at Kay. "I'm curious." "What makes you keep coming back to murder? And I might add, you muttered about something tying into Mr. Templeton's death."

"It's just a funny feeling that I have. Alex always chides me about them. But most of the time I'm right." Kay tapped her chin. "And yet I... I, it was Toady. He called us last night." She sat forward with an intent look. "But I was already thinking it could be foul play before he said anything."

Ujima smiled to herself, Kay was a character and she would use her friendly roundabout tactics to joggle her memory. "Your phone's finally hooked up?" Ujima said, with a look of surprise.

Kay pointed to an ancient apparatus that crouched like a gargoyle on one of the upright apple boxes. "Oh yes. The landline is working. The telephone company finally took us under their wing." She stopped moving in her chair. It slowly sagged. "Alex insisted on it even though we have our mobiles. Evidently week long blackouts on the Island are not unusual in the winter."

"Ha. The local phone company," Ujima exclaimed. "The islanders refer to them as Bradestone Bell, the Bungler's Branch. You'll find out why, soon enough. But that's quite a phone. Where on earth did you get it?"

"Oh, leave it to Alex. He has a penchant for things of yesteryear, particularly, if they're ugly and don't work. It's an old Belgian police department phone. He got it at a place called Wayward Antiques."

Ujima laughed then gently turned the conversation.

"About what time did Toady call you?"

"It was after eleven in the evening."

"Why so late?"

"He said he saw our car lights coming up the road, and just wanted to talk to someone." She paused then said emphatically, "it wasn't his idea though, murder I mean. That's my hunch. I told him so on the phone."

"What did he say?"

"That's what is funny. He seemed quiet for a while then actually sounded upset. He said that Mr. Templeton's decision to convert all his island holdings to a nature sanctuary has caused some trouble in high places. Evidently, there were more than just a few shaken board members in California; and when they found out Templeton had thrown even more acreage into it, the 'fit hit the shan', so to speak. But I can't see why the ruckus? If the investors don't like it, can't they just vote the decision down? I told Toady it would be a stretch to murder for that reason alone. Then he said if it were murder it would surely be an off-islander. That did it."

"Interesting, I wasn't aware that Toady was in on that particular rumor. However people have been murdered for far less. Do you recall anything else that Toady mentioned?" She wrote something on her notepad. "When you were helping Ms. Laven, I mean."

"No," Kay replied. She felt slightly uncomfortable; she hadn't meant to single out Toady. "No, not really, after Ms. Laven fainted it was pretty much chaos." She concentrated on her palms then sighed. "No, no nothing, nothing right now."

"Well, if there is anything you recall, no matter how insignificant, let me know. Now, let's hear about your complaint." Ujima leaned forward expectantly. Her gut feeling told her she could trust this woman.

"It happened Monday. Alex and I had a very unpleasant run-in with two of Superior Island's finest."

When Kay finished describing the altercation, Ujima noticed Kay's flushed face and shook her head. "People like Justice and Caen don't get where they are by being nice guys."

"Oh, I know. The whole thing is perturbing. Personally, I feel a wildlife sanctuary is a great idea. And I hope the Superior group comes up with some sort of compromise; something that satisfies the environmentalists and the corporate-develop-everything-mentality, but I doubt it."

Ujima's eyes flashed. "Superior will do what it's hard-wired to do. Most CEO's don't give a damn about the environment or people. As long as money keeps rolling in, they're happy. The prime directive is: profit, profit, profit, regardless of the cost to humans, wildlife or the planet. Profit is numero uno."

Kay's jaw dropped. "Phew! I think I've just uncovered a rabid environmentalist."

Ujima's smile was tight. "Maybe; just remember those two yahoos are putting the squeeze on you, for a good reason. And I'm wondering what it is. And what's the urgency?"

Kay frowned. "It could be that if they slip these so-called new plans in fast enough, it will be a 'fait-accompli' before any Islanders can rally to the cause." She cautiously leaned forward in her chair. "From the short time we've been here I feel a lot of locals will be up in arms when the news gets out."

Ujima nodded. "So true, and I'm not surprised. Rose told me Templeton's company was involved in a similar environmental fiasco in California. It isn't the first time Superior has given one impression and then turned the other side of its Janus face. But so far, they've kept a low profile on the island. The complaints here revolve around problems at the new Gull Condos."

"What happened?"

"The scuttlebutt is that Superior used defective materials and took some very dodgy shortcuts. It also appears there were bribes involving certain building inspectors. We've looked into complaints, the ones we're authorized to look into, and it's like nailing Jell-O to a tree." She shook her head. "Records have been lost. Files altered or deleted, the usual nonsense. But so far no one has been taken to court."

Ujima looked up from making notes on her pad and winked. "You know, there's a way the Islanders could fight this. You've shifted the devious part of my mind into overdrive. Let's suppose someone, I'm not saying who, makes a little preemptive strike. I.E., the Spindrift gets a whiff of what's going on. I know Cal Smith, the editor; I believe he talked to you at the party.

"Oh yeah, the hulk with the wild body art."

"You can't miss that man. He also has a rather complex Greenpeace logo tattooed on his back, and others in places unmentionable. But he's a nice Harley-driving kind of guy."

"My, my, we seem to know a lot of intimate details about certain ah, um, individuals."

"I never was meant to lead a celibate life, Kay. When I came to the island Cal was the first person to take a friendly and genuine interest in me. We met when he interviewed me for the paper; from there things became far more interesting." Ujima smiled. "He's also the ad hoc leader of a Madrona environmental concerns group and they're very feisty watchdogs. Cal would be delighted to spread the news all over the front page."

"I like your devious side," Kay said out of the side of her mouth, "and sister, tain't such a bad idea. You've a mind like mine. We like to stir the compost."

Ujima laughed. "Seriously though, if the bad boys from Superior progress to worse let me know. I'll harass them with trespassing. And if they get more out of line, I'd be quite pleased to slap a restraining order on their butts. Whatever you decide, the Bradestone Police force will help you put some teeth into it, pun intended."

Kay guffawed. "Thanks for the suggestion. It hasn't seemed to upset Alex, but it's been troubling me."

"Don't mention it." Ujima looked down at her notes. "Anyway, back to Mr. Toda and your phone conversation. Was there anything else?"

"No. But Toady did go on about how well the party was going before that infernal announcement. It was odd when I told him about the gruesome twosome's unpleasant visit to the farm. I had the strange feeling he already knew about it. I figured I was giving him an opportunity to vent, about his snarling match with Caen and Justice. But he never said a word."

"So, they did have an argument. Did you hear from anybody else what it was about?"

"No. And when I finally came out and asked Toady he just brushed me off."

"How so?"

"He made a big deal of loudly shuffling papers and then reading from a list he'd put together for us."

"A list?"

Kay nodded. "When we first met Toady we told him we were in the market for furniture, among other things." She took in the entire room with one sweep of her arm. "We desperately need chairs," she said and wobbled forward, "and more substantial than these."

Although Ujima was listening, her thoughts were on Toady, his reticence with Kay and the nature of his public row with Caen and

Justice. Mr. Toda was next on her list, she thought then looked up from the notes.

"I'd like to speak with Alex for a moment."

"Ha! The lout's not here, took a break." Kay lowered her voice. "He's having his first tennis lesson at the Madrona Golf and Country Club."

Ujima smiled and shook her head. "Ah, Toady. He does love the game, among other things."

Kay chuckled and ran a hand through her hair. "Oh yes. I know I'd be as welcome as tennis elbow. However, I like to swat the ball around occasionally too."

Ujima brightened up. "Me too, we'll have to get together for a game," she paused, "but my first love is sailing."

"Sailing? That's all Alex and I did for relaxation when we were staying with friends in Upstate New York. We'd beg, borrow or steal a boat and escape on the Hudson. The river is beautiful, particularly around West Point. Romantic castles and forested estates dot the scenery everywhere."

Ujima tapped her pencil against her teeth. "Kay. I've got an idea. How about just us taking in a sailing day? There aren't any castles around here, but we do have a few chateaus. And the scenery's different but just as beautiful. Ah, that is when it's not raining too heavily. We'll sail when it's a slapping good wind and 'the boys' have a lot of manly things to do. It'll be a grand tour of this part of the Sound, and maybe we'll have time to squeeze in Elliott Bay."

"Sounds great, you're on. How about having a girlie-do and include Rose? That's if it isn't an imposition. She was very friendly at the party, and very helpful in getting us squared away with the farm property."

"Why not, Rose actually is an excellent crewmember. Uh, that's when she doesn't have a drink in her hand. I hooked her on sailing.

When I came to Bradestone I rented an apartment for what seemed to be years. Then of course, after gregarious Rose arrived, she tried to sell me a house. But I told her I wanted something different. I told her I yearned for the sea-faring life, sort of like her houseboat. Eventually Rose realized I was serious and found me an actual boat, a Cal 30, and at a good price too."

"Well, enough schmoozing, back to business. I wonder, could you write down every detail about Rose's party that you remember, to your last Margarita? I'm very curious about Toady and Caen's confrontation." She glanced at her wristwatch. "And you're in luck. I have to leave in about fifteen minutes. I'm expecting a call from the coroner's office. She shook her head. "And my hunch is that Templeton's accident will be chalked up to death by misadventure."

CHAPTER 13

# *Smoke and Tricks*

"Take a hike," Alex shouted in exasperation. Kay, painting the ceiling in the main living room, was still mulling over Toady's phone call and the threats of the two bozos from Superior. She babbled out her frustrations to no one in particular and, more paint got on the ladder and her clothes than the ceiling.

"Go visit Willie," Alex grumbled while he placed drop-cloths over the book shelves that flanked the fireplace. "You're useless here. I'll finish it up by my lonely... but tidy self."

Alex was a royal pain, particularly when he was right, Kay thought then yelled, "Poor baby," over her shoulder, stashed the paint things, and walked out the door.

Jogging down the trail beside the pond lifted her spirits. Willie Cloudmaker, he'd help her sort the gadflies in her mind, much like her Grandfather did, years ago.

Willie sat on the porch, whittling a large piece of wood. He didn't look up. "Hi there trouble, was expectin' you." He leaned closer to his carving. "Gotta concentrate here. Mind gettin' us a pot of lemon-balm tea? It's warmin' on the back of the stove, guaranteed to calm shot nerves. If you like, put in a spoon of fireweed honey too and bring it all out here. I'll join you in a cup." He chuckled then looked up at her. "You seem skinny enough."

Inside the cabin the scent of citrus, punctuated the rich aromas of cedar and smoked fish. Kay eyed the cabin's interior as she placed the pot and two cups on a well-used, red lacquered tray. The kitchen was compact and neatly arranged, like his sleeping space. Above the workbench, tools were placed in their designated outlines on the pegboard. The area was swept and clean and a small cook stove gently heated the room. She carried the tray outside and sat down beside Willie. He enriches his life with simplicity she thought as she poured the tea, raised her cup and carefully mouthed the complex flavors of the steaming brew.

She glanced at the features on the oblong-shaped block of wood.

"Willie, what's that you're carving? It looks pretty scary."

He rotated the large piece in his hands and eyed it critically. "Well, it's that all right. Started a Kwakiutl tribal mask, called Tsonoqua. Sorta the boogey man or woman, if you please, of their ancient culture. Takes a lotta thought." He gently set it down on the porch and picked up his tea mug. "Got a commission from a shop in Canada. They wanted a Tlingit mask, but for some reason this goldang character's been jumping through my dreams." He smiled then continued, "or nightmares. The boys will be a little upset, but in the end, they'll like it. I'll do the Tlingit one, eventually. Every little bit of work helps." He took a long sip of his tea. "Thanks. Isn't that refreshing? Now, this mask is bothering Willie, but what's bothering you?"

"Willie we're being pressured." Kay paused. "No. Actually threatened, threatened by that Superior Island group. Several days ago two of their top suits came out to grill us. I can't get it out of my mind. They actually tried to bribe Alex and me into granting them a right-of-way. When we refused, they tried to intimidate us into selling the whole place." She thought of what they'd said about Willie. "Have they been here too?"

Willie looked out at the pond for a long time. "Well. It's like this. They gave me a bad time…once, in the past. But they found out that old Willie has some high cards up his sleeve. I've been around much longer than those tads and I've nosed into a few things, things they'd rather others don't know about."

"What kinds of things?"

"Like where the bodies are buried," he squinted at her over the top of his glasses, "so to speak."

Kay shifted on the porch and said in a low voice, "That's an ominous answer."

"Don't you worry none. Just hold tight, there ain't a thing they can do. Don't sign nothing. And don't sell." He rubbed his chin and peered at her intently. "Has Rose shown you any old papers on the property, anything involving land deeds?"

"No, nothing like that, just the current title papers. Uh wait, Rose had us sign an agreement on building codes that concern historical landmarks. They mainly apply to any changes to the foundation, exterior restoration and the tearing down of outbuildings. They're not too limiting. And oh, she did show us some papers on shoreline restrictions that we have to honor. But there was nothing about early land agreements or deeds. Why?"

"Hmm, it isn't Rose's nature to be holding back information." He shook his head. "Then she probably ain't aware of them."

"Can you give me an idea of what you're talking about?"

"Not my place to. Wait till all the legal dust settles. Then, if it's a necessity, I might be able to help out. But I do know something that'll catch your interest. Years ago I paid a visit to the county courthouse. I was curious about this here land's history and the adjoining parcels. I can't recall all the details. But there was something about water rights. Good water's scarce on this island and with that new 'Gull' development it just got scarcer. The Bradestone's water district is pretty touchy too." He suddenly slapped his knee. "Ha. We might just send that snooty committee a bug huntin'. But you'd better hear it from Rose, not me. She can hunt up copies and tell you exactly what's what." He grinned. "Then if there's trouble, maybe that lawyer fella of yours can sort it out. It's more legal-like."

Kay fretted. "Thanks Willie, just what I need on top of threats, some mysterious papers to stew about. I don't enjoy being near the center of this conflict and neither does Alex. Besides, one would think the legal eagles from Superior already have found those papers. And would have read them before they came around shooting their mouths off?"

"As I said, they don't know everyth'n. And it's to their advantage if they can panic people into doing something rash; makes it easier for em." Willie took Kay's hand. "Stop worrying. They've hit a wall. And like most people, they don't like it."

Willie shook his finger at her. "I think you need someone like Edgar to cheer you up. The poor fellar's been watching you like a hawk ever since you came up the path."

Kay looked around expectantly. "Where, I don't see him?"

"Edgar. Come on you old filcher. It's chow time."

There was a caw from the woods and in a flash of amber and white Edgar swooped onto the porch. Willie gently stroked the crow's back feathers. Then took a piece of dried fish from his pocket and offered it to him. Without hesitation, Edgar gobbled it down then strutted back and forth demanding more.

"Here." He gave Kay the packet of food. "You feed him," he said then got up and went inside the cabin. "I'll show you a little trick he likes to do," he shouted back. "Ha! I sure don't let him do it inside no more."

Willie returned to the porch carrying a large box of wooden matches. Kay had noticed them earlier in a metal scoop-shaped container, attached to the wall by the cook stove. Willie opened the box, set it in the porch and took a tobacco pouch from his pocket. He filled the bowl of his large pipe and leaned back. "Okay Edgar. Light er up."

Edgar hopped over to the box. With his head cocked he studied the matches carefully. Then, selecting one by the correct end and holding it in his bill, he scratched the red and white head on the rough porch. On the second try, with the match lit, Edgar jumped quickly onto Willie's shoulder. Willie held his pipe under the burning match. The tobacco puffed into life.

"Thanks Edgar," Willie said and reached for the lit match.

Edgar promptly dropped it into Willie's lap and with raucous caws took off for the woods. Flailing his arms, Willie leaped to his feet, after brushing furiously he shook his fist at Edgar's fast retreating back.

"You trickster!" Willie yelled. His pipe wobbled then fell from his clenched teeth: "I've tried to train that dratted crow to do the last bit correctly. Don't do this inside no more, almost burnt the place down last summer!"

Willie, his face red, scooped up his pipe and turned to Kay.

Holding onto her knees, Kay rocked back and forth with laughter. "I'll probably never see man and crow do such a wild dance again," she choked out, tears running down her face.

Willie closed his eyes and said with great solemnity, "I guess the lesson is, if'n you play Prometheus, you'd better expect to get burnt!" Kay laughed even louder.

Willie opened his eyes, they sparkled. He laughed and dabbed at his brow with his red bandana. "I suspect the boys at Superior are beginning to feel the heat about this time too," he spread his hands, managing to look quite innocent, "and not because of me neither."

Kay wiped her eyes and shook her head. "As Alice said, 'things are getting curiouser and curiouser'." She got up and placed her cup on the tray. "Well, I'm going to ignore what you just said, and those mysterious papers you won't discuss *and* your other cryptic comments.

She massaged her temples. "I told you before; I don't need more to stew about."

Willie tamped a few remaining tobacco shreds back into his pipe bowl, struck a match on the seat of his overalls, re-lit, and took a long satisfied draw as he leaned back against the porch rail.

"There are times when one needs something more to chew on." He winked at her. "It makes your stew that much richer and therefore, that much more interest'n." The smoke curled around his mouth as he squinted at her. "Don't want you to get too complacent, life has a habit of turning around and biting you in the rear." He took another puff on his pipe. "Edgar knows all about that."

## CHAPTER 14

# *Weather Change*

**The water in Scoon Bay** moved sluggishly. It insinuated an oily presence into the suddenly gray afternoon. Myriad bits of seaweed and drift slogged back and forth along the tide line. Kay breathed in the heavy scent of salt and decay. The atmosphere was thick, fetid, and oppressive. The morning's fine weather may have traveled in the opposite direction. But Edgar and Willie had boosted her spirits considerably.

If I were an old salt, she thought, I'd cast a beady eye on the barometer and say a storm's a brewing. She walked along the edge of the beach then jumped back as a rush of water swirled over her sandal-shod feet.

She found a Madrona branch with a y-shape at its end and thrust it into a limpid swell. Strands of green seaweed clung to the stick as she probed the depths. A styrofoam cup and a worn yellow Zori, drifted toward her. Kay grimaced, more beach trash she thought and dragged the objects in to take back to the house.

Above the tide-line she placed her collection next to several abandoned beer cans. She looked back to see if there were more flotsam when something bloated and whitish caught her eye. It appeared to be a canvas bag and from its top a piece of colorful cloth fluttered in the water. Convenient to put the other junk in she thought, but the tide grabbed her quarry and sucked it back. "Well here goes", Kay said aloud, took off her leather sandals; cast them up on the beach and then gasped at the depth of the water and its coldness.

She stopped, rolled her cuffs higher, then carefully felt with her toes along the sandy bottom. Last week she'd cut her foot on a shard of broken beer bottle and the occasional barnacle covered rock was a danger too. As she waded deeper a swell washed up to her waist. She breathed in sharply as the push almost knocked her over. Quickly recovering, Kay thrust her stick forward.

"Got it hooked, and on the third try!" The water, reluctant to give up its treasure, sucked greedily at her jeans. Grabbing her quarry she was surprised at the heaviness. It took all of Kay's muscles and grit to drag it up above the tide line. Someone lost a descent sail bag she thought as she sat on the sand and pulled out the colorful piece of cloth. Wow, it was a type of sarong. That was one wild party; she thought and ran a hand over the bright material.

Invigorated by her activity she returned to the water, sloshed the dress back and forth, releasing bits of seaweed and debris. The label was faded, but still attached. It read 'Sabra's Fine Fashions and Accessories', and under it, 'Bradestone's Best Ladies Apparel'. She placed the dress on a convenient log. Now, what else is in that bag that makes it so heavy and rigid? This is odd, a large piece of indoor-outdoor carpet, rolled up and tied with rope. Something glittered. It was a contact lens caught in the fibers of the carpet. She carefully picked up the piece of plastic then wrapped it in a very wet Kleenex. She shoved it carefully into her pocket.

The contents of the bag bothered her. She searched further. Near the bottom her hand touched the smooth surface of several large rocks; someone wanted to make sure the bag stayed on the bottom. The stones were flat and disc shaped, like ones found in rivers or creeks. She replaced the dress and carpet, put one stone in her back pocket then dumped the rest on the sand.

It took her a good half-hour to drag the sodden burden up the path. Alex took one look at her and laughed. "Ah, the bedraggled beachcomber returns. And what a prize you have there. Someone's last week's laundry?"

"Maybe, but I want to clean it up. And find out, if possible, who the owner is. It's almost brand new. And I have the peculiar feeling that something's wrong." She showed him the flat stone. "There were more of these in the bottom of the bag; I left them on the beach." She looked at him. "I think they were used to weigh it down."

"Hmm, we do have a mystery here. Let's take this around to the outside laundry sink. I've just finished cleaning the paintbrushes. We can wash it there." As he hefted her find, Alex made a joke about wet beach-bag ladies. Kay ignored him and pulled out the sarong.

"Alex, I'm certain I've seen this somewhere before," she paused; "now I remember. It was at the party on Rose's houseboat."

Alex gave a wolf whistle. "It looks like one of the very expensive Sabra jobbies. The day we went to the hardware store, Toady pointed out something like it in her window." He winked. "I was thinking how good it would look on you. But egad, it cost more than a month's expenses and we're not members of the reckless rich."

"Aren't we the observant one, Major Hoople. You're really enjoying those old newspapers you bought from Thom aren't you?" Alex nodded.

"Well, that's exactly what this is; see the label, something's not right here. I've a hunch this was meant to stay down in Davie Jones's locker." She thrust her fist through a large tear in the seam. "This is where most of the rocks fell out."

He put down the bag and hefted the rock Kay had given him. "It would be a great skipping rock for giants. My buddy, Roland and I use to have contests all the time with the smaller ones." Alex grinned smugly. "I was usually the winner." He placed a hand on her shoulder and sighed. "You and your sixth sense... but egad again, you're right, things look peculiar. Maybe you can satisfy that wild imagination of yours and check it out at Sabra's."

Kay nodded. "Great idea," she smiled sweetly at him, "I just might find something I like too."

"Whatever" Alex replied gloomily and picked up the sarong; he rinsed it under the faucet. After wringing it out, he held it up to his body and swished the garment back and forth. "Well it's not my color, but on the right person. Say, Dorothy Lamour, perhaps?"

"Dorothy who?" Kay asked innocently as she began to rummage through the sail bag.

"Tis a pity how we forget the famous movie stars of yesteryear."

She grabbed the sarong from him. "Oh, I remember all right. You've pointed her out often enough, usually on the 'road to somewhere' in your old movie collection. Hmm, you know Alex; we could take this down to Sabra's shop, now."

Alex gave her a pleading look then rubbed her arms. "Look, not we. There's plenty of work to do here. And shopping, for me, is a drag. Do you mind going by yourself?"

"Oh no, not at all; I wouldn't dream of dragging you to a woman's shop and watching you collapse in throws of laughter."

Alex smiled. "Right on." He paused and pulled at the piece of dripping carpet. "What should I do with this?" He asked and opened it up. "Hey, it's like new. There's just this stain, I'll cut it into a rectangle. It'll make a great pad in front of my workbench."

"Look handy man. Before you get carried away, dry it out with the bag and store everything in the tool shed. It might be important." She shrugged her shoulders at the expression on his face. "Humor me. I still have that weird feeling." She reached in her pocket, took out the piece of tissue, and un-wrapped the lens. "I found this too." She placed the contact in his hand. "It was stuck on the carpet."

"Looks more like crushed, you're giving me the creeps." Alex held it up and looked through the blue tinted plastic then handed it back to Kay. "You know. Maybe you'd better talk with our lady-Sergeant friend." He growled out of the side of his mouth. "Egad, this could be evidence of some sort of skullduggery."

"You jest, but that's possible." Kay paused. "But it also is possible that it will turn out to be something very mundane. I'll check Sabra's first."

Alex grimaced. "I notice the lack of conviction in your voice, but just remember my dear sleuth, tomorrow we have to be at Toad Hall to see about the rugs we need... and other bare essentials, like chairs and tables? I've reluctantly come to agree with you. Apple boxes aren't the only thing that makes a place homey."

Kay smiled. "Says he, who hates shopping. Anyway, I haven't forgotten our date with Toady. And I'm glad you're coming around to my more practical point of view." She paused at the corner of the house. "I won't be gone too long, why I'll probably be back before you unpack the rest of the books."

"Ah, leaving me with the dirty work? He pulled at his chin. "You know. On second thought, I'd like to go with you. You've made me very curious."

"Curiosity killed the cat."

"Hopefully that's all that it killed," Alex replied dryly.

CHAPTER 15

# *Necessities*

'Gala Spring Reopening the 26th of this month, check out our New Arrivals!!!' read the sign in the window. Sabra's was closed.

"Ah shucks podner, we should have called ahead. We won't be able to do any sleuthing till Wednesday." He thrust his hands in his pocket and started back toward the car.

Kay grabbed his arm. "Hold on to your horses Alex, as long as we're in town let's mosey over to Toad Hall."

"Ha. Hopefully they're closed too!" Alex looked at Kay. He paused. "Okay, give me your mysterious bag and I'll put it in the car. Then we'll check Toady's store out. It's only down the block. "

Peering through the front window they shaded their eyes and watched a man, with a feather duster, hop from object to object. Stooping and bending he carefully attended to the furniture. He moved like a bird. Bright, tight-fitting green slacks; accentuating his slender legs, furthering the avian impression. A snug, tartan sport-jacket completed his plumage.

As Kay opened the door the man, with every brandish of the duster, loudly hummed 'The March of the Toreadors'.

At the sound of the overhead buzzer, the man stopped. Then, balancing on the toes of his highly polished shoes, he closed his eyes, clutched the duster in both hands and danced toward them. Pirouetting three times he whirled to a perfect stop and bowed.

"Ah my dears, how may I help you?" Staring through his granny glasses he opened his eyes wide. "My word, a ravishing red head and her stunning mate; the island underground has not failed me.

Incestuous communities are so much fun, don't you think? Why they're more entertaining than the soaps. No. No. Don't say a word. Toady told me what you would need. I'm sorry to say he's not here. The naughty boy's gadding about in Seattle. My dears he simply can't settle down. Today he's buying marvelous things for 'Toad Hall'. And tomorrow, he may even start a new restaurant. I can't keep up with him. Alas! The young and impetuous, their tastes run from unimaginative to the ridiculous. It's all very frantic." He nodded. "And at the same time so limiting ... don't you agree?" He popped his eyes open in a daring stare.

Following a long silence, he thrust out a slender hand. "The name is Thommy Jay. A somewhat loose associate of Toadies," he giggled then shook an admonishing finger, "not to worry, I'm not that loose. And don't think for a minute that Toady can offer me a fig of competition. You see I deal in documented, authentic antiques. Now, what Toady trades in," he paused dramatically, "I'd rather not say."

Kay burst out laughing.

Delighted with her reaction, Thommy Jay saluted with the duster. A shock of premature white hair and jet-black eyebrows lent him the look of perpetual surprise; yet his Cheshire cat smile suggested that he was tuned in to some cosmic joke that he alone was privy to.

Mr. Jay indicated the entire shop with a sweep of his duster. "Remember dears, everything, and I do mean everything, is on sale, including me," he laughed and cocked an eye. "And by the way, my friends call me Thom. That's Thom with an 'h'."

Alex grinned, looked at Kay, and shook his head. "This is Kay Roberts, my fiancée and I am Alex Beahzhi." He extended his hand.

"Delighted to meet you both; now look around at your leisure. Any questions you have I'll gladly answer." His eyes sparkled. "Remember, this place is like Aladdin's cave, one never knows what they'll find."

Elegant furniture, shelves and cabinets were side-by-side with arrangements of dried flowers and old books. Fussy porcelain figurines jostled for place with Victorian oil lamps. A myriad of smaller bric-a-brac and linens was stacked neatly in wingback chairs and on table tops.

Alex found the closeness of the shop a bit overwhelming. But he followed Kay as she pointed and asked questions, then becoming curious about a large blue and white china chandelier that hung with the many above their heads, he asked: "What's the story on that?"

Thommy Jay pursed his lips. "Ah. The man obviously has taste, and hopefully the bank account to match. *That,* is a very rare piece of Blue Onion. I bought it myself in Antwerp, last year; quite a find. How Toady got it away from me, I'll never know. Fortunately, I have to retract my first statement; it's the only item not for sale." He shrugged his shoulders. "But, I do know what you came for. Toady tattled about my marvelous Kerman's, didn't he?" Thom made a dramatic gesture toward the back wall where a pair of apricot-colored rugs glowed with an inner light. "There, aren't they marvelous?"

Kay grabbed Alex by the arm and pulled him over to the wall. At a closer view, the carpets were even more stunning. A multi-colored border surrounded an intricate field design.

"Oh Alex, they're exquisite."

Thom moved swiftly to her side. "Yes, aren't they? I brought them over from my house in West Seattle. Very old, but they've had excellent care." He placed the back of his hand against his brow and shook his head. "When I think of my two dear puppies, the endless teas, not to mention the champagne and pate they and my friends went through. Of course I've had the carpets professionally cleaned and Kermans are as impervious as steel. That's if they're worth their salt." He ran long fingers through his thick hair and shook his head.

"I entertain on too, too lavish a scale," he muttered to no one in particular.

"According to the sizes marked here…" Alex swallowed as he saw the price tags, but continued, "I think they could fit in the day room."

"Day room!" Thom exclaimed. His eyebrows arched over the top of his granny glasses.

Kay laughed. "Alex is an ex-Army brat. He means the front room in our house that faces Scoon Bay. It's large, about twenty five by fifteen feet?" Kay asked and looked at Alex. He shrugged his shoulders.

"They're yours," Thom said with a vague gesture then turned to Kay and asked softly, "When do you want them delivered dear?"

Kay nudged Alex. "Oh. We're not through yet. I've just begun to shop. There, between those large armchairs, that pie crust table for instance, and then…" Alex stood back, his face as passive as a pallbearer's. Kay winked at Thom, "and the two lovely wingbacks?"

"Bargains, my dear; bargains in tip-top shape, and they're half-price today."

"I'm sure we'll need more things, like lamps etc., but let's set a delivery date. Would next Tuesday be fine? How does that sound to you Alex?"

He smiled thinly. "Sure. It's okay. I just don't want to blow our budget."

"Budget?" Kay asked. "Remember, I do the books, and so far we have mucho liquidity. When the axe is going to fall you'll be the first to know."

Alex swallowed and nodded his head. "Right, but what about my basic apple-box philosophy? We can use them as end tables, until…" He looked at Kay. "Er, with certain reservations of course. But yes, Tuesday around noon sounds good. In the morning I want to prune some of our fruit trees and I promised Toady that I would help buck-

up some downed maple branches. He said we could have the wood."
He nodded. "Yeah, I'll definitely need a break around lunch time."

Thom stood back and tapped his fingers together. "Ah yes. Toady
told me he has taken a, shall we say, neighborly interest in you two."
He grinned. "I'll be there with furniture truck about oneish. That'll
give our splendid Alex plenty of time to finish his labors of Hercules
and have lunch."

Alex smiled lopsidedly; his mind had begun to wander as pangs of
hunger were quickly getting his attention. "By the way Thom, is there
somewhere you would recommend for a late lunch?"

"Yes, as a matter of fact there is. But first, as it appears you're
already in the throes of starvation, there's coffee, pate, crackers and
homemade cookies on the table by the office."

Thom shooed Alex away and put his arm through Kay's. They
strolled off together.

"Now, my dear, what other marvelous things can Thommy Jay
interest the lady of the manor in?"

CHAPTER 16

# *Sabotage*

**Thommy Jay stood on the porch,** nose in the air and hands on hips. He took a moment to glance at his watch. Ah, it was exactly ten to one o'clock. He made three sharp raps. The door opened instantly.

"My dear Kay, you must have heard the truck struggling up the drive?" he asked then removed a blue silk-kerchief from his rear pocket and wiped his brow with a flourish.

"Yes, I heard the mad shifting of gears. It's a bit steep in places." She paused. "Thom, that delivery man outfit makes you look quite the professional."

He held his arms out and turned slowly around. "Isn't it marvelous? My armoire has a complete costume for every occasion." He removed his mover's cap and bowed. "I'm well aware that I'm an hour early. But, I can't be too careful for I do like to dawdle. And I'm not going to give Toady the satisfaction of finding out I was tardy with your delivery. When it comes to covering his... er business I automatically build in a cushion for error." He pointed dramatically to the large truck in the drive. "I've got your rugs and other goodies." He rolled his eyes toward the ceiling. "As usual, Toady is languishing in Seattle." Thommy growled the comment through his teeth then crammed his hat back on.

Kay was delighted; for she'd experienced previous delays from other merchants on the island.

"Come in, I'll show you where things go."

Thom vigorously wiped his shoes on the cocoa doormat and strutted into the hall. Eyes wide, he came to a halt at the center of the living room. "Kay, this is overwhelming." He looked at her intently. "I've never been inside this farm house before. These are the original cove ceilings and I love your paint choices. What are the other chambers like?" He didn't wait for Kay's reply, but strode to the archway that led to the stairs and the rest of the house. "You simply must give me 'Le Grande Tour'. Little Thommy will be very upset if he doesn't see everything."

As they walked through the rooms he kept up a flowing commentary. When they were back in the living area he went directly to one of the bay windows. With fists on his hips he raved about the view then sighed. "Well, let's start playing the butch, moving men bit." Then he whirled around. "Just where are you hiding that hunky husband of yours? We're going to need all the muscle he can flex."

Kay shrugged. "I don't know. Alex said the job would take some time this morning. But he should've been back by now." She looked at her watch. "He finished pruning the fruit trees three hours ago. He's probably still splitting wood at Toady's. It's a large pile of maple and it's on the other side of the creek. Toady told us we could have as much as we wanted. It's peculiar, he has that huge fireplace, but said he didn't have time to bother with it."

"I know. The poor boy's busy, busy, busy. But waste not, want not, I say." Thom shook his head then looked puzzled. "But where does Alex plan to put all the wood?"

"He's already started to stack it by that out-building." She pointed to a large structure hidden by a growth of morning glory and blackberry vines. "You can see it from this window. The wood will dry there all summer; later in the fall, we'll store it inside."

"There's a building under that vegetation? Good grief, that mound reminds me of a less than charming comic book character called 'The Heap'." Thom sat down on the window seat, a look of concentration on his face. "Ah yes, now I remember. His name was Baron Eric Von Emmelman. Shot down in the first world war."

"Why Thom, I didn't think you were that old," Kay said with a wink. "And why was he called 'The Heap'?"

Thom sat up straight and closed his eyes. "My dear don't be catty. I found the comic in a box of 1940 to 1950 books someone dropped off; like an abandoned child on the very doorstep of my antiques shop. If I remember correctly, the good Baron's body morphed into a large collection of plant material. And after his vegetative mishap, the creature wandered around the country side." Thom regarded the mound warily. "Doing mostly good deeds...I think."

Kay laughed. "It does look like the entire mess could creep up here and carry us off. But, in fact, there's quite a large, out-building under it. Alex and I paced it off yesterday. He says it was probably used to garage farm machinery. There are remains of a car dock on the bank beside it. We found old oilcans there. Alex said that the do-it-yourself mechanics of yesteryear drove cars out on wooden ramps. There they could change oil and lubricate fittings from below." Kay threw up her hands. "Ah, to the joy of any future environmentalist, if your grandfather or great grandfather had a dirt bank handy, one had a ready-made grease pit."

"Regardless, there's something lurking under there. It's just hidden behind a thicket of blackberry bushes and those lovely morning glory vines." She sighed. "It's on the list of our projects for clearing this summer. Liberating the house and barn come first. You know I think I will call it the 'Heap'."

"It appears that Alex has stacked a goodly amount of wood by it already," Thom commented.

"It's almost like magic, because I've not seen hide nor hair," she said with a tone of concern. "Anyway, let's remove a few of the lighter things from the truck?" She arched an eye. "When Alex gets back he can help us wrangle the heavier stuff."

Thom spread his hands. "Okay by me, but usually with my luck, we'll have it all done by the time he gets here."

"Not if we drag our feet and take tea breaks," Kay said licking her lips.

An hour later, Kay and Thom were sitting in her bargain wingbacks.

Thom patted the arm of his chair. "I'm thrilled you bought these. I had them for only two months in my house in Seattle. The chairs actually go better with your country-kitsch than my pseudo-Victorian décor." Thom shrugged. "But I like both."

"Are you the previous owner of everything we've bought?" Kay chided.

"Well, not exactly everything," Thom said with a sly smile as he rubbed the chintz pattern. You know, this material used to be illegal in jolly olde England? Anywho, Little Thommy likes change. He can't stand anything that remains the same too long. I become terribly bored." He quickly looked up. "Don't wish to change the subject, but where do you think our Alex is?"

"He said he would be back by lunch, and I've never known him to miss any promise of food, that's his middle name. What time is it?"

Thom checked his watch. "It's almost two thirty, wherever can that naughty child be?"

"He might be still chopping wood. Alex doesn't pay much attention to time, just his stomach." Kay paused, "Which, I might add, is usually pretty accurate. Look, you must be as hungry as I am. How does tea, tuna sandwiches and fruit salad sound?"

Thom clapped his hands. "I just love playing Martha Stewart. Let me at that kitchen."

Kay stood up. "If Alex isn't back in forty minutes we'll go down and throw apple cores at him. He could be hanging out with Willie for all we know."

To Kay's surprise Thom was inept in the kitchen. Even the manual can opener was a challenge to him. Eventually he swore her to secrecy. He was currently taking lessons in baking, but at the moment he yelped, "I can't even boil water correctly, but my one saving grace is that I can select excellent wines and have a running account at the most 'marvelous' deli in West Seattle." He mused, "I'm certain our little Thommy has dropped a small fortune there. It's so easy to drive to and be back in a flash with all the fixings for gourmet noshing. Julia Childs, eat your heart out! And they have the most heavenly pate with truffles," he said with closed eyes.

Finished with their quick lunch they walked back to the living room. Thom looked at his watch and announced it was almost three thirty. Kay was worried. With all Thommy's witticisms and tall stories she hadn't been watching the time.

"Thom. I'm going to take these sandwiches down to him. He splits the wood before he barrows it up here, and unless he's had a nosh with Willie he's going to be starved." She went into the kitchen and packed a paper bag and filled a thermos.

She was half way out the door when Thom said, "Look, if you don't mind, little Thommy would like to tag along. You might need an extra arm for the wood… or something."

In a short time they were well along the path. Thom nattered on about Toady's charming footbridge. Together, they'd built it last summer. Kay and Alex had walked over it many times to visit Toady, as it connected their properties.

They could hear the sound of crick water rushing over the rocks as it tumbled down to Scoon Bay. Rounding a fern covered bank, Kay stopped. Had they taken a wrong turn? "There's no footbridge," she exclaimed.

"Are you sure? I know for a fact it was there yesterday," Thom quipped. They heard a loud groan and broke into a run.

The footbridge was split in half and in the water. Alex lay to one side. The wheelbarrow and the wood it had carried were strewn across the moss-covered rocks below him. He groaned again as he tried to sit up.

"Stay there! Don't move!" Kay shouted as she slithered down the muddy bank. Alex looked at her with unfocused eyes. Blood flowed from his mouth and pink water pearled around his right hip. "You're hurt!" Kay howled. She rubbed his hand as Alex moved again. "Sit still," she commanded.

Thom stood white faced on the creek bank above. "Go for help!" Kay shouted then pointed to the opposite bank. "Toady's house is closest."

Thom shook his head slowly. "No. Remember he's still in town. And I don't have a key. I'll run back to your place and call 911. Can you stop the bleeding?"

Kay looked around in desperation. "I'll use his shirt. His mouth is cut inside too and his lip. I don't want to move him. Thank god the water's cold!"

"No!" Alex managed to blurt out. "No don't call 911. Nothing's broken. I've been testing my body for what seems like two hours. Of course I was out for a while. But everything moves, even my ankle. But I'm freezing my ass off." He groaned again. "There. See my foot's okay, it's just a bad sprain."

"How's your old back injury?" Kay asked anxiously.

He shook his head. "Seems to be okay, fortunately I landed on my face," he said dryly.

"We can't carry you back, you're too heavy. Besides, you seem to have a cut on your right side as well." Kay tried to examine his hip.

"Probably a rock," Alex mumbled. "I hit something sharp." Oblivious to Kay's protest, Alex gingerly pushed himself up then promptly fell back. "No. Don't fuss; I think I can make it. Everything's numb anyway. You guys can steady me. I'm only bruised," he panted, grimaced in pain, and then started jerkily forward. "Don't worry. I'm not in shock, had a lot of time to think things over." He was shaking involuntarily. "F-F-For Christ's sake, what took you two so long? I feel like an icicle."

"Well, neither of us is clairvoyant." Kay snapped back. "And, Mr. Macho Man, why don't you stand here for a moment and see if you really feel like going back under your own steam." She nodded at the wheelbarrow. "We could put you in that. I don't think it's broken." She looked up the bank at Thom. "Close your mouth and get down here, we'll see if we can support Mr. Stubborn."

Thom clawed his way down. "What happened?" he asked with a twisted smile. "Toady and I built it strong enough to support a herd of elephants."

Alex nodded his head in agreement and slowly ran a shaky hand through his hair.

"It was okay when I walked over it with the barrow the last couple of times," he said angrily. "And I've had the leisure, thanks to you two, to study it as I was cooling my b-b-butt in the crick." He pointed with a shaky finger at the collapsed structure. "If you'll notice the support four by fours have been partially sawed through. See how the runners have splintered."

Thom squinted. "I'm not wearing my glasses as I was resting my eyes, but I think I see what you mean."

Kay waded over to the struts and bit her lip.

"Alex you're right. Not only that. But some of those support blocks on the ends have been undermined." She turned to him, pain reflected in her eyes. "Why would someone do such a thing?"

Alex began to shake uncontrollably as he headed toward the bank. Kay hurriedly splashed to his side. "You're suffering from hypothermia. We've got to get you into the sunlight. Thank goodness I put a thermos of hot tea in the lunch bag. Thom, open it when we get to the top."

Standing between them on the bank, Alex shakily sipped the hot tea. Favoring his left leg, he looked down at the broken bridge and cursed.

They'd taken off his shirt and rubbed him vigorously with Thommy's small jacket then wrapped it around him as best they could. At Alex's request they massaged and rubbed his limbs. "Its okay," he told them, "can't feel a thing, I'll yell if I have to."

"It doesn't make sense, I've walked over that bridge hundreds of times last week," Thom babbled. "It probably wouldn't have broken under my weight. At least I don't think so." He looked wide-eyed up into Alex's ashen face. "Someone must have set a trap. A vicious trap for Toady, and you happened to fall into it."

"Why would someone do that?" Alex stuttered out as he tried to control his vibrating body. He took another sip of tea. "Or, or a t-t-trap set for a person who would be h-hauling heavy loads of wood, like yours... like yours truly," he managed to blurt out.

CHAPTER 17

# *Tantrums?*

**Alex replaced the phone's receiver** and limped over to the window. He looked out at the leaden afternoon and grabbed a handful of popcorn from the bowl on the window seat. Rainwater gushed over and through the rotted gutters. Occasionally a sudden gust would blow the water further onto the porch. He chewed thoughtfully and said aloud: "Rose was nuts, saying she didn't like a verandah. Whoever built this place knew what they were doing. They had to be Northwest natives."

A large fire crackled in the freshly cleaned fireplace. Kay put her book down and crossed the room. She rested her head on Alex's shoulder.

"I don't know about you," she put an arm around his waist, "but this weather is making me edgy." She winked up at him. "By the way, who was that on the phone?"

"It was Toady, calling from Seattle. He said that he and Thom would be here tomorrow with the rest of the furniture. He also went on and on about my pratfall in the creek. The way he kept apologizing I think he was afraid we'd sue."

"Well, it certainly wasn't his fault."

"No, probably wasn't," Alex said vaguely then smiled slowly as he pressed back against her.

Kay pushed him away. "You're not getting on Toady's case? Ujima said those supports had been cut a while back. So Toady could have been injured if he had something heavy to haul over it. And besides, he and Thom are very proud of that bridge. And what could Toady possibly gain by your accident?"

"That's what I was wondering," Alex said as he shrugged his shoulders and nodded at the bowl of popcorn. They munched in unison as they stared at the dreary weather.

Kay shook her head. "Ujima chalks it up to vandalism. But, she isn't going to ignore it. She was angry. She said, if it had happened to someone not as strong or as agile as you, they could have been severely injured or even killed."

"I guess my injuries are only superficial," Alex said then sniffed with exaggerated self-pity.

"You know what I mean. My man was lucky, sprained his ankle. And yes. Your cuts were superficial, and by some miracle you didn't re-injure your back."

"Hey! A lot of sympathy for my side, but yeah, you're right." He waggled his temporary walking stick and shook it at the room. "We'll be busier than a one-armed furniture mover when the troops get here tomorrow."

Kay rubbed his shoulder. "You mean they will be busy. You're not putting any unnecessary stress on that ankle."

Alex leered at her. "I wouldn't mind putting the stress someplace else." He nuzzled her hair. "So, you do care."

Kay squeezed his shoulder. "Of course I do. But sometimes, when it comes to your health, you can be such a wimp. I'm not going to encourage it."

"Ha! You'll be sorry. Remember, guys statistically check out sooner than the ladies. But don't worry. Toady said Thom would stick around and help." He closed his eyes and stuck out his jaw. "I do feel a little twinge in my low back and left knee. But, I'll be extremely careful. I want to be back on my feet as quickly as you do." Then he changed his voice to a whisper. "Of course, some things don't have to be done on your feet. Like the necessary things." He pulled her closer.

Locked arm in arm, they gently moved toward the stairs. He was still whispering in her ear. "Toady said they're going to bring everything in one load. He's leased a larger truck and ....hell! What's that noise? It sounds like someone's gargling outside."

Kay ducked out of his arms and hurried over to the peephole in the hall door and peered out. "It's Edgar. He's perched on the umbrella table."

Alex slowly moved over beside her. "Must've got caught in the storm, that bird has a nose for interrupting at just the wrong women." He looked at Edgar in disgust then burst out laughing. "He looks as mad as a wet crow. Too bad he didn't drown on the wing."

"Oh Edgar, rescue me from Alex's lousy groaners," Kay said as she opened the door.

Squawking impatiently Edgar sailed into the room. He made a rough landing on the floor, paused, then with a disdainful air, hopped across the rug and up onto the window seat. Promptly he began scattering popcorn out of the bowl.

"Hey, cut that out!" Alex shouted. "The little bugger is eating our popcorn. What a freeloader." Edgar paused and regarded him with a baleful eye.

Kay chuckled as she closed the door. "That's okay. I like a crow with chutzpah." Edgar appeared to nod his head and resumed eating and scattering popcorn.

Alex looked accusingly at Kay. "He's going to be like stray cats. Feed 'em once and they come back, again and again." Edgar stretched his wings, cawed as if in agreement and resumed his hungry attack.

"He's definitely not a cat. At least not in this present life," Kay said then paused and peered closer. "Don't you think it's strange that he's out in this storm, and at this time of day?" She glanced at her watch. "It's almost 4:30 and is he hungry?"

"You don't think anything has happened to Willie?" She asked anxiously.

Alex sighed deeply. "No, I don't. Crows are just like men. They will grab a free meal anytime, anyplace, anywhere. He most likely caught the scent while you were popping it in the fireplace."

Kay went to the hall closet and began putting on her boots. "I'm going to check on Willie. I feel something's not right. Maybe he suffered some sort of injury like you did. That bridge-so-called-accident has put me on edge."

Alex groaned, waved both arms then tapped his cane to get Kay's attention. "Don't be so hasty. Willie's probably fine. Maybe he's had too much Marionberry cordial, and is sleeping it off."

Kay stopped tugging on her boots and looked up at Alex. "You're as bad as that man, Justice. You of all people, stereotyping," she said through clenched teeth.

"That isn't what I meant at all. You're going to get soaked for nothing." When Kay started pulling her rain gear out of the closet Alex limped toward the phone.

"Okay, okay. Let me at least call Toady. He can go over there with you." Alex shook his head. "Hmm, there's no answer."

Kay stood ready at the door.

"Maybe he's still at Toad Hall."

Alex hung up and dialed. "Good old Bradestone Bell has got the lines crossed again. I'm getting a radio program for Chrisakes!" Alex gestured impatiently as he replaced the receiver. "Look Kay. This is totally unnecessary. It's soon going to be dark and…"

Kay made a face. "I'll be all right. You stay here, soak your ankle in some hot water and Epsom salts again, and keep Edgar company.

There's no sense in the two of us getting soaked. If I'm not back in twenty minutes call out the Marines or better yet, call Ujima."

"Thanks loads," he replied as she blew him a kiss and disappeared into the rain.

A sudden squall slammed her in the face as she clutched her yellow slicker and started down the path to the beach. The door flew open behind her.

Edgar hopped across the porch. He paused, looked back accusingly at Alex then flew after Kay. Alex cursed under his breath then hobbled over to the door and shut out the storm.

Kay was making good time. The path by the creek was muddy, but easier to negotiate than she'd expected. She glanced up and uttered a "thanks" to the tree-covered ridge of Heron's Hook. Alex had explained how it sheltered most of the pond from the prevailing southerly winds. All well and good, she thought, but unfortunately the clouds were getting darker. Damn, in her haste she'd forgotten a flashlight. It might be difficult going on the way back. Maybe Willie had one....that's if he were there.

She picked her way carefully. Alex's fall had been a great reminder to be cautious. Funny Alex, he didn't complain much and he teased a lot, but she knew he was in considerable pain. It was his 'Silent Sam' routine. She could tell by the way he walked that the accident had aggravated his old skiing injury. Kay looked behind her. What was that swishing noise? She made herself calm down, probably the large willow by the pond, its branches whisked over one another in the wind.

The cabin was dead ahead. Not good, it was dark. She hesitated. That seemed odd; the front door was open. She strained to see.

Cripes, it wasn't there, only a dark, cavernous opening gaped at her. To the left of the porch were pieces of broken wood. She must be extremely careful.

Gliding out of the storm, came Edgar. The wind rocked his body as he circled the clearing and landed delicately on the edge of the porch roof. Peering down at the yawning doorway he made no sound. Cautiously, Kay crept forward.

Torn paper and bits of debris blew across the grass. There was no movement inside. For the first time Kay considered her reckless behavior then yelped as she heard an oath muttered behind her.

Alex grumbled as he limped forward; flashlight in one hand, cane in the other.

"Lady, you walk too damn fast. I almost went pond diving back there."

"Oh Alex!" Kay exclaimed with a mixture of relief and anxiety. "Something awful has happened. Look at the cabin."

Alex flashed his light toward the black opening. "Well, if there's anybody in there, they've already seen us."

From the top of his perch, and leaning forward with great curiosity, Edgar watched their stealthy approach.

Alex's flashlight swept into the room. It appeared as if a tornado had hit the interior. Cabinet doors hung off hinges, shelves were strewn across the floor. The kitchen table had been thrown, knocking over the stove. Soot and bedding was everywhere. What could be seen of Willie's carvings lay smashed and buried in the debris.

"It's a shambles, luckily there was no fire in that stove," Alex whispered.

Kay wrung her hands. Her questions came rapidly. "What's happened? Do you see Willie? Is he under all that?" Alex played the beam over every suspicious pile and into every dark corner. His light finally settled on an ancient, gallery-railed desk.

"I don't know, no, and no." He paused. "It looks like a struggle, maybe a fight. Obviously someone was searching for something."

"Robbery?" Kay's eyebrows shot up.

"Could be, but look at that desk. All the drawers have been gone through and carefully stacked by it. Everything else is a mess. But it looks like the desk was meticulously searched."

"Hello. Look what I have here?" Kay picked a circular earring off the floor.

"I think we'd better leave things as they are, Kay."

"Oh don't harangue. This is completely different. It's a simple pressure fit and it's odd."

"Tsk-tsk, Nancy Drew tampering with evidence?"

"Well, it obviously doesn't belong to Willie."

"Not unless he's into cross-dressing," Alex said dryly.

"Don't joke. He could be kidnapped. Or worse," she said nervously and pocketed the bauble.

"I don't think so. He's a pretty shrewd old codger." He looked around the room. "But he has something, something that somebody wants desperately, and might be willing to kill for. By the looks of this mess I'd say they were in a rage, because they didn't find it."

Kay took Alex's arm. "We'll go back and call Ujima. Whoever did this might return." She paused. "Wait a second. Let me have the light."

She cast the beam on an old clothes bureau that had been tipped over. Her voice changed. "Now, that's strange."

"What? What now?"

Kay's answer was interrupted by a sudden movement behind them. Both shouted and clumsily stumbled out of the way.

It was Edgar. He glided in and landed on the chaos in the kitchen area. From her seat on the floor Kay flashed the light on him.

Nonplused, Edgar pecked at the rubbish. He turned over a cardboard box and pulled at its contents.

"Look, he's trying to tell us something." Kay whispered.

Alex got up and limped closer.

"Oh yeah, that he has a penchant for Ritz crackers."

Ujima's uneasiness increased as she down shifted for the curve ahead. What next! She thought. Alex's mysterious 'accident', Willie's cabin trashed, Kay and Alex wanting to slog around in this awful storm to look for him. At least the wind and rain had let up a little since they called. It was the kind of twilight that swallowed up car lights and left the road a twisting, glistening black snake. Ujima gritted her teeth and drove as fast as conditions permitted. She had cut the huzzah of sirens and flashing lights. It was too nerve-wracking.

She slowed the squad car down to a crawl and turned onto the old logging road to Willie's cabin. The vehicle bounced and swayed. The road had seen little use over the years. Ujima knew that Willie usually left his truck at the head of the road. It wasn't there. That could be good or bad, she reflected as she skillfully maneuvered around a large pothole of water.

Fir boughs and uncut brush slapped the windshield. Ujima made a mental note to talk to the local volunteers at the fire department. The men and women were always ready to clear and make a road more accessible. They were all aware of the vulnerability of living in heavily wooded areas. If they had another dry summer and a fire in here…she shook her head.

Kay rushed off the steps when Ujima came around the edge of the cabin. Alex stayed in the protection of the porch. After a few questions, Ujima gave them directions on how to systematically search the perimeter. Then she went in to examine Willie's cabin.

When she was finished, she asked for their assistance in yellow-taping the area and nailing what was left of the door back in place. She then took their statements. It was a somber moment as they discussed the possibilities as to what might have happened to Willie.

When the rain and wind started to pick up again, Ujima insisted on driving them home. It would be considerably drier, and as Ujima pointed out, Alex's limp had become more noticeable.

As they quietly got into the car, she told them, due to various storm problems, she was the only one on duty that night. And she'd immediately start checking out her sources when she got back to the office. "A policeman's job is never done. Neither rain nor sleet nor snow," she quipped. It helped to alleviate, if only slightly, the gloomy atmosphere in the car.

## CHAPTER 18

# *Recognizance*

**Early the next morning** Ujima called Kay and asked them to go to Willie's cabin. There's the off chance that he might've returned," she said. He hadn't.

"I can't believe Willie's missing," Kay said and sat down on the outside bench near the porch.

Alex sat beside her and hugged her, as tears welled in her eyes.

"Look, there are no traces of blood. Nor, and remember I and Ujima agreed, was there any other evidence of a physical struggle. Whatever happened, we're pretty sure that Willie wasn't here."

"I hope you're right." She wiped her eyes and got up. "Who's going to take care of Edgar? Willie said he's become too dependent on humans."

"Ah, crows have savvy. They can fend for themselves. Don't forget how he zeroed in on our popcorn last night. Anyway, if push comes to shove, there's always the humane society."

"Ouch!" Alex clutched his shoulder. "Physical abuse will not bring Willie back." he yelped.

"You're so callous. It's impossible. Aunt Nellie was right. When she first met you she said you were an uncaring adventurer."

"Gad, don't bring your aunt into it...though I agree with the adventurer part." He reached for her. "I was kidding anyway and I love it when you get mad. It's a real turn on."

Kay stomped off to the rear of the shack.

"Channel your testosterone into something useful," she tossed over her shoulder then paused. "I know; we'll take Edgar home to live in the barn. He can stay with us."

Alex reluctantly followed her to Edgar's lair; a large open hutch attached four feet up at the side of the house.

"Kay, be reasonable. We have rats in that barn and the occasional owl, they're very crafty predators that can serve Edgar up, feathers and all."

Kay laughed. "According to Willie, Edgar is as sharp as any human. I'm sure he'll be able to take care of himself. After what Willie showed me; he's one moxie bird."

Straw littered the floor of the hutch. Against the back was a wide shelf. On it a white dish held a few pellets of dog food. A broom handle served as a perch.

"He has very comfy quarters." Kay said, hands on her hips. "And look at that loot in the corner of the shelf. Willie said Edgar would scavenge anything. He certainly maintains his reputation," she said as she picked up a shiny half-pack of cigarettes and a pair of wire frames without the glasses from Edgar's hoard.

Alex was studying the back of the structure. "Yeah, we can detach the hutch easily from these hangers. It'll be a cinch." He started to lift it. "Ugh! It's heavier than it looks. I think we should dump Edgar's treasures and food bowl, it'd make it lighter."

"Watch your ankle and back. Here, I'll grab this end."

"It's not as light as it looks." Alex grunted as they lifted the cage off the wall. Suddenly his smile evaporated. "Watch out for that clump of grass behind you!"

It was too late. Kay abruptly sat down and the hutch tipped over. The contents of Edgar's cage tumbled over the ground.

Alex was at her side. "Honey, you okay? You hit the ground pretty hard."

"I'm all right, but my butt's going to feel it tomorrow." She massaged her hip and got slowly to her feet. "I guess I'm trying to pull an Alex," she said testily. "Speaking of aches and pains, you appear to have recovered."

"Yeah, those yoga-exercises of yours and that detestable ice-pack are doing the trick." He paused. "You know, this hutch is too awkward. I'll get Toady to help me carry it back."

Kay waved him away. "It'll be lighter now. After all, everything's on the ground. And anyway, it doesn't seem that Toady is all that available these days."

They righted the cage. "Well. Look at this. Edgar went in for fine jewelry," Alex muttered as he pulled a silver object from the pile of debris.

That is a nice cufflink." Kay turned it over. "He does have a passion for things that shine or sparkle."

"Looks like something I'd go for too." Alex winked. "That's if I had French cuffs." He paused. "When you find its mate hiding in there, I'll be in the market for a fancy shirt."

Kay knelt down. Her hands sifted through the straw. "There's plenty of beach glass. Hmm, some odd blue beads, one rhinestone dog collar, a fancy comb, shells. Oh, some gardener's going to like this. Look at these plant tags," she got up and rubbed her low back, "nope, nada." She stopped suddenly. "Let me see that cufflink again. It isn't cheap, but it is gaudy. I'm sure I've seen this somewhere before."

"Here we go again; before what, BCE?" Alex snorted.

Kay took the cufflink and pocketed it. "Very funny, but I may just find the other one. And if I do I'll buy you that shirt. Now, let's get Edgar's cage back to the barn."

They replaced some of the necessary contents, carefully hefted it, and staggered forward. It was awkward going.

"You know," Alex panted, "You're assuming that Edgar will like his new location. He'll probably keep coming back here. How exactly are you going to deal with ye-olde homing instinct?"

"Easy, I'll bribe him. The route to a crow's heart is just like a man's, through his stomach. Maybe I'll bake him a long-pig pie," she grunted.

"My, what a dainty dish," Alex said as he wiped his brow with a free hand. "You know. Willie could have made this a little heavier. He could have added doors."

"Stop carping and save your energy. We'll be…"

Ujima stood in front of them, hands on her hips, blocking their way. "What do you two think you're doing?"

"Ah…ah, carrying Edgar's bedroom back to our barn?" Kay answered vaguely.

"You realize you're interfering with the 'scene of the crime' I'm surprised at you two. Put that back where you found it."

They set the hutch down carefully. Alex raised his arms. "Don't shoot Sergeant. We'll tote it back this instant. I wouldn't want a good crow to go bad."

Kay rolled her eyes. "Ujima, this wasn't in the cabin. It's an outdoor hutch. Edgar's birdcage, to be concise; we took it off the side of the cabin. Someone's got to take care of Edgar until Willie returns. That's if he returns," she said in a small voice.

Alex smiled. "Kay wants to play mother hen to that damn crow. But, I'm pretty sure Edgar will have his own agenda." His face became sober as he looked at Ujima. "You're right though. This may be an important piece of evidence," he stage-whispered. Out of the side of his mouth he said to Kay, "she's not exactly overjoyed about this."

Ujima shook her head. "Definitely not, and here I thought I could rely on you two bozos."

Alex pointed at Kay. "It was completely that Bozo's idea. She's the one you should arrest. I'll be more than glad to return this to where it belongs. I'll bet when Willie shows up, he'll sue us for cage and crow theft."

Ujima smiled briefly. "I wouldn't count on Willie returning very soon."

Kay stepped forward. "Why, what's happened?"

"I shouldn't encourage you amateur sleuths, but it'll be all over the island by tonight." She pulled a newspaper clipping out of her shirt pocket and handed it to Kay.

"It's an item that appeared in the 'Spindrift' this morning. It was under personals."

Kay read it aloud: "Willie Cloudmaker visiting relatives. Address all correspondence to New Halem Oregon P.0. Box 9702."

"There you are. See Kay, Willie's all right. "

"I remember him mentioning something about Oregon and his berry canes."

Ujima nodded. "Ah his famous Marion-berry vines. I believe the berries were developed in Marion county Oregon. Hopefully the nutcase who wrecked his cabin doesn't have a clue where that is. With Willies truck gone, I'd figured he made tracks to somewhere safe." She paused. "I seem to remember him mentioning a niece somewhere. It should be in his file in my office."

Alex grumbled. "Willie knows something. It's good he's out of the picture."

Ujima nodded. "Yes it is and he could be staying somewhere nearby New Halem. All he has to have is a friend to pick up his mail. He's pretty savvy when he wants to disappear. To put your mind at rest Kay, I'm checking out other leads too."

"Like what leads?" Kay challenged.

"Humph. Like the man who delivers the Seattle papers. He's certain he saw Willie's truck parked at the dock on the Fauntleroy ferry side yesterday morning. But if he did, it's not there now."

Alex clapped his hands to his head. "You know, I thought this was a peaceful, quiet island, a place where a weary body could retire and rejuvenate. Now we're faced with vandalism, threats and possible mayhem. What the hell is going on?"

Ujima sighed and took a deep breath. "You think that's bad. I've got more jolly news. The mayhem you mentioned has actually occurred. The coroner's report came in this morning. Templeton's death was no accident."

Alex and Kay looked at Ujima in disbelief.

Ujima nodded and shrugged her shoulders. "Oh, yes. He was bludgeoned with the usual blunt instrument. Then his body dragged and flung over the cliff."

## CHAPTER 19

# *Tea and...*

**Two days after the cabin incident,** Kay found herself heading in the direction of Willie's. She was surprised to see the tape down and Ujima and her officer, cleaning up the site. Officer Reynolds was a tall, angular, pleasant looking young man. But his slow smile and laid-back attitude gave the impression that he was perpetually sleepwalking through his tasks. Kay, frustrated by his slowness, volunteered to pitch in and help restore a modicum of order to the mess. Surprisingly, Ujima gave her approval. And 'yes', she assured Kay, they had carefully sifted through the debris hours before and there was no evidence that Willie was there when the trashing occurred.

Later, after most of the debris had been sorted and cleared, Kay bid them goodbye. But she felt guilty that she had said nothing about the earring she'd found, nor the cufflink in Edgar's cage. Withholding evidence, she thought. But on the other hand she hadn't mentioned the sail bag and its contents either. In for a penny, in for a pound, she thought. Anyway, they were only random 'artifacts.' It would be fun to suss them out alone and avoid getting anyone else involved unnecessarily and she recalled times when her hunches had proved to be embarrassing. Even Alex wasn't listening to her speculations. In fact he discouraged them, and seemed completely involved in becoming a tyrant in residence.

He dispensed orders with relish, claiming his ankle and back injury had flared up again. He was particularly over-bearing in directing the placement of the newly arrived furniture. Finally, when Raymond,

Thom and Kay had had enough, they bodily picked Alex up and sat him in a chair on the verandah. There, banished to the outside, he and Edgar eyed each other warily.

The day after the furniture was moved in, a troubled Kay parked her car near Toad Hall. Thommy Jay was in front with his head cocked bird-like to one side, hands clasped behind his back. He was solemn as he strode up and down the sidewalk intently studying the window

Kay smiled. He reminded her of Edgar making a critical decision about what to pounce on next.

"Good morning, Thom. Is Toady in?"

He gave her an odd look and took a deep breath. "No. In fact the silly child is in Seattle, again. I've not been able to open my shop for several days. He owes me." Thom waved his hand at the window. "I removed the dreadful moose head and that odious stuffed peacock. It looks better, doesn't it?" Kay nodded. The window emanated the inviting aura of an English tea shoppe; wingback chairs, piecrust tables, fussy doilies, and a plethora of china and silver. Toady's aggressively masculine items had been shuffled to the back.

"Anyway, what brings you into our thriving metropolis?" Thom paused. "I hope you haven't had a change of heart." He shook his finger at her. "Toady has an unwritten policy. No refunds. No exchanges. And that goes especially for newbies," he chuckled.

"No. No, everything's good. Even Alex is begrudgingly enjoying things."

"Oh yes. My. Wasn't he a pain in the... In the other day? But let's forget Alex."

Thom grabbed Kay's arm with a flourish.

"Take another look, dear. Is my front arrangement a shade too Nellie? Have I overdone it?" He feigned concern. "We wouldn't want a bunch of butch leather-bikers destroying Toady's window. What's a poor friend to advise?"

Kay examined the display closely. "Well. It is a wee bit cluttered," she answered tactfully then paused, "but, talking about advice, I could certainly use some now."

Thom peered over the top of his glasses and studied her face. Then he hooked his arm in Kay's. "My dear, you didn't come to hear Thommy Jay criticize Toady's lack of taste. I can see it in your eyes. Tell mother all about it. Did naughty Alex not come home last night? Wishful thinking on my part, I'm sure." Kay traced a crack in the sidewalk with her toe.

Thom's jaw fell slack. "You mean he really didn't come home last night? I thought his ankle would've…"

Kay laughed. "Thom you're incorrigible. Alex hasn't moved from the house. And besides his ankle and back, there are other things bothering me. And I don't know who I can discuss them with. I thought I could bend Toady's ear a little." She turned her mouth down. "But at the critical moment he's never here. Ujima's far too busy with this Templeton thing. And I don't think she'd appreciate my bouncing ideas off her just now."

Thom loosened his grip and clapped his hands. "Not another word! Remember. Little Thommy can remain as silent as Cleopatra's tomb." He winked. "Besides, Toady is too involved with a new love interest."

Before Kay could ask any questions, Thom quickly dashed into the shop, changed the sign to 'Closed' and locked the door behind him.

"Kay, I'm always lamenting. Why can't little me be as lucky as Toady? It's been nothing but the good, the bad and the ugly this morning. A good ferry crossing, a really bad butter-horn, the hunky cashier who always tenders me the wrong change," he shook his head then said with a sigh, "but the fellow never talks to me, just grunts. Now, that's what I call an ugly morning."

Kay laughed and shook her head. "Thom. All you have to do is be your charming self."

While a part of Kay's mind listened to Thommy Jay's lamentations about his love life, the other part wondered: Where is a good place for a quiet tête-à-tête?

Kay turned in the direction of the 'Bradestone Inn and Tea Room'; where lace curtains in mullioned windows, framed by cheery flower boxes, beckoned.

Thom clutched her arm. "My Dear, we're not going in there. Oh heavens no. Once it was a bistro, then a sport's bar. The owners can't make up their minds as to what they want to do. They haven't a clue. Toady detests the place. And for once, I agree. It's overpriced, pretentious, and the food is ptomaine on a plate."

Kay could hardly hold back her laughter as she glanced at Thom's stricken face. "But I don't want grease dripping from my elbows at the 'Fish Bank'. I've my mouth set for a hot cup of tea. And that's what I need right now, tea and sympathy."

"Don't we all," Thom replied sotto voce as he reluctantly followed her into the tearoom.

## CHAPTER 20

# *Table talk*

**The place was empty.** The tourist season wouldn't begin until the middle of June and the noon ferry had not yet docked.

Thom selected a table far from the window. "I don't want to be seen here," he explained as they sat down, "and my dear, avoid the desserts. They're all, shall we say, well-aged."

The waitress stomped to the table. She appeared terribly inconvenienced. "So, is it water, or something else?" she asked.

He put his hand on Kay's and whispered, "Seriously, let me order."

Pad and pencil in hand the server rolled her eyes toward the ceiling.

Sitting up with an authoritative air, Thom removed the menu from the chrome condiment rack. "We want a large pot of hot, black *real* tea, none of those aluminum packets of straw-filled pillows that taste like chick-mash." He put the menu down. "And we'll have two plain veggie burgers. Omit the flabby fries and substitute two packages of potato chips."

The waitress left, protesting the substitutions and what the chef would say.

"Chef? Ha, look at this." Thom flourished the menu. "'Beef stew bourguignon, in spring? I ask you, featuring anything seasonal is beyond their grasp." He shook the menu at Kay. "This is precisely why I'm going to be the new owner of Toad Hall."

Kay looked puzzled. "What? The new owner of Toad Hall, have I missed something?"

Thom waved his hand airily. "I'm going into the furniture business along with my antique shtick. Lord knows, I've got enough in storage as it is." He leaned forward and lowered his voice. "Toady is selling Toad Hall... to me.

Thom grinned at Kay's surprise. "He intends to open a real restaurant on this provincial atoll. He'll make a mint. He's a much better chef than he is a furniture dealer. But don't tell him I said that! I won't ever hear the end of it." He nervously dabbed at his face with his napkin and looked furtively around the restaurant. "I probably shouldn't have said a thing. Let's keep it a secret, okay?"

Kay nodded. She wondered if Thom could be as silent as the "tomb" he had alluded to.

"Open a restaurant," she said in a whisper. "Does he know what the Islanders and tourists will go for? Gourmet dining? Asian? Family style?"

"Actually, a bit of all of the above." He wiggled in his chair. "I know it's eclectic, but Toady knows what he's doing. He's going to have a complete, well-stocked bar, and the menu offerings will appeal to many tastes. A sort of Med-Asian-Mex-Mix, but it will be seasonal." He smiled smugly. "He's going to name it 'The Bloated Toad'. I don't think that's the best moniker, but there you are."

"It sounds overly ambitious, to me. However, in the short time I've come to know Toady, I'd say he certainly seems to have the drive and personality to make something like that succeed."

"I agree completely. I'm amazed *this* place has stayed in business as long as it has. You must never over-tax the kitchen here. Believe me! They only survive because of the trapped tourists. The poor souls have to choose between this food and the ferry food. In both cases I use the word 'food' loosely." He burrowed back into his comfortable wingback chair. "But that's enough blithering. Now, tell Auntie all."

Kay played with her fork. "Well. It's hard to be specific. And I know Alex thinks I'm reading a lot into it. But, too many weird events are following on the heels of others." She paused at Thom's eager but puzzled look. "I'll try to put it in order."

"First of all, I know Superior Island has their fingers in the pie somewhere. They've made vague threats about us being sorry if we don't sell."

"Threatened you? Sell what? I didn't know this. What happened?"

Kay told Thom about the visit of the unpleasant duo then brought the conversation back to Alex. "And I thought it was strange that bridge accident occurred shortly after we rejected their offers."

Thom picked up his glass and stared into the water. "Anyone could have walked over that bridge and fallen through. I thought it was intended as a joke, but a very dangerous one at that. Rose probably has the right solution: vandals again." He fidgeted in his chair. "Every week the Spindrift has articles about rambunctious teenagers. They've vandalized mailboxes and picnic tables in the local parks. The poor babies say they're bored and have nothing to do." He swirled the water in his glass and stared at it. "It was fortunate that Toady called the law last year, or there wouldn't have been any charming farmhouse left for you to buy."

"But that's just it. Ujima's pretty sure it wasn't vandals. And she doesn't think it was kids; too well organized."

Thom waved his hand. "Ujima sometimes is as suspicious as the CIA, a conspiracy in every corner." He frowned at the water in his glass. "Yuk, *this* is pure Clorox!" He clutched his throat. "They're trying to poison us."

Kay ignored his histrionics. "But don't you find it strange that these events have all occurred around Heron's hook? Even Templeton's murder happened there."

Thom's reply was interrupted as the steely-eyed waitress clunked down their meals. "Sir, there will be an extra charge for the changes in your order." Thom sputtered as she continued. "Your tea will be up shortly. We don't usually get requests for loose-leaf tea. It takes longer!" She stomped back to the kitchen.

"You see what I mean?" Thom hissed. "She probably took it out of teabags. They don't have the slightest clue as to what the name Tea Room means," he hissed. He paused then noted the concern on Kay's face. "I can guess what you're thinking. What would the knuckleheads at Superior Island gain, particularly if they did have a hand in weakening the bridge? I can answer that. They're trying to intimidate you. They think you two will cave." He looked abashed and said weakly, "like the bridge."

Kay nodded. "Ujima said they've used similar strong-arm tactics in the past."

Thom dabbed his mouth with his napkin. "They do have that reputation. And recently Rose has been on their case more than usual." He spread his hands. "But, when I first came to the island the Superior boys were extremely helpful in locating a beach house for me. That hunk, Justice in particular, outdid himself. He gave me valuable tips on the location, and why high bank was best for what I wanted. Of course, at first he tried to wangle me into the Gull condos." Thom wrestled with his bag of chips. "Now Templeton was a different can of tuna, very aloof; he gave me the impression that the entire island should be one big nature reserve. Now they say he's had a change of heart... go figure." Thom paused, balefully eyeing the recalcitrant package. "Kay, can you have a go at this? I think it's hermetically sealed in super-vinyl."

Kay, her thoughts obviously elsewhere, tore the chip bag open with ease and handed it back to him. Eyes arched in surprise, Thom crunched on a chip and then took a tentative bite of his burger.

Kay regarded hers thoughtfully. "That's what's odd. Why his hidden agenda? Everyone I've talked to has been surprised by Mr. Templeton's complete turnaround."

"Dear Kay. It's simple. His company is out to make m-o-n-e-y. Their history is developing properties, and not too nicely." Thom picked out a leaf of suspect lettuce. "So, Templeton put one over on the Bradestone community. What's new? Greed runs the world." He winked at her. "Speaking of greed, any development will mean more business for yours truly, particularly when I become the new owner of Toad Hall. You can see why I'm not complaining." He paused. "Of course the greenies will be up in arms. They'll fight this new resort through the courts with impact studies and whatever." He sighed wistfully. "It'll probably be a long time before Superior builds a resort at Heron's Hook. But eventually it'll lure enough bodies and boost poor Auntie Thom's business into the million dollar mark. And it will also help defray my commuting costs from West Seattle." He put his burger carefully on his plate. "And what else is bothering our Kay?"

"Willie's disappearance for one thing and the senseless destruction of his personal property," she leaned forward and whispered, "Alex and I think there's something in the cabin that someone wants. And it's obviously not Willie's valuable art work." She looked down at her plate. "They thoroughly smashed that."

Thom adjusted his tie and tsk-tsked. "You think a lot of Willie, don't you? I really don't know him very well. But I do know he gets himself involved with some very peculiar characters. It's not too surprising that his cabin was ransacked. Could be dope," he said, then his voice dropped, "and the word around here is that he practices some sort of witchcraft!"

Kay's eyes flashed. "You really don't know him at all. He's a kind, gentle, man. Maybe he is eccentric and has eccentric friends to boot. Who cares? He might even have psychic abilities. That's beside the point. He's an artist and a humanist. So naturally he would be involved with many different types of people. And it would never cross his mind to censure them or their lifestyles. Personally I'm surprised at your attitude. And I resent it when silly rumors are spread about him."

Thom's eyes were huge. "Whew! My, my, aren't we sensitive on this subject. Auntie offers a thousand pardons."

"You bet I'm upset. We haven't had a word from Willie nor do we have a clue where he might be."

"Hmm... I've heard something positive through the Island grapevine. It might put your mind at rest. The rumor is that he is staying in Oregon with a relative."

Kay looked shocked. "Where did you hear that?" She knew Sergeant Washington wouldn't have told anyone.

"I never divulge my sources," Thom said primly and dabbed his napkin at his lips.

Kay rolled her eyes to the ceiling. "Well I don't think it's true. And I wouldn't spread it around." She paused. "Anyway, on top of it all, I have other problems. I found a sail bag of strange personal items washed up on the beach last week and I haven't told her anything about it, yet."

"Well. Now this is getting interesting. Who lost their undies overboard?"

"That's just it. I don't know."

Kay rummaged around in her shoulder bag as Thom glanced nervously around the room. "Odd bodkins, you're not going to air the dirty laundry here... are you?" He rubbed his hands together. "You won't hear any protests from me. It's that waitress, Ms. Ratchet, I'm concerned about."

Kay lowered her voice. "There actually was a dress from Sabra's shop. But there was also a piece of odd-shaped carpet. You know, like the kind that's used in boat cabins."

"No. I don't know. I just drive onto the ferry dock and I'm seasick. I try to give any boat a wide berth, and Auntie is not making a pun."

Kay opened one of the side pockets of her large leather purse that Alex always referred to as her 'feed bag'. She carefully unfolded a piece of Kleenex. "I also found this embedded in the carpet. It's slightly damaged."

She handed him the tinted contact lens, the earring that was wrapped in the same tissue fell into her hand.

Thom pointed at the silver bauble. "Where did you find that?"

"Oh. You mean this cuff-earring?" Kay watched his reaction closely.

"I think I know whose it is." He poked at the earring. "Yes, I'm certain. It's Toady's. He'll be grateful. I was with him when he bought the pair at Sabra's. They cost him the earth. That's white gold."

Kay starred at Thom. "I- I found it in Willie's cabin, the night it was vandalized."

"Well, it's obvious how it got there. That damned crow. If it glitters and isn't nailed down, off it goes. Why don't you give it to me? I'll see Toady before you do." He winked at Kay. "Maybe we could extract a reward from him, say dinner at Salty's in Redondo?"

She hesitated then handed him the earring. Thom was probably right, she thought. She and Alex had wondered why the earring hadn't been buried when the cabin was trashed. The likely scenario was that Edgar had flown in the open door and dropped his treasure there.

Thom smiled as he patted his pocket then opened his other palm. "Now, this contact lens, it could belong to anyone. When little Thommy was wearing them he was always losing them. I recall one night, at a dinner party, my friends and I looked everywhere for twenty minutes, we simply couldn't find my left lens. Later, I ate it. It had fallen into my potatoes! That's why I refuse to wear contacts." He preened slightly then made a face. "Even though they do make me look younger, I don't think a diet of contact lenses is beneficial to one's digestion." He tapped his granny glasses. "Can't swallow these; however, some people would insist I have a big enough mouth." He looked at her. "You mentioned a dress by Sabra?"

"Well. It's not actually a dress it's more of a sarong. The label says it's a Sabra original."

Thom arranged his napkin into a neat square. "What does our gorgeous Alex say about all this?"

"He's more concerned with his injured foot and sore back right now. But I had him keep the scrap of carpet, and the sail bag it was in." She delved deeper into her own purse and pulled out a clear plastic bag containing the sarong. "This is it. We tried to take it to Sabra's last week, to see if she knew anything about it, but the shop was closed."

Thom spoke very slowly. "That my dear is definitely a Sabra original; to the tune of eight hundred dollars. I saw Elanor Lavin and Janet Holmes almost kill over that scrap of material."

Kay made a grimace as she neatly tucked the dress back into the plastic bag. "Well, I hope Elanor didn't carry through with it."

"My dear Kay, you're such an innocent. Women have killed for less." He shoved his chair back.

"Now, I think it's time we played Nancy Drew and dragged our tired little bodies over to Sabra's. I haven't been in her shop for ages. Not since last Halloween. We'll stir up a little excitement on Bradestone." He looked at the bill then threw his napkin onto the table with disgust. "Anything to take our minds off this dreadful lunch!"

## CHAPTER 21

# *Haut Mode*

**The shop bell tinkled** as Kay and Thom entered. Sabra, a pleasant looking woman with a heart-shaped face and unruly red hair, knelt in a large alcove near the back of the shop. She glanced up then went back to the dress she was working on. The silky material seemed to barely cover the mannequin.

"Why hello, Ms. Roberts and Mr. Jay, I'll be with you in a moment," she mumbled through a mouth full of pins.

Kay shot a look at Thom. Sabra knew her name. The Island's telegraph working again she mused then turned to poke through a rack of size ten's. Humph, expensive material and not surprisingly, the styles ranged from gorgeous to god-awful.

"Ah, that's done." Sabra patted the mannequin and came into the main room. "Thank you for waiting. Now, how can I help?" Her large eyes were fixed in eager anticipation.

Kay quickly put a seven hundred dollar frock back on the rack. A brief look of disappointment crossed Sabra's face.

"I'm sorry," Kay said, as she searched in her purse. "I'm not shopping today. But I do have this I'd like to ask you about."

"Wherever did you get that?" Sabra said, hastily removing the garment from the offending grocery bag. "I've only made two of these. One was for Ms. Lavin and the other for Janet Holmes." She nodded. "Elanor wore hers to the symphony soiree on the mainland last year. Janet saw it and loved the material. She wanted it in a different style, of course." Sabra held it at arm's length. "Yes. This is the one I sold to Janet, strapless, and a smaller waist." Sabra's blue eyes flashed. "It's in terrible shape. Ms. Roberts, where did you get this?"

Kay glanced at the amusement on Thom's face. She would have given anything to say she found it at a garage sale for five dollars. Instead, she carefully measured her words, "It was over a week ago, about eight in the morning, near high tide."

Sabra's mouth formed a small 'o', as she clutched the dress. "My creations are not thrown away like bits of garbage? Never, never, I simply can't imagine…"

Thom looked around for a chair and scooted it under the folding Sabra.

"I don't think it was discarded on purpose," Kay said. "But there has to be some explanation as to why it was there."

Sabra looked straight ahead. "Janet wanted this for her trousseau. Do you know Martin Gray? He's the lucky groom."

Thom leaned over and whispered in Kay's ear, "Mr. Gray makes those small and rather odious carved miniatures. You can see them in his shop window on Front Street."

"Oh yes. I have," Kay said as she elbowed Thom. "It's that eclectic art studio. There's interesting pottery and paintings along with the carved creatures. But the shop seems to always be closed."

Thom flipped his wrist. "That's the one. It's across from the Grange building." Sabra smiled and nodded in agreement as Thom wondered aloud, "I recall his crow and heron studies. They seem difficult to tell apart." He sniffed. "And it appears that he'll be plaguing Burn with his creations too. That's if he ever finishes remodeling that derelict boathouse he bought there."

Sabra's shoulders stiffened. "He's a budding artist and doesn't only carve birds. He did a 'Creatures of the Wetlands' series recently; it was very lovely." With a look of adoration on her face, she launched into considerable detail.

Thom's lips twitched. "Yes Sabra, they do sound like splendid works of art." He grimaced. "But I don't have the, er capacity to appreciate his technique. I'm more into 'Victoriana' anyway...but, back to the wedding. I wasn't aware that this Gray fellow was marrying anyone." He stroked his chin. "Of course, picturing them together, they would make a lovely couple."

Sabra was slightly mollified. "Yes. Yes, definitely. Janet is a beautiful girl and very much in love with Martin. It's so romantic. They met last winter at the 'Bradestone Mollusk Festival'. They just couldn't leave each other alone. It was shortly after, they decided to run off and get married."

Thom asked innocently, "Who, the mollusks or Janet and Martin?"

Kay shot him a withering look and asked, "When was this?"

"It was about a month ago, during that awful wind storm." Sabra shook her head. "Janet is a great help, and a good seamstress. She works for me part time. The poor girl isn't paid very much for her secretarial work." Sabra nervously examined the backs of her hands. "It's not only me, but many of her closest friends were surprised at their elopement. I was to give Janet away." She sighed. "But she did leave me a note."

"Do you still have it?"

"Yes. I always file my personal correspondence." She got up and put the dress on top of an ancient, green file cabinet. After a few moments of going through manila folders she said: "Here's the one. It's on Janet's lavender stationery. I'll read it."

"Dear Sabra. I'm off on one of life's greatest adventures, my honeymoon. Don't try to contact me. I'm sure you'll understand. We're going to New York then Europe. But I'll send postcards; then you can follow us on our travels. We haven't any idea as to where we'll be after New York. I want Paris but he wants London. Martin is so spur of the moment. It's already a fabulous honeymoon; all my love, Janet."

Kay took the note and skimmed it. "Do you have any of their postcards?"

"No. Not me. But some of her friends have. That's what hurts my feelings. I thought we were closer than anyone else. She had no family that I know of." Sabra sat down. "Of course, they're both very young and silly." She stared at Kay. "And nobody knows exactly where they are, seem to flit from place to place, but that's understandable, neither one is the tiniest bit concerned when it comes to certain social graces."

Thom nodded. "This, er, Gray fellow, does he have any relatives on the island? Any close friends?"

"You know. I can't think of anyone here. But, Martin does carry on about his family and the friends he left in New York." She smiled. "He's always saying New Yorkers are far more sophisticated than any of us country bumpkins." She smiled and looked up. "Though I do remember him mentioning one friend in particular, I forget his name, but they shared some sort of art studio space." She looked confused. "Or worked together in a studio there, I'm not really sure."

Sabra sat up in her chair. "Why are you asking all these questions? Their affairs are no concern of yours."

Kay looked out the window at the sunny day and carefully considered her answer. "I don't wish to worry anyone unnecessarily. But three things puzzle me. One, an expensive and much valued frock of hers washes up on the beach. Two, no one seems to know her whereabouts, and three, you haven't received any postcards from her, and she specifically said she would send them on to you."

Sabra dropped the note in shock. "You aren't saying that something has happened?!"

"No. There no doubt are perfectly good explanations for everything. But I do think Janet's whereabouts should be established." Kay paused. "Uh, just one more question. What color are Janet's eyes?"

"Why, they're blue."

"I have another question. Does she wear glasses?"

"Well, yes. But she wears contacts when she...why do you ask?"

"Oh nothing, I'm just curious."

Thom cleared his throat as he picked the note up off the floor. "I don't wish to add to Kay's fanciful speculations, whatever they are. But I think it's peculiar that this note is typewritten. There's not even a personal signature. Was this the usual way she handled her correspondence?"

Sabra looked disoriented. "No. But I, I assumed she was in a hurry."

Kay sniffed the lavender-colored note. "This is, er rather distinctive paper."

Sabra nodded vigorously. "Janet always used it; the scented stationary was a gift from Martin."

Kay turned to Thom. "You sir have got a point. And I hope I'm not being hasty about this, but I'm going to alert Sergeant Washington. She has the means to locate Janet and Martin, even if they're knocking about Europe at random."

"Oh no, not the police!" Sabra's hand covered her mouth as she walked over to her desk.

"It's all right," Kay said gently. "I think we all can handle this with discretion. Where do you keep your phone?"

Sabra reluctantly pulled an antique phone from behind the green cabinet. "Here. Remember, speak loudly, and be careful of the mouthpiece, it sometimes unscrews. Darling Martin fixed it for me but..." she shrugged.

Why do people like these accursed phones? Kay thought as she dialed. She listened to crackling sounds then shouted into the receiver, "Hello Ujima? It's Kay Roberts. I don't know an easier way to say this. But besides Willie, there may be another missing person or persons to report." There was silence. She raised her voice. "Hello Ujima. Are you there?

"Kay. You don't have to blow my ear off. You're coming in very loud and very clear." There was a long pause that ended with an audible sigh. "Now, what's this about missing persons?"

Kay lowered her voice. "There might be two more. Their names are Janet Holmes and Martin Gray."

"Did you say Martin Gray? Just a minute, that name sounds familiar." Kay could hear Ujima shuffling through papers on her desk. "Ah, here it is. I have a fax from the Idaho department of motor vehicles. It concerns an automobile registered to a certain Martin Gray."

Kay said, "Just a moment," into the mouthpiece and covered it with her hand. She looked at Thom then motioned to the doorway with her head. "Ujima wants to have a private chat. Could you and Sabra get us some coffee and maybe doughnuts? Make mine a cafe-au-lait."

Thom fumed, but after Kay mouthed, "Make yourselves scarce or my lips will be sealed tighter than any proverbial tomb." They reluctantly left.

Kay whispered, "Go ahead."

"What's going on? Too many ears?" Ujima asked cautiously.

"You could say that."

"Kay. I'm only telling you this since you've been hounding me for the last few days. Keep this under wraps, okay?"

"Sure. You know me. I'm as silent as.... er, go ahead."

"Mr. Gray's vehicle was found last week, abandoned. It was near the road to Blanco pass in northern Idaho. The report indicates that the car was totaled, evidently a fire. Fortunately no victims were found. But the Idaho police think the vehicle was stolen as the plates were removed. They located me by the VIN number. Now, do you have something else to add to this?"

Kay told Ujima about the sarong she'd found, and the incommunicado couple. Ujima's voice increased in volume at the end of the line.

"Girl, you and Thom get your butts down to the station. And bring that dress and anything else you may have. Also tell Sabra I'll need that note," she paused for a moment, "and the names of those who said they received postcards." There was a longer pause. "Dammit Kay, things are too quickly becoming too complicated!"

*CHAPTER 22*

# *Disguises*

**Rose fumbled** with the ignition key as she eyed the three motorcyclists waiting in the ferry line ahead of her. They certainly didn't seem in any hurry. They were laughing and showing- off for the girls that stood near the dock railing. One macho, leather-vested young man punched the other on the shoulder. Then the other countered with a challenge to arm wrestle. When the lead biker shook his fists in a victory stance, the onlookers were provided with a show of tattooed biceps, well-muscled abs and an occasional flash of earring.

Rose envied the aura of adventure and excitement that surrounded the young men. Too, she secretly admired the hint of minimally contained recklessness.

But, after all, she was having an adventure too. It was her first night off the island in a long time. Surprisingly, a neighbor who couldn't make the opera that evening had called and given her his ticket. Rose quickly closed the office early. She was determined to be at the front of the line destined for Fauntleroy.

I've needed this, she thought, then grimaced as she closed her eyes. What she didn't need was this loaner truck. The starter groaned. What a wreck. To add to things her morning had been awful. It started when Kay snubbed her. Rose tried to wave her down three times. But, to be fair, it did seem Kay had been preoccupied. And then, soon after that, Ujima showed up to question her about Martin Gray and Janet Holmes.

Rose told Ujima that she didn't much care for either one of them. Of course Rose did keep track of their affairs and the juicy gossip that surrounded them.

However, with Ujima's encouragement, Rose recalled more than she thought she knew. Rose squirmed in her seat. But she hadn't told her everything.

There were the instances when Rose spotted her and Martin leaving her opponents real estate offices several times, and late at night. Janet was a part-time employee so she might have had a legitimate reason for being there, but not him. Rose had a hunch they were using the office for more than just catching up on paper work. And then there was the obnoxious way Janet had thrown herself at Toady. Obviously Janet was jealous because of her close relationship with Toady. Well, Rose thought with an audible sigh, Janet had made the correct choice in running off with a Greenpeacer like herself. Toady didn't take risks, unnecessary risks, no way. They would have been completely incompatible with his character. Ah ...finally engines snorted into life.

With a casual glance at the girls, the young men revved their engines and drove slowly down the ramp onto the ferry.

"Gad!" Rose exclaimed aloud as a deck hand beckoned her hastily forward. While she had been daydreaming, the cars ahead had moved. Nervously, Rose shifted her truck into gear. It lurched forward. What a dog. Right after Ujima left, Rose had gotten into her sweet little Mazda. The car decided not to be so sweet and had to be towed into Barney's garage, the only decent service station on the island.

Barney shrugged his massive shoulders then with a greasy paw, gave her keys to, "the only rig I've got left on the lot". When Rose saw it, her heart fell. It was a 76 Ford truck. Barney grumbled, "I'll throw in a free tank of gas cause it's a guzzler compared to your sweet little

M." He should've also said that the truck had a grabby clutch and moved like an ocean-liner on bedsprings. Well, at least everything else worked, hopefully.

Cautiously she eased into the lane the deck-hand indicated. Rose's shifting was a little rusty, but she still took pride in being able to use a clutch. It was a relief when she set the brake and stopped the engine without killing it, like an amateur.

As the other vehicles thunk-thunked onto the car deck behind her, a heavy smell of exhaust fumes wafted into the truck's cab. Rose grimaced. As soon as she could, she would head for the upper deck.

In front of her, two of the bikers had already left. The third stretched, removed his helmet and slowly, sensuously ran a gloved hand through his long dark hair. Carefully he shook it loose. Rose glanced at her watch.

She'd have to kiss the first part of Florencia en El Amazona's goodbye, but she'd be there in plenty of time for the second act. Toady had told her it was a 'fabulous' production and proceeded to describe the opening scene. She smiled. She wouldn't miss a thing; his re-telling had been so vivid that she'd already memorized the first act.

However, Rose felt a little miffed that he hadn't asked her to go with him on the opening night. Then she waxed philosophical. After all, he had his own life to lead, and he couldn't ask her to every social event.

With one eye on the last cyclist's broad shoulders she started to open the door. She stopped. It couldn't be! She adjusted her glasses as he turned slightly in her direction and made small adjustments to the side pack on his bike. Rose gaped. It was. It was him! The light was poor, but there was no doubt.

He dismounted, ran his hands sensually over the bike, and then casually strode toward the stairs. Rose shrunk down behind the wheel. He was going to walk right by her. She held her breath. The sound of heavy boots trod past the driver's side of the truck.

She hadn't been mistaken. Imagine, dressed like that. A sleeveless, frayed denim shirt exposed his muscular arms to the shoulders. The tattoos! She had seen him with his sleeves rolled up before, and there hadn't been any tattoos. And earrings, in both ears…not to mention the long hair hanging past his shoulders; it had to be a wig and a good one at that.

Rose's heart beat rapidly as she pushed her glasses further up on her nose and squinted surreptitiously in the large side-mirror. As he started up the stairs a slinky, leather clad figure fell in step beside him.

Dazed, Rose slowly sat up. Thank the powers that be she didn't have her own car. Obviously he wanted to disguise himself. If he had seen her, they both would have never lived it down. Well, this was definitely his darker side, she thought. A side she'd certainly never suspected, but mentally insisted that all men had. She couldn't wait to tell Sabra. She would be just as shocked as she was.

At first, Rose was determined to stay in the truck. She didn't wish to run into him, not at all. Nor the female he was with. But, her innate curiosity and the capriciousness of nature intervened.

Damn! She had been so worried about missing the opera that she had neglected to use the facilities at the garage. She squirmed in the seat for a few minutes. The ladies room beckoned, that's all there was to it. It would be okay. She could easily blend into the crowd. A dash up and then a dash back. Or would she? Maybe, if she was careful, she could find out what he was up to. She giggled. He wasn't too difficult to spot. His hair and those ridiculous studded boots added four inches to his height, at least.

Easing herself out of the truck, she joined the crowd milling and walking up the stairs to the view decks and the cafeteria. At the top,

Rose scanned the area. Good, he was nowhere in sight and the ladies was on her left. It must be an overload night, she thought, as the larger ferry was on for the evening run. She had to be careful. It would be easy for her to become disoriented. Rose took her bearings, made one last look around and shot into the restroom.

Afterward she skulked down the corridor. Skulking was difficult as people kept bumping into her. One careless passenger almost dowsed her with a brimming cup of lethal ferry coffee.

She peered around a corner. Why would he dress like that? And who was the girl? Rose never thought he would rub shoulders (literally) with bikers. She smiled. This was more intriguing than she ever imagined.

Cautiously, she did a complete circle of the inside deck. It was packed. After a full day on the island, tourists were returning fatigued and sunburned to the mainland. Her quarry wasn't in the snack area and they weren't sitting down. She would have to try the outside decks. Carefully she slid the door open. A cool, breeze rushed by her as she stepped out into smoker's haven.

It was dimly lit, particularly near the outer railing. She stopped. Sure enough, there they were. The foursome were on the opposite side above the car deck, taking advantage of a semi-sheltered area, and leaning against the railing with their cigarettes. Occasionally they tilted their heads together in intimate conversation and blew sensuous streamers of smoke into the air. Rose reasoned that if she walked around to the other side of the observation deck, she could hide behind the metal support near the doorway. Once there she could easily eavesdrop and not be detected. Rose crept stealthily forward.

"Lady, you just stepped on Booger!"

Rose tottered. A tiny, earnest face stared up at her.

"Booger, who's Booger?" Rose's said plaintively, her voice artificially high.

The boy pointed at her foot. "He's… nope, probably was, my pet ant."

Appalled, Rose quickly lifted her foot.

"I'm, I'm terribly sorry young man," she said then red-faced asked, "How do you know it was I that stepped on him; and how did he get away from you in the first place?"

The boy knelt down, grabbed her shoe, turned it over, and inspected her sole. Rose, arms flailing, yelped and demanded he let go.

"Nope, Goober ain't there," he said solemnly and stood up. "I guess the wind could've blowed him away."

"Yes. Yes. How unfortunate," Rose said and grabbed the handrail. The boy shot her a, 'Lady you sure are weird', look.

After accepting Rose's multiple apologies, the youngster left and Rose began edging back to her hiding place. That silly kid, they'd probably spotted her. She groaned. They must have. They were nowhere in sight.

Rose warily circled the child (he was on all fours scrupulously examining the deck). Where on earth were his parents? Rose thought, as she stepped onto the unsheltered deck.

Here it was exhilarating and secluded. There were no car or smoker's fumes and it was a safe distance from 'that child' and his wayward ant. Rose walked over to the railing.

An arm shot out of the darkness. Strong fingers gripped her wrist. She felt she was clutched in the talons of a giant bird of prey.

The odor of cigarette smoke and fetid breath followed. Rose gulped as words rasped in her ear. Her heart held still.

"Oh. I am terribly sorry, Rose. I didn't want to startle you for the world. But I saw you hopping and creeping about back there," Elanor gestured toward the windows with her cigarette, "and I thought you were ill." She eyed Rose intently.

"Any way, what are you doing here?" She demanded huskily. "You've always avoided Seattle like the plague."

Rose looked back at the windows. Everything was visible from out here. She could see the small boy, his nose and lips pressed against the glass in a squashed mask as he peered at them. Rose's own mouth was agape. She felt the fool. Angrily she thrust out her jaw and simultaneously jerked her arm from Elanor's grasp.

"Well. I might ask you the same thing!" Her heart was pounding and the adrenaline rush ran her words together. "I thought *you* hated ferries. You... you said they made you seasick and were 'the transportation of the smelly masses' or something like that." Rose inhaled sharply. "Why, you're wearing a leather dress."

Elanor gave her a withering look, then turned and tapped her cigarette against the railing.

"Since Eric's death, I've made a lot of changes in my life. I've even decided to take a much larger role." Her look challenged Rose, "Not only in what I want do and where I want to go, but also in running the company as well."

Rose was impressed. Elanor's overall demeanor was still that of disdain, but she could see a subtle change in her face. For the first time she looked stronger and comfortable with her age, less defiant. Her hands were the only part of her body that betrayed a shaking undercurrent of vulnerability. Rose lightly touched Elanor's arm.

"I was terribly shocked at the news of Eric's death. And when it turned out to be murder! I... I just couldn't believe it." Elanor dropped the arm Rose was patting and turned away.

"I couldn't either," she whispered into the night. Rose could hear the deep sadness in her voice.

Elanor took a long drag on her cigarette. "It was really terrible, and the entire responsibility of keeping Eric's business on the right track has fallen to me and the board," she said then pounded the railing. "And that stupid board of gray beards in California is useless." She coughed at the end of her outburst. "In fact, that's why I'm on this tub right now, for some inane reason, the helicopter is grounded." She sighed. "I've called a meeting the day after tomorrow at the Four Seasons in Seattle. " She took another slow drag. "I decided to stay over this evening because I haven't slept well in weeks. I've booked a suite. At least I'll be able to catch up on my rest in between the Board's tedious squabbles."

Rose's ears picked up.

"I wondered what would happen, now that Eric's not at the helm. Will the real estate end of it still be on the island? Or will the company rename itself and continue with the new policies of land preservation?" Elanor seemed to have not heard. Her back was still turned away. Rose rambled on, "You know. The direction the newspaper said Eric was taking the company in, the last few months anyway."

Elanor turned around. Her lips portrayed her familiar, deprecating smile. "Don't worry that pretty little head of yours. I'm going to convince the board to go ahead with all its former building plans; they're still in the works. After all, I tend to do real business. I won't follow in Eric's shoes. It only led him off the deep end," she growled, then hesitated when she noticed the appalled look on Rose's face.

"I'm sorry. I don't intend to sound callous. It's really that damned fool Janet's fault. She manipulated Eric around each little finger. He was a fool to let her." Elanor closed her eyes, her voice hissed. "I'm glad she ran off with that Martin fellow. I say good riddance to both of them. She left everything at the office in an absolute mess and no wonder. And that's Eric's fault. He hung on every single one of her detestable utterances, to the point of neglecting the business's the company runs on, she led him by the nose." Her laugh was a short hacking cough. "He actually was going to marry her. Did you know? She had him donating huge sums of money to the 'Worldwatch Institute' of all things."

"I think that's a terrific idea. Why if it wasn't for their work in promoting education and ways to provide sustainable development in this era…"

Elanor interrupted. "Ha! It's an organization Eric once said was an anathema to progress." She took a nervous puff. "Why Janet even had him throwing his money at the local Bradestone Nature Conservation group, literally dragging him to their meetings." Elanor grimaced. "I remember when she had him excited about visiting some bog for Chris-sakes!" She took a deep drag and blew the smoke out the side of her mouth. It slipstreamed in Rose's direction; she coughed.

Elanor inhaled raggedly then dropped her cigarette on the deck and ground it out with her heel. "Even if he'd lived I would've convinced him to fire that bitch. The board and I are going to make certain that Holmes woman's plans are kyboshed."

She looked up. "Don't worry Rose. There's plenty of prime real estate left on Bradestone." She grinned lopsidedly. "We can carve it up to suit ourselves."

"I wasn't thinking about carving up anything," Rose said slowly. "And personally, I thought Eric had good ideas, particularly when it came to the Hook. We need to keep natural habitats undeveloped for wildlife and …"

"You sound exactly like that whining Janet and her cohort, Martin. Oh. That's right. You attended those propaganda meetings too." She took a deep breath. "Look. Let's have no hard feelings. That's why I'm letting you stay on the island as my only competitor. You can handle most of the existing developed properties. And my agency will go where the high end money is."

Rose's face was tight-lipped and red. "Well, Empress of the Island, that's very kind of you. I've-," Rose was interrupted by the announcement for passengers to return to their vehicles.

Elanor glanced behind her. "We're almost there. That's if they don't wrap this tub around the pilings," she said dryly then turned to Rose. "Don't think it was a pleasure talking to you, because it wasn't." She spun on her heel and quickly walked away.

Rose was boiling. She shouted at Elanor's receding back, but a blast from the ferry horn drowned her out. Only her gnashing teeth and rapidly moving tongue were evidence of her anger. The little boy, watching everything, looked amazed. Rose glared at him then crouched, gnashing her teeth she raised her arms like a monster. He turned and ran.

Shaken, she walked toward the stairs to the car deck. She felt diminutive and drained, but something made her look up.

Her heart beat wildly. He was there, looking directly at her! No. No. He wasn't. He was staring brazenly at Elanor, who had halted several paces in front of him. She gestured as if to say something. He leered broadly at her, tossed his mane of fake hair then turning with a panther-like grace glided to the stairs.

So, Elanor had been with *him* on the ferry. Rose glanced around. What if someone else from the island recognized them in those get-ups? Rose would certainly keep her ears tuned in to the island network. It really was the most outrageous thing he'd ever done. This time, if any rumors came up, she couldn't defend him.

Rose watched Elanor gather her coat and walk rigidly toward the stairs. They must've argued about something. She felt a shiver run down her back. She wondered if the opera would be as exciting.

*CHAPTER 23*

# *Nosey Parker*

**Kay sat upright** in a cushion-less, metal chair. Her eyes studied the space around her as she waited for Ujima to finish her phone conversation. The office was cramped. It occupied only a small part of the squat, cinder-block building. And even though it was hot outside the interior felt clammy. Glancing down a grim corridor to her left she spotted a second barred door leading to two small cells. It was understandable why Ujima preferred being outside and on patrol most of the time.

Ujima hung up the phone, swung around in her swivel chair and swore under her breath, her face unreadable.

"Thanks for coming, Kay. I'm office-bound this afternoon." She opened a manila folder on her desk then picked up a pencil and licked its tip, a habit that Kay had noticed before.

"Now, I'd like to review Sabra's typed letter for a moment. Then we can go over what you said when you phoned from Sabra's." Ujima read the note twice, placed it in the folder on her desk and said, "Okay. Shoot!"

Kay was deliberate and thoughtful in answering. Occasionally Ujima asked terse questions. This time Kay included more details, but didn't mention the carpet, it seemed irrelevant and Alex had found an excellent way to recycle it. After relating how she'd found the dress and the lens she placed them on Ujima's desk.

Ujima turned the dress over and looked at its label. "Janet could have become tired of it, loaned it to someone, given it away." She put the garment aside and picked up the lens. "As for this ...," she said as she held the blue piece of plastic up to the light, "It too ..."

"That's not what Sabra thinks." Kay interrupted. "She said the kid paid a lot for that sarong, and was excited about taking it on her honeymoon. And yes, I know lenses are easily lost. But, you mentioned Martin's car had been found. That's just one more thing that I don't like about this whole rigmarole."

Ujima leaned back and sighed. "We're looking into it right now. It appears it was abandoned, and not where we found it. It's highly likely that some country joy riders drove it for a while, cannibalized any useful parts then burned it. From talking to Barney at his garage, the vehicle was never in great shape and was always breaking down. Barney said Martin wasn't much of a mechanic and wasn't exactly poor either, but held onto the car for some environmental reasons." She winked at Kay. "If you'd taken off like that when you were young, car trouble would be just part of the great adventure. Right now I'd say they abandoned the vehicle and went to a train station or airport."

"Where, in some obscure place called Aardvark, Idaho? They've got to have left a trail somewhere."

Ujima became angry.

"Hey! How in the hell am I supposed to locate newlyweds who are hot on their honeymoon, traveling who knows where in Europe, and don't want to be found? Do you have any suggestions, bright eyes?"

"Okay, okay. I know you're under a lot of pressure. If you can't look into Janet's disappearance right away, I can. From the beginning, it bothered Sabra that she hadn't heard directly from Janet. She says they're more than close friends, she felt like a daughter to her. Janet stays in a small apartment above the sewing shop. So finding this discarded dress really upset her."

"Hmm, do you know if Sabra is acquainted with Janet's family?"

"She doesn't have any. Sabra said she lived in foster homes ever since she could remember, and when eighteen hit she gathered what little she had and boogied."

"If Sabra's as close as she claims, why doesn't she call them? I'm sure Janet's parents would let her know where the couple is. So far there is no evidence of foul play or missing persons, and I can't make a move until there is."

Kay shook her head. "For some reason Sabra doesn't want to get involved with the police." Kay waved her hand, "so...I'm offering."

"Why am I not surprised? You don't leave stones unturned. That's your nature." She leaned forward, her chin resting in a cupped hand. "How about this young man, Martin Gray; have you dug anything up on him?"

"Not exactly... but Sabra has the phone number of a close friend of his in New York. Evidently he stays with this person when he visits the Big Apple. Sabra gave me his number and name, a Wick Wilding. He's sure to know something. I intend to start there."

"Look Kay, be discreet. You don't want this one lonely police department under siege. As you indicated, I've enough to do; dealing with pressures from the mainland to sort out Templeton's murder, not to mention trying to locate Willie Cloudmaker. I can do without extra worry, particularly of the unsubstantiated kind." She smiled indulgently. "Let the kids have their fun. When they finally get tired of sewing wild oats, they'll send a fax or make a phone call." She smiled. "And it'll probably say: 'please send money'. Right now, if I were in their shoes, I'd want all the privacy I could muster." She hesitated. "But, I *do* want that sail bag. Okay?"

Kay stood up. "Okay. I'll be discreet and you're right. I'm probably being a nerve end. But I am going to start with that friend of Martin's in New York. I'll find some pretense, like I'm interested in renting space in Martin's studio, and where can I find him."

"Now you're cooking girl, I might deputize you yet." Ujima said this lightly then her mood changed. "Look Kay, I don't want you to think I'm not concerned about these two. I am. And if you find out anything concrete, and I mean concrete, tell me. No funny business or holding something back." She paused as she held up the dress. "Like this."

Ujima got up, walked around her desk, and stuck out her hand. "Thanks Kay." Her grip was warm and solid. "Hey. Don't forget our sailing date. I've been dunning out the 'Talaria' so you won't think I'm camping in the remains of a shipwreck."

Kay laughed. "Don't kid me. Toady told me about what a tight ship you run. Spotless deck, spotless shoe soles, stowing the fenders away immediately, and a complete wash down after every sail. He went on and on about the last time he was crewing with you."

Ujima smiled to herself and looked around the four walls. "Well, it's just like this office. Well... not really. Far more livable, but just as small, so I have to keep it shipshape. Remember, a sailor is like a good politician, always looking smart, even if they don't know what the hell they're doing." She laughed. "And don't believe anything Toady says. He's more of a stickler at captaining than I am."

"Hmm, for some reason it didn't register on me that Toady sailed."

"Oh yeah, he has an old Islander 29, named it the 'Toady Go Too'. A beautiful boat, she's moored at the marina in Peavey Harbor. Occasionally it's tied up at his dock in Scoon Bay. As old as that boat is, he keeps every inch repaired and shining. It's his baby."

Kay looked at the clock. "Well, if I'm going to make those calls..." She paused. "Oh. I almost forgot. I've got to call the airport too."

Ujima sensed Kay's sudden excitement. "What's up?"

"It's my daughter and son. They'll be here in two days. I have to double check the flight bookings and the E.T.A at Sea-Tac. Their Aunt Olive is a little cavalier when it comes to details. I think the kids encourage her." Kay shrugged. "I know they don't like the term 'kids', but I can't help it, even young adults are still kids to me."

Ujima chuckled. "Alex told me about Teri and Byron at Rose's party. He sounded as if they were his own, 'Kids'. He is really fond of those young people. You're a lucky woman."

Kay shook her head. "You're right there. I've never ceased thinking about how lucky I am."

Ujima wanted to ask Kay if she'd thought enough to change her mind about marriage, but said nothing and glanced toward the door.

"Well, don't let me keep you. There's a pay phone down the hall. Like the rest of us, you'll have to throw yourself at the mercy of 'Bungling Bell'. I'll give the phone-boys credit though; at least they keep the emergency lines working. And we recently have acquired new cell-phones."

Kay shrugged and looked steadily at Ujima. "You'll keep the dress and the lens, then?"

Ujima nodded wearily. "Oh yes." She looked at Kay intently. "I haven't the slightest idea why, but one never knows, *do* one?"

Kay laughed. "I'd better make myself scarce," she said and stood up then paused. "When my tribe gets here I want you to meet them."

"I'd like that very much, and..." The phone rang. "That'll be Seattle, hopefully with good news." Ujima picked it up. "Hello, Sergeant Washington here. Will you hold please? Thank you." She put her hand over the mouthpiece. "Kay. I know you're excited and I don't blame you. But keep any of your speculations about this from the kids and Alex too. Will you?"

"Anything the boss says."

"Thanks. Teenagers can be so infernally inquisitive. And if they're anything like their mom, well you know what I mean. Catch you later." Ujima turned and said "Yes?" loudly into the phone. Kay waved and quietly shut the door behind her.

## CHAPTER 24

# *Family*

**The 'red-eye' flight from New York** had just arrived. Kay watched the passengers begin to listlessly debark. I desperately need another cup of coffee she thought and headed for the nearest mall restaurant. She checked one of the Sea-Tac monitors then looked at her watch. The youngster's flight wouldn't be in from Sedona for another forty minutes.

She yawned. The kids were saving money, a good thing, except this incredibly early arrival. She yawned again and decided to use a coffee machine. It would be raunchy, no Seattle's Best, but at least she'd get the jolt she needed.

Might as well people watch, she thought then wandered over to a bank of seats and sat down. Slowly she sipped the tepid coffee and gazed in the direction of the unloading New York flight.

A small girl, clutching the strings of three deflating birthday balloons, ran down the ramp. A frustrated mother hurried after her and managed to grab her waving free hand. The girl giggled and promptly sat down on the floor. A stern looking man, who had been watching the chase, broke into a smile and walked over to embrace them.

Then, with a welcome-home sign wobbling between them, screaming men and women rushed forward to embrace an athletic looking girl. The boisterous mob clustered around her. The girl blushed through her tan as they grabbed her carry-on bag, and thumped her boisterously. Behind them, a young man gracefully stepped around the worshipping crowd.

He's about Teri's age, Kay thought. But considerably taller and appeared quite shy, not at all like Teri. He brushed a healthy tangle of chestnut colored hair out of his eyes as he glanced around. No one to meet him, Kay thought as a look of concern crossed his attractive and sensitive face. Oddly, he seemed familiar. Taking a sip of her coffee she watched the young man turn to study the monitor, re-shoulder his backpack, then lope off in the direction of the tram that returned to the main terminal.

Kay looked at her watch. If the plane were on time, and she drove 'skillfully enough' as Alex would say, they could make the next ferry to Bradestone and not have to wait another hour for breakfast.

She smiled as she remembered Alex's grumbling and pulling the covers back. He was tired and not feeling very well. She said okay, I'll go it alone. She suspected he was conjuring up a surprise 'breakfast welcome'. He couldn't conceal the truth; his expressive brown eyes always gave him away. That was one of the reasons she loved him.

Kay swallowed another sip of the paper tainted brew. Why was it so hard for her to say 'yes' to marry him? He was incredibly patient. She had to stop running away, and to make a decision soon. Alex couldn't wait forever. Her eyes were moist as she got up to look down through the gigantic glass windows. Baggage carts snaked across the tarmac.

Slowly, a plane taxied toward the Sedona gate. People meeting the flight were queuing up at the side of the entryway. An attendant, sandwich and coffee in hand, rushed to her desk. In a flurry she placed her early breakfast under the counter and began readying herself for the incoming flight.

Kay smiled. The kids were the first ones to stumble zombie-like down the ramp. But things perked up as they helped her locate the car. Soon the ride to the ferry dock was raucous and satisfying, everyone talking at once. Byron kept begging to drive, but Kay was adamant and they made the ferry in ample time and in one piece.

She set the hand brake and waited for the ferry attendant to signal the cars in the lane next to her to stop. Then doors slammed as Teri and Byron took off for the upper deck. No waiting for old mum, she thought. Fumes from the vehicles swirled around the car while Kay checked that Barney's loaner was locked, then hurried toward the stairway.

Kay felt the thrumming of the powerful engines that stabilized the ferry in its berth. Looking back a young girl and a man, wearing orange life jackets and heavy gloves, ran the safety chains and posts together into the deck holes. The girl mouthed something into a hand phone. The ferry shuddered; they were off.

The smell of salt air mixed with diesel fumes assaulted her nostrils as she opened the passageway door and started up the steel stairs. Her stomach protested. Ferry food was pretty mediocre and the smell wasn't helping things. But another jolt of coffee and something artery-blocking would not go amiss at the moment. She headed toward the cafeteria. It was great not having to herd the kids anymore. Now they were young adults and could do "their own thing." Of course she still had twinges of concern, but they were essentially on their own. She set her chin forward. It was time she focused on herself, Alex, and their new life together.

CHAPTER 25

# *Friend?*

**As they slowly pulled away** from the dock, Wick Wilding pushed the mop of unruly hair out of his eyes and gazed sleepily out the ferry window. The sound of the engines coupled with the whirling of seagulls mesmerized his tired mind. He stretched his lanky frame and yawned. It hadn't been at all difficult finding a cab this early in the morning.

Thirty minutes later his eyes popped open and he shifted his sleepy gaze ahead. There it was, Bradestone Island. At least that's what the ferry map in his hand said. It was still far away and parts of the shoreline hid in the distance and the mist. Distant tops of fir trees shredded the fog. The occasional shard of sunlight bounced off the water and the far shore. Wick read that it always rained in the Northwest. Whatever, he thought and shrugged. So today was an exception, because an awesome spring sunrise was coming up behind them.

Wick shivered and stretched again. His young body easily shed the stiffness and damp. Everything out here seemed so far apart and oddly quiet, he thought as he looked around. Where were the people? There was hardly anyone on board. Already he missed the excitement and action of New York. He sniffed the air, it smelled pretty good though, but he still felt that this place, the Pacific Northwest, was a little creepy.

Wick had almost dozed off again when his sixth sense perked up. A girl, munching a doughnut and swigging coffee out of a paper cup, was leafing through the tourist brochures at the magazine kiosk. He grinned. Even though her back was to him he could see by her shorts she was tanned and gorgeous. He appraised her full feminine form as she walked around the kiosk. He didn't know if it was the long reddish- brown hair, the bulky-knit green turtleneck, or her tight cut-offs. Whoa! He had fallen in love, again. Running his hands through his hair he slowly got up, stretched and yawned audibly, but not too audibly, and slipped into his best leisure slouch.

The girl turned around and adjusted her sunglasses. She stared at him. He couldn't see her eyes, but he bet that they would be a marvelous green. He smiled and attempted to look even cooler. Whoa, she was smiling too. As he moved toward her, a young man suddenly tackled her from behind. His hair matched hers in color and he wore the same type of sweater. As they wrestled it was obvious he had the advantage in height and weight. They laughed and twisted. The girl tried to save her coffee from spilling and at the same time held her doughnut high in the air. The young man quickly snatched the doughnut and held it far above her head. He smiled, offered to give it back, and then stuffed it into his mouth.

"Oink, oink," the girl mocked and pushed him away. The young man opened his mouth and displayed its contents.

"Don't be so gross!" the girl exclaimed and shoved him again.

Wick cast his eyes down. Why did he always become attracted to attached females? Martin, his best friend, said it put him on safe ground. Suddenly, blind to the beauty of the unfolding sunny morning, he slouched back to his seat and stared glumly out the window.

"Hello," her voice, soft and tentative, startled him out of his melancholy.

She did have green eyes! At least the one he could see was green. A long copper tress covered her other. Casually she brushed it away and asked: "Do you mind if I sit here?" He numbly shook his head.

Taking Wick's open-mouth stare as an okay, Teri slipped gracefully by him and sat down next to the window. Wick wondered what had happened to her rambunctious boyfriend.

"Brothers, they can be a royal pain," she said to the window then turned around. "Do you have any?"

Her hair had fallen over her eye again. He hadn't been listening. Did he have any what? He asked himself. And who did she remind him of? His thoughts sorted rapidly. She looked like an old movie star from the past. Lake, that's it. Veronica Lake.

Teri looked at him; she was concerned by his silence. "Do you live on Bradestone?" Teri nodded her head in the direction of the island and pronounced each word carefully, as if he might have difficulty in hearing and possibly speaking.

"No. Uh no." he said quickly. "I've come to visit." He shrugged. "Well, I'm not really visiting. I'm looking for a friend whom I haven't seen for a while." He felt an overwhelming urge to tell her everything; to share his dilemma then warned himself to be careful.

"How about you?" he croaked out. "I mean, how about you? Do you live on Bradestone?"

She shook her head. She had a marvelous throaty laugh.

"No. My mother and her fiancé bought a house on the island. My ratty brother and I thought we'd check it out, before they completely tie themselves down to one place." She shook her head at the view out the window. "Everything seems so far from civilization." She looked at him with those intense green eyes. "Don't you feel as if raw nature is staring right over your shoulder?"

He swallowed hard and looked at her most excellent shoulder. "Er, yes. Definitely, I feel the same way." He paused then said, "I'm really a New York City kinda guy." He frowned, then with a serious look pointed to the window.

"See all those trees. There's so much…green and space. I bet there are dangerous Indians lurking out there. It's going to be hard to get used to. From the plane, I know we were over five miles up, but the Midwest looked the same way, miles and miles of emptiness. It makes a guy feel incredibly, well, isolated, as if his life is pretty insignificant." He looked at her, embarrassed that he had said so much.

She nodded gravely. "It's a big change, particularly if you've lived on the East coast. I grew up in Oregon. So I'm pretty used to greenery and open spaces. I visited New York though once, and really loved it. We'd wake up at three in the morning, look out our hotel window, and everything was just as busy as it was at ten in the evening." She settled back on the hard plastic bench. "Are you in a college back there?"

"Not now. Just finished my degree in Fine Arts at Metropolitan University," he said then wiggled his eyes and his left hand. "I'm a puppeteer." He looked at her, willing her not to laugh. She didn't. Encouraged he added, "And I hope, someday, to start my own troupe."

"Cool! I've never met a puppeteer before. Do you use marionettes, rod, shadow or?"

Wick was in his element. "I perform with all types, but basically I use hand puppets. They're easy to make, especially for youngsters. Last fall I started teaching classes at a private school for low income kids. It's great, because they can make the puppets and scenery from stuff they find in their homes." He leaned back and said smugly, "I also teach them how to act and how to write their own plays."

"So, you're an instructor as well!"

"Yeah, you could say that. I'm cadetting in a program that will eventually lead to a Masters. When I'm free-lancing, I'm mainly a one-man show. My troupe will come later. " He squinted, pulled his sweater sleeve over his left hand and deepened his voice. The cuff became a toothless mouth. "Ah ha, my fair beauty; I am zee Count of Transylvania. Unt you're unter mon shpell, resistance is useless." He chortled evilly, "so I've lost my teef, a shlight misshap...I still vant your blute!" Teri leaned back and giggled.

A smiling Byron flopped down beside Wick. "I leave my sister for a minute and she is in the gloms of the evil villain." He stage whispered, "Who is this rude dude, anyway?"

Teri covered her mouth with her hand. "Oh. I am sorry. I forgot to ask your name."

Wick stood up and with a sweeping bow doffed an imaginary hat. "The name my good sir is Wick, Wick Wilding, puppeteer extraordinaire. And I'm at your service fair lady and most gentle of gentleman."

Brother and sister laughed with delight. "I'm Teri, Teri Roberts and this is my weird brother Byron, 'Byron the blob' who manages to make my life miserable most of the time."

Byron leaned forward, wrinkled his nose and said in mock seriousness, "She always whines." Then both young men laughed and ritually slapped hands. Teri rolled her eyes. Byron had begun his usual merciless questioning. She mentally grimaced. He was so impossible when they met new people.

Teri watched the two guys chatter away, it looked like they were going to become fast friends. She contrasted her brother's strong, animated face and Wick's graceful and theatrical gestures. It was obvious that Wick was a natural for the theater, but why had he been so shy and awkward at first? Teri crossed her arms and settled back in her seat. She felt intrigued by his complexity and his odd habit of not always looking one directly in the eyes. But more importantly at this time, she felt excluded.

"My, my, enough of this male bonding," they looked at Teri in surprise, "Wick, where did you say you were staying?"

"I didn't. But my friend is restoring a boat house. Actually he's making it into a theatre for local talent." He smiled. "If he's finally returned from his honeymoon I'll bunk there...if not." He spread his hands and shrugged. "I'll find something."

Byron piped up. "If your friend hasn't returned yet, you can stay with us. Our mom won't mind." He cast a slightly guilty glance at Teri. "I don't think her boyfriend would mind either. They bought some sort of farm house. Anyway, Alex said 'there's lots of rooms'." He enthusiastically pounded Wick's back. "Hey. You'll be their first bed-and-breakfast guest."

Teri shook her head. "Byron, don't mess with the fates. You know how mom feels about that subject, it's strictly taboo."

"Sorry, sorry," he said then stuck his chin out. "Personally, I think Alex's bed-and-breakfast idea would be a lot of fun. I'm one hundred percent behind him."

Wick shook his head. "I wouldn't want to cause anyone any trouble. Er, what's this about a taboo?"

Teri winked at him. "Don't worry. It's an old argument. A few years after our dad died, Mom met this great professor at the university, Alexander Angelo de Beahzhi." She nodded her head. "Yes. Try to say that around a mouthful of biscotti. Anyway, as the name sounds, he's an Italian-American and tremendously good-looking. He was a teacher like Mom, but was able to retire early." She took a deep breath "And he has this nutty idea of opening a bed-and-breakfast. Mom, who's hopelessly in love with him, doesn't agree. I think that's the only thing they ever argue about." She poked Wick's shoulder. "But, I'm certain they wouldn't mind if you needed a place to stay."

Wick felt a tingle course through his entire body, but the sudden feeling of elation faded. "Uh, your last name. I didn't catch it."

"Oh, it's Roberts. Our mother is Kay Roberts." She looked at him, the pride evident in her eyes. "She's an artist. She makes baskets and pottery, and teaches yoga too."

"I had a hunch, a lousy hunch." He groaned. "I know your Mom. She talked to me on the phone." He shrugged his shoulders. "That's part of why I'm here."

Teri clapped her hands. "What? You and Mom know each other? That's great!"

Byron looked doubtful, "But how, how so?"

In a flash, Wick became overwhelmed by the memories of the phone call and the magnitude of his decision to stop everything and fly out to the state of Washington. He slumped in his seat, head in his hands. Instinctively Byron and Teri moved closer. "What's wrong?" they demanded in chorus.

He wrung his hands. "You see. I have two great, really great friends." He looked at them. "Your Mom says no one has heard from them or knows where they are. I haven't heard from them either. And they've not contacted any of our friends in New York." He paused. "But it makes sense. They are on their honeymoon. They planned to see me before they took off from New York." He looked down at the floor. "Martin was going to leave his car with me. I got a place where I can store it. But they never showed. Of course both are a pretty wild," he gulped, "but after your Mom called I thought about things and it seems a little weird. You see, Martin and I are pretty tight."

Teri and Byron looked at each other, then further confused Wick by peppering him with questions at the same time.

Kay finally gave in to the demands of her stomach. She bit into a half a tuna sandwich then gingerly sipped a paper cup of what had to be hot Drano. Nothing like the complementary flavor of wax and paper in the coffee, she thought as she searched for her errant brood.

I'll probably find them on the forward view-deck she mused, their young and highly metabolic bodies, braving the mist and salt-air. She stopped, took another hesitant sip and then spotted them.

Byron, saw her first, and gestured excitedly. There was somebody with them. From the back, she had thought it was... but no, he was on the island. It was some very young stranger they had cornered.

Teri gesticulated animatedly at their hostage, then saw her mother and waved. He turned around slowly. Kay waved back. It was the same young man she had seen debarking from the New York flight, the one that had caught her attention. But why on earth was his handsome face twisted with fear as she walked toward them?

## CHAPTER 26

# *Houseguest*

**Teri groaned.** "Oh Mother! Don't be so negative. Wick's a nice guy. He wouldn't have dropped his obligations and traveled all the way out here if he really didn't care about his friends."

Kay fussed. "But, we don't know anything about him. You can't base everything on just what he told you. Thankfully, Ujima's checking him out, but that takes time."

"Honestly Mother. Did you have to turn him over to the gendarmes! And besides, it's because of *your* phone call that got him here."

Kay gritted her teeth, "I didn't turn him over to anyone. And I did not suggest he come out here, at all. And under the circumstances, I think it's a good idea to confirm what he's told us."

Teri tossed her head. "Listen to you, a classic case of paranoia. You know more about him than we do. He said you talked to him on the phone for over an hour."

"It wasn't over an hour and frankly, you surprise me. But he's in luck. There just happens to be enough room at the inn tonight, and I use *that* term loosely." Silently she argued with herself, of course I don't know about the other nights. True, he's a charming young man. But having him under the same roof could be a problem. And Alex was exasperating. He didn't disapprove, but agreed in a nebulous way.

Kay looked at Teri. Fortunately, Byron and Wick had taken off to explore Scoon Bay. Now she and Teri had had this time to talk. It was unusual for Teri to remain behind when anything was happening.

Probably not too unusual though. If it were her, she would stay to argue the young man's case, too. Like mother, like daughter, she thought. Teri read her mind.

"Mother, he explained himself very well on the ferry. I did want to go with the boys, but I sensed I should stay behind and well, smooth ruffled feathers. And you're right; it was after he heard from Martin's dad, not you that he decided to come out here. Mother, Wick dumped important things to locate his friends. That at least says something about his character."

"Teri, you know me well enough; I always feel better when I can see actual facts before me. I told you about the odd things that have been happening here." Kay considered Ujima's asking her to keep a tight lip. Oh well, she hadn't told the kids everything she reasoned, then said aloud, "And we can't blithely ignore every stranger that suddenly appears on our doorstep. Especially when they're directly or indirectly associated with what I feel are missing persons."

There was a forceful knock at the kitchen door. "I'm not expecting anyone," Kay said and jerked the door open, "Yes!"

On the threshold stood Raymond Toda; he seemed to fill the doorway. How many form-fitting, crispy-white tennis duds did this man own anyway? Impatiently Kay beckoned him in.

"I'm terribly sorry to interrupt...ah... Ms. Roberts. But Ujima asked me to come over." He brushed a lank of hair out of his dark eyes as he stepped gracefully into the room. "It seems your phone's down." Behind her she heard Teri's sharp intake of breath.

Oh cripes, here we go again Kay said to herself as she forced a smile. "No problem Raymond." She turned around. "I'd like to introduce my daughter, Teri, she's home from college this summer. Teri, this is Mr. Raymond Toda. He's our next door neighbor."

Raymond's big hand engulfed Teri's. For one of the few times in her short life, Teri remained speechless. Kay had to appreciate

Raymond, though. The guy was used to instant female adoration and handled it well, even as Teri kept squeezing his hand.

"Nice to meet you Teri, but please, don't call me Raymond. Call me Toady instead. All my close friends do," he said and gently released her grip.

"Oh, ah yes, Mr. Toady. I mean Toady," Teri said. It was one of the rare times Teri was having trouble completing sentences. Raymond cleared his throat and turned toward Kay. "I've a mysterious message from Ujima. She says, and I quote, 'So far, the man checks out A-Okay'. Whatever that means, I...."

Teri at once recovered. "See Mom! I knew he was all right." She did a semi-nod at Raymond, then added, "Nice meeting you, but excuse me," and ran out the kitchen door.

Raymond smiled. "Your daughter is most interesting," he murmured then turned to Kay with a puzzled look, "What was that all about?"

Kay sighed. "She and my son Byron have found a new friend. And you know mothers. I had him vetted by Ujima."

"Oh," Raymond said, still looking bewildered. "Isn't that overdoing things a bit?"

Kay bristled. "The kids just met him yesterday, on the ferry. Suddenly he's staying here, and we don't know anything about him." She avoided mentioning Wick's connection to the missing Martin and Janet.

Toady shrugged his shoulders, "Okay… sounds good to me. Ujima eventually gets around to checking out everybody anyway. Oh. And there is a second message. She wants to know if you still can go sailing this Friday. It's her day off."

Kay clapped her hands. "Great! It'll be a joyous and wondrous thing to toss the mop and broom aside. Did she say what I should bring?"

Raymond stroked his prominent, clean-shaven jaw. "Something about a potluck lunch you'd promised her and Rose. Said you'd know what she meant. She also said she would provide the beer." He grimaced. "But unfortunately, I have another message. Rose called me about ten minutes ago. She said she couldn't go; mumbled something about up-dating office files this weekend. Must be a lot to do, she sounded very uptight. "

"Oh? That's a shame. Couldn't she work on the files later? She was very excited about our all ladies day-sail."

"I don't think so. Once Rose tackles the office it's murder to get in her away," he paused, "but, why don't you give her a call when your phone's working. It's worth a try." He looked thoughtful. "Be wary though, she's really miffed about something."

Toady clapped his hands. "Anyway it sounds like a great escape, I'd volunteer to crew, just to get away, but we're really too busy at the club."

Kay chuckled. "Rose and I've been planning it for weeks. Ujima's been so busy lately, what with trying to solve the Eric Templeton case and other things." Her voice trailed off.

Raymond didn't seem to be listening; he was looking at the ceiling, "Uh, there's one slight problem, not a very big one, really."

"What's that? Bad weather, gale warnings?"

"No. It's Ujima's boat, she planned to take hers. But the Talaria's engine is acting up and Ujima doesn't want to be stranded with the funky auxiliary. You never know when the wind will die and you're in the doldrums."

"So?"

"So… I've offered the services of my boat. The 'Toady-go-Too'. It's a 29-foot Islander, slower than Ujima's, but a lot of fun. You have handled a tiller before?" He asked hopefully.

"Many is the time, Matey. Don't sweat it. Alex and I have sailed the Hudson in up-state New York in all kinds of weather." Her eyes brightened. "We'll have fun, I'll tell Rose not to cry her eyes out, but we will miss her. And it's very neighborly of you to lend your boat."

Toady laughed. "I've done it before and it's the least I can do for Ujima, she helps me out a lot. I owe her. And don't be concerned about Rose. I'll let you in on a secret. Though she lives on a houseboat she frequently gets seasick on a real boat; go figure," he said and shook his head. "Anyway, my boat's rigged so if there is only one person at the helm, they can handle it." He started for the door then turned around.

"I'm glad you ladies are getting to know one another. Ujima's a cracker-jack sailor. She won the 'Blakely Rock Race' two seasons in a row." He hesitated. "I'm going down to my boat this afternoon and get everything shipshape. If you don't mind, I'll come over this evening with a map and show you how to find the marina."

"No problem with me. Why don't you just come for dinner? She said she'd pick me up here in the morning."

"Hah, knowing Ujima, she'll be on your doorstep at six." Kay groaned as Toady smiled and nodded. "My boat is currently at Peavey Harbor." He thrust his hands into his pockets. "I had to sail it over last week for some bottom work."

"Where do you usually moor the boat?"

"Oh. Most of the time I tie up to that lonely float in Scoon Bay, you know, the one you can see from my place."

After Raymond said his good-byes, Kay walked into the living room. She was delighted with the freshly cleaned bay windows. The view was terrific and there was a strong and steady breeze. If the wind was this good on Friday, they could sail all the way to Seattle.

She looked down and spotted Teri standing on the gravel with Toady. They were gesturing toward the path that went down to the beach. Kay shook her head. Without a doubt Teri would confer with Byron and Wick about Wick's new status the minute they were back, but now she was taking the time to chat up Toady.

The shadow of a large bird skimmed over the porch. Edgar landed noisily and clomped across the verandah roof. Kay craned her neck and her head hit the glass. "Stupid thing to do," she exclaimed aloud and rubbed her stinging brow. Funny, here it was a fantastic day and an ominous foreboding had suddenly washed over her.

I'm going to ignore this. It's probably guilt I'm feeling. Edgar was looking for his cage; they hadn't put it up yet. But he seemed satisfied with his makeshift perch on the verandah. And besides, when she left food scraps on the shelf attached to the porch post, they disappeared quickly enough.

She went back to the kitchen. There's still some work to be done if I'm going to put up with an unexpected guest. She retrieved the cleaning basket from under the sink and started for the stairs. Hesitating for a moment, she changed her direction and quickly headed for the front door. When there was housework to do, Teri usually made herself scarce. It wasn't going to happen this time.

Later that night, Alex couldn't fall asleep. Kay said she'd be up to bed shortly, but had a few things to do for the sail tomorrow. Toady had shown up for dinner earlier and explained a few things about the boat. Kay for some reason had called Ujima and said she'd rather meet her at the dock. Toady's directions to Peavey Harbor were easy to follow. But, he seemed bothered about something and left right after dessert. The kids shrugged and went upstairs excitingly talking to Wick.

Alex looked at the clock on the dresser. It was 11:30. Humph, I usually hit the bed like a brick. What's bothering me? I know. He punched the pillow. It's that new friend of Teri and Byron's, Wick Wilding. Interesting name that. Oh well. And along with his name, the kid was oddly unsettling. Alex had worked with men in the Army. And before that, he and his college buddy, Roland, banged around the world; they ran into a lot of characters. But there was something about this Wick guy that didn't ring true. He said he was here to find Martin and Janet's whereabouts. But it seemed he was holding something back. Alex yawned mightily. Ah...I'm probably stepping into the 'jealous father routine', trying to protect Teri. Look Alex, she's handled herself pretty well in the past. There had been the occasional creep, but nothing significant. He did worry a lot about her though. This Wick guy, seemed to fascinate her and there was also Toady... Alex's eyelids grew heavy.

It was a dream, it must be a dream. Edgar perched on the canopy's post, near Alex's side of the bed. That damned crow was peering sideways at him. It was Edgar's snide look.

He pecked at the bed post. It was a challenge. Then Edgar spread his wings and they began to grow. The ends twisted, became tipped with red and moved, searching like fingers through the room. The walls dissolved into in an ominous, sepia-light. Then to Alex's astonishment the entire bed headed toward the window.

Where was Kay? He reached for her and everything tilted precariously. He gripped the back of the mattress as he plunged headlong through the window. The wind howled and the bed fell rapidly toward Scoon Bay. It bucked and the posts and frame peeled away. He held tighter as he plunged toward Heron's Hook.

He was fearful, yet fascinated. He could see Willie's cabin to the south. Then, poking through the trees was the modern slant of Toady's roof. A Harley with a hooded biker made perfect circles in the driveway. He had seen the bike before. Then it disappeared.

Alex detested heights, and this, this was scary.

In a few seconds he realized he could control the dream. All he needed to do was concentrate on his hands that clung to the mattress.

Below him a thick mist crawled over Scoon Bay. Someone was swimming in the water. He flew closer. No. They weren't swimming. They were floating. Face down. Gauzy, auburn tendrils caressed ivory shoulders. It was Kay! Her hair spread like blood around her naked body.

Alex yelled. The mattress plummeted. Automatically his muscles flexed him upright. He was awake and soaked to the skin. He felt for Kay. His heart thudded. She wasn't there.

Kay stood at the end of the bed, a strange smile on her face. "What's happening? I heard you call me."

He had thrown the top sheet off. He was naked and sweating. "Uh, nothing… nothing really, I was having a miserable nightmare."

Kay nodded solemnly. "I said not to have that second piece of cherry pie." She suddenly looked at him in surprise. "My, my, I thought you wouldn't be feeling romantic with all that pastry in your stomach."

Oddly, he was aroused, quite aroused. He sat up and patted the mattress. "I'd never let a piece of pie come between me and my, er our recreation." He winked lewdly then quickly became somber. "Tomorrow, you and Ujima, don't take any unnecessary risks, okay?"

Kay unbuttoned her shirt slowly. "We're both experienced sailors. What's the matter? You want to be captain all the time?" She removed the rest of her clothes and slipped onto the bed. His hands moved over her body.

"Umm," Kay said. "And I bet you're going to be captain now."

He skillfully rolled her beneath him then whispered hoarsely in her ear, "You bet sailor. You're learning well." He paused then quipped, "This is going to be the X-rated version of *Two Years before the Mast.*"

## CHAPTER 27

# *A Capital Ship*

**A steady wind blew from the North.** Halyards snapped and clanked a mesmerizing beat against aluminum masts. Although the marina was well inland from Puget Sound, pennants and wind indicators fluttered and jumped. Kay loved the kinetic symphony. It was the portent of a great sail. She placed her backpack on the dock; her eyes traced the trim lines of the sloop in front of her. On the stern the name stood out in bold, gothic letters, "Toady Go Too".

Kay cupped her hands to her mouth, "Ahoy Captain, requesting permission to come aboard." There was a scuffling sound from the cabin and a grinning Ujima stuck her head out of the hatch.

"Hey sailor, permission granted. Toss me your gear and we'll cast off in minutes."

Kay held out her backpack. "Handle it gently. I've appropriated some of Alex's homemade fudge-cake and two generous meat-loaf sandwiches."

Ujima licked her lips. "I can taste it now. Your man does know how to cook." She removed the lunch pack and took it down to the galley cooler. Over her shoulder she said, "I brought that dark beer you like and my barbecued chicken and potato salad. Too bad Rose isn't coming; we're going to feast like Queens."

Together they stowed the rest of their gear under the deck seats and installed the regulation life preserver on the aft guy-wires. Putting on bright-orange preservers, Ujima slapped hers. "These are great confidence builders," she shook her head, "and if you're accidently overboard for just five minutes, wham, hypothermia takes over. But it looks like the sailing gods are with us," she said and grinned.

Kay stepped back onto the dock as Ujima threw her the bow line then the stern line. "Step lively now!" Ujima shouted as Kay firmly pushed the bow away and jumped on board. They drifted out into the inlet.

Ujima glanced at the telltales. "Ah, a spanking north wind," she winked at Kay. "Girl, when we hit open water, we're going to scoot. Now, get those fenders in. Wipe them off with that old towel then stow everything under the starboard seat, and fold that towel so the wet side is in."

Toady was right, Kay thought. Ujima ran a very tight ship.

As they drifted, Ujima sat relaxed at the tiller. "Hold on to the safety rails and go forward and release the jib. I'll crank the sheet out and we're out of here."

"Aye, aye Captain," Kay said with a salute and felt the excitement of the moving deck as she scrambled towards the bow.

Strong winds and white caps greeted them as they left the shelter of the inlet. With the main reefed, the boat healed over and flew through the water. Ujima squinted. "When we're out, we'll round Bradestone and tack up the Sound. If the wind holds from the North, we can eat our lunch on the way back. We'll return wing-on-wing. It should be a smooth sail."

Kay inhaled the exhilarating salt air. The peculiar events of the last few days had created plenty of tension. With Ujima at the helm, Kay was finally beginning to relax. She smiled. Alex would be chagrined if he knew that Ujima was as skilled a skipper as he was, and handled the sheets with considerably more finesse.

On the return trip, the sunlight danced in silver prisms atop the waves. Kay fumbled with the bottle opener. She was giddy and ravenous. It was calming; they were cupped in the hands of the wind. And by watching the landmarks that Ujima pointed out and eyeing the swells, she could tell they were moving fast. Who said the Islander was a slow boat?

Ujima took a swig of beer and wedged the bottle behind her seat cushion. She felt the bow dip. When the boat rose again, it was sluggish. She frowned then read the water, and looked at her watch. It wasn't time for a tide change, must be a heavy rip here, she thought.

Kay removed two slabs of fudge cake from the lunch bag. She offered one to Ujima. "This cake tastes really good with dark beer," she said and then asked, "the two people, Martin and Janet, any new information?"

Ujima shook her head. "We're not coming up with much. The girl's family was like a slab of frozen fish." She paused to let the main out a little further and take a bite of cake. "But they thawed enough to admit they'd received a postcard from Janet about a month ago. They sent me a fax of it. The postmark is Paris, but the card's content is useless."

Kay brushed hair out of her eyes. "Were there any similarities to the missive Sabra shared with us?"

"Too much; absolutely generic, anyone could have typed it." Ujima frowned as she moved the tiller. "After I compared them it was obvious both were written on the same machine."

"That's a little old-fashioned. Why use a typewriter?

Ujima shrugged. "Sabra said Janet found it stored in the closet of the room she was renting. She asked if she could borrow it; got a kick out of using it for short notes and labeling. She wasn't a Luddite though. She was computer savvy, and liked using the latest in electronic gadgetry."

Kay looked thoughtful. "Janet probably typed the post cards so they would be handy to mail from wherever the couple wound up." She paused. "But Sabra said she liked the personal touch of handwriting. And they were on their honeymoon, seeing exciting things. If there wasn't any added handwriting, it doesn't sound too good."

"No it doesn't." Ujima pulled again on the main sheet. "Even worse, later we contacted a hotel whose address was on one of the postcards she'd sent to a friend. The staff there was very helpful. They checked registration entries as far back as September, but found no record of our twosome; nor did any of the staff recall persons fitting their description." Ujima finished her cake and wiped her hands on a large napkin. "We're circulating pictures and details; that's all we can do for now."

"How about Martin's parents," Kay asked as she finished her beer and held out another piece of fudge cake. Ujima shook her head.

"At least Martin's father is concerned and has cooperated with us," Ujima said tightlipped as the boat seemed to dig into the next wave. Ujima continued, "Actually we owe a lot to Martin's father. He told us the couple had planned to spend a few days with Wick Wilding in upstate New York before they left for Paris." Ujima glanced at Kay. "Martin's father doesn't seem to care for Wick. Says he can't be trusted. And you were right; Martin was supposed to leave his car with Wick, which his father did not approve of."

Ujima felt the bow dip again. She glanced at the shoreline and corrected her heading. "The car is keeping the police department busy in Idaho," she continued, "but so far nothing too out of the ordinary has turned up. The one positive thing is that we've been able to corroborate everything Wick Wilding has told you. He seems to be what he says he is, for now."

Kay looked in the same direction as Ujima's intense stare. "It's obvious that Martin didn't tell anybody where they were going. Not even his parents...or his supposedly close friend, Wick."

"Ah...right," Ujima said with distraction. "It might be because the older Mr. Martin is quite vocal in his belief that Wick is a poor influence on his son. He says that the young man thinks he's a know-it-all, has no business sense, is irresponsible, too cavalier, etc. etc." Ujima made another move with the tiller. "Hmm, back to your house guest. Evidently Wick usually stays with a group of artists in a large studio in New York. One of his resident friends told me that he's usually difficult to get a hold of. Evidently he doesn't keep any itinerary of where he performs. When your call went through to him, he was somewhere in up-state New York." She glanced at the telltales and told Kay to pull the jib in slightly. "I hope to know more when I talk to our Mr. Wilding in person."

Kay licked the rest of the fudge frosting off her fingers as she mulled over Ujima's comments and adjusted the jib's sheet. "You know, those postcards, they really bother me. Sabra told me that Janet was an avid enthusiast of the personal, handwritten note. But those are typewritten and..." Kay noticed the concern on Ujima's face.

"What's up?"

There was a long pause. "I don't know. The bow seems, well, like a plow. Toady's boat usually handles much better than this. Kay, could you go below and see if everything's shipshape?" Ujima said with a thin smile.

"Sure, I've got to use the head anyway." As she scrambled toward the hatch the boat gave a sudden lurch. Kay steadied herself at the bottom of the ladder. She loved the layout of the cabin. Yellow cushions and polished wood contrasted with the blue and red curtains edged in tiny white anchors. The galley was on the starboard side. Attached to the opposite side was a swing out dining table flanked by two spacious bench seats. Typical Toady tidiness, she smiled. The entire table top was a large, laminated, nautical chart of Puget Sound. To the left of the galley was a neatly made bunk. Forward was a small, but adequate, double sleeping compartment. It was then she noticed the carpet.

Between the table and the bunk side a section had been replaced. The new material was a fairly close match. But it was the shape of the cutout portion that made the skin on the back of her neck prickle. She knelt down. It was identical to the section she'd found in the sail bag drifting in Scoon Bay!

She stooped to examine it and the boat slued then dipped. Kay braced herself, her hands on the carpet. Jeez, it was wet. Suddenly a cascade of salt water surged up from beneath the flooring. The chill water washed over her fingers.

"Ujima!" She shouted. "We've a leak! Water is coming out of the bilge."

"Shit! I thought something was wrong," Ujima yelled back. "We must've hit a piece of drift. Kay, come up here and on the double. We'll have to take the main and jib in. Wait, before you do, flip the toggle on the panel. The one labeled bilge-pump."

Kay nervously scanned the electric panel to her left. She flicked the chrome switch. Nothing…she flicked it again.

"It's not working," she yelled as she shot up the hatchway.

"Christ! We're in trouble. Take in the sails. Lash the sheets to the safety rails as best you can. Just get them out of the way. I'll start the engine. If we have to… we'll beach her," she said grimly.

Kay glanced at Bradestone. They were at least a mile offshore.

The sails managed easily. The wind had fallen off sharply. Ujima turned the engine key to prime and counted to ten, allowing the diesel plug to warm. She turned the key. No response. She looked at Kay. "Quick, let's get below. There's a manual pump. I'll set you up and then we'll send out a mayday on the radio."

Back in the cabin, the water surged over their shoes.

Ujima glanced behind her. "Look! It's coming from beneath the door to the head!" She jerked it open. "The hoses, they're loose. Here's the leak!" She grabbed the tubes. Black tape fluttered around the gushing fittings. The clamps were gone.

Ujima jumped past Kay and slid open a cabinet door. "I'll see if I can cut off the flow from the toilet while you bail. Ever use one of these before?" She held up a manual bilge pump.

"You bet!" Kay grabbed the contraption and positioned it as Ujima opened a porthole.

It was an awkward piece of equipment, but it could save their lives. She thrust down. The handle separated. Kay panicked as she attempted to reattach it to the unit. It was impossible. The pivot bolts weren't there. "The pump's broken too!" Kay yelled.

Ujima turned to her, face ashen. "These hoses have been sliced in several places and the radio isn't working either. I checked everything yesterday afternoon. Right after Toady was here. Someone…someone sabotaged us last night." The boat took another sluggish dip.

The water, ankle deep, cascaded across the cabin floor. From nowhere a sodden, blue handkerchief caught, it floated over her shoe. "Where are the flares? Maybe we can get somebody's attention."

Ujima was angry. "I've got a feeling there aren't any," she said and charged up the ladder. Her face was set and determined. "Not to worry, I've got something better," she yelled back, tore open the seat hatch and pulled her duffel bag out of the inside compartment. Clutching a black object in her hand, she grinned at Kay, "I know at least this will work." She flipped open the cell phone and made her mayday call.

A thin gray light filtered through the verandah's bay windows. Evening was rapidly fading into night. Kay and Ujima huddled on a couch near the flames in the front-room fireplace, each cocooned in a large wool blanket.

"Here you go ladies and you too Alex, this ought to bring the roses back to your cheeks." Teri placed a tray of steaming hot toddies on a table and handed them around.

"I'm still chilled," Kay complained as her hands shakily lifted the steaming mug.

Ujima thanked Teri and Alex nodded, took his drink and settled back into the wingchair near them. He stretched his long legs and looked wearily into the flames. "It's been one helluva six hours," he paused, "for all of us."

Ujima took a cautious sip. "I've got to hand it to those Coast Guard guys. They were terrific. But it seemed to take forever before they let us go. I don't think my feet will ever be warm again."

Alex smiled and blew on the surface of his drink. "Ujima, you're just pissed because you got a taste of your own medicine. Now you have an idea of what we poor civilians go through when we have just a traffic violation. There are questions, forms to fill out ... then more questions and forms."

Ujima looked at him with an unsympathetic eye. "You poor dude. If I had the energy you'd be stretched out on the carpet with this swizzle stick rammed up... up your nose."

Teri guffawed then covered her mouth.

"And I would be a most able assistant," Kay mumbled and then ended with an explosive sneeze. She groped through her pockets for a tissue. "Oh great, all I need is a cold."

Alex smacked his lips. "Teri, this is delicious. Where did you get the recipe?"

Teri spread her hands and looked at the ceiling. "Oh Alex, you know, dorm mixology 101." She grinned. "And I hope you don't mind. I floated some of your 151 proof Demerara on top."

"Mind? Yummy, just the right kicker."

Ujima stared into her drink. "I'm just happy we're not singing 'Yo-ho-ho,' down in Davie Jones' locker. We came awfully close." She stretched and yawned.

Teri, standing behind the couch, shook her head. "Wait till the Coast Guard finally gets a hold of Toady. He'll have a herd of cows."

Ujima sighed. "I'm thinking of all that beautiful woodwork. Even though they have fans running it's going to warp and it's going to take a month to dry out. If he never loans anything to me again, I won't blame him."

Teri cupped her chin in her hand as she leaned forward, her elbows on the back of the couch. "I wouldn't worry. It doesn't sound as if it was your fault. Just rotten maintenance, and once it's fixed Toady can get Byron and Wick to help clean the boat up. After all, he's letting them stay at his house for free, you know."

"Teri," Ujima said softly, "that was not poor maintenance. Toady keeps everything on that boat shipshape."

"You mean it was sabotage?" Teri said shocked.

"Yes. And nothing goes beyond these walls until I'm certain, everyone got the message?"

"Yes ma'am," Teri said wide-eyed.

Kay nodded her head in affirmation then turned a steely eye on Alex. "Now what's this about the boys and when did this happen?"

Teri eased herself down on the arm of the couch. "Oh Mom, now don't *you* have a cow. Byron is hoping to buy Toady's dune buggy. He told the guys he doesn't use it anymore. And it was Toady who wanted them to stay there. He said they could get the buggy running, try it out and keep an eye on his place at the same time. I guess when he's not at the tennis club he has business in Seattle. He's a little worried about leaving the house empty. He said that he's had too many weird things happen lately."

Kay tapped Teri's hand. "Next time, you see the dynamic duo tell your brother I would like to be informed before they take off, particularly for any stay overs." She looked at Alex again. "Did you know about this?"

"Yep. He did ask me. I assumed it would be okay with you." He looked at Kay's expression. "Hey, they're young adults. But you know guys, they like to get away and do their own thing. And Byron's pretty excited about that buggy."

"Yeah Mom," Teri exclaimed, "It isn't as if we're little kids anymore." She stood up. "There's the phone. I bet that's them now. I'll get it upstairs," Teri said excitedly as she left the room.

Alex arched a brow at Kay. "Teri's right. And it would be a good thing if Byron had his own set of wheels. We can't keep borrowing one of Barney's loaner every time we need a large car. In fact, Wick asked me this morning if there was any bus transportation to Madrona. I had to tell him there was nothing close by; only the island cab and it doesn't always run where and when you want it too." Alex looked chagrined. "He made a rude remark about being in the sticks. I sort of set him straight."

Ujima looked into her drink. "Mr. Inch is getting quite old and his cab is usually geared to ferrying foot passengers to Madrona."

Alex nodded. "How true, but eventually Byron or Teri will need to use the car. Not that they've asked yet, but an extra vehicle would certainly keep them and their friends busy and out of our hair."

Kay chuckled. "You don't know everything; Teri already asked if she could take a trip into town, tomorrow."

Alex looked intently into the flames and sighed. "We're going to need the MR-2 available when *we* want it and I'm super protective about that car. So I wouldn't get upset over the buggy, or the fact that they're looking after Toady's house while he's off island."

"I guess I am tired and a little rattled," Kay said as she rubbed her forehead. "It's strange but I have mixed feelings about Toady." She shook her head. "I know this sounds ridiculous but would he sabotage his own boat. There was that carpet..."

Ujima's mouth fell open. "That *is* ridiculous. But what's this about a carpet? What are you saying girl?"

Alex glanced at Ujima and drew a circle in the air with his finger. "A touch of water on the brain," he whispered. Kay stuck her tongue out.

He shrugged. "Well. What do you mean? It's a pretty lousy thing to imply he wrecked his own boat. And the last time I saw him he was crowing about the fact that he made everything shipshape so you ladies would have a great sail. Think about it, it looks like someone else messed with things after he left."

Kay shook her head. "Yes. I know. But who would be the target, Toady or us...and why, in either case?"

Alex licked his swizzle stick. "Aha, super sleuths, he did it for the insurance. "

"Oh Alex, get serious! There's something... something I saw before we started to shift into submarine mode."

Ujima closed her eyes. "Is this something about the carpet? I've a peculiar feeling, that in a few moments I'll be saying: 'Here we go again.'"

"It was that scrap of rug. Remember Alex? The yellow one peppered with dark gold. I brought up from the beach."

"Yes. I'm using it in front of the tool bench. What about it?"

"I'm glad I insisted we keep it. That scrap is the exact match to Toady's boat carpet, same color, same cutout shape. The mending lines were faint, but I spotted it when the water came in. And it's newer than the rest of it."

Ujima set her mug down and threw up her arms.

"Whoa! Hold on, hold on. What are you two talking about? I've a hunch that someone's been concealing evidence.... and worse, mucking it up."

Kay closed her eyes and said in a weary voice, "It wasn't intentional. I wasn't even sure it was important. It's a remnant of carpet. It was in that sail bag I found. Alex thought it was a scrap from the top or side of a dock."

"Yeah, many people use indoor-outdoor carpeting for buffering the side of a dock or covering part of the actual dock," Alex said.

"I get the picture. So... was this with the sarong and the contact lens you found?" Ujima pursed her lips "And is there anything else you haven't mentioned?"

Alex swirled his drink and studied the bottom of the mug intently. "Well, I do think that Kay has something to share." He glanced up. "Maybe even a little more than something?"

"You fink!" Kay exploded. "I was going to tell Ujima about the other thing. But just like the piece of carpet, it didn't seem relevant." She grimaced. "But, maybe parts of the puzzle are coming together."

Ujima leaned back against the couch and sighed. "Let the investigating officer determine what pieces are fitting in this puzzle of yours and which are not." She shook her head. "As Thommy Jay would say, 'Tell mother all'. Hm, I don't have my notebook. But I do have my mini-recorder handy."

She reached over and pulled the compact object out of her parka on the end of the sofa. She talked into the machine, mentioned the date, time and those being interviewed and set it on the coffee table. "Speak calmly in the direction of the recorder please. For the sake of my patience, which is rapidly running out, make it short and succinct." She sighed audibly. "Kay, you're first... and don't forget the 'other thing' or is it 'things'?"

In fits and starts Kay again related how she found the sail bag, the dress, the lens, the stones and the piece of carpet. Then, she reluctantly mentioned finding the earring in Willie's cabin.

Ujima settled back in her chair. "I want that earring. Where is it?"

Kay grimaced. "I think Thom gave it back to Toady," she said meekly then related her conversation with Thom at the restaurant.

Alex stroked his chin. "You know, I've got an inkling of what Kay's thoughts may be. And I'm wondering if you're getting the same drift that I am?" he said, squinting at Ujima.

Ujima grimaced. "Okay you two. A lot seems to have gone on behind my back. Not only is the inquiry into Janet and Martin's disappearance becoming exceedingly sticky. But Elanor Lavin and the county marshall are putting pressure on me to resolve Templeton's murder, and quickly. I would be grateful for ideas on either situation that might be helpful," she said holding up the recorder. "And, like Tricky Dicky, I'm going to get this all on tape."

Kay hesitated then slumped. "I don't think this has anything to do with Templeton's murder... but here goes. Something awful may have happened on Toady's boat. It could be that Janet was somehow involved, I think...maybe."

Teri burst into the room, frowning.

"It was the guys on the phone. They said they're having a ball, playing games on Toady's new computer. And before I had a chance to invite myself over, they said it was Men's-only night. I told them they were being stupid and not cool." She flopped down next to Kay and stared at her.

"Mom, you guys, you all look spacey. Anyway, the good thing is they got the buggy running and I made them promise to pick me up tomorrow on their way into town. Wick's going to find out more about Janet and Martin." Teri assumed a stiff posture, stuck her nose in the air and said in an affected accent, "He says the most logical thing to do is to begin by asking some of their friends on the island."

Ujima snorted, reached over, turned off the recorder and scratched the side of her nose. "I hope he has more success than I've had. And young lady, if you or your young Sherlock find anything out, I want to know what it is… and immediately, if not sooner."

Teri looked warily at her. "Well, sure, that's okay," she said then turned and poked Kay, who still seemed in a catatonic state. "Mom, your friend Edgar's been tromping around on the roof so I fed him some of my chips. Does he have his own space or is he going to be a permanent resident at the chamber door?"

Alex chuckled and cleared his throat. "He likes to roost on the verandah and sometimes in the tree near your window. And count yourself lucky there's no bust of Pallas, or your chances of sleep would be nevermore."

Everyone groaned.

Alex smiled smugly and continued, "but it would be great if you helped us put up his cage tomorrow. That is, of course, if the princess will rise early, say about noon?" He nodded at Ujima. "Thanks to Officer Washington, we now have the go ahead."

Teri blanched, "Oh sure, sure."

"I've got it!" Kay shouted and grabbed Ujima's arm. Ujima and Teri yelped and Alex swore profusely as some of his drink sloshed on his jeans.

"Mother," Teri exclaimed, "I'm glad none of us have a weak heart."

Alex took in Kay's wild-eyes. "And just what do you have, besides a death-grip on Ujima's arm?"

Ujima pried Kay's fingers loose and took a deep breath to calm her adrenaline rush. "Teri, would you mind leaving us alone. Your mom and Alex have something to discuss with me and it may have a direct bearing on a case I'm working on."

Teri nodded her head.

"I knew you wouldn't mind," Ujima smiled, "and that hot toddy was just the thing. It started our little gray cells working again."

Teri stood up slowly. "Uh, thanks," she said and then paused, "They're not in any trouble, are they?"

Ujima shook her head. "Not right now, but maybe later I'll have to throw them into solitary."

"Okay, okay." Teri grinned and patted Ujima on the shoulder. "It's all right to use thumbscrews on Alex, he's tough. But not on mom, okay?"

They waited until the upstairs bedroom door slammed.

"Now," Ujima said and reached over and flipped the recorder on. "Go ahead Kay and with a little less enthusiasm, please."

"I think Janet was killed on Toady's boat. The dress and the carpet must have had blood on them."

Alex and Ujima stared at each other as Kay patiently continued. "It was her dress. And she wore contact lenses. Sabra said so. One of the lenses must have been knocked out in a struggle." Kay sat down suddenly, both hands to her face.

"That would put Toady in deep doodoo," Alex said as he stirred his drink.

Ujima nodded. "Thank you Alex for your, succinct, insightful and scatological deduction; now, if the Bobbsey Twins will read my lips: At present we have no evidence that Janet has come to any harm." She stared at them and said very slowly, "nevertheless, since you still have that section of carpet; forensics can determine if there was any blood, and also the type."

Alex was surprised. "Even if it has been in cold salt water for who knows how many weeks and I've walked all over it?"

Ujima nodded. "The sail bag would have given some protection. And things may not have been in the water that long. I noticed that new section of replaced carpet in Toady's boat a week ago. But there was no reason I should attach any particular significance to it," she looked pointedly at Kay. "Important *evidence* was being withheld." She gestured for Kay to remain quiet as she continued her answer to Alex. "Once a substance has the chance to soak into fibers, it can be pretty tenacious. I'm just happy you didn't put it in the garbage."

Both heads nodded quickly. Ujima got up and shut off the mini-recorder. "Well it's time yours truly got herself down to the station. Looks like it's going to be another long night... thanks again to you two."

Kay stood up too. "We're really sorry, Ujima. But you should get some rest. Look, if I can be of any help?"

Ujima shook her hands and head wildly. "No. No, No! You've helped a lot already. Thanks for your concern. I squeezed in a little cat-napping while we were at the Coast Guard station." She smiled. "You're the ones that look ready to cave." Then she looked glum. "I'm not looking forward to hauling Toady's ass in. His boat's a wreck, and that suspicious piece of carpet." She closed her eyes. "It's not going to be a pleasant task. He is...maybe was, a close friend."

## CHAPTER 28

# *Cagey*

**It was early** the next morning when Kay and a yawning Teri knelt beside Edgar's nesting box. Alex winked at them. "I attached these new brackets at the top. They'll make it easier to fasten to the porch, and to remove when Willie returns."

Kay smiled tentatively up at Alex. "Do you really believe he will, or are you saying that just to make me feel better?"

"Both," Alex replied. "Come on, help me lift. Teri, you steady the front. Kay and I'll grab the back. Remember, chin in, tighten your gut and lift with your legs."

"Yes Sir!" Teri said with a snappy salute then squatted and took her end.

"It's much lighter," Kay exclaimed.

"Yeah," Alex grunted. "I removed the shelf and with the front off... Ouch!"

"What happened?"

"I snagged my finger on this damn piece of back trim. Let's set the cage on its face, I'll nail it tighter." The three easily moved the box to the ground where Alex studied the offending corner.

"Funny. I didn't notice that before."

"Funny what?" Teri asked.

"This whole bottom strip, it's loose." Alex looked at Kay. "It must have separated when you dropped it at Willie's."

"Me! I wasn't the only one carrying it."

Alex smiled. "You're right. But you're the only one who fell backwards."

"Ha," Kay mocked. "You weren't exactly mister twinkle-toes either."

Teri's small fingers tugged at the trim. "The whole thing moves, it's a piece of veneer." She moved it from side to side. With a ripping sound it came off, revealing a narrow slot.

"That's an odd opening." Kay remarked as she peered into it.

Teri held her nose, "maybe an old poop catcher?"

Alex peered over her shoulder. "I don't think so. But someone, probably Willie, replaced the original wire bottom with these thin sheets of plywood. Here Teri, let me see." Alex tried to fit his hand in the drawer-like space. "There's something in here. My fingertips say it's part of a plastic bag." He chuckled, removed his hand and poked Teri, "Okay slim. I can't get my hand in past my knuckles. Whatever is in there, see if you can pull it out."

Teri wrinkled her nose. "You just want me to get my hand into something nasty. I've got a better idea. Why don't we turn it over and shake it out?"

Alex turned to Kay. "Ah. Young minds, they're so agile. Okay let's turn it over...now, to the count of three, everyone. One, two..." A slim paper package, sealed in plastic wrap, fell to the ground. They set the cage down quickly.

"Maybe it's money. Or Willie's last will and testament." Teri said excitedly.

Kay squatted beside the packet, and studied it carefully. "I do admit Edgar would make a great watchdog for such things." She poked it with her finger. "Alex. I have a hunch that this is what those thugs from 'Superior' were looking for when they tore up Willie's cabin."

"Wow, another one of your wild speculations."

Teri was puzzled. "What are you two talking about? Superior... oh, you mean that Real Estate Company, the one whose CEO was murdered?"

Kay pursed her lips. "Yes. They want to buy Alex and me out and seem to go to any length to get their way."

Teri was shocked. "They want you to sell this beautiful place?"

Kay sniffed as if there was a really bad smell. "I'll tell you all about it later. And, I'm pleasantly surprised you're beginning to enjoy our new home."

Alex nodded in agreement then gave a low whistle. "So Kay, you think those were the jerks that trashed Willie's cabin?"

"Yes. After the tactics they tried to use on us, I do." She smoothed the plastic so they could see through it. "The ink has faded to a sepia tone. I can hardly read it."

Alex sat back on his heels. "Okay Jane Marple. Stop surmising and open it up. Let's see if these could be the mysterious papers Willie has us wondering about."

Kay bowed to him. "Monsieur Poirot that is a most excellent suggestion."

Kay hunched over the papers on the desk, and examined them with a large magnifying glass. The pages were surprisingly coarse, thick and spotted with age. The ink, faded to a light ecru, contrasted only slightly with the brown stains and mottled background.

"Alex, according to the title, that I can barely make out, this is indeed the document Willie was elliptically referring to."

"What document?" Teri asked as she leaned over Kay's shoulder.

"Well, it appears this top page is the original deed that refers not only to our land, but also to Willie's. The language is a bit archaic and the writing almost impossible to decipher." She glanced at Alex. "Willie did say that at one time our land and his was one big parcel."

"Wow, the date with those other signatures. And even those stamps on the back of that folder are probably very valuable," Teri said excitedly.

Alex studied it closer. "These aren't fakes. I've seen and smelled plenty of old papers when I worked with Role at the museum. But how did Willie get a hold of this? And why did he only tell you about it? And why didn't he put it in a safe-deposit box?"

Kay stood up. "We'll have to ask him." Her smile wavered. "That's when we see him, of course." She tapped the magnifying glass against Alex's shoulder. "It wouldn't be in his nature to trust a bank. Probably has his life's savings buried in an iron box under a tree by the cabin."

"He didn't even trust me enough to tell me about it," Alex said contritely.

"Well, you certainly are a suspicious looking character and Mom definitely looks more trustworthy." Teri laughed. "Anyway, I've read that people of his generation hid everything in a coffee can under a rosebush. From what you say, he's super cautious and that's only natural if he was in the great depression."

"Oh, he's old enough," Kay said as she gestured for Alex to look through the magnifying glass. "See this title. The Superior island group would gain plenty from destroying these."

Alex nodded. "Or, with the right computer technology, change it to suit them."

"And they could chemically age any of it to match," Teri interjected. Alex looked at her quizzically. "Er, that's if these guys are as sneaky as they seem to be."

"They most certainly are," Kay said then turned back to the documents. "I remember when Willie took me into his confidence. He implied Rose knew about these and had a copy. And was surprised Rose hadn't mentioned anything to us about the papers."

Alex spread his hands. "If there aren't any records of this at the county courthouse, Rose wouldn't run across it in a title search. The papers she showed us were recent."

Kay shook her head. "I wonder how recent they are, like hot off the press? But now let's get this to Ujima. I will be more comfortable with these in the hands of the law, and we can get Max in on it. He'll have things deciphered and authenticated, then tell us what it means."

"Okay by me," Alex said. "But what I still want to know is how, if Rose didn't find out about this, the Superior boys did."

"It's just a guess but Willie may have been using the existence of these papers as his ace in the hole. Probably waved their existence in their collective faces, I hope he didn't go too far. I feel those guys could play for keeps."

Alex put his hands on Kay's shoulders. "Willie's psychic, he knew what these guys might do and made himself scarce."

Teri grinned. "Yeah Mom, don't fret. Willie sounds like a real cool guy."

"You mean like the cool cat with nine lives?"

"Yeah… sorta."

"And I have a hunch he hasn't used them all up," Alex muttered then raised an eyebrow at Teri, "not yet, anyway."

*CHAPTER 27*

# *Barn Dances*

'Be at the old Bremmer's barn, midnight tonight, NO police or anyone else. Bring four-thousand dollars in cash in hundred dollar bills, or you can forget about finding your precious Janet Holmes. Put the grocery bag of money and this note on the old tractor's seat.' Sabra Whitestone tried to smooth the wrinkles in the piece of paper on her sewing table and nervously lit a cigarette.

"What kind of hoax is this?" She asked herself aloud. Then reread the note and blew a puff of smoke toward the ceiling. Bremmer's barn, the barn on Toady's land; where Toady and Rose promoted music festivals every year. When Sabra was a child the original Bremmer's farmhouse burned down one night. She remembered that the flames lighting up Scoon Bay, but somehow the ancient barn had escaped the flames.

Come alone? They must think I'm stupid, Sabra thought; and four thousand dollars for information. They must also think I'm crazy. Where would she get that kind of money on the weekend? Sabra smiled. I'll leave a fake ransom with the note and see who picks up the bag. But she would have to have someone with her, someone whom she could trust with her plan and make things appear that she had come alone and left alone.

She'd only met Kay Roberts a few times, but she liked her confidence and no-nonsense attitude and she was as concerned about Janet as she was.

The number rang interminably. Ms. Roberts just had to be home. Suddenly the line went dead and a faint low buzzing ensued. Sabra hastily re-dialed, her hands shaking. Bungling Bell in their usual competent mode, she thought. "Damn!" She exclaimed aloud as she dropped her cigarette on the desktop then furiously mashed it out with the ashtray. Her whirling desk filter and scented wicks kept most of the smoke smell out of the shop and clothes. She felt a pang of guilt. She knew it was dangerous to her health. But it relaxed her in times of stress. And this was stress in capital letters.

She couldn't ask Ujima. She was too nosey and besides she was the police. Her mouth twisted. The less interest they took in her the better. Beads of sweat began to accumulate on her brow as she counted each ring. The phone eventually picked up when she reached fifteen.

"Hello?"

It was Ms. Roberts. Sabra's mouth was dry, her voice a whisper.

"You'll have to speak up. This is a terrible connection," Kay said.

Sabra moved the mouth piece closer. "Ms. Roberts. Kay Roberts? Hello? This is Sabra Whitestone. Can you hear me now?"

"Oh. Hello, Sabra. Yes. You're loud and clear." There was a long pause. "Is there something I can help you with?"

Sabra took a deep inhale then coughed uncontrollably. She recovered and wiped her mouth. "As a matter of fact there is. I...I just don't know where, where to begin."

Kay listened. There was only the sound of short breaths. Sabra was frightened. "Well," Kay said cheerily, "as a befuddled King once said: 'Begin at the beginning and go on till you come to the end; then stop'."

Sabra laughed hoarsely. Her tension eased. Yes. Kay Roberts had been the right one to call.

"I...I didn't want to bother you, but I was closing the backdoor of the shop this evening and I found a note. It was sticking out from under the doormat. It's about Janet and I know you want to know her whereabouts like I do."

"Yes?" Kay's voice was suddenly cautious. "Who's it from?"

Sabra shakily picked up the note. "Well that's just it. There's no signature and I don't like it." She reread its meager contents to Kay. Sabra coughed. "I don't mind the money." It'll be fake anyway, she thought. "But it's worth it if I can find out where Janet is." She smiled to herself. And it would be a real coup to be one up on Sergeant Washington. "Here's what I've planned."

Kay replaced the receiver and glanced at the clock in the hall. Eight... they had four hours. She got up from her chair and made her decision. Teri and the boys were at the movies in Madrona. Alex was out, which was fortunate. He would come up with a million reasons why she shouldn't go; or worse, he might insist on coming along. His body size had certain drawbacks, particularly when it came to hiding.

However, she being small could easily hide on the floor in the back seat of Sabra's tiny car. They had agreed to dress alike and wear hats that Sabra would bring. The only difficult thing would be crouching beside the car when Sabra went in, then scooting into the driver's seat when Sabra returned. Sabra knew of a place near the barn entrance that was heavy with low brush. They'd make the transfer there.

Sabra stressed that they keep the whole escapade to themselves. That wasn't a good idea. To hell with Sabra, Ujima had to be in on it, if only for their protection. She dialed the police station.

"Police desk," the sleepy voice said with uncertainty as it came on the line. This was followed by a stifled yawn. "Dispatcher, Officer Isaac Reynolds speaking....can we be of any assistance?"

"Yes. Yes, *we* can. My name is Kay Roberts and I'm wondering if you could please put Sergeant Washington on. I need to talk to her."

"Is this...an emergency?" The voice asked wearily, punctuated with another yawn.

"Well no. But I'm Kay Roberts and I'm..." Officer Reynolds interrupted her.

"Sorry Ma'am, but Sergeant Washington is in Seattle. She's working on a very important case at present. And I don't know when she's due back. If you'll leave a message, I'll see that she gets it." He yawned again. It made his offer sound extremely doubtful. "Of course, she'll check in before tomorrow. But if you think this is important..."

Kay envisioned the somnambulistic dispatcher falling asleep, pencil in hand, and injuring himself. "No," she said, "I don't want to overtax anyone. Just tell her that Kay Roberts called and will call back later. Thanks, anyway."

"Whatever," Officer Reynolds replied as his voice slid off the phone in an even more magnificent yawn.

Kay stared at the receiver in her hand and listened to the irritating dial tone. My god, she thought, I hope no one has to call 911 tonight. By the time Reynolds responds; this year will be over.

Well, she and Sabra would have to go it alone. Kay rummaged in the top drawer of the hall commode. "This time I won't forget my flashlight," she announced aloud.

Sabra Whitestone inched her Jaguar up the gravel road. Kay whispered that she switch off the headlights. The sudden dark was impenetrable and terrifying.

Sabra stopped the car and strained to focus her eyes on something, anything ahead.

"The barn should be around that last turn, but I can't see it without the lights," Sabra carped. But, slowly her eyes made out a break in the trees. "This must be it," she hissed, then turned to Kay, huddled behind her on the backseat floor; a blanket covered her small frame.

"Why isn't there a moon? It would have made things so much easier," Sabra whined.

Kay started to reply then hastily covered her mouth and sneezed. Cripes! Nothing like a doggy-blanket to hide under. Sabra said it was all she could find. Kay wondered about this as she rubbed her nose vigorously and quietly growled, "Don't talk so much. Whoever is out there might see your lips moving." Kay's voice sounded spooky and muffled.

"Don't be ridiculous!" Sabra snapped back. "It's as black as ink. Even I, who has more visual purple than most, can't see a thing!"

Well, goody-goody for you and your visual purple, Kay thought. It was evident their nerves were wired.

Sabra rolled down the car window and glanced nervously at her watch. "It's damn cold tonight. At least you've got that wool blanket, while I...I must have a cigarette." Keeping an unwavering eye on the barn, she lit up and puffed a large cloud into the damp air.

"If someone's going to be here they'll have to pass this way," Sabra hissed.

"Not necessarily," Kay hissed back. Why didn't the damn woman stop talking? She paused to brush blanket fuzz and dog hair from her lips. It was like talking to a small child. "He… or she could have come up the back way," Kay whispered.

"There's no back way." Sabra snapped. "I was here last summer at the Musicale. There's only a steep bank behind the barn. And it's covered with blackberries and brush. This *is* the only approach." The tone of her voice implied that any person who didn't know that fact had the IQ of a nit.

Why had she ever agreed to come along? Kay lamented. All evening Sabra had been alternately unpleasant, then tearful, and only happy when she talked about Janet. Janet was her closest friend, the daughter she never had. Sabra had gone into exhaustive detail; how Janet was the most creative young person she had ever worked with; how for uncountable evenings Janet insisted on staying on helping Sabra with rush orders and refusing to go home until they were done. Sabra had marveled at Janet's boundless energy; as she not only could skillfully sew, but worked part time at Templeton's agency and was the driving force behind Bradestone's Nature Conservation committee.

It was sad, Sabra went on, but Janet's parents actually avoided her. They told Janet that her life style was frivolous and beneath their economic station. Janet, being rebellious, refused to have anything to do with them.

Sabra became giddier when she described the plans she held for Janet, intending to offer her a full time position in the shop, with the possibility of becoming co-owner in the future. That's if Janet was interested, Sabra said wistfully.

Stiffly alert in the front seat Sabra checked her watch and relished a deep drag on her cigarette. They had fifteen minutes.

Everything was so different from last summer, she thought. The budding Madrona's Citizen's Chamber Group had handled close to a thousand music enthusiasts over a two-day weekend. On opening day, the sunlight had streamed down. It made the metal folding chairs, standing in rows outside the open barn, almost too hot to handle.

Sabra smiled as she remembered the panicky ushers trying to accommodate the overflow of people. Comically they stumbled into each other while blowing and shaking their hands as they set up the scorching metal chairs. No one escaped a hot seat that day. And then there was Toady; running back and forth, making sure there were plenty of refreshments, and that the toilet paper in the port-o-potties hadn't run out.

The event proved popular beyond all expectations. Even the backers were amazed at its financial success as most of the advertisement had been by word-of-mouth. At present, Toady, the pro-tem director, was pushing to make it an annual island "do." And Sabra and Janet had encouraged him. After all, his barn was in a convenient location and the event had brought many more visitors to her shop than the dreary season the year before. Without a qualm, she and Janet had enthusiastically volunteered to help him solicit funds for this year's event.

But now the barn loomed. It had become the prow of some gigantic ark, run aground in the shadows of the wooded road, black and brooding.

From the trees an owl hooted. There was an answering trill inside the structure. Sabra shivered, and again glanced at her wristwatch. It was 11:55 p.m. She bravely stepped out of the Jaguar and ground her cigarette into the weedy drive.

"Don't forget. If I'm not back in five minutes or you hear something, push the alarm switch and drive up to the barn with the lights on. Okay?"

"For Pete's sake stop gabbling," Kay snarled through the fuzz. "I remember everything we agreed on. With all this palaver you've probably spooked your informant and they've left!"

"Humph!" was the last comment Kay heard.

As she walked up the road, Sabra wondered why she simply hadn't come alone. Kay had turned out to be a dictatorial nag. She snorted in disgust, wrapped her coat tighter around her, and headed for the dark mouth of the barn.

Standing in the gapping opening she took her pencil flashlight out of her pocket; the feeble beam was almost useless. Sabra recalled that the building was large. About forty by eighty feet, Toady said. She sniffed. It was the familiar smell of last summer, the odor of animals, damp hay and rotting wood, the breath of an old barn. She sniffed again. Was that perfume?

The dull light revealed that everything was covered with dust and cobwebs. The rusty tools she and Janet helped arrange were still artfully positioned along the back wall. The stacks of metal chairs, tables and bales of straw had been pushed into a far corner. She stood by an ancient John Deere tractor; the one Toady had insisted on pushing inside for atmosphere.

She removed the fake money bag from her coat then swept the flashlight back to the tools. Something made her uneasy. Something wasn't right. Carefully she walked over the uneven planked floor. The beam of her light played over the business end of a large shovel. It was the one she had donated to the tool collection. Sabra picked it up, rotated it and nervously ran the beam of the light over the blade. Part was shiny, but the blade was covered with a dull coating of moist dirt. It had been recently used.

A scratching noise came from behind her. She dropped the shovel with a clang and spun around. The tiny flashlight trembled in her hand and the blackness of the barn greedily swallowed up the wavering beam.

The stillness made her increasingly uneasy. It probably was somebody's macabre joke anyway, she argued with herself. No one was here. She really wasn't going to find anything out about Janet.

The scratching came again, this time, from overhead. Quickly she flashed the thin beam into the dark, web crossed rafters. There was a whoosh sound as something brushed by her hair. Sabra yelled and jumped forward. The flashlight flew from her hand and spun away. She clutched the bag, waiting. Waiting for what? There was a screech outside the barn, then quiet, then an answering trill.

Shakily she got to her feet. "My cripes, owls, just owls, you almost gave me a heart attack," she said aloud. Laughing a bit hysterically she willed her pounding pulse to calm down, felt for the dropped bag then ran her trembling fingers up the side of her scalp. "My hair...it's a mess." Speaking aloud comforted her. She patted at the stray strands. Her eyes had become accustomed to the dark of the cavernous room. She hoped Kay hadn't heard her temporary outburst of panic. And damn! Where was that accursed flashlight? Her eyes slowly searched for it in front of her.

There it was. A thin beam glowed from beneath the joint of two rough-hewn planks. She gasped as her heel caught on the edge of a loose board. She stumbled to her knees.

"Will this hell never end?" she snarled through clenched teeth then tugged and pulled a board aside to retrieve the light. A terribly sweet, rotting odor wafted up from beneath the boards. She held the bag to her nose as she felt in the direction of the beam. Sabra sucked in her breath and clutched the light. The smell gagged her. There was something else. It was soft to the touch. She scrabbled backwards, suddenly screaming in small piteous gulps.

Back in the car, Kay jumped. She thought she'd heard a strange sound moments before. But now, those were real screams. Kay dove over the back seat. In her enthusiasm, she slammed her head against the dome light. Yelling in pain she hit the alarm switch. Frantically she searched for the keys. They were not in the ignition. With the alarm deafening her, Kay thrust the door open and promptly fell out of the car. The dog blanket tangled around her ankles.

With the car beeping and blinking behind her she staggered to her feet. Kicking the odious blanket aside she charged toward the barn.

"Hold on Sabra I'm coming!" she yelled at the top of her lungs.

Kay honed in on the wailing Sabra and wrested the flashlight from her grip.

Sabra's car lights flashed grisly shadows in the barn and along the floor, but this time they were becoming blood-red and siren sounds over-rode her cars bleating. It was a police car.

The combined light and cacophony was enough to wake the dead. But Janet Holmes was beyond hearing.

*CHAPTER 28*

# *Brandy and Questions*

**Officer Washington eased her tired body** into the nearest chair and opened her notebook. Merde, it was too early in the morning. She focused her protesting mind and surveyed the people and the modern living room. Toady's decorating influence was in aggressive evidence. His selection of furniture bordered on severe avant-garde, but was still eye-pleasing and comfortable.

Ujima motioned to Sabra and gently asked her to sit down. What was that odious blanket wrapped around her? It had a strange smell. She sniffed. That's it, essence of wet dog. Fleetingly, Ujima wondered if this was to become one of Sabra's newest fashion statements. She licked the end of her pencil. There was a greasy, fishy taste. Cripes. It wasn't a pencil. It was a ballpoint pen. She swallowed hesitantly and looked up with a sour face. The four wide-eyed adults regarded her expectantly.

"I'm not getting much sleep," she said acidly then nodded in Kay's direction. "What with somebody trying to drown Ms. Roberts and yours truly, Willie's disappearance, the vicious accident intended for Alex, or possibly Toady and all topped off with Mr. Templeton's homicide, then this! I'm not usually a whiner, but I think that I'm rapidly becoming one. And I'm definitely not pleased. I'm not pleased because the Mayor and the county Sergeant are not pleased." She glanced at her watch and continued. "Again the forensic team and their ace detective should be here in about forty-five minutes. I'm sure they won't be pleased either. However, they overlook the finer points, that here in the provinces communication is not instant, our so-called man power minimal and the geography demands a slower pace. Worst of all, the ferries run infrequently, if at all, after midnight." She snorted. "They have to come by launch, and are already quibbling about where the department funds should come from."

She looked at Sabra's pale face then nodded at Toady. "Can you scare up a shot of brandy?"

"Not a problem. The good stuff is in the kitchen cupboard," Toady said wearily and got to his feet.

"I'll help," Alex offered and jumped up. They left the room together. In contrast to Alex's chipper self, Toady was pale and drawn. Ujima noted that he'd only had time to grab a tank top and a pair of tennis shorts. She also noticed his hands shook, his tennis shoes were uncharacteristically grubby, and there was moisture in his eyes. Had he been crying? Maybe he was in shock about the condition of his boat. Or was there something else she wasn't considering?

Then there was Kay, her red hair all a-tumble. How could any woman turn up a corpse, calm a hysterical companion, enlist the aid of a possible murder suspect, then turn around and look so ravishing at two-thirty in the morning? Ujima sighed resignedly and turned her attention to her notebook.

"We'll start with who found the body." At that point Alex entered the room and with a flourish handed a snifter of brandy to Ujima.

"It's not for me. I think Ms. Whitestone is in need...not that we all couldn't use one!" Ujima groused.

Alex handed the glass to Sabra. Her fingers trembled. She spilt almost half onto her blanket as she struggled to take a sip.

"I'm terribly sorry," she apologized in a faint voice.

Kay leaned forward and whispered, "Don't worry Sabra. It's only brandy." Personally she felt it would smell a helluva lot better than the doggie odor wafting from the blanket.

"Okay Ms. Roberts, you're first," Ujima turned on her small recorder and wrote in her notebook as Toady wandered into the room with a glass of water in his hand. He sat quietly at the end of the dining table. It was strange she thought. Someone, it must have been the murderer, called Officer Reynolds and said there were kids vandalizing the old Bremmer's barn, but wouldn't give his name. Fortunately she'd just returned from the mainland and gotten to the barn just after the gruesome discovery. She glanced sideways at Toady. Was he the anonymous caller?

"Sabra found the body. I heard her yelling. The commotion awakened Toady too. He must have called the police department first then ran to help us. I thought you were still in Seattle though?" Kay said, expecting an answer from Ujima. But Ujima only nodded and said for her to continue.

"Toady told us he thought the barn was on fire." She looked at Toady. "I wasn't aware that the road to the barn is almost directly below your house."

He stuttered then said slowly, "Yes but as you said, when I heard the car alarm, the first thing I thought of was fire. I was groggy and it all sounded like it was in my front yard. And then I saw the lights flashing by the barn and I thought it was those goddamn vandals again. But then...." His lips trembled.

Kay turned to Ujima. "Were we glad to see him! He helped us to the car, checked to see that we were okay and then called for help." Toady's eyes closed and he nodded in agreement.

Ujima regarded the end of her offending pen. The taste lingered nastily on her tongue. "I might ask what you were doing there, Kay," she said aloud, as her inner voice said: but I probably don't want to know.

"Well it's obvious. Sabra couldn't go alone. Someone had to be with her."

"Why on earth didn't you contact me first?" Ujima asked. "You both might have been in real danger. It's most likely Janet's killer set you up to find the body."

Alex nodded grimly and was visibly upset. "Ujima is right. The two of you gallivanting off without police support? It's foolish."

Kay was exasperated. "I tried, but Officer Reynolds said Ujima was in Seattle. And your friendly policeman, Drip-Van-Wrinkle, was too asleep to be of any help."

Ujima looked down at her tablet. It was her mistake. She'd told Officer Reynolds to hold calls that were not of an emergency nature. He'd only done exactly what she'd requested.

"Officer Reynolds has recently been assigned to me. But that's no excuse. I'll go over procedures with him, this time in extensive detail. I don't foresee any future problems," Ujima added ominously.

Kay wasn't to be mollified. "He was totally uncommunicative. I could have gotten more information out of a turnip. At the time it wasn't an emergency, but it was urgent. At the least it would have been convenient, to have planned something with you before we tackled the situation."

Ujima ignored Kay's frustration, and her own anger at Kay's amateur sleuthing. She wrote details hastily in her notebook. "I take it you were in the car?"

Kay looked down at her feet. "Uh, yes," her voice became small. "I was hiding under a blanket in the back seat." Alex couldn't restrain a guffaw.

"Ah." Ujima looked at her. "No doubt, in a location where you would be most effective if Sabra ran into trouble."

Kay was clearly embarrassed. "Well, well we both…thought so. After all, the note did say, 'Come alone'. We didn't want to spook anyone, particularly if they did have information about Janet's whereabouts."

"When you arrived at the barn what did you find?" Ujima faced their stares. "I'm sorry Sabra. But you'll have to tell me it over again." She had hesitated to ask the poor woman anything. But it was necessary while the events were still fresh in her mind. "This time I want even the tiniest detail."

Sabra began her story. At first she seemed bewildered, but with her eyes closed, she launched into a surprisingly coherent telling of events. Ujima interrupted the narrative with the occasional question and was pleased. Sabra had managed to get through most of the inquiry without breaking down, and with the exception of a few details, matched what Ujima had gleaned from the first rush of hysterical babblings she'd heard. When she was through, she turned to Kay.

But, Sabra was not finished with her statement: "I was in shock and so was Kay. Kay told me that we shouldn't try to...to do anything. And that the money was a ploy to get us there. Nobody was around, only Toady after he heard all the racket." She gave him a weak smile. "The poor man, he went back to the barn to see what could be done, if anything." She flashed a hostile look at Ujima and said peevishly, "And I know you were there as quick as you could be, but it seemed like hours before the police showed up."

Toady, whose attention was elsewhere, suddenly turned his ashen face to Alex. "You know. I could use a brandy too and no water, please. I've this," he said as he held up the glass of water he had not touched. "That's if you don't mind."

Alex stood up. "Sure sport. Good idea. I'll get a shot for everyone." He paused and wagged a finger at Ujima. "With the exception of the investigating officer who and I quote: 'at all times must remain sober and alert'." He grinned and walked into the kitchen.

"Alex feels like I do," Kay said in a quiet voice. "There has to be a connection between these things that have happened recently." She held up the fingers of her left hand and ticked them off: "Templeton's murder, Willie's disappearance, threats from Superior, Alex's so-called accident, now Janet's murder."

"We can't assume anything yet," Ujima said stiffly.

"Oh give me a break," Kay said angrily. "Janet didn't exactly crawl into that barn and pull those boards over her head."

"How could you be so crass!" Sabra exclaimed with a sob.

Kay acknowledged her crying with a grimace, but plowed on, "Regardless of how we feel, there's a connection, and we have to find it." She leaned forward. "Who left Sabra that note? The bribe for information was to get her there. She'd of found the body by the smell. It has to be the same sicko that's doing this. And whoever it is, they're on this island!"

Ujima finished up a postage stamp sketch in her notebook then turned to Sabra and said, "I understand that Janet has an apartment over your shop. I'd like to have the key. Or, if you have an extra one...."

Sabra looked at her lap. "I do." She paused, "You just reminded me, a funny thing happened several months ago. Her apartment was broken into. Whoever it was, walked across the back porch roof and climbed through the upstairs window. We found faint pine needle footprints on the carpet." Sabra blew her nose. "Janet said nothing had been taken, but the papers and items on her desk had been disturbed. She thought at first I'd been in the room, but then noticed that the window ledge had black marks on it. She said that she didn't want to report it." Sabra sighed and continued, "I don't know why but she does keep a diary. It's in a special hiding place. I'll show you where."

Toady cleared his throat. His voice had recovered and he spoke in a surprisingly firm baritone. "I know you all think I had something to do with the sabotage of my boat. But all I can say is you're dead-wrong. It would help if you didn't think the worst of me."

Kay and Alex raised their hands in protest, but he went on.

"I've been thinking about these terrible events too. And with me it started when that bridge collapsed under Alex. Kay's right, there has to be some connection with Templeton's murder. From the damage to Willie's property to the vandals last year at the Petoskey farm. I don't know how the rest of you feel. But we'd better level with Ujima and tell her everything we know." He wiped his brow with the back of his arm. His eyes were red.

He had been crying, Ujima thought.

Alex smacked his hands together. It startled everyone. "Okay. Here's my two centavos. The Superior dogs came sniffing around here right after Templeton's death. Someone is pulling their leashes, someone who is very clever. And that someone, or someones, plural, stands to gain here. As usual, money and greed will be at the root of it."

Ujima looked chagrined at Alex's statement. "I haven't run across any money motivation yet. But I'm beginning to suspect some sort of financial cover up. Janet was only a temp but she might have seen or heard something. And if there is someone acting behind the scenes, their motivations aren't obvious, yet." She glanced at Kay. "That reminds me, your lawyer Max called. He wants to talk to you as soon as you're available."

"Thanks," Kay said.

Ujima pointedly looked at the face of each person. "And now *I'm* taking it from here. I know I've said this several times before, but I'm saying it again. No more looking for clues and no more getting involved in sticky situations. That's what I get paid for." She paused to see if her last comment had any effect. "Good. I concur with Toady. You must at all times level with me. I'll be taking further statements when I interview you individually. But now, there's a certain young man that comes to mind. Do you know where he may be at the moment?"

Kay took Alex's hand. "He's with Byron and Teri. They're in Madrona tonight. They went to take in a movie and said something about pizza afterwards."

Ujima glanced at her watch. 'They should be tucked in their beds by now,' she thought for a moment. "If you two don't mind I'd like to reconvene this meeting at your house." Ujima sighed. "With the forensics team coming, it looks like I'll be up all night anyway. I can take care of Wick and finish my interviews there."

She looked around at the surprised faces. "Look, if mama suffers, you all suffer. Well, it will help me get the paperwork done." She looked at her cell phone. "And forensics knows how to get a hold of me when they get to the barn."

Alex looked askance at Kay then at Ujima. "How about the murder scene, shouldn't it be secured?"

Ujima got up and put on her hat. "Not to worry," she said as she tapped her cell phone. "The inimitable Officer Reynolds is already there."

All were settled in the farmhouse living room when Ujima looked at her watch again. "Those kids must be making a night of it. Are they usually out this late?"

In answer to Ujima's question, a throaty noise could be heard rumbling up the farmhouse road. Bright lights swept over the ceiling of the room, the wall-shaking noise reached a crescendo then suddenly cut out.

Toady looked out the closest bay. He could see Byron sitting behind the steering wheel, caressing it, with a dreamy look.

"It's them all right," Toady said as he turned around, a crooked smile on his pale face. "You can't mistake the sound of that yellow squash-bug."

Wick's hand gripped the side of the sand buggy. They had been talking and laughing so hard he hadn't noticed the parked police car until the last moment.

"Christ on a crutch! It's the wicked witch of the East. What's she doing here?"

Teri stopped laughing. "Why? What do you mean? It's only Ujima's police car." She laughed uneasily. "Mom probably called her because we're so late. Gosh! All the lights are on."

It was tight, sitting in the back seat of the bug. Teri's breast brushed Wick's arm as she leaned toward him. Her scent enveloped him. Wick's breath became uneven. Instead of following his desire to crush her to him and bury his face in her hair, he gently took her arm and pushed it aside.

"Ujima probably wants to see me again. She's been on my case ever since I got here. For some reason she hates my guts." He paused and dropped his voice lower. "I don't think your mother likes me either. She's always watching me. It's creepy."

Teri's expression was unreadable and only inches from his face. "That's not true. I know that she..." He couldn't hold back. He pulled her close and kissed her. It was gentle, at first.

Byron made an unpleasant sound with his lips, "Hey you guys, don't get all jiggy in the back seat. If those plastic seat covers melt you'll pay for them. I've got enough to repair on this buggy as it is."

Wick pulled back. His pulse was racing and so was Teri's.

"I've got to get away from here," Wick panted, "I've got to have time to find Martin and not be under everybody's eye while I'm doing it. The fearsome threesome, your mom, Alex and Ujima seem to clock my every move."

Byron lowered his voice. "There's an island really close to Bradestone. It's called Blake Island. A girl at the dock told me all about it. She said there are a lot of neat places that not everybody knows about." His eyes lit up. "The Island is so close that deer can swim to it. Most of it is a public park. Nobody would think of looking for you there."

Wick was exasperated. "Why would I want to go to another island? The work I've got to do is here."

Byron swallowed. "Well it's just a possibility." He stuttered, "It's a small island. Remember? We saw it that morning when we first came in. A millionaire owned it once. Now the state has it. And there's an Indian center there too. It sounds like a pretty cool place to me," he said hesitantly.

Wick didn't wish to alienate Byron. "Okay, thanks. But we'd better get inside." He jumped out of the car and paused. "If I do need to hide out, how do I get there?"

Excitement crept back into Byron's voice, "That's easy. Toady said anytime we needed to borrow his powerboat we could. He keeps it moored near the ferry landing. It's in case the ferry isn't running and he has to get to Seattle. And he's real good at keeping secrets. He hasn't even told mom I bought the bug, yet."

"It sounds like a good idea to me," Teri said as she steadied her hand on Wick's shoulder. "And if you have to hide, we can loan you some of our camping gear and foodstuff, no problemo." Wick turned away. He hoped she couldn't see the look on his face. He was a city guy, the thought of 'Le Camping', was an anathema.

"Wick would need someone to be look-out for him. I'll go too," Byron said.

Teri glared at him as she jumped to the ground. "If you go, I'm going! You're not leaving me behind."

Wick intervened, "Hey, hey! Take it easy you two. I'm not going anywhere right now." He saw Byron's face, and then qualified, "Only of-course, if it's absolutely necessary. And anyway, I'd go by myself. I'm not getting anyone else in trouble, no way."

"Wick's right," Teri said. "It's a great idea. But only as a last recourse." She reached over and tweaked her brother's nose. "And hey, sly one, who's this girl you met at the docks?"

Byron looked sheepish and shrugged his shoulders. "Just a girl, she works at that tacky fish and chips place. You know, at the landing."

"Aren't you the smooth operator?"

"Hey, she's a nice girl!"

Wick lounged against the buggy, a worldly look on his face. "What's her name?"

"It's Jennie."

Teri smirked then snapped her fingers in rhythm, Wick joined in, "Oh Jennie, Oh Jennie, Oh Jennie Oh!" they crooned.

"Cut it out. I've only talked to her a couple of times and ..." The door to the porch swung open. Kay stood framed in the backlight.

"How was the show?"

"It was really good, Mom," Teri shouted back as she and Byron ran toward the house. Wick hadn't moved.

Sherriff Ujima's uniformed silhouette stepped in front of Kay's. "Is Wick Wilding there?"

He crossed his arms and grumbled, "Yeah."

"Good. Stick around. I'd like to talk to you in a little while."

"Yeah, yeah," he said aloud; then to himself, 'Where the hell does she think I'm going to run off to? These woods are probably full of bears, cougars and snakes.'

"Hey Mom, Ujima, what's up?" Byron asked brightly as he stepped onto the porch. He hesitated when he saw the looks on their faces and hoped that whatever it was, it didn't involve Wick.

Teri frowned as she took Kay's hands. "Mom, what's wrong?"

Ujima shrugged, "Something unfortunate has happened tonight. I'm merely talking things over with your Mom and Alex. Toady and Sabra are here too," she replied slowly. Her smile was suddenly tired, "It seems, whenever I meet you Teri, I'm discussing things of a confidential nature. Well it's happening again. This time I hope your brother and you..."

Teri nodded her head. "Yes. Yes. You'd like us to go to our rooms until you're finished." Then out of the side of her mouth she said, "I'm quickly catching on to the routine around here."

Ujima nodded. "It'll only be a short while. When I'm finished interviewing them, I'll talk to Mr. Wilding before I leave." Teri nodded as she watched Wick lurch onto the porch.

"Whadaya want to see me about?" He asked belligerently.

Teri reached out and shook his arm. "Hey, shape up! Something serious has happened and Sergeant Washington just wants to ask you a few questions. That's all."

Kay kissed Teri on the forehead. "Thanks dear. That's it, in a nutshell."

Byron was already rushing up the stairs, "Come on! The last one up is a lame duck." Teri reluctantly followed after Byron.

It was Wick, who with a churlish look over his shoulder, made a show of grabbing the railing and swinging up the stairs.

Alex heard only one door slam. He knew the kids would be into immediate and heavy conferencing. "Well. They're out of our hair, temporarily at least."

Alex turned to Toady, "I've a hunch, Mr. Toda, that you've sold Byron your bug. I hope I'm right."

Toady smiled weakly, "Well. Negotiations are in progress, but..."

"Just as I thought, don't worry. He's got the allowance to pay for it. And it will loosen up the vehicle situation around here." Alex clasped his hands on his head. "How about a little more brandy to finish the night off? It'll soon be daylight." There was no response. "Okay. I'll bring the bottle in. I also have some expensive stuff and it's everyone for themselves." He left the room.

Even though the youngster's arrival had provided a welcome distraction, Sabra huddled in her blanket, still in shock. "I can't believe Janet is dead." She shivered and dabbed at her eyes, "That means Martin's dead too. And maybe..."

Ujima kept the sound of her voice as neutral as possible, "I don't think that would necessarily follow."

"What she means..." Kay paused and bit her lip. "I'm sorry Ujima, but earlier tonight I told Sabra about Martin's car being found in Idaho. Supposedly, they were traveling together, and if...," Kay paused and looked miserable. "Things are getting serious. And I don't want us to find any more dead bodies. All I want us to find is a live one, and put that murderer away for keeps."

Sabra's voice was low and she hiccupped. "If Martin were alive we would have heard from him...somehow."

Ujima followed Alex with her eyes as he walked into the room and put the brandy bottle and a pitcher of water on the coffee table. She had to keep her own council. They knew nothing of the evidence that had been found near the car. But, like a chameleon, the whole complexion of the case was changing. Along with Toady, Martin and his friend Wick were prime suspects. Although Wick, it was very odd... she was getting a headache and her throat was parched. She looked at the feeble rays of dawn outside the window. "I'll just have a glass of water and two aspirin," she said aloud, and then to herself she mumbled, 'it's going to be a rotter of a day.'

CHAPTER 31

# *Sacred Glade*

**Three days had passed** since Janet's body was found. And now rumors and conjectures were all over the island. Seattle media bloodhounds had panted in on it, embellishing their articles with gory details and wild scenarios.

The news accounts of the mayhem and mystery inspired Kay Alex and the kids to make their own guesses. Each tried to trump the other with more realistic motives and theories. Wick, sour faced and closed mouth, remained silent.

When it was two a.m., and there was still no consensus, Alex called it quits. He shooed the youngsters upstairs, shoved the remains of their dinner into the fridge, promised Kay he would clear up the kitchen in the morning and then pushed her upstairs.

It was an unusually warm night and the sound of revelers on the beach echoed over the water and drifted up through the open bedroom windows. Alex passed out instantly. Nothing seemed to keep him awake. But the sounds of the distant party, coupled with her own thoughts, would not let Kay sleep. Toward morning, Morpheus gathered her into a fitful slumber.

When Kay completed her morning yoga regimen, she left the house refreshed and energized and headed down the path to Scoon Bay; a lone walk on the beach would be a first rate meditation.

Far from the shore, jewels of sunlight glinted off the water. Kay shaded her eyes from the brilliance and inhaled deeply. The minus tide smelled surprisingly fresh. She paused; a faint odor of charred wood mixed with the sea-weedy scents wafted near her. Then she spotted the source. It was to her right, on the bank, further up the beach. A thread of smoke curled lazily from the center of a stand of trees.

The remains of a beach fire from that party last night, she thought. The raucous bunch no doubt hadn't bothered to douse it. The sounds of yelling and jolting music had kept her sleepless almost till morning. "Better make sure the fire doesn't spread to the woods," she grumbled aloud and picked up her pace.

A movement, to her left, caught Kay's attention. Two seagulls and six black crows were working an exposed mud and gravel bank. Edgar was among them, he wasn't going to be left out. His amber plumage was quite distinctive as he sauntered among the birds. Eyeing a special tidbit he pecked it swiftly from the muddy edge. It was a small clam. He flew a distance up the beach, hesitated in the air then dropped his prey on an outcropping of exposed rock. Kay applauded, at Edgar's crow-way of shelling mollusks for his breakfast. He uttered a triumphant caw and eagerly swooped down. The other birds flew over to the exposed meal. They stalked around Edgar, eyeing his breakfast, but not daring to interfere.

Kay enjoyed watching the pecking order. But Edgar, having quickly eaten, was busy working his way up the beach. Behind him his camp followers argued over what he had left. Then, disconsolate, the crows fanned out in separate directions. True to Edgar's nature, he hadn't left the tiniest scrap.

When she reached the smoldering fire it was at the center of a large cleared area of sand, surrounded by a circle of trees and shrubs. She kicked pieces of charred drift to the side then picked up a Madrona branch and swept sand over the remaining coals. Strangely, remote thoughts of last week events whirled into her mind. She wished she could extinguish the troubling thought of murder as well as she had the fire.

Then Kay heard the sobbing. It came from behind a large log in back of her. The sounds of misery and despair were intermittent. They were the sobs of a man. Kay dithered for a moment. She didn't wish to intrude. She ought to turn back or continue down the beach, not invade someone's privacy. But the crying was potent with grief. Kay had heard Alex cry, but this sound was far worse; as if it was wrenched from the man's very being. Softly she made her way toward the log.

The man occasionally hiccupped. His back shoulder muscles moved under his light tank top as he held his knees and rocked back and forth. A maroon cashmere sweater lay carelessly tossed on the ground beside him. Kay sighed. A weeping Adonis in this sylvan glade, she thought and made her way to Toady.

She softly called his name several times before he hastily stood up, turned and rubbed red knuckles across his tear-stained face. Then quickly he blew his nose into a blue-silk handkerchief he'd fished out of the pocket of his shorts.

"Are you all right? What's the matter? What's happened?" Kay stood next to him, her hand on his forearm. She asked what she considered trite, but necessary questions.

Suddenly, with a chest-rattling gulp of breath, he hugged her until she thought she would be crushed. She could smell the sweat and salt of his grief, then letting go he sat heavily on the sand, his back against the log.

"Kay. I'm so glad it's you," he said in almost a whisper. "But there's nothing you can do. Nothing anyone can do. Janet's gone," he hiccupped then sobbed. "And we loved each other so much. She, she understood me, completely. What am I to do? What is my life to be without her, now?"

Kay drew back. "But, but I thought..."

For the first time she was able to look him full in the face. She was appalled. His lips were swollen and crusted with blood. He had only one good eye; the other was purple and puffed shut. His right earlobe, minus an earring, was bloodied and torn. And his chin bore the unmistakable print of a square ring-cut.

"Toady. What's happened? Looks like you've been in a bar fight royal. And where did you get that hideous black eye? It needs attention."

"Ah, the noble male of the species; he's always fights to protect the lady's honor."

"Which Lady?"

"Janet," he said and waved his hand. "I know. I know. You thought I ... I was only attracted to men. Believe me that would be a helluva lot easier." He looked down at his sandal-shod feet and took in another deep and shaky breath. "Janet and I were lovers." His tone changed to belligerence. "She was only *fascinated* by Martin. It was her nature to be kind to everyone that was not run of the mill. But she loved me."

Kay was confused. "But I'd understood she'd married Martin and they were away on honeymoon."

He looked up, squinting through his good eye. "None of that's true. They didn't get married. And Ujima knows that. Janet talked the marriage shtick up to tease me, and everyone else. She always did things like that. She even had Sabra believing her. But it was only a ruse. I have to admit though, Martin intrigued her. He's unbelievably artistic and intelligent."

"Did you and he get along?"

Toady paused and took in a deep, ragged breath. "Martin was totally different than me. And yes, we had our arguments. Because I was the athlete and he was the brainy one, he always stuck up for her. He always justified her actions, no matter what…what crazy things she did." He drew a finger across his swollen cheek.

"But then why did she go to New York with Martin and not you?"

"She told me she needed a complete change...from everything, from the rain, this backwoods island. She also wanted to see Martin and his friend, again. You know that...that Wick Wilding."

"Why was she so keen on seeing Wick?"

"The three of them were students at the same art school and planned on putting together some sort of yuppie art gallery. She said Wick was very skilled with puppets and the like. I would have been a third wheel because I don't have any art background or creative talents," Toady said with a sour look on his face, "besides I have my business and run the gym and tennis club.

"I didn't know that Janet was involved in the arts. I thought she only did secretarial work. But Sabra did say she was a great help at her shop."

"She made special costumes for local theater productions in Issaquah, Federal Way and Tacoma. She even had parts in some of the plays. Her degree was in costume design. She knew that I liked the arts and I promoted them, but she said that I didn't have any innate, creative talents in that direction. She called me a...a philistine." He smiled, "But she wasn't nasty about it."

Kay put her hands on her hips. "We should do something about your eye. Come back to the house with me and we can make some, er necessary repairs."

"Hah, I'll be alright. I've been in fights before. That, at the least, is what I have the talent for."

"Well, personally, I think you have many talents," Kay paused, "but I'm curious. Where was the...um... art gallery supposed to be located, Upstate New York?"

"Originally yes, but then they decided to have it here on the Island, in the town of Burn. Martin found an old boat house that is in great shape there and bought the building from Rose. Janet told me that after they would firm up the details with Wick, then she and Martin would take off for Europe since it was so close." He shrugged. "I told her she was making me feel like a second-rate lover. I was hoping all the time she would stop teasing me. And things would be better when they got back." He began to sob quietly. "Who would do such a horrible thing to her? She was a terrific person and my real soul-mate, I..."

"Look, if it helps any. Ujima told me that Janet died instantly, she... didn't suffer."

Toady gestured toward the sky and let out a deep sob, "Oh that certainly helps a lot! She's dead and I think that bastard Martin killed her." He wrung his hands, "and for what reason?" He paused and said under his breath, "as if any reason would justify murder anyway."

"What," Kay exclaimed. "Why do you think Martin killed her?"

"Who else could it have been? She left with him. No one's heard from him, either. He's got to be the one. Obviously he's in hiding... maybe in France somewhere."

Kay could think of a few jealous men who might have a 'reason'. She remained silent; his naive defense of Janet irked her.

"You know, if you think about it, Janet was very unkind to you. Maybe she wasn't aware of what she was doing. I'll give her that benefit of a doubt. But in the sensitivity-to-others department I think she had a lot of growing up to do. I don't want to be judgmental, but from what I've been able to put together, it seems her main interest was in hooking men like fish. And the more splashing there was in the pond, the more the merrier."

Raymond looked up angrily. He hissed through his teeth. "It sounds like you've been listening to Edward. He says the same things about Janet. Edward thinks he knows everything. But he knows nothing. He was here. Him and his cronies, they told me what a fool I was and said Janet was a whore. Edward implied that she and Templeton were... but it just isn't true. Mr. Templeton was like, like a father to her. She told me so." He closed his one good eye. His face twisted in pain as tears slowly trickled down his cheek again.

"And now she's dead!" He cried quietly, dabbing at his eyes with his handkerchief and shaking his head back and forth.

Kay moved behind him and massaged his tense shoulders. "I'm sorry. I just said what came off the top of my head. You know, I'm sorting through things too. But with Janet's er, type of personality, she made many men jealous. And when jealousy enters the stage, the players usually say outrageous things about each other and the more mendacious they are the more lies they stir up." Toady appeared calmer.

"Anyway, how did you get that black eye?"

"It was Mark!" Toady growled. "He said Janet had the hots for him, because she was always putting the moves on him. He even bragged about how good she was in bed. But I know he's lying. When I told him the truth, about me and Janet, he said I was a 'shitty, lying fag' and started to punch me out. We'd been drinking." Toady smiled lopsidedly, it lent his face a twisted and sinister look. "But I took care of him, a fast kick to the groin, then a slam on the back of his neck." He chuckled deep in his chest. "That Norse God fell like a chopped spruce. He won't mess with Toady for a long time." He sniffed then grabbed his sweater and drew one of the sleeves across his nose.

Kay winced. "Here, why don't you use this?" She handed him the soaked, blue handkerchief that he'd dropped on the log.

Toady took it then he held it out like some offending rag. His one eye focused unsteadily on it. "That's not mine. Where did you get this?"

"You were just using it," Kay said. He looked at the handkerchief again, shook his head in confusion and threw it on the ground. Kay pulled a packet of tissue from her pocket. As she handed it to him, she wondered who else had been at last night's 'Beach Party'. She was going to ask, but he interrupted her with a ragged laugh.

"Always pays to be prepared, thanks." He paused to dab at his swollen eye and blow his nose. "Thommy Jay was here too. He saw it all. He told me, before he left, that I deserved to be punched out!"

"Why would he say that?" Kay asked, surprised.

"He was angry because of the ladies we were entertaining last night, even though they were Edward's friends." Toady gulped. "Thommy says I keep my feet in both camps. He's no help at all. Says I'm as queer as a three dollar bill and just won't admit it." Toady inhaled a long, dry sob. "He's not in my head. He can't see through my eyes, and he never will be able to."

Toady made a spiral motion with his hands. "Oh, you can let your hair down with him, but only part way. Then he expects you to pay your five cents and listen to him. He tells you what life's all about. And pity you if you have an idea of your own. The trouble with Thom is that he puts everyone in little boxes. He never takes into account that they may be on different paths, or for that matter, have different feelings. He says my 'situations' are inconsequential and my reactions to them, romantic and unreal." He sighed. "With him conversation is always that one-sided." He wiped his sleeve across his eyes and groaned. "I do need an ice bag. My eye socket is throbbing."

Kay was relieved. Toady was finally paying attention to his physical problems. He paused and drew a small infinity sign in the sand with his left hand. "Now I'm alone... again."

He looked so dejected that Kay moved forward and hugged him. "We're all alone in this life," she said. "When you reach my age, you'll look back and see that the road is traveled alone, and most of the way. But if we're real lucky we'll meet someone who will share that road. But you have to find completeness in yourself, in your heart. You're going to have to... oh, oh!" She put her hands to her mouth. "I'm starting to preach. Just like Thom."

Toady laughed shakily, "Yes, Mother Roberts. That's funny you're not that old... gad, I must bring it out in people. No matter, I know what you're saying's true. But, I'll probably not make it to an age anyway, where I can look back with such wisdom."

Kay stared at him. "Why on earth do you say that?"

He shrugged his shoulders and flapped his hand. "Oh you know... AIDS and all that stuff; I'll probably lose my senses in the passion of the moment. And that'll be it."

Kay shook his shoulders. He seemed so much like a kid, only a very big kid.

"Don't be a twit. All you have to do is what nine out of ten doctors' recommend, abstain, or practice safe sex. You'll survive."

For the first time, Toady seemed his old self and barked a laugh. "Kay, you're crazy, but I love you just the same."

"That's the old toughie I know." She massaged the part of his back between his shoulder blades again then patted his back. "Come on; let's go up to the house. I've ice bags in the freezer. Alex keeps them on hand for his back and other bruised-muscle events."

Quietly she reached over and picked up the crumpled handkerchief. She tucked it in her back pocket. "I keep telling Alex to build up his resistance to accidents. He needs to practice Hatha Yoga. But he can be as single-minded as Thom." She paused. "Or me, for that matter."

Toady swung his sweater over his shoulder then leaned on Kay as they started up the beach. "Phew, I guess I had more beer than I thought." He stumbled frequently and things were out of focus even through his one usable eye. Kay supported him the best she could.

They reached the verandah when Toady hesitated. He patted Kay on her arm and said unexpectedly: "Alex is a great guy. Why are you holding out? Why aren't you marrying him?"

Kay stopped then blushed as she recognized he'd nailed a nerve. Toady had confided in her, let his 'hair down' so to speak. Now it was her turn. But, it would be a difficult question to take apart, to look at closely, and to answer. She smiled ruefully to herself. She had been adept at avoiding it.

She sighed deeply. "It is, as the weary sages say, a long and involved story. Are you sure you want to hear it?"

Toady smiled lopsidedly. "You bet I do."

Kay glanced back at the graceful curve of Heron's Hook. The water flashed silver shards of light in the inlet. And the giant firs on the opposite side broke up the view to Puget Sound. They lent an air of shelter and intimacy to Scoon Bay.

"When Frank died, I found I could make decisions. And I could direct my life the way I wanted." She looked down. "I really began to enjoy my independence. It wasn't that Frank was dictatorial, far from it. But we married very young and at that time I wanted him to be the one in control, to be the man who made the decisions. I suppose you could say I was lazy. Anyway, Alex may not look or appear to be a man of steel, but he steadily and determinedly gets his way. I call it passive steam-rolling. I like that part of him, and I don't like it at the same time." She paused. "For instance, he wants to start a bed and breakfast. He may joke about it, but it's for real. He's putting pressure on me, subtle pressure that I thought I got away from when it was just me and the kids." Kay was beginning to sweat a little.

"So," Toady said quietly. "Go on."

"Alex's true nature, and he would never admit it, is to always be in the driver's seat. Oh he's diplomatic enough, but it's like trying to sway the rock of Gibraltar. And that messes with my own identity, my own independence. I know it sounds selfish. But that's how I feel."

"But you've gone ahead and bought this place together," Toady said, his arm made a sweeping gesture. "Why would you do that?"

"It's selfishness again. I love him and don't want anyone else to have him. Besides, we both have to start somewhere. We've got a lot of interests in common and both agree that as one gets older it's tough going it alone; and I've learned to trust him and give a little." Kay became serious. "I think that in any relationship, compromise on both sides is essential, or it won't succeed. And I'm tough enough to stand my ground when I need to, and successfully negotiate when I have to," Kay said, a determined look on her face.

Toady laughed jerkily. "Oh you're tough enough all right." He sighed and looked up the path to the Petoskey farmhouse. "Now let's see if you're tough enough to help me up the steps." He patted her hand. "When we get there, I'll take one of Alex's ice bags for my eye, a couple aspirin for my aching head and Tums for the stomach." He grinned down at her, "and how about a beer or two to wash down the aspirin?"

"Mr. Toda. Beer is not a good idea. Well, maybe one for me, but only tea for you." Kay laughed. "Now don't resist, Mother Roberts is going to dress those fists. I'm glad you didn't hit me with those huge knuckles."

Toady gave her a shocked look. "My dear lady, on you I'd only use my tennis racket and at fifty paces."

## CHAPTER 32

# *The Plan*

**It was two o'clock in the morning.** As agreed, the clandestine meeting was to be in Wick's bedroom. It was the farthest removed from Kay and Alex's. Teri arrived first.

"Mom would boil me in oil if she knew I was meeting a strange man." Her voice was breathless with excitement, "and in his bedroom." She paused, cast a sidelong look in Wick's direction, then made a show of patting the foot of the bed and sat on the edge.

Wick sat ridged, in a cross-legged yoga pose, his back against the headboard. He started to say something, shook his head, then closed his eyes and resumed meditating.

Byron was next. Opening the door stealthily, he stopped and puckered his mouth in a low whistle. "Dad, er Alex might have something very short of murder on his mind if he caught you two here, and alone."

Teri bounced up and down on the corner of the bed. "Now we're not alone...are we?"

"I could leave and rouse the household or," his expression became crafty, "I could be generously compensated for not saying a word."

Teri gave her brother a withering look. "Oh come on, Byron. It's all for one and one for all. Or has that pea-sized brain of yours forgotten?"

Byron stuck out his tongue, circled his right ear with his pointing finger and sat down alongside his sister. "Okay, okay. Why don't we get started?" They looked expectantly at Wick.

He was barefoot and in a full-lotus. A slight smile played on his lips. Eyes were partially closed; he paid no attention to the brother-sister interplay. The small bedside light cast deep shadows in the spartan room. Byron admired the muy macho look of Wick' black jeans and bulky black sweatshirt.

Teri thought Wick looked like a romantic leader, handsome, dashing, and he wasn't a bad kisser either. As Teri continued to stare at him she thought how weird it was that he reminded her of a younger Alex, without the broken nose, of course.

Several years ago, when she was first introduced to Alex, she had developed an instant crush on him. It was like that now, with Wick. She took in a sharp breath. Wick had turned to adjust the bed lamp. In profile, he resembled Alex so much that it startled her.

Wick ohmed quietly then opened his eyes and frowned at the smiling Byron.

"Hey fellah, I thought I was meeting with you only. How come Teri's here? It's too awkward with three people."

Byron rolled full length on the bed then cupped his chin in his hands. "Well," he muttered through clenched teeth, "Sisters can be a royal pain! She knew something was up and grilled it out of me. I wouldn't hear the end of it, if we don't include her." He looked sideways at Teri. "She might even rat on us."

Teri looked considerably put out. "I wouldn't do that. But you said if we were going to do something we would do it together. We took an oath on it." she said defiantly.

Wick waved his hand. "Whoa, sorry, I'm already uneasy about what's going on and I especially don't want to create any problems between you and your parents. They've all treated me so...so well. At least Alex has...but if you want to help," he said and sighed. "It's frustrating just sitting around and not being able to do anything. I've got to find out what happened to Martin. Byron said he would help me. But actually, I really could use input from you too," he finished diplomatically.

Teri, mollified, leaned forward. She nodded at her brother. "I can speak for both of us. We're in with you one hundred percent. Aren't we Byron?" He nodded vigorously. "Now, what's up?"

Wick slowly rubbed the left side of his nose. "I've told you before; I came here to find Martin, or at least where he may be hiding, or whatever. I can't do it alone. He may have left a message for me at the dock gallery he was putting together. But I have no idea where it's located. And I wouldn't know how to get there if I did." He pulled a well-worn 3x5 card out of his pocket.

"This is his last mailing address, but it's his art store in Manzanita, and General Ujima seems to have searched the place thoroughly and found nothing. Martin told me his new place was in a town called Burn." Wick gestured helplessly. "But with no directions and no transportation, I'm totally lost." He opened the drawer on his nightstand and removed a large folded paper. "When we were at the restaurant last night I took this map of Bradestone. But it only shows the main roads, and you can't read any of the tracings of the secondary roads."

Teri took the offered map and laughed aloud. "This is one of those hokey place mats that are on the table at the restaurant!"

Wick was offended. "I know that. But it's the only thing I could find. I didn't think I'd need a map. I didn't know things would be so primitive out here. You've got a better idea?"

Teri put a finger to her temple. "Actually I do. Number one: I happen to have a detailed map in my bedroom. I picked it up on the ferry. We'll use that. Number two: Mom and Alex have an appointment in Seattle with Mad Max our family lawyer, the master of tight purse strings and boring detail." Byron nodded vigorously in agreement. "And they plan to shop at the public market, and take in an old show at the Egyptian, so...." She clapped her hands and continued, "We'll have the entire day to ourselves. Number three: Rose, our resident yenta, knows everybody's business on this island. I'll call her in the morning, I bet she'll tell us exactly where Martin's other art building is located." She pointed a finger at Byron. "And number four: Your job is to get the bug's ignition working again. We're *not* going on bicycles."

"Oh thanks, great poobah! You've saved the easy job for me."

She shook her head. "It shouldn't be too difficult. The other night it ran like the greatest sand-sifter on four wheels. Besides, Toady told us it could be touchy at times; and if it needed any parts, he has an ongoing agreement at Barney's garage."

Byron's face lit up. "Yeah, Toady's a real cool guy. He said if I couldn't do some of the repairs on the buggy I could take it to Barney's and have him put it on his tab. That's one of the conditions he insisted on before selling it to me."

Wick leaned forward. "Is everything legal on it? All we need is to get stopped by General Ujima, or one of her minions."

"Yes. The buggy's been inspected and licensed. And I'm covered on Toady's insurance. That is, until I get full title. Then I go into real debt."

Teri smiled and took Byron's hand. "I've an idea. Since we need the bug right away, early tomorrow tell Toady you want to go on a tour of the island with Wick and me. I bet he can repair the bug faster than us having it towed to Barney's garage."

"Thanks for the vote of confidence, sis." Byron said, though secretly relieved.

"There's no reason he couldn't make the repairs, he doesn't open Toad Hall until noon. Anyway, I have a hunch he'll say 'yes'. I can tell he really likes you," she teased.

Byron blushed. "Yeah, he's pretty neat. And I like him too, but not in the way you're implying."

Wick sat up and shook his head. "Hey, I don't think it's a great idea using people... just because they're that way. It's not cool. No. I don't want anything to do with it." Then he crossed his arms and stuck out his prominent jaw; Teri thought he looked more than ever like a silly Alex.

"I don't agree with you Wick," she said. "Toady isn't being used. He likes any opportunity to show off his skills and abilities. The first time he let us take the car out, he said, any troubles just bring it back to him. If it's an electrical problem, he said he'd know what to look for."

"That's right. He rewired it this winter," Byron added eagerly.

Wick shrugged. "Well, I guess it makes sense. We don't have any money to be running around all day in a cab or waiting on a mechanic. Also, I don't want anybody else knowing what we're doing." He thought for a moment. "Okay, tomorrow is going to be here pronto, so we're going to have to hustle. And it's imperative that we get back here with everything done before your mom and Alex return, agreed?"

Byron pursed his lips. "Yeah, but they specifically told us not to get involved in this Martin-Janet thing."

Wick opened the palms of his hands. "So big deal, we're exploring, we'll just have to be real careful."

Teri nodded then lowered her voice. "Before we adjourn, did you hear all that noise on the beach the other night?"

Wick and Byron exchanged a quick glance. "Yeah," they said quietly.

Teri picked at the bedspread. "Well, Mom and Toady were talking about it. I saw Toady yesterday. He was here at the house. You should have seen his face. Evidently he got into a fight at the beach. I tried to hear more details, but every time I was around they were pretty tight-lipped."

"It wasn't Toady's party!" Byron blurted out.

Wick put his finger to his lips. But it was too late.

"What? Well, how do you know?" she paused, "Oh, I get it. You two went to the party and didn't invite me?"

Wick shook his hand. "No. It wasn't like that at all. We weren't invited." He looked at Byron. "It was too hot that night and I couldn't sleep. Byron was awake too so we snuck off to see what was up."

"Oh great, poor little female me wasn't even considered."

"That's not true," Byron said. "I did look in, but you were sound asleep. Besides, it was dangerous. We went out the window and crawled along the verandah roof." He paused, "remind me to tell Alex there's a lot of loose shingles up there."

Teri snorted. "You turkeys, you could've just used the front door."

Wick looked sheepishly at Byron, "We didn't want to wake anybody up and it was more... fun."

"Oh sure, breaking your neck is more fun," Teri snorted. "Anyway, what did you mean it wasn't Toady's party?"

"It was those two guys from Superior," Byron said softly.

"You mean Mr. Caen and that dreamy blond guy, Mark Justice?"

"That's them. And they were sure having one wild party. Also there were two other dudes, and four hot looking ladies. There was a lot of wild music and a lot of beer. And plenty of messing around."

Wick smiled and said with a leer, "When Thommy Jay and Toady showed up, things were getting pretty rad. Everyone was really making out."

Teri tsk-tsked, "You two are a couple of voyeurs!"

Wick laughed. "It was better than any show on T.V."

Byron said, "Yeah, and that's when the fight broke out. We heard Toady tell them to pipe down and stop making a mess on the beach.

That's when one of the big guys got up. I thought Toady was history."
He winked at Wick. "Didn't you?"

"Yea man," Wick agreed. "But that Toady can really fight. Man! He
used some wild martial-arts moves. The big guy crumpled. And when
that Mark guy threatened Toady, he got really angry. I've never seen
a cat move like that."

Byron punched his fists into the air. "And then those thugs were
going to jump him he kicked one in the groin and threw sand in the
other's face."

Wick laughed. "Even Thommy Jay got in a few shin-kicks; that's
when the women hauled the guys off, man they were all drunk and
swearing. We stuck around until it was just Toady and Thom. Then
they shouted at each other for a while, Thom left in a huff and that's
when we decided to cut out too."

"Did you hear what was said?"

"Oh, some of it, but we didn't want to get too close and be caught."

"Wow that must have been some scene. Do you know who those
other people were?"

Byron yawned. "I've seen the girls hanging around the snack bar at
the ferry landing, but the two guys, I don't know anything about
them. They looked pretty tough, though. They were wearing t-shirts
with the South Bay Resort logo on them. Maybe they work for that
Templeton's real-estate company." Byron smiled. "But I wasn't about
to ask them."

Wick laughed. "I've seen those guys in town. They're glued to their
motorbikes. At least I'm pretty sure it was them." He looked at Byron.
"Later, bike engines were revving up, but they sounded really far
away. Did you hear um?"

Byron shrugged. "People park their vehicles at the bottom of the
bluff by the road then walk in. Sound doesn't carry well from there."

"Tomorrows going to be a long day," Teri said then yawned. "I don't know about you two, but I'm going to get some shuteye."

"Sleeping Beauty has to get her zees," Byron teased.

Teri ignored him and got up. "From now on, when you men are off to the wars, I'm included, or I will put a bug in Mom's ear."

Byron shrugged again, "Okay okay. That's blackmail. I guess you got us where you want us... sis."

"Yeah, you drive a tough bargain," Wick held out his hand, "but let's shake on it."

The conspirators decided on an awkward three-musketeer's handshake (Byron's suggestion). Then brother and sister returned quietly to their rooms.

Wick leaned back on the headboard and crossed his hands behind his head.

"I've got this far," he said to the ceiling, and then grimaced. "I hope the brother and sister team don't get in the way." He yawned. "Things have been going pretty smoothly, though. But it'd be better if General Ujima and Suspicious Sister Kay were out of the way." He grimaced, punched the pillows hard and was instantly asleep.

## CHAPTER 31

# *Burn*

**After an hour's tinkering,** Toady assured them he would be 'Silent Sam' about what they were up to. He gave them the high sign and they took off, skirting through the back roads of Madrona. When they reached the Island highway, the two lane road was a smooth ribbon. At first it curved gently through a checkerboard of farmlands and orchards. But too soon it became narrow and precipitous; taking sharp twists that clung to the sides of a hair-raising cliff; no guardrails to obstruct the magnificent view. With its light fiberglass body and oversized rear-wheels, the dune buggy fairly flew over the road. Byron, at the wheel, was relaxed and smiling. As the wind blew through his hair he shouted that the bug was easy to steer and gripped the road most excellently. Wick, white-knuckling his side of the bug, wasn't so sure.

Teri was thrilled. The speed and the scent of the salt air furthered her excitement. She glanced sideways at Wick. He'd puzzled her ever since they'd left Madrona. At first he'd been giddy with chatter, but now he stared straight ahead. Ignoring any of her attempts at shouted conversation.

She turned away and watched the occasional house or garden whiz by on the opposite side of the road. She sighed to herself. Wick could be really obtuse and reticent. Although he was an enigma, she was steadily growing attached to him. Maybe he was worried about what lay ahead.

Byron glanced in the rear-view mirror. He, too, noted Wick's stony face. Byron's thoughts were similar to his sister's. He wondered at

Wick's loyalty to a friend, a friend whom Wick seemed to say little about. It was exemplary, yet strange that he would travel to a place he considered the 'wilds' of the United States, to trace this buddy. Byron shrugged, but Wick did have an impetuous nature. That'd explain some things, and he *was* a terrific generator of adventure. Byron's college friends definitely paled in comparison.

Teri suddenly shouted and pointed to the turn-off to Walsh point lighthouse, a place they had been enthusiastically planning to visit. She was disappointed when Wick didn't respond.

Without warning the car shot down a steep dip in the road. On the right was a lone sandy beach, rimmed with logs. It appeared then, just as quickly, disappeared as they shot up the opposite side of the road and back into the tree line. The dense woods temporarily eclipsed the sweep of shoreline and water. In the trees, the air was chillier and thick with the scent of fir.

Deprived temporarily of the view, Teri turned her thoughts back to the early morning when she and Byron visited Rose's office. At first they had been daunted by the questions Rose flung at them, but Byron wandered away and left Teri to deftly field Rose's questions about the daily goings on at the Petoskey farm.

After complementing Rose on her acute observations on island life and life in general, Teri soon began ferreting out the information *she* wanted. An effusive Rose said that Martin's newest gallery was an abandoned boathouse in the historical town of Burn. She smiled smugly when she told Teri it was she that'd sold him that building. Then Rose looked perplexed. Martin's old art shop, the one in Madrona, he'd bought through her nemesis, Templeton Real Estate. She felt Martin must have had some sort of deal with them as he was able to buy the rundown building 'dirt cheap'.

Martin confided in Rose that Janet didn't like the Madrona shop, but she was more than happy to help him remodel the place in Burn.

They planned to eventually live in the building, anyway. No. Wick Wilding's part in it had not even been mentioned.

But Rose did remember that Martin was particularly excited about an upstairs office-loft that he planned to expand. Teri also found out that Burn was a good forty minutes from Madrona.

As Rose talked she warmed to her story. She fascinated Teri when she launched into the history of the town of Burn. Even Byron, reading an old Vanity Fair magazine, wandered closer to hear.

"The story's not pretty." Rose said with a thin smile, then continued, "The original name of the town was Hope. At that time it was a thriving community. Most of the people were Chinese. You know, the lucky few who'd survived the building of the railroads; of course there where others too." She made a nervous sound in her throat. "Some were local Indians and settlers who had toughed out the deforestation of the island by the lumber barons. Together, the people of Hope had a vision of the future, a vision of planting and reclaiming this beautiful island. The old saying, 'When the tide is out the table is set', is literally true. And the ground around here is amazing, your mother already started her vegetable garden; she knows how rich the soil is. Plants grow at the drop of a seed. The new Islanders too had great plans, but they were not to be long-lived."

Rose went over to her desk and sat down. As Teri followed her, she noticed Byron leafing through a collection of pamphlets stacked on a table by the door. Teri was glad he wasn't boring them with endless questions, or his I-know-more-than-you-do attitude that he sometimes fell into.

Rose doodled on her desk pad as she continued her story. "As is typical of people, anger and jealousy arose among a few of the wealthy mainlanders. They wanted the farming and fishing holdings of their prosperous neighbors on Bradestone. They cited infringements on their commerce, and profits. The mainlanders had

278 | THE AMBER CROW

the ear of the local press. And enough influence to persuade the uninformed that Hope and its surrounds were a detriment to the mostly white communities. The nature of the newspaper articles were that with the different religions, unusual methods of farming and peculiar assortment of peoples, the southern part of the Island was becoming a nest of unnatural practices and lifestyles. Religious, racial and cultural prejudices were stirred up to justify the grab for Hope's markets and land. The driving farce behind all of this was the envy of the progress and financial success the people of Hope enjoyed."

Teri interrupted, "This sounds really lousy. I minored in social anthropology and the ethnocentrism of 'you're different than me, therefore no good' is mankind's basic nature."

Rose nodded. "That's a harsh judgment, but it gets backed up here. One night, several boatloads of angry Mainlanders and hired thugs, rowed over under the cover of darkness, and set fires in the trees and slash, that's the piles of brush and log debris left over from strip-logging. Later, the marauders said they only intended to harass and frighten the Islanders. But the fire spread and the surrounding became an inferno. Completely out of control, and with a strong northerly wind; the fires burned everything, right down to the beach line. The southern destruction of the island was complete. The few people that survived had nothing to come back to."

"That's sick!" Bryon exclaimed. "When did all this happen?"

"Sometime in the late eighteen hundreds," Rose said with a grim smile. "In the early forties after a town was built there, the site was renamed Burn, so people would never forget its past. The few locals, who had a conscience, persuaded the Island bigwigs to grudgingly put up a plaque to commemorate what happened there."

At once Teri decided to throw herself into reading about Burn and research the events behind it at. But that could keep till later. It was time to get directions to Burn and the location of Martin's boat dock.

CHAPTER 32

# *The Loft*

**Screeching brakes and spinning gravel** announced the buggy's stop in front of the boathouse. Rose said that the present day Burn was small. It was an understatement.

A dreary one-pump gas station and a lone grocery store with an Old-Western facade bordered by a few run-down houses were all that stood on Main Street.

The three jumped out of the car and gazed at what had to be Martin's gallery. It was on the opposite beach-bank side and about fifty yards down from the gas station. Rose mentioned that the building was part of the original boathouse that had survived the fire. The large structure stood on pilings near a slough that fed from South Bay.

The newly painted building stuck out like a galleon in full sail. It was painted dove-gray and trimmed in blue-black, and had the spare but flowing lines of a ship. Above the tall, double dock-doors a strong line of white-mullioned windows reflected the sunlight and on top of that the fake front sported a freshly painted sign in brass lettering: "Old Town Burn, Founded 1895" then below, in smaller letters, "From Hope that springs eternal".

Teri didn't say anything but felt the bitter-sweetness of the sentiment.

It was the first time, since they had started out, that Wick was upbeat. The building had been restored exactly the way he would have done. Particularly with the rear beams and their hoisting pulleys and rigging that looked like masts. That's of course, if he had the money. It was a testament to Martin's character. It demonstrated his flamboyant but passionate respect for preserving things of the past.

Teri and Byron glanced up and down Main Street. Had anyone taken notice of their noisy arrival? No. Their sole greeter was a golden-retriever. The dog happily thumped its tail as it watched from the gas station's door mat, but it didn't move from the shade. Further up the street, on the grocery store's leaning front porch, an elderly man in coveralls sat in an ancient rocking chair. Byron thought he was either asleep or dead as nothing moved.

No wonder. It was a sleepy, sunny morning in the town of Burn. The pungent, egg-odor of salt-marsh flats pervaded all. Two gulls screeched overhead as Wick quickly disappeared around the side of the building.

Teri and Byron peered into the soap-smeared front windows. It was impossible to discern anything. Since Wick had not returned from the back, they took one last look around and followed the dock that wrapped around the three sides of the boathouse.

The changing tide left a beach of brown mud and green algae. Occasionally, with a squirt of water a clam burrowed deeper in the ooze. In several places, foam burbled to the surface; marking the movement of things that moved beneath the mud. To the right and left, protruding from the muck, were rotted pilings; the burned, skeletal remnants of structures that once were. Mussels and barnacles clung to their sides. Teri thought they were perfect; accusing, ancient fingers pointing to the sky.

The overhead wheeling and squawking of gulls was interrupted by the argumentative cackle of two crows that settled onto the flats. One was jet black, the other shiny amber.

"Look!" Teri shouted as they caught up with Wick. "There's Edgar. He must know every nook and cranny on this island. Isn't he beautiful?" Edgar strutted up the beach, seemingly unaware of the effect his plumage had on admirers.

"Let's not stand here gawking at wild-life all day," Wick snorted. "Crap, look at these back windows. They're soaped up like the front ones, you can't see anything."

Byron chimed in, "Those humungous doors in front, and even the small ones on the side seem to be nailed shut. I tried them all when we walked back here, nothing budged."

Wick signaled them to lower their voices. "I'm going to try and open these double doors back here. They seem to move easier and are hidden from view."

Teri thought his skulking and secretive manner was silly, there wasn't a soul around. But Byron and Teri's eyes widened as Wick removed an assemblage of metal objects attached to a ring from his pocket. He grinned and informed them they were lock-picking tools.

"Geez Wick. I thought only locksmiths, police and criminals were allowed to use those." Byron said with partially veiled admiration.

Wick's grin was sinister. "You can buy anything in New York. Hah. I was a jewel thief in my other life. Now step aside and let a professional get to work. You two can be lookouts."

Keeping one eye on the road and the other on Wick, Teri and Byron watched with fascination as he skillfully manipulated the tools in the padlock. "This one here is a special type of rake," he whispered as he moved it gently back and forth. He worked something else beside it. There was a solid click.

"Ah, this baby was easy." He stood back, doffed an imaginary hat and bowed. "Sir Byron and Lady Teri may now enter at their leisure."

An incredible cacophony sprang up. "Shit!" Wick exclaimed and flattened himself against the door. Startled, Teri and Byron swung around. Three crows stood on the dock's railing; led by Edgar, they raised wholly hell. With wings spread and forward thrusting necks they cawed raucous warnings at the interlopers.

"What the Hell? Wick growled, red-faced. "The last time I saw those jerks they were on the beach. What are they playing at? They've seen us before."

Teri grabbed Wick's arm. "They're trying to tell us something. Willie said that Edgar has a sixth sense... about things."

"Yeah, that he usually knows when there's a handout about," Byron said nervously.

"Shoo, get away!" Wick yelled and waved his hands at them. "Cripes, They remind me of the witches from Macbeth, all they need is a cauldron."

The two black crows flew off immediately, but Edgar stood his ground. His caw changed to a soft call with a clicking at the end.

Byron smiled but pointed a shaking finger. "I'm getting spooked. He's looking right at me."

"Here," Teri said and reached into her shirt pocket. "Here Edgar, I've got treats for you." She threw several small biscuits in the air; they landed on the beach below. When the other two crows dove toward the food Edgar took one last baleful look at Byron and plummeted down to the mud. Squawking and then scattering his friends, he managed to fly away with most of the morsels.

"Whew," Wick said in a shaky voice. "I thought they'd raise everyone in the neighborhood."

"It's like snooze-ville here, I don't think we have to worry," Terry whispered.

Byron shrugged his shoulders. "Sis is right and anyway, Mom and Teri always carry kibble in their pockets for Edgar. That's how they train him, right sis?"

"I disagree brother, mine. Edgar is as smart as any human. He'll only train to do something if he wants to."

"Hey, thanks Teri, I was getting ready to throw a rock at them," Wick frowned, "let's get inside before someone sees us. Hurry Byron, help me drag the door back then shut behind us, it's gonna be a real dog."

At first, the interior of the large boathouse seemed empty. But when their eyes adjusted to the gloom they could make out stacks of packing crates against the right wall. The smeared, tightly shut windows trapped in a stifling dusty smell. It made the air thick and fowl.

Teri shivered; though the temperature was easily over eighty outside, in this cavernous space, she had goose-bumps.

The gallery project was an immense undertaking. Teri's eyes traced the forms of the ancient beamed trusses above them. A stage was being assembled near where they stood. But the interior remodeling had a long way to go before any 'grand opening'. Teri wondered why someone wasn't working on it now. It was weird that Martin and Janet had rushed off to Europe and left the project they were so passionate about, unfinished.

Wick walked over to one of the crates. He tried to pry a lid off with a hammer he'd found on the floor, and shook his head. "How could Martin expect to make any money out here in the boonies? Tourists will never come this far south." He looked exasperated. "We're totally in the wilderness." He attacked another crate.

"I beg to differ sir." Byron's voice came from above them. He stood on a flight of stairs that led up to the window-enclosed office at the front of the building. Gripping the wooden railing he managed to appear taller. Teri groaned, she could see he was in one of his lecturing modes.

Byron took a well-crumpled brochure from his jeans pocket. "Ahem. According to my research, the South Bay environs are home to, and I'm quoting here: 'A Budding Art-colony'. Not to mention a

Yuppie-haven (my own words) called 'Gull Crossing'. 'An Exclusive and Charming,' he paused, studied the pictures further, "they look like rabbit hutches to me; 'State-of-the-Art condominiums, courtesy of Templeton Enterprises'. It goes on to say: 'A Premier Gated Community on Bradestone Island, eventually supporting a friendly boating and leisure community of five thousand'. " He continued, "'The Gull owners are able to access their spacious units by tranquil Blackbird slew and its adjacent canals'." Byron interjected again, "What a lot of hooey. I can smell the rotten egg-gas already. It says that a private golf course is to come later. It also says that Gull Condos is the home of the South Bay Marina; another 'Superior Exclusive'. Etc. etc., 'We have an Aggressive Emergency and Security System' "Whatever that is. And..."

Wick slammed his hammer down. "Where did you get all that crap?"

Byron was taken aback, but only slightly. "These are brochures from Rose's office. While Teri and Rose were schmoozing over Martin and his art work; I was being the dutiful detective." He wagged the leaflets above his head like a fan.

Wick nodded. "That figures. Martin is always clever at sniffing out where the bucks are. But the funny thing is; he doesn't need to work. His family's got beaucoup bucks."

Byron smirked and continued up the stairs to the office. "Let me remind you, I'm plenty useful at times. I got the buggy running with just a little help from Toady and Barney. And I picked up some vital information. And..." he continued as he jumped to the next stair, "I can leap over small buildings in a single bound."

"Be careful." Teri called up anxiously. "Those stairs don't look very sturdy and there's nothing up there to see anyway."

He was already at the front of the loft office and peering into the mullioned glass of the door window. Teri was right, there was nothing to see. Hah, she complained of the musty odor down there. Teri should smell it up here close to the ceiling.

He tried the locked door. It wouldn't open. He swiped off some of the soap-smeared window. No. There *was* something there. Through the cleaned patch of window, he could make out a small table with a bottle and what looked like two wine glasses sitting on top. Everything was covered with dust. Next to the table was an oak swivel chair and then...beyond that.

He blew on the cleared spot and rubbed harder. Outside sunlight filtered through the hazy panes. It was difficult to focus. Byron cupped his hands around his eyes and squinted.

There was something dark in the corner. It looked like a lump piled in another swivel chair. He blinked his eyes. The shape had a black coat draped over it. Then Byron could make out bony hands, white and twisted. They rested on the table.

The blood quickly drained from Byron's face as he turned away. His breathing was shallow. Far away, he could see upturned faces, their expressions fuzzy.

"What, what's happening?" Wick's voice croaked below.

"You all right?" Teri asked anxiously.

It was terribly hot near the room's ceiling. Byron closed his eyes and took hold of the rail. He swallowed and gripped harder. He could hardly hear them below. White tennis balls were moving up and down against a black background in his vision. He blinked, they didn't go away.

"Uh... uh... call 911... but, but, it won't do any good," his voice faded into a mumble and he crumpled against the railing.

CHAPTER 35

# *Questions*

**Ujima growled** and tossed the sheaf of papers on her desk. The interview with Toady had not gone well. Not well at all. He'd ended up shouting at her. She hadn't done much better. Her words were short, her voice harsh, and her questions dripped with acid. She wiped her brow. It was hell interviewing your friends, triple hell when they were murder suspects.

Although Toady had left an hour ago, Ujima was still tense. She took a deep breath, closed her eyes halfway and inhaled again, this time it was measured and she watched her breath. It was the yoga breath that Kay had taught her. She breathed in to the count of four, held it for two counts then exhaled slowly to the count of eight. After six reps, her mind drifted back to her surroundings.

Ujima grimaced as she pictured Wick Wilding, cooling his heels in the tiny room outside. This interview wasn't going to be easier either.

Wick had insisted he was Martin's best friend. But, a week ago, Martin's parents said not possible. They brushed off the name Wick Wilding. It belonged to some obscure acquaintance that Martin had mentioned in passing. They stated that, to their knowledge, he was *never* a friend of their son. They added that it was suspicious that said person, 'who they had heard from others, was a scam-artist, notoriously unreliable, and whose financial resources were dubious at best. And it was strange that such a person, would at considerable expense to himself, travel all the way from Upstate New York to the Island of Bradestone, wherever it was'. They further claimed that they had never heard of any 'art gallery scheme'. They were aware of a

Miss Janet Holmes, but only in the capacity as one of Martin's usual retinue of female followers. It was not long before they said they could offer no further help and had 'more important matters' to attend to and terminated the call.

Ujima found it was amazing that they showed so little interest in their son's welfare. They had effectively squashed her suggestion of placing a missing person's bulletin regarding him. She also found it interesting that for Wick being Martin's 'obscure acquaintance' the parents had an in depth litany of Wick's faults. Well. They were in for the ultimate reality check today. They soon would receive the notification, by the New York State police, of their son's murder. Then Ujima knew that doors would start flying open. She would have to move discretely as they were wealthy and could cause trouble.

But what bothered Ujima more was that Wick broke into that gallery in Burn and was the first to discover the whereabouts of Martin. Had he already known the body was there? And did Wick conveniently drag Byron and Teri into the middle of the mess as witnesses?

She organized the papers on her desk, tapped them straight and placed them in a manila folder for later filing. She willed her shoulders to relax and massaged the back of her neck. In the first interviews, Wick appeared to be genuinely upset over finding Martin's body. Still, there was something he was holding back, something she had not been able to shake out of him the day before. It was natural that during the interviews with Byron and Teri they'd been quite defensive and it was unfortunate that Byron had suffered the worst of the situation.

The other thing that annoyed her was the skill with which Wick had wormed his way into Kay's family. Granted he appeared to be a personable young fellow. He had all the gifts of a Good Samaritan, but these were also the gifts of a good con-man, and a clever murderer. But there was something else... he reminded her of someone, someone she recently had seen on the island, but the person and situation eluded her. Or it might have been a face she had seen in a police file. The problem niggled at her and she rubbed her eyes.

The other day he certainly had become obstinate and defensive. She got up, shoved her chair back and walked to the door. Maybe she could get under his skin a little more.

Outside the office, Wick coughed in rapid succession. Damn! He always did this when he was nervous. What was the matter with Sergeant Washington? From the first time he met her, she had something against him. She'd grilled him over the coals twice before, and here she'd called him in again.

When she beckoned from the door she didn't even look at him. It made him feel like garbage. His lanky body slumped into the chair that she pointed to. He tried to clear his throat. Did she suspect him of murdering Martin and Janet? He told her they had all been tight for Christ's sakes! He had an alibi. He'd been in Upstate New York, when Janet was killed, and he had witnesses when they'd found Martin's body. How did she think he knocked them off, murder by telekinesis?

True. The police in New York wouldn't have anything good to say about his record. What did it matter? He knew there was no way anyone could determine the exact time of Martin's death, or for that matter, Janet's. Besides, his friends were a nomadic bunch, they were true artists. And another thing, they didn't weasel on each other and they didn't keep tabs on everyone's coming and goings.

Yesterday he'd said he didn't know how long he would be on Bradestone. He told her, due to financial reasons; he couldn't be away too long from his gig in Upstate New York. Hah, what gig? No, he'd stay just until he found what he was looking for and then nada. What did she know anyway? He could disguise himself easily if he wanted to. He might just get a theatre job on the mainland and fade in.

Wouldn't that be a ripper, just to spite her? He snorted aloud. Anyone could disappear completely in this wilderness. And he was used to living by the seat of his pants anyway and probably would, the rest of his life.

He smiled nervously. He'd almost had a cow when his dipso uncle had shipped his trunk to him. The drunk just wanted to get rid of him and everything he possessed. Damn what a millstone he had now. Of-course Ujima insisted he go through it with her. Luckily he hadn't hidden anything in it. But it still felt like he was going through a prison inspection. She'd made him take all his clothes, art materials and puppets out and spread them on a counter. He snorted to himself. What did she think? He was hiding an Uzi up their skirts? He'd hoped he could get her on his side and convince her to help him. But man, that was not going to happen.

God, why was she looking at him that way? They'd said they found Martin's car; what was in it, something incriminating, his files maybe? She was driving him crazy.

Ujima took her time and made final touches to the desktop. Good. Let him sweat. He'd be more liable to make mistakes, say more than he intended. She turned her back to him and sharpened her four pencils slowly; carefully inspecting each tip. Then she leaned over and flipped a toggle on the recorder. Mechanically she read the day, date, time and subject into the machine. Finally she looked directly at him.

Ujima recalled the first time she had met Wick at Kay's. She had been impressed. He was clean, polite and intelligent. She'd particularly enjoyed his entertaining the family with his mastery of ventriloquism, his ingenious on the spot creativity, and amazing voice alterations. But, as the evening wore on, she had the impression he was too glib, too self-consciously honest, too subservient. It annoyed her that Teri was instantly taken by him. Unlike her daughter, Kay was more observant. Ujima appreciated Kay's circumspect treatment of Wick and her questioning attitude. After all, if you summed him up, he was the consummate actor. Even now he appeared relaxed, and regarded her with a sham, innocent look.

She'd fix that. Ujima's eyes bored into his.

He could see gold flecks that flashed, almost like a tiger's eye. Inside, Wick fought to retain any shreds of bravado that he had when he first entered the room.

"State your name, age and other vital statistics. Speak slowly and clearly. I'm starting the interview now."

Jeez. She wasn't kidding! She was dragging him through it all again. He couldn't help it; he had to cough to clear his dry throat. He tried to hide his shaking hands and leaned forward to talk into the machine.

Ujima shook her head. "Mr. Wilding, it's not necessary to be that close. Just sit back. Relax, and be comfortable while you talk." She tapped a pencil against her teeth. "This little baby can pick up the noise of a pin hitting the floor a mile away. It detects even the slightest catch or waver in your voice."

Relax! Was she losing her mind? He ahem'd three times while Ujima scribbled fast notes on her tablet; what could she be writing down? He hadn't said a thing.

"Now... I want to go over this again. We missed something yesterday. Start with your relationship with Janet?"

He coughed then blurted out, "I told you before. It wasn't a relationship, exactly." He paused and fished a handkerchief out of his pocket, "Well, it was in a way... she was a friend. We graduated together from The Amos Toller School of Fine Arts in New York." He cleared his throat, "we saw each other only... occasionally. But we, we wrote to each other." He covered his mouth and coughed. "She was into stage acting, went for the drama end entirely and really, she was Martin's serious girlfriend... not mine."

"What do you mean by, 'serious girlfriend'? There were others?"

Holy crap, this was awful. He coughed again and cleared his throat. This time he pulled out his lucky, blue kerchief to wipe the sweat off his brow and quickly stuffed it back in his pocket.

He stammered, "No, not exactly. I didn't keep track of his love life... but *she*, she said she was his serious girlfriend."

Wick was tense. How should he phrase this? Fortunately the phone rang. A sweating Wick Wilding took his handkerchief out again and quickly blotted his nose and mouth.

Ujima held up her hand, spoke into the recorder then flicked it off. She picked up the receiver, turned her back to him, and spoke in hushed tones. Wick closed his eyes and attempted to settle back in the chair, it was metal and cold. He wondered vaguely if he would be allowed to use the bathroom.

In one terse gesture, Ujima put a hand over the receiver, swiveled around and turned a steely gaze on him.

"You might be interested in this phone call, Mr. Wilding. It's from New York. From one of the detectives, who's working for us. This morning he informed me that the notification of Martin's death moved his parents close to hysteria." She paused and looked at her note pad. "But it seems by now, which is evening back there, they have just gone ballistic."

"Why? What's happened, what's different?" He tried to sound casual, but his smile was sickly. What had they found? Had they found the papers?

"Their lawyer has just finished with them. It seems that Martin changed his will several months back."

"So? What's this got to do with me?"

At this point Ujima spoke into the phone again. Then he heard her say: "Okay. When? Thank you. You've been very helpful. Yes, goodbye," she said and replaced the receiver. She made a few more notes on her pad then looked up.

"According to their lawyer in New York, Martin Gray Junior's Will is legal and binding." She paused; her smile was cynical and held a question. "It's an unusual and interesting document; evidently the sole beneficiary of the Will is a Mr. Wick Wilding." Ujima leaned forward on her elbows and clasped her hands. Her eyes, like those of a hawk held him in their golden stare. "It seems you've become one, extremely wealthy young man."

The room was filled with silence.

"When did you first become aware of his wishes?"

Two hours later Wick was urgently shaking Byron's shoulder. "Remember plan B?"

Byron said groggily, "Yeah, what's up?"

"It's in effect, as of now. Grab your gear, let's get the boat and vacate, ASAP."

"Why, what's happened?"

Wick turned on his heel. "I'm going to load the dune buggy, no more questions. I'll tell you later. It's all coming down."

"Should I tell Teri?"

"No!" Wick turned with a snarl. "She'll just ask a lot of dumb questions. Just do it! We meet outside in five minutes."

Byron found his shorts and sandals, dumped things into his backpack and took the stairs, two at a time.

## CHAPTER 36

# *Confidant*

Ujima **opened the folder** marked 'Templeton' and placed it in the middle of her desk. "Kay, what I'm going to say must go no further than", she pointed, "that door, agreed?"

As Ujima tapped the file with her pencil, Kay scooted closer. "Sure."

"Thanks," Ujima said then grimaced, "We've been thrown together into this maddening murder case by proximity; and worse your family's involvement has increased exponentially." She fingered the folder. "Most of the involvement was of course unintentional and some wasn't; and right now I need to bounce ideas off a person who is not only familiar with the current imbroglio, but whom I can trust and has been thinking a lot about it… in short, you," she said and smiled lopsidedly, "I considered Officer Reynolds, but he's a novice, very new very green and very conventional. I need someone who can think outside of the squad car. Currently I'm keeping him in the loop, but I don't want any loose cannons running about, just yet. "

"Well, I'm your man," Kay said feeling a little silly but extremely excited.

Ujima leaned back in her chair. "The department on the mainland has tossed this case entirely in my lap. Since I've been in situ since the beginning, and so far they approve of the way I'm running the show. Typically the overlords want it solved, yesterday." She rolled her eyes to the ceiling. "I've been patted on the head and told it's time to get my sea legs. But, I want to emphasize that I can depend upon Officer Reynolds for most anything and again I must stress I don't want you playing at Nancy Drew." She leaned her elbows on the desk, "But it seems that when we girls get our heads together…"

Kay relaxed. "Of course, I like to help anyway I can. And it's true, I've been very worried about Alex and the kids and I want to know the whys of how's of what fates sucked us into this."

"Good," Ujima said as she took several pages out of the folder. "I'm going to share this with you. Most is available to the public, or soon will be. And please, feel free to make any contributions or…," she eyed Kay carefully, "share certain things that may seem trivial, or for one reason or another you thought not worth mentioning," she said and pursed her lips, "as you have on certain occasions."

Kay squirmed in her chair. "I'll do my best."

"First, this report was faxed to me from the Idaho State Patrol. The weapon used to kill Templeton was a hydraulic carjack. Surprisingly, it was located in the vicinity of Martin's vehicle

"Templeton's, not Martin's! In Idaho? How do you know it's that weapon that killed him?"

"The blood analysis and hair samples match exactly. Besides, as you now know, Martin was poisoned." She paused. "The jack was found a considerable distance from the car, wrapped in what is evidently Martin's clothes and stuffed in an old suitcase. Scraps of blue silk material were also found on the weapon. They may be evidence of an attempt to wipe the jack clean."

"You're sure about all this?"

"Yes, forensics confirms it."

"Blue silk? Not like the handkerchief that I took from Toady?"

"Unfortunately, it's very much the same. But, he claims he doesn't like or use silk handkerchiefs, only organic cotton. However, he vaguely remembers a gift of these from a friend a few years back. But, he said he rids himself of unwanted gifts by donating them to charity."

Kay thought of the handkerchief on the beach and said, "It is possible that it was someone else's."

"Yes, but who could that someone be; and did they drive the car to Idaho with the jack to get rid of or destroy the evidence? That doesn't seem likely at all."

"Obviously Martin's car was taken there because it was a remote place and wouldn't be found. The murderer must have placed the weapon back in the car. And the person driving the car wasn't aware of it. Or Martin was the murderer, or... wouldn't Idaho be way off any route the couple planned to take to New York?"

"Actually no, Janet left a travel itinerary with Sabra. And it mentions stopping at a mutual friend of theirs who lives only a few miles from where the car was found."

"Ah, so there's your major suspect."

"I thought so too. But, the friend is in her seventies, a well-known ceramic artist and has had a long bout recuperating from pneumonia in a local recovery center."

"Talk about a literal dead end."

"There is the slim possibility that they could have run afoul of highway thieves, if for some reason they had to abandon the car."

"This is getting messy."

"The police say the car was stripped, before it was set on fire. And the burn site is close to off-road cyclist trails for the locals. Also luggage and related contents were scattered 'over a country mile'. A direct quote from the Idaho police statement."

"So they could've run into a nasty group of survivalists, or back roaders."

"Those are possibilities; then there might have been looters after the car was abandoned." Ujima said.

Kay frowned. "Hmm, maybe, for reasons unknown, Martin killed Templeton. Janet found out and then he killed her; possibly transported her body in the car to the barn. You said she wasn't killed there. Too, he could have had an accomplice, someone to take the car to an obscure place, burn it and destroy evidence. Kay looked puzzled. "But then, who killed Martin... the accomplice? And who gave Sabra the tip about the barn? Whoever it was knew about Janet's murder in order to send Sabra that note. I'm sure it wasn't a Good Samaritan. Maybe one of those supposed accomplices of Martin's decided to take him out. Could there have been blackmail involved?"

"At the moment I don't think Martin or Janet ever left the Island."

"Well then maybe..."

"Hold it, hold on, one speculation at a time. I said Officer Reynolds could be a loose cannon. Your mind is a gerbil wheel running at full tilt. And you're omitting the evidence from Toady's boat and the attempt on our lives."

"I know Toady is your primary suspect, but he doesn't seem capable and he says he loved Janet...and whatever is the case there seems to be other persons involved, someone we're not considering and..."

"If you're thinking of Templeton's dynamic duo, Caen and Mark, I've interviewed them twice already. Not only do they have sound alibis for the probable times of the murders they are in a panic trying to keep Templeton enterprises afloat, i.e. minimizing the fallout from the press *and* keeping shareholders happy. Ironically it was Janet who seemed to know the intricacies of Templeton's operations and plans. Caen and Mark are running around like chickens sans heads. I hate to have to agree with Elanor Lavin, but they appear to have learned little about the business. It is amazing that he kept them employed and let a temp like Janet hold them and it together."

"Well, what about the lovely Elanor?"

"She is a control freak and not a pleasant one... that's true. And she is more interested in being seen at Seattle's upper echelon social functions, gallery premieres, operas etc. Templeton's death, from all indications, will augment her own fortunes substantially, but at present she seems angrier than anything."

"Humph, not too unusual. Anger is the first stage of grief, they say."

"Her brother was her top preference for his knowledge and use as arm candy at events."

Ujima twiddled her pencil. "Don't think, from what I've said, that I'm ignoring anyone as a possibility. But I have to be careful in making the right connections in solving this case. And Toady is not my lone suspect. Actually your house guest, Wick Wilding, benefits admirably from Martin's death. And he so conveniently and recently dropped into view. We're still tracking his whereabouts before he got here. So far all we've turned up is the date he left NYC. As to where he was and what he was doing prior to these murders we have nada." Ujima paused. "I can see by your face you've already heard about the inheritance."

Kay nodded. "Yesterday evening. I had a call for Wick. It was from a law office in New York. I gleaned from the rather circuitous conversation that he had come into money of some sort. They called again this morning, but I couldn't find Wick anywhere. Teri was no help, she has her nose out of joint and said she hasn't seen him or Byron since yesterday and doesn't care where they are. Byron did leave a note about going camping for a couple of days, but he was his usual vague self. They took the dune buggy and it appears that they're camping and fishing, just to get away. Finding Martin's body was a real shock to both of them."

"My, I didn't think our city-slicker would know one end of a fishing pole from the other," Ujima said growling then tapped the desk. "The first thing I want you to do when you get home is find out where the boys are, and if Teri knows anything. She's a lady, much like her mother. Keeps her ears to the ground and pretty much knows what's afoot. Call me as soon as you have any information."

"I'll do that …er, is there anything else I should know about?"

"I'm not sure, but there's a lot Wick has not told me about his coming here and specifically how he was involved financially with Martin," she paused, "it's important that both Wick and Byron be on the spot for immediate consultation when necessary. I don't want them any deeper in this than they already are. We still have a vicious killer or killers on the loose."

"Then you don't think Wick is the killer?"

Ujima looked exasperated. "I'm not saying he is or isn't, but he is hiding something and behaves suspiciously, we need to be wary and alert."

"But it hardly seems that Wick... anyway, let's get back to the murder weapon. How heavy is that jack? I mean could a woman have used it? And does the jack belong to the car? And was it used to kill Janet too? Were there any prints?"

"Whoa! I'll answer the questions that I can, but not so fast. The jack weighs over five pounds and yes; it could've been used by a woman. As to the jack's ownership, we're checking now. And it is not the standard jack that came with Martin's car," she made a wry face, "it's definitely a heavy duty hydraulic type. Barney's garage sells them. Toady said he bought one from Barney to do work on the cars in his own carport. Toady said he hasn't used it recently. Usually stores it in the work bench. But he'd search for it and tell us when he locates it. And yes, he doesn't know why we were looking for it."

Ujima extracted a small plastic bag from the folder. "Now, this earring you found at Willie's cabin, Toady says it's not his, nor his style. But he was pretty shook up when I showed it to him. He's lying about something, if not everything."

Kay poked the earring. "I think he's telling the truth. His ears are pierced. This is an ear-cuff." She laughed. "Usually worn by fakers who want to pretend they're walking on the wild side."

Ujima smiled. "My, my, we are knowledgeable." She smiled. "And our Toady doesn't need to fake that."

"No." Kay said quietly, "But I'm sure it belongs to the person that vandalized Willie's cabin."

"Why so?"

"It was lying among the debris. Of course it might have been one of Edgar's treasures, but he usually takes shiny items to his cage. And if it were a plant it would have been on top.

Ujima nodded her head. "Okay, I'll take note of that." She removed a photograph from the folder and tapped it with her pencil. "But know I've got something more serious to share. Maybe you can help me with this too. It's about Wicks involvement in this. I didn't want to unsettle you since he is your guest."

Kay grimaced and prepared for the worst.

CHAPTER 37

# *Snapshots*

"**Gad!** You've already implied Wick's a multiple killer and living in my house. Could there be anything worse?" Kay attempted a smile, but it faded at the look on Ujima's face.

"At first I thought Wick was giving me some cock-and-bull story about a job that Martin was doing for him. But now I'm not so sure."

"A job, what kind of a job?"

"Wick said that one of Martin's hobbies was genealogy, and he was tracing Wick's parentage for him."

"That rings fairly true. I remember Wick said he was brought up by an uncle after his mother died. He never knew his father. And his uncle is some sort of a crank. I know that much."

Ujima nodded. "Wick's mother died of cancer when he was about eight years old. Evidently Wick's uncle had to care for him but wanted little to do with him. And his uncle is not a crank, but a drunk."

Wick was interested in who his father was as evidently the mother never married. He got what little he could out of his uncle and gave it to Martin. Martin traced the father to Oregon. Martin told Wick that he possessed papers and addresses that concerned the last ten years of Wick's father's life. Of course he was going to let Wick have them, but not for money. He wanted Wick to exchange work for his extensive research."

"What kind of work?"

Ujima shrugged. "Evidently, Martin intended to use Wick's considerable artistic and creative abilities in stagecraft, carpentry and puppetry at the new art gallery; this is of course according to Wick. Wick also said he was going to be used as a chauffeur and general dog's body on the so called honeymoon trip to Europe after the pair got to New York. At least that's his story."

"Have you checked this with the inebriated Uncle?"

"Oh yes. But he isn't cooperative and glad to be rid of the boy, 'nothing but a trouble maker'; he said he was overjoyed when he cleared out. Evidently the feeling is mutual. Wick took odd jobs, and according to past academic records was able to work his way through high school and college. His achievements are pretty impressive. Luckily, he had a free apartment when he was going to school," Ujima nodded, "that's true, he was the building's custodian and maintenance man." She paused then looked at Kay oddly. "However, Wick's uncle was considerate enough to send a package of some photos. I think you may want to see this one."

Kay swallowed. "Why? What have you got there?"

Ujima pushed it across the desk with her pencil.

A woman in a bathing suit smiled back. She was young and pretty. In the background, a slender young man leaned casually against a boat hull. His arms were crossed over a muscular chest and curly locks of hair hung down the sides of his smiling face.

Kay felt a twinge in her stomach. The girl and the boat looked familiar. "Who's this?"

"Look on the back."

In tiny, cramped, writing were the words: Wick's mother, New York. Age twenty? 1977?

Kay turned the photo over and studied the front. "It looks like Wick leaning against the boat. But it couldn't be. He's only twenty, now, isn't he?"

Ujima regarded Kay closely. "About, he turned twenty-one this January. But I wasn't thinking of Wick. I thought... I thought he looks much more like a younger...a younger Alex."

Kay's eyes closed. The chair seemed to move. She opened her eyes and looked again. "But the nose and, and the hair."

Ujima pursed her lips. "Didn't you tell me that Alex got his nose broken when he was in the Army? And if you cover up that hair with this piece of paper."

Kay recoiled and dropped the photo on the desk. A snake had bit her. "But, if this is Alex!" In her thudding heart she knew it was. She recognized the girl. She was the same girl in his photo album. The one called 'Emily'. And that was the small sailboat named the 'Fanny Dunker'.

Kay was in a trance. She remembered after they'd moved in together she found the album stashed away in a box of books. In the evening, over wine and dessert, he said the woman had been older than him and turned him down and 'that was that'. She knew he was silent about the other women in his life. But this relationship had soured him and he decided to never marry...until he'd met Kay.

Kay blinked. "Alex never claimed he was a monk when he was young. He made a point to tell me he'd led a pretty wild life. But I know he wouldn't lie to me. He said he never married and he would have told me if...if he had a son."

Ujima spread her hands. "That's assuming he knew he had one." She leaned forward. "Kay. What do you really know about Alex's past?" She toyed with the photo. "And how did you wind up on Bradestone in the first place. Was it Alex's idea?"

Kay stood up. She was shaking. "Ujima, I realize that everyone connected to this murder investigation is a possible suspect. But this, this is going too far, and, and I know Alex. As to this photo..." Her eyes were beginning to blur.

"I'm sorry Kay. But I thought it was important you should know." Ujima stood up. "I'm trying to solve these murders. And people aren't telling me everything. In fact they're telling me very little. And some are lying. And when that happens, everyone's toes get stepped on."

Kay was at the door. She stumbled into the outer hall then headed for the outside. Ujima was right behind her.

"I, I don't want to talk about this now. It's too much," Kay blurted out.

As Kay opened her car door, she attempted to calm herself. She tried to think, to sort things into some logical order. If it was true and he didn't know, Alex would have to be told, and Wick also. It had to be a strong resemblance. But hadn't she noticed it? Hadn't it been in the back of her mind all along? Even Teri remarked on how odd it was and the similarity in their actions.

Ujima tapped on the driver's-side window. "Are you going to be all right?" She paused, "Call me when you get home. I've got to know Wick's whereabouts."

Kay nodded numbly then slumped behind the wheel. She felt her world beginning to separate. But she had to find out. She started the car.

When would be the right time to confront Wick? He was so touchy, like a young colt. She angrily wiped tears from her eyes as she steered out of the parking lot. And she knew Alex. It would stun him. But it should be his place to tell Wick, not hers. She yanked the wheel to the left. Maybe it was all a mistake. Her thoughts raced as she pushed the throttle down. But damn it, there was the photo of that girl and the boat! Kay ground her teeth. All she needed was two hysterical males on her hands. She was hysterical enough right now, thank you.

*CHAPTER 38*

# *Bad Connections*

**Alex couldn't concentrate on the book** Kay had given him for his birthday. It wasn't the topics: Virtual Time Warps, Dark Matter and Black Holes. Those ideas intrigued him. But it was the real black hole that Wick and Byron had dropped into that plagued him; it hadn't been too soon after Ujima put the pressure on Wick that they'd vanished.

Alex closed his eyes and recalled his best friend, Roland Shakleford. They'd pulled many a disappearing act too, when they were young and foolish. He smiled and wondered if Roland would be up to the same shenanigans now that they were old and foolish. There was one incident in particular that he recalled with relish. It was at a big dig in Sicily where novice graduate archaeologists and any live body with two good hands, who knew one end of the shovel from the other, were eagerly sought. Small artifacts had gone missing. Both thought they might have to make tracks to Brindisi. Luckily, in the end, the stolen items had been recovered. Alex and Roland exonerated and certain ladies were forgiven for their involvement with 'professional site thieves' in the nearby town.

Alex drifted from reminiscing and focused on the present. Of course, Kay had shifted into her search and rescue mode. She was in Madrona, at Thommy Jay's Antiques, one of the main rumor nodes in the island's pipeline. Oddly, Kay hadn't gone to Rose, another main node in the line. For some reason there was friction between those two, but what it was Alex couldn't fathom.

Teri, the other part of what he and Kay dubbed 'the terrible trio', hadn't been included in the boy's escape. When questioned, she'd snarled something about 'macho men' and stomped off to her room. Alex chuckled. In a remarkably short time she placed an epistle on her door, it read, among other things: 'And Do Not Disturb, unless Godzilla is on the loose, or the house on fire.'

The phone rang. Alex quickly put his book face down, a habit Kay loudly objected to, and barefooted it out to the hall. Maybe it was the guys. They probably needed money, or gas. Well, he'd play the hard-nose. They'd be the brunt of his best drill-sergeant voice.

"Yes?" There was a clicking noise at the other end. His clipped question fell into a hollow silence. "Speak up. I can't hear you." Something made a whisking sound on the other end; followed by a muffled voice.

"Hello Alex?" The voice was low and hesitant. "It's me, Ujima; don't put Kay on. I want to speak to you, privately." The statement ended in a familiar hollow laugh.

"Ujima? What a miserable connection! Sounds like you're speaking from the bottom of a barrel."

"I'm calling from Seattle, on my new cell, that's part of the problem." There was coughing at the other end. "I also have a wretched cold. I'll try to speak louder. Is that better?" She sneezed.

"Nah, but don't strain yourself. Everything's coming in loud and clear," he lied then asked: "What's up? Did you finally corner the two desperadoes?"

The phone crackled, "Who? What, desperadoes?"

"You know. Kay talked to you this morning. Wick and Byron still haven't shown up."

"Oh that bunch. We've located where they are," her voice rasped. "And I'm glad they've the sense to stay out of trouble. But this, this is far more important. Something has come up on Bradestone and it's urgent. I'm going to have to rely on you."

Alex was immediately at attention. "Okay, shoot."

"It concerns Raymond Toda. I have information that has to be checked out this evening. And for some strange reason I can't raise Officer Reynolds."

Alex laughed. "If he's living up to his reputation, he's probably off the road for a snooze. But, if I can help."

"You can," the voice crackled. "One of my informants says that Raymond Toda has been holding out on us. It appears that Mr. Toda knows the names of the person or persons who killed Janet Holmes, Martin Gray and Eric Templeton. From what my source tells me, the names and facts are all there on Raymond's hard drive. And there may also be a backup disc. I want you to find those discs for me."

Alex snorted. "If he's involved, why would he keep a record of anything incriminating? Not smart."

"It would appear so, at first." The phone was silent for a moment. "Hubris, perhaps but my guess is he's intending to use the material for blackmail. It will put him in grave danger."

Alex considered. "Isn't this a bit unorthodox? Why don't you just get a search warrant?"

"As I mentioned before, that takes time, and it's time we don't have." Her voice was tinged with impatience. "Our Mr. Toda left for the mainland late this afternoon. I'm tailing him here, in Seattle. I don't want to lose him. My hunch is that he's getting ready to go into hiding; he has many friends and can carry out his blackmail scheme from the mainland. As soon as you find the evidence, we can make an arrest, and nail the murderer."

Alex swallowed hard. "Well. What do you want me to do?"

"Go to Raymond's house. Find those discs and download anything you find pertinent." There was a long pause. "He does have a fax machine, if you know how to use it I'll take it from there. His password is: Toady2Todasaucy."

"But, isn't there the minor matter of breaking and entering? And if I'm caught..."

"Don't concern yourself with legal aspects. I'm temporarily deputizing you. It's an emergency and I'm taking care of it from this end. Of benefit to you is that Raymond doesn't lock his doors and has no alarm system. Call me as soon as you retrieve the data. Here's my number." Alex hastily grabbed a pen and copied it down.

The crackle became louder. "Look. You may not find anything. He could have hidden it elsewhere. But if you do, it will greatly assist us in wrapping things up, and quickly. And wear latex gloves."

"Should I....?" Alex managed to blurt out before he heard a click at the other end. He slammed the receiver down. "Damn!" Alex exclaimed aloud. "Bungling Bell's at its best."

He rubbed his chin. What Ujima was asking him to do wouldn't be too difficult; no one was home and he'd seen where the computer center was located, it was no big deal. But he fussed about obtaining access to the incriminating discs. Kay was a whiz at breaking codes, and searching and retrieving information. Kay and Byron played a computer program from time to time that basically challenged their hacking skills. At the moment, Kay was ahead.

But this was no game. Alex didn't like invading another man's space. However, if Toady was up to no good, he'd brought it on himself.

Alex glanced out the window at the weather. It was getting dark and fog was coming up in Scoon Bay. The mist writhed like tentacles of a sea monster. Wispy tendrils wafted over the water onto the beach then snaked into the trees. Curling menacingly it crawled up the bank below the house. Alex shivered. "No answers there," he muttered aloud.

He felt pumped as he turned from the window. Ujima could count on him. It was a long time, actually since the Army, that he'd seen some real action. Alex grinned. He knew she meant it when she said she'd cover his ass if anything went wrong. He chuckled, deputized!

At the hall closet he grabbed his parka, slipped into his loafers, found a pair of tight rubber gloves and the emergency flashlight. If he was going to accomplish anything, he'd better motate.

He scribbled a quick note, dropped it on the hall floor, and in a few seconds was hastily jogging along the path to Toady's.

He quickly detoured around Toady's reconstructed bridge. Questions still nagged at him. Who had given Ujima the tip? And how would anyone know what Toady kept on his computer? Could be Thommy Jay, he seemed to always be in Toady's hip pocket. And Ujima could be wrong. Toady might not at all be involved with blackmail. He could be the one behind everything. It was Toady who had been working on Ujima's boat the day before her engine quit; and kindly offered his boat as a substitution. It was discovered later that Ujima's engine malfunction consisted of unconnected wires behind the ignition panel. There simply was no 'accidental' way this could have happened. As he neared the house, his speculations seemed to coalesce.

Toady, he'd been behind it all along. It made sense; monkey-wrenched his boat because he felt Kay and Ujima were onto something. He obviously wanted to sink the evidence of the carpet and two busy-bodies in one nasty 'accident'. Ergo, Toady's sabotaged boat was intended for the ladies, not Toady, as Kay had insisted.

The collapsing bridge too, was a cinch for Toady to arrange. He had been insistent that Alex collect the wood that particular day. Knock good old Alex out of commission and Toady could smoothly move in on Kay and acquire the Petoskey farm. And if that didn't work, bump her off? Murderers are capable of anything, Alex reminded himself.

Property seems to be at the key. With that happy-go-lucky handsome face of his, Toady could maneuver slickly. It would be a great addition to his acreage. But why hadn't he just purchased it earlier? According to Byron, he definitely was chummy with the Templeton 'gang'.

Then there was the attempt to steal those papers from Willie. They involved property too, and good old plodding Max still was working on them. Someone had wanted the documents, maybe enough to kill for them? They definitely were important to someone. Maybe Toady knew what they contained and wanted to modify or destroy parts of them. And if he'd harmed Willie when he'd tried to get them...

Alex got angrier by the moment. If it all was true, Toady was turning out to be a genuine gold-plated turd. But there must be concrete proof.

Then there was Janet's body. The barn was almost in his front yard. And so isolated he wouldn't have to worry about witnesses. But why would he bury Janet Holmes in his own barn? Alex shivered. Kay said Toady had been very much in love with Janet. Maybe Janet's death had been some sort of accident and Toady panicked. Or Janet knew too much about something.

At first Alex's money had been on Thommy Jay. He and Rose were the Island's premier busybodies. They found out everything before it happened. But Ujima said Toady was the one. Kay would be surprised. She'd been adamant that Toady and Thom were innocent.

And what about Rose? She'd become more hostile the further Ujima's investigation had gone. And now she was being secretive and not talking to anyone.

As Alex opened the gate to Toady's yard, thoughts swarmed around his head. Unlike bees, the pros and cons kept bumping into each other. He and Kay had chewed over the seemingly unrelated incidents many times; but had reached no agreement. This new information, if he could find it on Toady's computer or desk, would bring it all to a head.

But why, besides blackmail, would anyone keep a record of their own criminal activities? Maybe Toady thought he was too ingenious to be caught. Maybe it made him feel powerful. Or maybe the records served unconsciously as a reality link for a psychotic mind.

Alex stepped softly onto the gravel drive. For the first time he focused clearly on what he was doing. Calmness, analytical and cold, descended on him. But somewhere, a little nagging voice whispered that his own present 'no fear' actions could easily qualify *him* as the psychotic.

## CHAPTER 39

# *Pigs is pigs*

**Rose smiled complacently** as she checked the odometer on her dash. Her Range Rover was really roving at a comfortable 55 mph on the 40 mph road. She checked her rear-view mirror. Sergeant Washington and her minions were hopefully busy, or lounging with their feet up in the Beach Cafe and shooting the bull with the locals. On Bradestone that was an important social activity. The doughnut and coffee crowd used the time to talk to their protectors in blue. Complaints, rumors and general information was shared, listened to and advised on.

Rose liked to attend the gatherings. The general palaver usually enabled her to pick up other tidbits of interesting news. Sometimes, even before it was hot-wired around the island. Rose shook her head. That wasn't the case now. Since the murders, she couldn't keep abreast of the current rumors. At least she'd tried to add some items that had a semblance of truth to the local gossip. But Ujima was always too busy, and also, extremely tight-lipped; but not when the questions seemed to come from a certain Kay Roberts. "Argh!" Rose exclaimed aloud in frustration. And pumping Officer Reynolds for information was as easy as wringing water out of blue Jell-O.

Rose squinted at the pavement ahead. A low ground mist was drifting through the trees and white threads lined the deep, boggy ditch that paralleled the road. She switched on her fog lights. She wouldn't need them now until she reached Dark Hollow; for in spring and fall, heavy mists were easily trapped between the hills that surrounded the small town.

She glanced at the paperwork on the seat beside her. The contractor, who'd called earlier in the day, wanted to list two new homes with her agency. She shifted her briefcase on the seat and felt inside. "Damn!" she said aloud. She'd forgotten her cell phone.

Oh well, she thought, as she flipped the case shut, she needed a break from messages anyway. She was accruing far more business recently; the market was definitely on the upswing.

Since Templeton's death, and the Spindrift's exposure of his company's environmental policies, the agency was viewed with skepticism and suspicion. Edward and Mark were working hard to mend the PR damage. But, according to the grapevine it wasn't hard enough. And Islanders had not forgotten the pressure tactics they'd used on Kay and Alex and most likely Willie.

Rose frowned. If she could believe all the rumors that surrounded the confrontations, Mark and Edward had been unnecessarily strong-armed. But, what was it about the right-of-way that they wanted? It wouldn't have cost them anything to be diplomatic. Or they could have bought it earlier. She smirked. But of course, at that time, none of them knew it was back on the market

Too, Edward and Mark, at times, had been pretty snotty to her. They were certainly a contrast to that marvelous Alex. But on the other hand, she wasn't exactly taken with Kay. Kay was overly chummy with Toady and Ujima. Naturally, he had assured her that there was nothing there, but good conversation. That was so like Toady, so naive when it came to women. She frowned. Janet had really thrown herself at him. It was terrible that she was dead, but that girl had led many a man on. And that was most likely her undoing, Rose judged.

But she felt for Toady. He had fallen hard. She shook her head and sighed. Of course, he would always be involved with attractive women, even older women, like herself. Well. All men needed a little mothering. She smiled again. She was lucky that she could be there for him.

Oh yes. And then there was Teri. Later on she could spell real trouble for Toady. And that young lady was extremely skilled at pumping out information. But it was dry-well-city when it came to reciprocation. She shook her head. Like mother, like daughter.

Rose's reflections were interrupted by the blinking parking lights of a car. The vehicle was stopped on the opposite side. Rose automatically applied the brakes. It was a long, lonely stretch of road. Someone might need help.

She recognized the car. Oh Lordy, Evil Elanor. The woman was standing helplessly by the open trunk of her huge prestige vehicle. I'll regret this! Rose thought, but rolled her window down anyway and stuck her head out.

"Anything I can help with?" She inquired reluctantly.

Elanor looked up and wrung her hands. Rose had never seen her nemesis in such a state. Rage distorted her well-preserved face.

"I've got a flat!" Elanor screamed, "A god-damned flat. How could this happen to me!" The 'me' ended in an even higher whine.

Rose eased over onto the shoulder of the road and set the brake.

Since their first meeting, three years ago, Elanor had always sustained a floating animosity toward her. The reasons were unfathomable. But nevertheless it was there. Rose usually was the forgiving one. After all, Elanor was a human being. But when Rose recalled the most recent incident on the ferry crossing, a brief and uncharitable thought crept into her head. Maybe she was being a bit generous about the 'human being' part. She paused; she had never considered Elanor as being helpless, but she put her feelings of unease aside and got out of the car.

"I have a meeting with a client in Dark Hollow in forty minutes," Rose said glancing at her watch. "But if you have a jack and a spare, I'll be glad to help you get rolling again."

Elanor kept wringing her hands, as if she hadn't heard Rose. "Nothing, nothing like this has ever happened to me before. Eric always looked after these cars." She kicked the flat tire with amazing fury. "The son-of-a-bitch," she snarled. Rose hoped she was referring to the car and not her brother.

Trying to smile Rose walked over and glanced into the trunk. Cripes! It was stuffed with luggage. The spare and jack would be buried, that's if they were even there.

Rose pulled a suitcase out from the right hand side; she guessed that was where the necessary equipment would be.

"Oh. I see you're going on a trip. A long trip by the looks of things," she mumbled as she tugged at another piece of luggage. The spare must be under the trunk floor she sighed and stood back.

"That's none of your damn business," Elanor shot back viciously. "Just fix the crappy tire." She lowered her voice and became more apologetic. "Don't...don't worry, I'll make it worth your while."

Rose gritted her teeth. Typical Elanor, she never changed.

"Elanor, I don't need your charity, and..." In her anger Rose jerked a paper grocery bag out of the trunk. The handles ripped loose. She grabbed for the contents as they spilled on the ground.

"Oh, I'm so sorry, I...." Rose stopped in mid-apology. A pink windbreaker and a brown clutch purse lay in the dirt. Embossed maple leaves intertwined along its surface. It was oddly familiar, definitely not Elanor's style at all. Rose frowned and leaned over to pick it up.

"I'll take care of that," Elanor said briskly. She bumped Rose aside with her hip. But Rose was quicker. She danced away with the purse clutched in her hands.

"Where did you get this?" Rose asked and felt the roughness of the broken clasp. "I've seen this before. This is Janet's purse. What are you doing with Janet's purse?"

"I'll take that. It doesn't concern you," Elanor said menacingly.

There was something about Elanor's stance. Rose backed further away. The purse fell opened and she could see inside. There was a small wallet and something odd--a passport.

"You're always sticking your nose in where it doesn't belong," Elanor said as she began rummaging in the open trunk. Rose rapidly scanned the passport. The date was recent. Then she saw several postcards. They were tucked inside the passport and identical to the one Ujima had shown her. The one Janet supposedly had sent to Sabra. Rose felt a queasy sensation. Suddenly, things were coming together. She looked up.

Elanor was standing with her legs apart. She had a very large gun clutched in her hands. It was pointed directly at Rose's chest. "I'm glad you found it. It gives me an excuse to get rid of you too. Not that I really need one." Her laugh was cold. "You know, I've never liked you or your boring parties. You're bourgeois, obtuse, stupid and a meddler. You're always rooting about for little bits of gossip, bleating your misinformed opinions everywhere, and never seeing what really is going on around you."

Rose's heart was pounding. She was terribly afraid, and peculiarly at the same time intensely angry. "Is that what you did to Janet? Did you shoot her?"

Elanor smiled. "Why do you care? You will be joining the others soon." She snorted. "When you get there, why don't you ask them?" She raised the gun higher and aimed it carefully. Rose's muscles involuntarily tightened. There was a loud click.

Elanor was incredulous. "Shit, the clip's not in!" Quickly she turned back to the trunk.

Rose's legs quaked like rubber, but she moved them into action. It seemed to take forever to run towards Elanor. Elanor pulled the clip out of the trunk then Rose rammed her hard on the shoulder; Elanor let out an indignant roar. Gritting her teeth Elanor swung the gun, side to side, as she staggered backwards.

"How dare you... you Bitch..." Rose shoved her again--harder.

Elanor flung up her hands and plunged backward into the ditch. Foul waters sloshed over her wriggling body. Howling and spitting, she rose out of the brown muck. Gripping at the forest of cattails she lost her handhold and fell back into the clinging reeds and slime. The gun and clip were gone.

Rose couldn't stop shaking, but she felt triumphant. She was amazed, she still held Janet's purse in her hand. "I've got the evidence!" she shouted, "the actual evidence."

Elanor began to struggle up the bank. The smell of rot and decay exuded from her, it was overpowering. Then the panting Elanor, dripping brown and green ooze stood up, a primordial monster, incarnate.

Rose ran back to her Rover, leaped in, and gunned the engine into life. She had to prevent Elanor from reaching the big car. Shifting her car into gear she cramped the wheels and turned in an arc directed at Elanor's open trunk.

Elanor screamed in rage as she realized what Rose was up to. A crash of grinding metal echoed over the swamp. The car was like a rock; Rose backed up and hit it a second time. She kept ramming the Rover's bumper into the rear of the other car. Again and again she hammered the vehicle. Then, with a loud clang, the giant sluggishly moved forward. Rose stepped on the gas. It was only a few more feet. "Please dear God!" Rose said aloud.

Elanor's car lurched ahead, the wheels turned onto the grade of the ditch and the huge nose dipped.

Slowly, ponderously the elegant vehicle rolled down the embankment. Then, with a loud porcine grunt, the car settled slowly into the ooze. Rose unglued both hands from the steering wheel and cheered. She flipped Elanor a birdie, re-gripped the wheel and backed into the middle of the road.

Elanor mouth agape, stood at the edge of the ditch. In the gathering fog she was a grease-covered automaton, her mouth opening and closing, hands working in a spasmodic unison.

Rose pulled the Rover onto the gravel shoulder and yelled out the window, "Next time you should use your usual mode of transportation," Rose's voice shook on the edge of hysteria, "A BROOM! It's a helluva lot easier on the gas and the repairs aren't as expensive."

Elanor, raised fists, staggered forward.

Rose jammed on the accelerator. The wheels spun with a scream before they caught. Rose gloated and glanced in the rear-view mirror. She had actually thrown gravel in Elanor Lavin's face.

The fog was closing in, but Rose clung to the wheel. Automatically she groped on the car seat beside her. Where was her cell phone? Oh mercy! Then she remembered. Desperately, she peered ahead. A few miles back she'd passed Barney's gas station and the lights were still on. With any luck Barney would be working late and Sergeant Washington was only a phone call away.

Oh Damn! She pounded the steering wheel. I'll have to use Bungling Bell!

CHAPTER 40

# *Ninja*

**Toady's Black Trans Am** usually had pride-of-place under the house and dominated the left garage bay. But instead, the space was occupied by a red Jeep Cherokee. Heavy mud covered the sides of the vehicle and obscured the license plate. Odd, Toady never struck him as a backwoods kind of guy, or even one to have a second car. Alex cautiously approached the strange vehicle.

He noted the clogged treads of dried mud, the grimy windshield and dust covered paint. He felt the hood; cold as ice. There was a faint whiff of gas, but the car had been there for a while. And the mud-splatters were from last week; this week had been fairly dry. Not an unexpected visitor then. And the jeep, definitely not used recently. He finished his scrutiny of it then focused on the under-eaves of the house.

Ujima had assured him that there wasn't an alarm system and doors were left unlocked on the island. Regardless, he would be cautious. After all, Toady was a city cousin and led a wild lifestyle. He might have some warning device that Ujima's informant wasn't aware of.

Alex headed up the spacious flagstone walk at the side of the house. The main door was located at the back. It was fortunate that the entry was hidden from the drive.

The screen door opened easily and quietly. He ran his finger over a hinge. It had been recently oiled. That figured. Toady, the fastidious bachelor, wouldn't tolerate a squeaky door. Alex grinned. The front door was unlocked and opened as quietly as the screen. He moved into the kitchen.

So far, no blinking lights or ear-piercing noises. He hesitated and scanned for a silent alarm. Hopefully, if there were one, and Officer Reynolds could be counted on, it would ring in an empty station.

Now, where was the damned computer? The last time it had been on the far end of the kitchen island. He walked through, past the antique bar and into the ultra-modern dining area. The eating space formed an integral part of the entire living space. In the evening, with all the subtle lighting on, the room was large and attractive. Now, in the fading window light, its basic bones dominated. To his right, a stone fireplace ran from floor to ceiling. It was the entire south wall. For the first time he took in the full-length hearth that architecturally anchored the massive stone facade to the floor. Books and bric-a-brac decorated a dramatic, thrusting mantelpiece. The vaulted ceiling created a further feeling of intense spaciousness and luxury.

Directly ahead, the large triple picture window overlooked the driveway. Beyond, the steeply sloped front yard was a wooded ravine. The trees had been skillfully pruned, creating a tantalizing, peek-a-boo view of the hook. Near the fireplace, two oversize wing-backed chairs angled toward the window. Alex shook his head. The room smelled of orange and sandalwood. The scent emanated from the potpourri in a gigantic Asian bowl showcased dramatically on the baby- grand near the windows. It was quite the bachelor's pad.

Alex inhaled deeply of the pleasant aroma then spotted the monitor to the left of the piano. It was housed in a customized armoire against the wall. He had noticed the ornate cabinet from his last visit, but it had been closed. Now all the components were clearly visible and the related computer materials were neatly stacked to the right. This was too easy.

A tingly feeling teased the back of his neck, a warning to speed things up. He liked the darkness of the room, but shortly it would be necessary to use his penlight. He walked over to the computer. Great, it was similar to several he'd used in the past. He reached over and brought up the main screen.

"I'd stop right there, if I were you." The cold, deep voice came from behind him

Alex spun around. He faced the dull glint of a metal gun barrel aimed directly at him. In the shadow of the farthest armchair, Toady sat sideways, his hooded look radiating hatred.

Alex's eyes widened. "What! What are you doing here? I thought you were in Seattle."

"Easy, she's following a friend of mine and...." Peering closer, Toady's expression changed to astonishment. He gulped visibly and growled: "So it *was* you! Why did you do it, you bastard?"

Alex didn't move. His thoughts raced to explain his presence and he was confused by Toady's question. Distractingly something reflected in the window. It was only a moment then the silhouette of a woman glided silently near the far end of the bar, outside Toady's vision, her head covered with a balaclava. It was Ujima!

She must have caught on to Toady's ruse and had no time to warn Alex. It was odd though, she told him she was in Seattle. No matter, that was a gun in her hand and she was a good shot.

Fortunately, Toady's attention was solely on Alex.

"I thought, when you came to the island, you were who you said you were. I even liked you." Toady's volume and anger increased as he continued, "But now I know. Who paid you? Or, better yet, who are you working for?"

There was a flash and a single, ear-splitting shot. Toady's gun flew from his hand while his body pitched forward in the chair. Alex hit the floor and rolled.

Nothing moved. The blast of the gun had depressed his eardrums. He slowly calmed himself, but kept his eyes on Ujima's reflection in the window. She moved like a cat. Alex shook his head. The window distorted her image into a much larger shape.

"Thanks," Alex said as he brushed his eyes with shaky fingers then pushed himself up. His voice rumbled in his head. "I thought he had me for sure and...." He sensed a swift forward movement. He was slugged quickly and efficiently behind his right ear.

First, his head throbbed relentlessly; second, something filthy had been stuffed in his mouth; thirdly his hands and feet were bound; fourth, a chair propped him up, if you wanted to argue a fifth, he'd been dragged into the dining area.

There were quick movements at the computer keyboard. Groggily, Alex's eyes shifted in that direction. A large, black shape uttered an exclamation of pleasure, cleared the screen, removed something from the computer then walked over to Toady's chair.

Toady's body was still and dark fluid seeped over the side of his face. Alex's mind couldn't focus. Ujima was just standing there and looked down at Toady. Had she intended to kill him? Had she made a mistake? And why was she dressed like... like a Ninja?

Alex struggled. The figure crouched and pointed the gun at him.

"Waking up are we?" The voice, deep and resonant continued, "Good. That'll be helpful, when we take our short walk." It was definitely not Ujima.

The Ninja, for that was the only label his fuzzy mind could think of, gestured at the body on the floor. "He's bleeding to death, a fitting end for the lousy fag." The faceless shape viciously kicked Toady's body then strode over to Alex.

"I won't need this, you can have it." Though muffled, the voice was familiar, but whose? Alex carefully moved his head. He tried to escape the nausea as he was pushed forward.

He felt cold steel thrust into his left hand and his rapidly numbing fingers pressed around the pistol's handle. Alex didn't hesitate. He twisted the gun backwards and aimed for the leg. The trigger clicked. No ammo. An elbow jabbed hard in the neck. Pain! Alex slumped forward and his mind blurred.

The Ninja's laugh was a sneer. "Did you think I'd put a loaded weapon in your hands?" He took the gun from Alex's weakening grasp, reinserted the clip, and kicked the gun across the floor. It skittered to rest, next to the computer.

"Tsk, tsk," the creature chided, then began to vandalize the room. Books, disc files, lamps and pictures were pulled down and thrown onto the floor. Furniture too was toppled and splintered under foot. Finally, laughing with pleasure, he kicked Toady's chair over. It fell on the lifeless form.

Unexpectedly, blinding car lights swung across the ceiling and illuminated the room; followed by the squealing of tires in the driveway below. The madman stood outlined in the picture window.

"Shit!" the figure exclaimed, glided to the corner and looked out. Alex could hear the man muttering in a jagged breath, something about a cabin and then in a pleased aside, "Excellent, they're going the wrong way."

Alex blacked out.

When he came to he was being shoved out the back door. The smell in his nostrils was of damp fir trees mixed with the acrid scent of his own blood. His legs, though numb, were no longer bound. He pulled back. A gloved fist slugged him again in the neck. Stumbling and in raging pain he was frog-walked down the path at the south side of the house.

A steel door frame scraped Alex's shins as his grunting adversary cursed and heaved his dead weight up and forward. He growled in pain then weakly smiled. It was no small feat to lift him; he weighed close to two hundred and twenty pounds.

When the floor hit his face, it knocked any remaining gloat from his thoughts. His nose gave. Not again, he groaned as the door slammed. Alex took a deep, belly breath. It held the swaying haziness at bay. Then, startled, he heard the piercing yell of a woman. She was very close. As his body rolled from side to side, the car made a wide arc then plummeted down the road. Behind them, a man yelled "Stop".

Alex started to pass out again, he smiled. He very much liked the sound of the first voice. It was Kay's, laced with expletives, and very loud and clear, she was pissed.

Thommy Jay tore up the north walk. He threw open Toady's door, then stopped cold when he heard Kay's yelling and the Jeep's engine roar into life. Thom turned abruptly, shouted "stop" again and charged down the opposite path in her direction. He barreled into Kay.

Stunned with the wind knocked out they tumbled to the ground. Painfully, taking short gulps of air, they tried to regain their breaths.

"I couldn't see who it was," Kay gasped. "Thank god it's not Alex. Whoever it was, drove like a maniac. Almost ran me down."

"Christ, you scared the crap out of me when you shouted." Thom choked out. "Naturally, our dear Alex has missed out on the action." He paused and took a shaky breath. "But we haven't. Toady's house is a complete shambles." He took a deeper breath. "Whoever it was tore the place apart. We've stumbled onto something, something very nasty." He took another gulp of air as he looked up the path, "And... it's not in the woodshed!"

Kay's laugh hurt. And her arms had shooting pains. "Oh yes," she said as she rubbed her elbows. "'Cold Comfort Farm,' a real hoot!"

"Just like us," Thom said as he gently massaged the growing bump on his head. "The Keystone Cop's routine is an added extra."

"You really ran fast!" Kay exclaimed.

"Yes Kay, I've had a lot of experience," Thom said. Then he looked back at the house and gestured with his head. "Whoever that was, we almost caught him in the act. Maybe we'll find what it's all about when we sort through the mess." He sighed deeply. "Thank the fates, Toady is in Seattle.

"We must call the police," Kay said, as she extended a shaky hand and helped Thom to his feet. "If Ujima's back, we'll find out where Alex went and what he meant by that peculiar note he left."

"It was rather cryptic," Thom replied as he looked around. "Now, more importantly, where are my damned glasses?"

"Here they are, in the bluebells," Kay said, fogged them, and then polished the lenses with her shirttail. "I can also give Ujima a good description of that car. I sure hope 'Resting Reynolds' will put me directly through this time. I've seen that Cherokee in town." Kay paused, "The driver though, was dressed in some sort of hooded outfit."

Dizzily they hurried up the path.

"Probably one of Toady's rough trade," Thom said with sarcasm as they entered the kitchen and switched on the lights. "You'll find the phone near the computer. That's if it's... Cripes, look at this vandalism."

"I can't believe there's so much damage," Kay exclaimed as she threaded her way through the debris. "It's just like what happened to

Willie's cabin. Ah. Here's the phone. I'll just... no good, Thom," she twirled the cord in her hand, "Yanked out of the wall."

"Well dear, I didn't pass the Girl's Scout's sending-smoke-signals requirement. So we'd best get back to the car." He suddenly froze and turned his face away. "Is it dead?"

Kay's stomach dropped at the strange tone in Thom's voice. He pointed to an overturned chair beside a battered lamp table. Kay's breath hissed through clenched teeth. She'd just walked by a body! It was lying right there...on the floor. Arms and legs sticking out from beneath a wingback chair.

She knelt down, pushed debris aside and looked closer.

Sheets of paper were stuck to the bloodied head. "Thom...oh no... it's... Toady!"

Thom jerkily made his way to Kay's crouching figure. "It simply cannot be. He's in Seattle. He told me..." His hands shot to his face. "My God, it is him. I'm going to pass out."

"Oh for Hell's sake," Kay growled. "Push this chair up. Sit in it. Now, put your head between your legs."

Thom sat and Kay quickly put her hand to the side of Toady's neck. She felt a weak pulse.

"CPR?" Thom asked faintly.

"Not necessary, and I don't see blood anywhere else." She examined his body and the clothes very carefully. "It's a shallow head wound." She paused. "He's lucky. It appears that a bullet creased the scalp." Kay searched her pocket. "We'll have to stop the bleeding."

"I can't stand the sight of blood." Thom gasped out as he clutched his stomach. Kay grabbed his arm and shook it.

"Don't you fade on me, Toady's in shock; I'm going to need all your help to keep him alive."

As she checked Toady's breathing, he moved slowly on the floor and turned his head. His voice was thick, "Am....am I alive?"

"Yes," Kay answered softly. "Yes, dear, there's a slight wound at the side of your head. It's not serious," she said and applied her kerchief to the seeping wound.

"Now think, Toady. Where's the first aid kit?"

"He, he...shot me," Toady said slowly, as if he doubted what he was saying. "Then he kicked and kicked me. He really hurt me. I.... I pretended to be dead."

Kay made Toady check his limb movements then, carefully raising his legs, helped Thom to put the chair cushion under them.

"Toady, listen carefully. You're going to be all right. But you're in shock. We've got to patch you up first. Now, where do you keep your first-aid kit?"

"It's…it's in the bathroom, under the sink," he said with effort then promptly passed out. Kay pushed at Thom's huddled form. "You'll have to get it Thom. I must keep pressure on this head wound."

"I'll get it. I'll get it. I'll get it. Being nagged is worse than the sight of blood, any day!" he shouted as he staggered through the kitchen.

She heard Thom retching into the toilet as he flushed it. But amazingly, face white, lips set in a thin line he was now at her side and rummaging through the kit. Solemnly he handed her scissors, and a sterile bandage.

"I'm thirsty," Toady said as she cleaned and dressed the wound.

Kay smiled through the mist in her eyes. "Sorry. You can't have water yet. And you can't sit up either. So, let's again do a routine check of the old bod. Can you wiggle your toes?"

There was a moment's pause. "Yes. And I can still move my arms," he said and crossed them slowly over his chest. He grinned lopsidedly. "It's my Tai Chi conditioning. It's paying off. Oops. I... I think I'm going to be sick."

"Join the crowd. Everyone's doing it." Thom remarked dryly.

Kay leaned closer. "If you have to throw up, turn your head to one side, okay? And not in my direction," she added hastily. "But here. This might help." Kay had located an ammonia ampoule in the kit and broke it near his nose. She wiped the perspiration off his forehead.

Toady took several whiffs. "Oh. That's better." There was a long pause. "I... I'm going to be all right. I think the nausea is leaving." Toady nodded painfully, in agreement with his last statement, then moved his hands to his thighs and stretched each leg slowly.

"I think I'll try to sit up."

"Whoa! Steady there, big fellow." Kay patted his hand. "I wouldn't try that, just yet."

Toady smiled wanly and managed to croak out, "I know. A brandy, I need a sip of brandy. That's okay, isn't it?"

Thom leaned forward and eyed Toady critically. "Now you're making sense dear. This is definitely a task for Nurse Thommy. Do you still have that vile stuff in the back of the bar?"

Toady nodded and gestured vaguely in that direction.

Kay heard the clink of glasses in the cabinet. There was a coughing and spluttering. "Yuk, it *is* that same old rot-gut."

"Why don't you just spend a little more money and buy a decent cognac?" Thom said and thrust a brimming glass into Toady's trembling hand.

"That's too much," Kay warned as she helped Toady prop himself up. "A sip with two of these aspirins is more appropriate."

"Don't worry." Thom expostulated with his hands. "It's diluted with lots of chlorinated tap water. It won't burn a hole in his esophagus like it did mine."

Kay took a sip from Toady's glass, "Um that's not as bad as I..." she gasped, clutched her throat and tried to catch her breath.

Toady grinned lopsidedly then carefully popped the aspirins and took a swallow from the proffered glass. "Gotcha, huh?" he whispered. "You two are real wimps. Willie told me that this brandy puts hair on your chest."

Kay glanced down her shirtfront and eyed him balefully. "Thanks, but that's not what I need right now." She patted his hand. "Look. If you feel well enough to be sassy, I think you feel well enough to tell us what happened."

"Okay. I'm...I'm just having a hard time remembering" he said softly then in a pleading voice, "but please help me into the chair. I hate looking up at you two and talking from the floor. I...I really think I'd do better sitting up. Maybe I'll even remember more."

Though Toady helped, it was difficult. And with plenty of grunting and groaning from all concerned they finally managed to push and shove his large frame into the chair.

Toady, listing to one side, rubbed his forehead and gazed slowly around the room.

"That miserable shit; he's destroyed everything. And all along I hoped he was telling the truth." Tears formed in his eyes. "He really tried to kill me!" A note of disbelief entered his voice. "And I trusted him."

Kay touched his hand gently. "Who, Toady? Who are you talking about?" Slowly, he turned his head away. Kay could tell he was blushing.

Thom pursed his lips and slapped the side of the chair. "It's obvious." He shook his finger. "I've always warned you about rough trade. You never listen to your dear old aunty, and now..."

Toady interrupted, "No, no. It's not what you think. We were ...," he gasped then looked up. "Geez, I just realized. We have to find Alex."

Kay was on her feet. He had her full attention.

"Alex! What has any of this to do with Alex?"

Toady made a helpless motion with his hand. "Somehow he was tricked into coming here. Now I know why. He was going to make things look as if I killed Alex. It didn't work. But, he'll kill him, just like he tried to kill me."

"Who? How? Where? What are you talking about? Please tell me, or I'll..." Kay, regardless of Toady's injuries, was short of shaking the daylights out of him.

Toady looked at Kay. "It's Edward. It seemed nuts to me at the time. But he's had this obsessive hatred toward you and Alex, ever since he first ran into you. Remember? It was about a land grant, or the right-of way, or something." Toady lowered his voice and started to mumble. "And he hated me because I fell in love with Janet." Tears began to fill Toady's eyes. "He killed her you know. I realize that now. And he's going to kill again," Toady, swallowed then continued, "He's taking Alex to Willie's cabin. I heard Edward tell him that, when I was pretending to be dead. Edward's going to kill Alex there. I just know it."

CHAPTER 41

# *Call out the Marines*

He held his hands to his bandaged skull and slowly slid to the ground. "Jeeze, my head's splitting," Toady whispered

"Now Sweetie, Thom hissed and patted Toady on his cheek, don't be a faint-heart just when we need you the most."

"Shh, listen!" Kay said, finger to lips.

Huddled beneath the window of Willie's cabin, they could hear something heavy being dragged along the floor inside.

Kay grabbed the handle of a mattock that was beside the cabin. Crouching below the window, she hefted it. "We can use this."

"Sure. A garden implement is always the first-line of defense against automatic weapons," Thom hissed.

Kay ignored him. "Thom. Slide up to the window and see what's going on."

"Me? I might get my head blown off!"

"Now who's being the faint-hearted?" Toady grumbled.

"Toady's right. Don't be a weenie. Just imagine you're looking into one of your neighbor's keyholes."

Toady smirked painfully as he nudged Thom. "Remember? Like the bedroom at Rose's party last year,"

"Thanks for reminding me dear." Thom said out of the side of his mouth and carefully edged up to the window.

"Can you see anything?" Kay whispered.

"Well. I see dashing Alex tied up like a Christmas package. Absolutely delectable...er with the exception of his bloodied face. Ah, here comes the evil queen. She's doing something; I can't make out...

at the back of the room." Thom glanced at Kay. "Dispel the long face. We're not going to desert you." He patted her hand. "We'll bag the bitch."

"Whatever you're planning is foolhardy," Toady said quietly. "We should've called the police and let Ujima know. Instead of...."

"Nag, nag, nag," Thom interrupted.

Kay touched Toady's bandaged head. Her hand moved to his pale face. "You were still groggy. And we had to hurry. You probably don't remember, but all the phone lines were torn out of the wall."

"And your cell phones looked like they've been crushed by some Sumo wrestler," Thom said grinding his hands together.

There was a movement inside the cabin. Thom peered into the window again. "Whatever he's up to, I'm certainly glad we girls are here to prevent it."

Kay clenched her fists. "It's all I can do to hold back; to keep from charging through that door and screaming like bloody hell." She forced her throat muscles to relax. "Can you still see his gun?"

"No, but oh, oh..."

"What does 'oh, oh,' mean?"

Thom held tightly to the window ledge. "He has a large can of something and is splashing it around the cabin. I don't think he's planning a tea party, more like a barbecue."

"That's not at all funny," Toady said crossly. "Argh, I'm going to be sick, sorry." He quietly gagged into the grass beside the cabin.

"Blame it on yourself; you wanted to come," Thom mocked then turned to Kay. "Seriously, if we're going to do something, we've got to do it now."

Kay nodded. "I've an idea. But it's going to require speed, coordination and more than a little risk."

"Fine, just my forte," Thom said snidely.

After a short, but intensely whispered conference, they positioned themselves according to Kay's plan.

The loud knock startled Caen. He cursed, heaved the empty kerosene can into the far corner of the room, and grabbed the gun from the table.

"Some son-of-a-bitch must've seen the light." He gestured toward Alex with the gun. "Don't get any fancy ideas. There'll be two charred bodies found in the cabin instead of one. Let Ms. Ujima wiseass, figure that one out."

Caen flung the door open.

Thom gulped. It looked like a canon pointing at him. A trickle of perspiration ran down his spine. His legs shook and he stammered.

"My, my, what a big weapon you have Grandma. I was just in the neighborhood and wondered if you'd be interested in my Girl Scout cookies?"

A sneer spread across Caen's face. "This is perfect. Getting rid of you will be doing mankind a favor." He grabbed Thom's waving arm, jerked him into the room and held him in a vice-grip. At that instant, a six-foot plank of cedar crashed through the window. Shards of glass and splintered wood exploded in the air.

It was just the right distraction.

Caen swiveled his gun toward the window. In one flowing motion, Thom's knee smashed up into Caen's groin. Caen yelled and bent forward. The gun went off. Thom pirouetted around with his hands locked in a single fist and slammed them straight down onto the back of Caen's neck. Caen dropped like the proverbial sack of cement.

Thom danced backwards, grimacing and massaging his hands. "Christ, sweetie!" he said as tears of pain glistened in his eyes. "That really hurt me more than you."

Kay was in the room. "I'll kill him, I'll kill him!" she shouted and brandished the mattock.

Thom reached up. "Naughty, naughty, let Auntie have that before you pull something."

Startled, Kay handed Thom her weapon. He mimed a look of surprise as his grip slipped and the mattock dropped on Caen's head. "Oh, my boo-boo," he said and poked the crumpled body with his toe.

"I'm not too sorry about that." Then he smiled. "Blame it on Ujima's self-defense classes every other Thursday night. They've paid off. "Besides, a girl's gotta do what a girl's gotta do, right?" He looked at Kay for confirmation who nodded dazedly while Thom squeezed his throbbing fists. "Cripes, I'll never be able to play the piano again."

Toady stumbled through the door. "It worked, it worked!" he shouted as he shook a hefty chunk of 2x4, but the smell of oily kerosene was overwhelming. He dropped his weapon. "Erk...I'm going to be sick again."

"You would." Thom said and put his hands on his hips. "Please barf outside. Then we'll free Alex; tie up Brutus Maximus, and shake our gluteus maximii to the police station."

Kay shook her head at Thom's continuous use of wit to lighten the situation, laughed nervously and pulled the gag from Alex's mouth.

"Whoosh," Alex exclaimed. "Sure took you a long time. I think he used an old sock." Alex blinked. "What? That's you Toady, you're alive?"

"Barely," he said and leaned against the doorway with a sickly grin.

Thom tugged at Alex's bindings. "A bit of tidying up and Toady will be just fine. He told us *all* about Caen's dirty old tricks, luring you to the house and all.... now hold still dear. Auntie and Kay will get these nasty ropes off." Thom paused. "My, my, how this takes me back to my S and M days."

Toady, who looked as pale as Alex, knelt down to rub Alex's wrists and ankles.

"Thanks, the numbness is going. I think I'll be able to walk now," said Alex, using Thom's small body to support his weight. They stood upright for a moment. Then Alex swayed, clutched Thom's shoulder for support, and staggered through the doorway where they fell to the ground outside.

"Sorry Thom, I should have waited until *all* my circulation returned."

"Alex, be careful," Kay yelled as she ran to them. "You'll make your injuries worse."

"How about me?" a muffled voice whined from beneath Alex. "I'm thoroughly crushed here. I need medical attention." Thom paused and looked up at Alex. "But, I'll kick myself later, for complaining.

Toady limped out of the cabin and sat on the steps. "I'm the one that needs attention. I feel worse."

"Toady has a mild concussion," Kay whispered. "His one pupil is dilated. We have to get him to the doctor," she said as she helped Alex to sit beside Toady on the steps.

Thom tapped Toady's shoulder and appraised him. "My, you really do look... and smell like last week's salad. But, not to worry, Nurse Thommy prescribes a shower, aspirin and bed rest."

"Thanks. I won't forget that," Toady said frostily.

While Alex massaged his ankles and legs, his thinking became clearer. "Thom, you and Toady go to his place. Phone the police, and ask the first-aid boys to look at your injuries."

"We can't," complained Toady. "When Caen went nuts, he wrecked the wiring, power chords, everything." He wrung his hands. "We'll have to phone from your house. Besides," he shook his head and looked blearily at Alex, "I don't want anyone near my house until I feel better and have the time to swamp it out."

Kay interrupted Toady's lament, "You guys start now. The key's in the ignition. We'll tie Caen up and wait for the marines."

Thom nodded and wrestled Toady to his feet. "Come on dear, she's right." With Toady leaning on Thom they walked toward Kay's car.

Thom's chiding voice rang out clearly as he buckled his dazed patient into the passenger seat: "I'm surprised at you Toady; this certainly is *not* the time to be house proud."

Alex gingerly stood up next to Kay. They glanced into the cabin. "Looks like sleeping beauty will still be out when Toady and Thom return with the police. Christ Kay, he's one nasty customer. He was going to torch Willie's cabin and me along with it."

Kay lightly touched Alex's bruised face and kissed his chin. His nose looked worse than usual. "I know dear. And I couldn't have done it without them. They agreed to follow my plan. Even with Toady half unconscious, if...."

He stroked her lips with his fingertips then pulled her to him. "Kay, you guys were very brave. You could be the leader of my Army squad any day." He steadied her trembling body. "Relax; we'll get the ropes on him now," he whispered then shook her gently. "Everything's all right."

"That's what you think, lover boy." Caen was slouched against the doorjamb. His small, 22 revolver pointed at them. The gun was steady. "Don't move. Don't even try to run for it." He smiled and wiped the back of his free arm across his mouth. "On the other hand, moving targets are more fun."

"You're not going to do anything stupid Caen," Alex blurted out. He was thinking, I've got to stall him. "Attempted murder is handled lighter by the courts than the real thing. Sure, you're into some serious crap. But murder? Murder doesn't strike me as your game. You're far too clever for that."

Caen's laugh bordered on hysteria. "You're crazy. I've already done, 'that', as you say. Two more won't make any difference."

"I don't believe you." Alex said warily.

Kay looked up at him. "It's true. Toady figured out that Caen killed Templeton and Janet. But he doesn't know who killed Martin. It makes sense..."

"That's right Ms. Roberts. I almost had the Toad convinced Alex was behind the murders, but tooty-fruity was coming too close to the truth. That's why I got rid of him." He laughed. "Actually, that'll make three. By this time, the Toad has bled to death."

Kay and Alex kept silent.

"I see your other fruity friend has gone for help." Caen smirked. "Too bad, Thom always likes a party, he'll miss this one, but you two will do just fine. I'll be long gone before Ms. Washington and her odd squad show up."

Alex shrugged. I'll keep him talking; I'll appeal to his ego. "I still don't understand.... what's this all about?"

Caen snorted. "You never did get it, did you? It started with that snoopy bitch, Janet. She found I was putting funds into a special Canadian account, a branch of Templeton's Enterprise that I had very cleverly set up, by the way. Then she snooped further and discovered I was altering some copies of old land documents. It was actually to Templeton's benefit. It would have made Superior even more millions. But, when Templeton found out, he said he didn't appreciate the deed alterations; told me he was going to handle it, 'differently' and with Janet." Caen smiled. "When he had his little accident, I of course went ahead with *my* plans. Templeton and his damn mid-life crisis, shit, he wanted to throw it all away on that, that slut, Janet." He laughed. "Then there was Martin, the inept blackmailer. He thought he was sooo clever."

Caen waved his gun at Kay. "Anyway, after the first, it becomes easier; in fact, it's almost more exciting than sex."

"But you didn't kill Willie." Kay blurted out, the relief evident in her voice.

"I almost got the sucker. But he was gone when I reached the cabin." Caen spat on the ground. "*He* was at the root of all this anyway. From the start, he refused to sell the original deeds he had. He was that typical uppity native, thought he was better than everyone else. Wouldn't take an offer, no matter how much we anted up." Caen glared at them. "I'm sure that sounds familiar."

"So, Mark Justice? Was he in on this too?" Kay asked.

"Justice is a wimp. He stumbled onto some of the papers I was altering. He was afraid he'd be sucked in. That coward is somewhere in Mexico."

Caen glanced at his watch. "On the table is my briefcase, my golden parachute. I'll be out of this country, pronto."

Alex was puzzled. "Out of the country, but the island's airport is closed. You'd have to go to Sea-Tac. At best, the ferry takes over forty-five minutes to get to Fauntleroy."

"Tsk, tsk, such concern for my welfare. It's warming my heart. But who mentioned Sea-Tac?" Caen chuckled. "I was a chopper pilot in the Navy. The Superior Island's personal helicopter is waiting for me, fueled and scheduled." He looked at his watch. "Someone told me the Canadian San Juan's are beautiful this time of year." He craned his neck listening, then licked his lips. "It's time to cut the foreplay and get down to business."

"But," Kay said hastily. "But, I threw the keys away to your Cherokee. How do you expect to get to the helipad? Fly?"

"My, aren't we the clever one. Sorry to disappoint you. I've a friend that drives a very fast car." He glanced at his watch again. "She'll be here any minute."

"She, who's she?" Kay asked.

"It's none of your damn business," Caen snarled and stepped off the porch

Kay moved back and softened her voice. "You know Edward. Maybe she finked out on you. Maybe something happened. She should've been here by now."

"Don't try playing mind games with me, Ms. Roberts. I'm the master at that. Just relax. It's inevitable." He aimed the small pistol. "I was an expert marksman in the Marines. It'll be quick and over before..."

A raucous scream echoed through the woods and a shadow plummeted over their heads into the cabin.

"It's Edgar!" Kay exclaimed.

"That god damn bird, I'll kill him." Caen swiftly ran up the steps and fired two shots into the cabin. "Ha, crow feathers." Caen swung back, "And now for you two."

"Edward," Alex said softly. "It's me you want. Not Kay. I'm the one. Just like Willie, I got in your way. I blocked the land deal. Let her go. Think about it. You'll be in Canada before the law can do anything." Alex shook Kay's arm and pushed her away. He had to get some distance between them.

"Better yet," Alex said, "you could use me as a bargaining chip. Especially if something happens..."

Kay's eyes widened. She pointed behind Caen. "Look, flames!"

"Ms. Roberts, that trick's beneath you. It..." There was a muffled puff. An orange glow blossomed behind Caen.

"What the hell? My briefcase, my money!" Caen yelled and flung himself back toward the porch.

"Run!" Alex shouted and grabbed Kay's hand. They sprinted around the side of Willie's shack. In the distance were sirens. Alex quickly grabbed Kay's hand, and pulled her down the trail at the back.

Kay resisted. "Why are we going this way?"

"It's Ujima. We have to warn her. Caen is loose, and has an accomplice. We'll flag her down at the curve, hurry."

There was an ominous roar behind them.

Kay stopped. "What's happened?"

"Shit, get down. The flames have ignited Willie's gasoline store."

The back of the cabin blossomed into an angry, orange-red ball.

There were four explosions. When they subsided Alex raised his head. He felt the heat on his battered face as the cabin's flaming roof gracefully collapsed into the inferno. He wiped his hand across his sweaty brow. "Caen didn't make it out of that."

Kay sprang to her feet and helped Alex up. He groaned; the effect of his adrenaline rush was fading.

Tears rolled down Kay's dirt-streaked face.

Alex stared at her, mouth agape. "I wouldn't waste any time feeling sorry for that bastard. He isn't worth it."

"It's not that," Kay sobbed. "It's Edgar. Edgar's in there too."

"Oh," Alex said. He straightened up and stared at the billowing flames.

CHAPTER 42

# *Sanctuary*

**Toady's eyes traced** the moldings along the ceiling. Everything was the same bland color, white and maybe off white. His left leg, the only part of him that ached, was being gently massaged through the coverlet. A chant, soft and low, filled his head. It was soothing and strange. It called him to awaken. The words were ancient, yet somehow familiar.

His name, it was his mother calling. He heard her clearly. He closed his eyes. No. No, it couldn't be. She had died shortly after his tenth birthday, on the beach, on the Big Island.

"Kavehekhalani, where did you go to?" The voice sang, "time to come back." The words were whispered in melodic Hawaiian. Then slowly, as if it were the most natural thing, the whispers faintly dissolved into English.

Toady blinked and slowly turned his head. Willie's face loomed over him, a brown moon fringed with white-whiskers.

"The young brave wakes. Hey, hey, hey," the moon said and winked, "and lives to fight another day."

Raymond's body filled with a sleepy joy. "Willie, it's you...and you've got a beard. I knew.... I knew you had to be alive."

"It takes more than thugs and murderers to put old Willie away." He harrumphed then sat back in his chair. "When things started happening, thought I'd take a little vacation, needed to see my family in Oregon anyway. It's a tad calmer down there, at least when the teenagers aren't home. Besides, my niece sorta insisted on it. 'For my health', she said."

Toady managed a weak laugh. "But, how… how did you know my Hawaiian name? I've never told anyone." Toady tried to sit up, but the moon face began to spin.

Willie continued to pat his leg. "Take it real slow. The doctor told us you had one bad concussion. But, don't worry none, between me and Thommy Jay we got everthin' covered, from both ends. My job is to keep your spiritual side in shape." He looked back at the door. "Thom's is to push this hospital staff over the edge." He leaned forward and growled. "I don't know how the man does it. He hasn't hit the hay since you got here. And that was two days ago."

"Two days!" Toady blurted out. "Oh and where… where is he now…and I still don't know how you know my real name. I never told anyone; they would've just harassed me." Toady gasped and closed his eyes; it was taking all his energy to talk.

"One thing at a time, young man; Thom charged out of here about an hour ago. He said you'd recover faster if you were home. In fact he's there now, whipping your place into shape." Willie leaned forward again. His clothes gave off a homey odor of smoked fish and cedar oil.

"The hospital staff gave a joint gasp of relief when they saw his backside." Willie chuckled. "He's one, take-charge man. Course he's gonna be upset when he finds out he wasn't here when you came to." Willie scratched his whiskers and continued. "Hope he's gonna realize that his mother-hen complex can't be everywhere at the same time." He paused. "And another thing, he's insisted I move into your place til I build me a new cabin. He sez I can pay you back by being nursemaid and gofer, so to speak. I don't mind at all. Course, it would just be until I build me a new shack."

Raymond moved his hand onto Willie's. "You're always welcome, you know that. It'll be great having you there." He took a deep breath. "Thom will be under a lot of pressure, I know he'll be keeping both our businesses running. And he'll be more intolerable, than usual. But you'd make a great buffer." Toady smiled. "Maybe even put one of your spells on him."

Willie shook Toady's hand. "Spells? Where'd you ever get that notion?" He chuckled then nodded his head vigorously. "But I'll do my best. Maybe slip a dose of valerian into his tea. I was thinking about doing just that, last night. I swear he left one half of the hospital staff with the Saint Vitus dance and the other half planning his murder. S'fact he's been a trial to them."

Toady settled deeper into his pillow. He focused on the uncomplicated ceiling. "Now, back to my Hawaiian name, how do you know it?"

Willie looked at the floor. "It was Edgar. Edgar told me, long ago."

"Edgar? Be serious."

"I am. It was when he was helping us move you in? He was pecking at a box of pictures marked, 'living room', remember? Most of the packing crates were stacked long the driveway. We'd all stopped for a tea break. I wondered what Edgar was up to, so I opened the box, 'twas a bunch of pictures. That was when he put his claw on one very particular frame. Made me curious, since he kept tugging at it, I took it out. And whadaya know? There was you and your Ma. Edgar gets real nosy at times."

Toady mumbled something about humans too, and Willie said grinning, "Edgar also pointed out the names on the back of the picture. It says that Kaveykahlana in Hawaiian means: beautiful mist on the mountains. That true?"

Toady closed his eyes with a grin. "Yes. Yes, I think so. I haven't heard the name for a long, long time. Thanks for bringing it back." He sighed. "How's that snoopy, feathered friend of yours, anyway? Still the old trickster?"

Willie looked at the floor and cleared his throat. "Let's say he got caught in one of his last tricks. He was in the shack when that varmint Edward blew it up. But Kay swears Edgar started the fire. If it's true, I should've never taught him that match trick, no how. Feel lousy about the whole thing."

There was an audible sniff behind them. "I think you should feel very good about it. Edgar saved Kay and Alex's lives."

It was Rose. She had been quietly standing in the doorway listening, her arms crossed.

"I see sleeping beauty is awake," Rose said stiffly and moved into the room.

Willie winked at Raymond then whispered, "Don't let her tone fool you none. She's been here every day, too."

Rose walked to the night stand and touched a vase of flowers then read the attached card. "I see Kay brought you these." She sniffed again. "Thom will have to rearrange them." She paused. "I guess you three are heroes; rescuing Alex and all."

Willie chuckled. "You didn't do too bad neither Rose; from what I heard, you sent that Elanor harpy a bug-huntin'." Rose studied her fingernails and smiled to herself.

Toady watched her intently. "Why are you being so- so stand-offish?"

Rose leaned against the nightstand. She looked steadily at Toady. "I didn't realize you were such a Don Juan." She closed her eyes. "And even with Janet. And I can't believe you were... were involved with Edward too."

"Now, now," Willie said with a laugh. "Don't be too hard on Toady. Just remember Rose, for some people, 'variety is the spice of life'."

Rose fiddled with a pocket on her smock top. "Okay. I can accept that. But Toady, what really gets to me is your constant confiding in Kay. I thought I, I was your best friend."

"You are. But Kay's a good friend too. And amazingly, at the very first, she understood me, all of me."

Rose continued as if she hadn't heard, "And you're always having intimate talks with her, and when I ask her, she turns around and tells me, everything's confidential. Teri's the same way. She digs up all the information she wants. But when the shovel's not in her hand... why she wouldn't even tell me about Wick and how he was involved." Rose shook her head. "I feel cut out. And it's not just by you, but...but by everyone."

Willie interrupted, "Well. I can answer a few things." He cocked an eye, "And I just found em out this morning. Concerning that fella Wick? Kay said he ain't involved; other than trying to find his friends of course. And you might want to know that Byron and Wick have taken summer jobs on that Island they scuttled off to. They used your boat too, Toady." Willie chuckled. "They were conned into the jobs by two park rangers who nailed them for trespassin'. Alex said it's the best thing that happened to those pups; maybe make them shape up, like the Army."

Rose leaned forward and looked accusingly at Toady. "You see. Not a soul even told me that!" She sniffed. "Thanks Willie."

Toady looked helpless. "But, I didn't know about any of this either. Now that I do, I'm wondering about the Blake island thing. Wick doesn't exactly take to the 'Wilderness out in this Wild- West'," Toady quoted. "And I feel responsible. I gave them complete use of my speed boat," he said sheepishly.

Willie made to reply, but Rose crossed her arms and plowed on, "Well, one thing, I know for a fact that Edward and Elanor made a killer team. And that's not a joke." She pointed a thumb at the door.

"And I found out that she's spilling her guts down at the police station, right now."

"Don't surprise me none," Willie said. "She was a pretty lonely women, and not very likable to boot. She'd practically do back flips for attention. Specially when a good looking guy like Caen came sniffing around."

Rose nodded her head. "She really fell for him. But I bet it sure turned sour when she discovered that he hadn't even packed her a toothbrush. I mean, I'm not surprised. I always thought Edward was a loner." Rose had a distant look in her eye, "Though he might have taken her at least as far as Canada."

Raymond nodded his head. "Oh right, as far as Canadian waters, then right out of the chopper." Toady became angry. "He was so good at creating fake evidence against me that even Ujima believed it. He said I wore cuff earrings, I detest ornaments of any kind, and he might as well have papered the Island with blue-silk handkerchiefs. He knew I liked the shorts he gave me, but the handkerchiefs I told him I would donate. Somehow he got a hold of them, cause he planted a few in my wardrobe."

"He gave you silk underwear?" It was hard to tell if Rose was scandalized or envious.

"Edward always flattered me with gifts, particularly of an intimate nature. Man, was I ever the fool."

Willie shook his head. "Now don't blame yourself. He was a clever, downright vicious man. You weren't the only one that he fooled."

Toady nodded. "I knew he was getting tired of me. It was probably just before he sabotaged my sailboat. I'm sure he figured it would be a slick way to get rid of Ujima, fool the authorities, and pin her and Kay's death and the other killings on me. And what gets me is that he didn't care who she might be with." Toady shook his head. "And I still can't believe he shot me and left me for dead… then he was going to shoot Alex."

"Obviously, that was so we all would think you were the killer," Rose said.

Toady shuddered. "I guess he didn't really love me. He was just thinking of all the ways he could use me." Toady took a wipe at his eyes. "Then, when he was through, just toss me out with the garbage."

Rose stared at Toady. If he was casting around for sympathy, he wasn't going to get it from her. She was hesitating over what she was going to ask next, then said to herself, 'Oh what the hell' and blurted out: "Was Edward a killer in bed too? I just want to know."

Toady blushed. It was a total shock, coming from Rose. "Well, that is an awkward question. But since you asked…"He cast his eyes down and thought for a long while. "I'd have to say yes. Yes, he was terrific."

Willie stood up. "Gotta be goin' now, promised Thom I'd help him range some furniture this afternoon." He patted Toady's leg again. "Looks like you otta be home by tomorrow."

At that moment a young nurse bustled into the room. She tucked a wayward strand of raven-black hair under her cap. "Oh, Mr. Toda," she said, her face was flushed. "I'm so glad to see you're fully awake. It's time for a check-up." She moved over to adjust his IV's, "And it's time for some solid food… like Jell-O," she giggled.

Raymond's smile was pale, but engaging. "I really like raspberry. But, if you don't have it, that's okay."

The nurse nodded her head. "If we don't, I'll make sure we do. And if there's anything else you need…" Her voice trailed off hopefully.

"Well later, if you're still on duty, maybe you could read me a bed time-story?" He winked.

"Oh, Mr. Toda," she simpered, "you say the sweetest things."

"My friends call me Toady," he said with the look of a chagrined puppy.

Rose made a strangled sound and quickly exited the room. She joined Willie as he walked down the hall.

"Hey Rose. Don't you worry none, Toady's gonna be A-OK."

"Oh, I've no doubt about that. No doubt at all," she said through clenched teeth.

## CHAPTER 43

# *Finale*

**The sun streamed** into the long verandah; the intensity of its light and heat diffused by hanging, bamboo porch screens. Ujima nestled into the plump, flower-patterned cushions of the new chaise. Bands of sunlight fell across her green print, cotton shift.

"Wow," Kay exclaimed and placed a tray of cut fruit on the table near Ujima's chair. You're really relaxed this morning, and that dress looks cool and comfy,"

Ujima fingered her collar. "Thanks, I got it at Sabra's. It was just my size and on the bargain table. Can you imagine?

Kay shook her head. "No I can't. I've never thought bargain was a word in Sabra's vocabulary."

"Meow," Ujima said and grinned.

"My only excuse is that I can grin like the Cheshire cat; cream in your coffee madam?"

The aroma of fresh brewed coffee was drifting onto the porch.

"It smells delicious and if I have a choice, I'll trouble you for half hot-milk and half coffee, but basic black is okay too." Ujima winked.

"No trouble. Alex prefers café-au-lait. I'll be back in a flash." Kay hesitated as Ujima, began humming 'My Reverie' and ran her slender fingers along the arm of the chaise.

"I could get used to this life; and at the risk of having my coffee dumped in my lap," Ujima made a sweeping motion with her arm; "this would make a charming bed and breakfast."

"You *are* living dangerously, "Kay said and paused in the open screen door.

Ujima chuckled. "After listening to Byron, one's personal walking-talking brochure, I think I can quote him, blindfolded: 'Discover your own private hideaway. This rustic B&B, with charming old-world accommodations, serves gourmet meals as the majestic view of Heron's Hook and the sun-drenched shores of Scoon Bay beckon. Continental breakfast is included. This is where magic begins and your personal Eden comes true.' Ujima blinked and looked surprised. "Whoa, actually Byron's babblings are very persuasive. I know I'd make reservations." Ujima kicked off her sandals, examined her lime painted toenails and burrowed deeper into the chaise.

Kay raised her eyebrows. "If you continue in that vein when Alex gets back, I hereby give notice that your next cup of coffee will be liberally laced with arsenic."

"I know, I know." Ujima shook her head. "He told me about your objections; even when I hadn't asked."

Kay let the screen door slam and slowly sat down. She was quiet for a long time.

"This is for your ears and your ears only. I *have* been seriously mulling it over. But, if it encroaches on my art projects and yoga teaching, it will not be a plus. Of course the kids have talked it to death. But they're young, full of energy and can afford to romanticize. Ha, like most people, they disappear into the woodwork when a real task rears its ugly head. It's one hell of a busy job. Ask any B and B operator."

Ujima tapped the arm of her chair. "I grant you a few arguable but not unreasonable points."

Kay picked up a large strawberry and bit into it. "When the kids return, I'll call a family powwow. We'll review the idea of a B&B. Even though they are naïve and have the ability to pander like a politician, I'll appreciate their input."

"Speaking of your brood, when do they get back from Blake Island?"

"In four weeks. Toady will use his other boat to pick them up. The speedboat's engine gave up the ghost. Alex is going along too. He's pining to be at the wheel of an antique Chris-Craft. They'll tow the smaller boat back. The guys will stay here till about mid-September, then off to the Universities." Kay became wistful. "I love having time for just the two of us, but we'll miss the hullabaloo."

Ujima picked up a slice of pineapple. "I've heard by the island grapevine, aka Rose, that Teri's working on Blake Island too." She munched thoughtfully. "How was she able to swing that deal?"

"As usual, she couldn't let the guys get away and suffer by themselves. So she wheedled a volunteer job in a nearby park facility. She said she needed to keep an eye on her long lost brothers. Now there's irony for you. Teri hasn't any idea how close she is to the truth."

Ujima looked intently at Kay. "Have you told Alex, yet? About Wick I mean."

Kay studied her fingernails. "I'm having a rough time with that. But..."

Ujima waved her arms frantically as Alex stood framed in the doorway.

"Hallelujah! I smell java." Alex put his good arm around Kay and gave her an enthusiastic kiss; then limped over to an empty chaise next to Ujima. "Hi Copper, I'm honored by your enthusiastic greeting. It reminds me of the Queen's wave, only more militant."

Ujima sat up and bowed. "The walking wounded. I thought I heard your car pulling up in the back." She winked at him; "By the by, how's Toady doing?"

Kay stood up. "If you'll excuse me, I'll get the coffees ready."

Alex blinked his bruised left eye. "Toady's overjoyed to be home. The major question is: Can he and Willie survive the uber-attentions of Thom? This morning, Willie prepared a fantastic breakfast. Exasperatingly, Thom was showing Willie how to cook everything. Cripes! He wants to go gourmet, all the way." Alex popped some grapes into his mouth. "Willie told him, rather testily, that he had at least fifty years' experience covering the kitchen floor. Luckily, Thom had the sense to stop criticizing, but then began moaning about running two businesses and having to hire extra help; he's a babbling, nerve-end." Alex gestured helplessly. "Thom should realize, Toady needs time to get up to speed. It was Toady who suffered the brunt of Caen's anger. The poor guy was almost kicked to death."

Alex shook his head. "Fortunately, Toady has the constitution of GI Joe. Even with a concussion he smashed that plank through the window and still kept on his feet, he's one tough guy."

Ujima nodded, mumbled something about the high testosterone levels of certain young males then said; "Thom's trying to avoid the fact that we could've lost Toady."

"Well, it'll be a much needed experience in team building now that they have to work together," Kay said and put down the coffee tray. She poured hot milk into two oversize yellow mugs, added streams of black coffee and then handed them to Ujima and Alex. Finally she sat down and took a sip of her own, neat, 100-proof. Kay licked her lips and nodded approvingly.

"A chaser of Jamaican rum would make this pleasantly decadent," Ujima said with a smile.

"I'll get the jug," Alex said and started to stand up.

Kay motioned for him to sit down. "No, save it for later. The radio says it's going to get hotter this afternoon and I'm going to make Daiquiris, or maybe a Rum-Collins. But, getting back to Toady and Thom; I agree with Ujima, I think there's a need for a greater communication on both sides." Kay omitted mentioning Toady's newest business venture, 'The Bloated Toad'. He wouldn't be making any official announcements until he completed an interview with Cal Smith at the Spindrift. She grinned; it would be an interesting name for a local bistro.

Kay glanced at her watch. "We expected you earlier, but I'm sure your endless stomach lingered without too much difficulty."

"It more than lingered. It indulged. It would've been blasphemous not to." He smacked his lips. "Apple Dutch-babies, side pork, Canadian syrup and...."

"Stop, you're making us drool." Kay nodded at the tray of fruit beside Ujima's chair. "It's unfair. We're watching our waistlines."

Alex smacked his lips. "Yeah, you don't know what you missed...but now, to a rather unpalatable business. All this brouhaha last week, just what drove Caen and Elanor to those murders? I sensed he wasn't particularly fond of me, but things got real excessive."

Ujima looked up. "He wasn't fond of you...in spades." She lowered her voice. "Contrary to Elanor's lawyer's advice, she won't stop talking. Spindrift Cal is always lurking in the bushes, pen in hand and I'd like you to keep what I'm about to tell you confidential."

Kay and Alex nodded in unison.

"Elanor had murder on her mind when Eric, her step-brother, began buying up prime building sites, then setting aside over 98% of the land as environmental sanctuaries. He was totally won over by Janet's idea that our planet's environmental health, including living things like us, dictates a necessity to create large connecting greenbelts. Janet claimed these 'set asides' were imperative for all of life's survival, including the continuance of genetic variability of local species. Of course this philosophy did not sit well with Elanor's greedy personality. She still refers to her brother and Janet as those 'bloody tree-hugging idiots'."

Alex chuckled. "Most of mankind seems to subscribe to the mantra of progress, regardless of the consequences." He paused, "But besides er... the disagreement with her brother's turnabout, why did Caen become such an avid sidekick?"

"That's simple. Elanor and Caen were lovers."

Kay guffawed. "My, my, he was certainly brave to cavort with *she* of acid-personality."

Ujima shrugged. "It was a case of necessity over bravery. Caen had to romance the boss's sister. It was just another hurdle in his path to monetary success."

"In a way they were well suited for each other. Especially when it came to the green of ye old greed," Alex said.

"You bet." Ujima nodded. "Caen was as avaricious as Elanor. He told her he would take care of everything. And he did. Elanor says she protested at first. But, she's cold and pragmatic. She said it became necessary, before her brother gave everything away. The faster she inherited the better. She was the sole recipient of the estate, which includes various Templeton Enterprises. There were no regrets at her half-brother's death, and I quote here, 'We never got along anyway. Eric was a groveling namby-pamby.'"

"Ah, one of the corporate credos, greed when necessary must trump familial ties," Kay commented snidely then paused, "but what made Templeton change from developer to one of nature's protectors? What lands are we talking about?"

"The first property he developed was on Squeak passage at the Peavey Harbor entrance. You've probably read about all the post-construction difficulties in The Spindrift. It's called the 'South Bay Marina'. His next big project would have involved the acreage in back of and including your properties. The acquisition would have given him a connecting parcel to Scoon Inlet. Eventually he wanted to develop the entire Hook. He must have had an epiphany concerning the environment, or merely the need to keep the love of his life, Janet, happy. We'll never know. He vowed to her that he would not develop the Hook. And would acquiesce on the other Bradestone properties he'd recently acquired."

Alex gave vent to a long whistle. "Caen did yell that Janet was the "Queen-Bitch of Greenpeacers, and it was all her fault" He winked. I prefer to think of her more as an enchantress."

"Oh yes. After Janet enchanted Templeton into turning most of his land holdings into permanent greenbelts, she then wanted to form a volunteer enterprise called the 'Templeton Conservation Group'. And she was working on bringing it to the world scene; a non-profit organization that would encourage and assist other developing countries to save vital lands from development. It was most ambitious. We found drafts of the plans and paperwork that would've gone to the 'Superior' board. According to legal, the greenbelt documents are airtight. No matter what people say about Janet, in her heart, she was an ardent environmentalist, on steroids of course, but she had beaucoup brains and the creativity to go with it."

"Unfortunately, Janet had to be cut out of the picture."

"Right, she had the dubious honor of being the first. Caen invited her out on Toady's boat for a romantic sail. Obviously he thought she was another female that couldn't resist his charms. But he underestimated her. She was aware of Caen maneuvering around Templeton to drop his plans of permanent greenbelts. And he was campaigning board members to develop Scoon Bay and the Hook. We can only surmise that Janet told him to back off, or she'd go to Templeton and the press and expose his embezzling games along with his behind the scenes manipulations of other various Templeton projects. We think that after she discovered he'd altered original land documents, she decided to rein him in. We found detailed accounts of everything in her personal computer files. Janet most likely felt she had the ultimate instruments to control him. She was wrong. He killed her that night."

"So, he was the one that dumped the sail bag, with the piece of bloody rug and dress, overboard."

Ujima nodded. "By that time, the movement of the salt water had washed most evidence away, at least to the naked eye. But the lab found enough remains in the fibers."

"But why didn't he bury the evidence somewhere or throw it in the garbage?" Alex asked.

"Something happened, we don't know exactly what, but he must have become rattled. After he cleaned up the murder scene and patched the carpet, he tossed everything into that bag and chucked it over the side." He explained to Toady that he'd spilled motor oil on the floor.

Kay looked grim. "It turned out to be a pretty solid frame-up for Toady, but I'm still puzzled. "It must have been Caen that came back that day Alex spotted a sail boat circling in the inlet. Later we found out it was Toady's boat, but he hadn't used it for weeks."

"Yes," Alex said and stretched. "I can postulate an idea as good as the next guy. And it wasn't the old wheeze about the criminal always returning to the scene of the crime. The tide was low that day and Caen was hoping that he could retrieve the bag," he paused, "and I bet if Caen had located the bag he would've planted something in it. Something that belonged to Toady," he winked at Ujima, "say a blue silk handkerchief? But, 'time and tide wait for no man', as the saying goes. Then later, along comes curious Kay."

"The scattering of those damn handkerchiefs got a little thick. I was building up quite a collection, almost enough for a quilt. And I took the bait. Toady was my prime suspect," Ujima said ruefully.

"But, I thought he was guilty too! For a while," Kay blurted out.

Alex put his coffee down. "Back to Willie, wasn't it having and flaunting the original land papers that got *him* into trouble?"

"That was a major part of it. Caen tried to buy his land." Ujima smiled. "It is in a prime location, another great access to the inlet's tidal marsh and ultimately the hook. But Willie told him to go soak his head."

Alex guffawed. "And when Caen found out that Willie had those original land deeds, it really got his shorts in a twist."

Ujima nodded. "Willie's father held title to the property and the Hook as well, that drove Caen over the edge; he told Elanor he was going to burn the cabin, the papers and Willie along with them. It could have made a difference though; months before, Willie had registered photo copies with the county. Willie thought he was safe. He didn't know that Caen was doing a pretty deft job of altering them. The stipulation that the Hook and his adjoining property would be designated as 'Green belts in perpetuity' was being eliminated. But I'm happy to say that the original documents, with the help of Max's and his capable minions, have been translated, vetted and stamped official."

"You remember Alex, the first day we met Willie? He was terribly worried about something. Later that week he confided in me that he didn't know who he could trust, either with the deeds or his wishes about the Hook. He was afraid that predatory real-estate and corporate interests could legally wangle him out of everything. Condo mania was afoot and growing. He didn't know a lawyer he could trust to fight the deluge of greed that would sweep his land and wishes away.

Ujima set her cup down. "Who does? I don't have much truck with lawyers, but after talking with your 'Marvelous Max' about Wick

Wilding's inheritance, if I had any legal troubles, I'd contact him in an instant.

Alex's eyes brightened. "Ah ha, that reminds me, I've a little surprise to tell one and all." He paused, "But it can keep till later. I still want to know why everything came to a crisis last Friday."

Ujima cleared her throat. "To begin with, Elanor and Caen knew yours truly was getting close to solving the murders and..." Kay hooted. Ujima glanced in her direction. "What? Don't be rude Doctor Watson, I *was* close, so let me finish. When you and Alex refused to provide a right-of-way down to Scoon Bay, Caen hit the proverbial wall."

Alex nodded at Ujima, "And with the long arm of the law beginning to make connections, it was time for them to cut and run."

"Exactly, it was Elanor who told Caen to take the money he'd embezzled and whatever they could grab and her along with it. Toady was the liability. He was close to Caen and became suspicious and was asking questions about Martin and Janet. So the quicker Toady was out of the picture, the better."

"But Toady was being framed as the murderer," Alex said.

"Ah, but things might not stick, that was the problem. So Elanor faked my voice and set you up. You would kill 'the murderer' in self-defense. And then die of a fatal gunshot. He tricked Toady into coming back from Seattle by saying that Janet's murderer would be sneaking in that night and downloading incriminating evidence into Toady's computer."

Alex put his coffee cup down quickly. "Then Kay and Thom show up and Caen has to make some quick decisions. Ha! That was an unplanned stumbling block. "

"You're right. But he didn't always stumble. He was very clever, planting red herrings and suspicions. Caen panicked Toady into believing I had enough evidence to pin the murders on him, which I did. And he also convinced Toady that you had something to do with the murders. He was set up very well"

"Me! I knew nada, zip about what was going on."

"For me, Toady became the premier suspect after we found his fingerprints on the wine glass in Martin's office." Ujima closed her eyes and nodded. "Oh yes. Caen made a few stupid moves, but also some very clever ones."

"Janet couldn't leave any male alone for too long could she?" Kay mumbled through a mouthful of grapes.

Ujima winked. "And, she knew how to use them wisely; but then clever women do, don't they?" She raised her coffee cup in a salute then paused, "It's just 'they' have to tread carefully when it comes to psychopaths."

Alex rubbed his jaw then looked at Ujima. "As long as they do it with finesse, we psychos enjoy it."

"Hah!" Kay exclaimed. "Speaking of a non-psychotic who is a great guy, namely Toady, why did Caen have such an intense hatred of him? After all they had been lovers."

"It was partly Janet's fault. Caen was not only jealous of her, but was aware she kept a hidden diary, and she intimated that she'd put detailed evidence of all his criminal actions on a disc and give it to her real lover, Toady, for safe keeping."

"Wow, Toady right in the middle of the fireworks! And just what kind of incriminating evidence was *she* talking about?"

"Well, it did take a while to find the actual disc, having to sift through the shambles at Toady's house. Caen thought he'd deleted everything, he didn't realize Toady had made duplicates and hidden them. The CD was a compendium of his embezzlements and had complete copies of the computer-enhanced changes Caen made to Templeton's land-grant documents. The alterations were very convincing, as I said." Ujima grimaced. "Toady did it for Janet, but the guy never looked at them. He trusted her completely."

Alex made a circular motion by his ear. "What did crazy Caen think he was doing when he enticed Sabra to the barn?"

"Ah." Ujima sighed. "He intended to force her to reveal where Janet's diary was kept and then get rid of her. He, no doubt, would have buried Sabra along with Janet." She shook her head. "He didn't expect tag-along Kay to muck things up."

Kay shivered then leaned forward. "It still gives me the whim-whams. He must have been hiding in that barn all the time we were there. Hmm…there's a person who's been sucked into the background. I'm talking about that gorgeous hunk, Mark Justice. Island underground says that he's in Mexico. But is someone going to find another dead body, somewhere?"

"Not a dead one. We've located a very live Mark Justice and yes, in Mexico. He's cooling his heels in the proverbial Tijuana jail. That is, until he's extradited to stand trial."

"Was Janet also involved with Mark?"

Ujima shrugged. "Most likely, but he wasn't totally pulled in by her…um shall we say charms?

"But Caen told us Justice wasn't involved in any of the shady business, right?" Alex said.

"Well, not exactly. He found things weren't making sense when he tried to resolve the company's accounts. At first he discussed it with Caen. But Caen stonewalled him and when Mr. Justice dug further, he realized he was in deep waters. He knew something was fishy but to protect his hide he just blew bubbles." Ujima tapped her fingers on the armrest. "Technically he wasn't directly involved, but is considered an accessory."

"A minnow among sharks," Kay quipped; Alex rolled his eyes.

"Right, so he packed his bags and stole into the night." She shook her head. "Fortunately for us, he did a miserable job of covering his trail."

"So the CD was hidden at Toady's all along?" Alex interrupted as he carefully felt the bump on his head.

"Yes indeedy, and we found it in the bottom of a broken potpourri container. Thom wept, said it was late Ming dynasty or something. Anyway, Janet gave Toady the CD for safekeeping, as I said he never read it. There's a backup somewhere too, but so far no luck. It may be hidden at Sabra's," she paused, "I think that Janet was just beginning to realize what a dangerous situation she was delving into. I'm no psychologist, but from what I've been able to piece together, it appears that Toady had been in complete denial about Caen's personality traits. But, Toady knew that Janet was suspicious of things going on at her work so he began asking questions about Templeton Enterprises, that's when Caen attempted to punch him out at the beach. After that Toady did a 180, he realized that Caen could be cruel and very dangerous."

Alex nodded. "So Toady's affections turned to Janet."

Ujima stirred her coffee. "They were already there, and Toady was happier with Janet. Unfortunately, Toady didn't see that Janet was manipulating him, too. She wanted Toady's popularity and money on her side.

Alex sputtered. "Janet was having an affair with Toady? Besides Martin er, Templeton or was it all of the above?"

Kay pursed her lips and glanced at Ujima. "It takes Alex a while."

Ujima smiled. "Poor naive Toady, he thought Martin and Janet were just good friends, he had no idea how involved she was with Templeton either. She had convinced Toady that he was the only important man in her life."

Kay took a sip of her coffee. "When did Toady finally realize Janet was having him on?"

"It was when Caen started the rumor that Janet had run off with Martin, and they were getting married in Europe. And that made sense to most people. Janet and Martin were seen together a lot. They were avid environmentalists; attending lectures and meetings together. And frequently they were the main speakers."

Kay leaned forward. "And how did Caen manage those notes from beyond the grave? When the postcards arrived, Janet and Martin were already dead."

"Leave it to Elanor; she was mailing letters to friends in Europe. Included in the letters were postcards, similar to the one Sabra received. She then asked her friends to mail the missives from various places the couple would supposedly be staying. Her friends were under the impression they were playing a joke on a mutually detested rival here in the States."

Kay spread her hands. "But couldn't the cards get crossed up somehow?"

"It didn't matter. The notes were brief and generic. It was the postmarks that counted. They threw us completely off the track, at least for a while."

"Why didn't Caen vamoose with the money after he killed Martin?" Alex asked.

Ujima shrugged then helped herself to a slice of melon. "All we know for sure is that he was dead set on incriminating Toady before killing him."

Alex shook his head. "What a weasel. But how did I fit in?"

"Initially, Caen planned to get rid of you and Toady at the same time. He staged things so that your murder would be pinned on a dead Toady. Elanor and Caen thought it was perfect. With Toady the primary murder suspect in Martin's death, and both of you dead, the case would come to an end quickly."

Kay laughed. "It wouldn't have been that easy. I would have created a big stink."

Alex raised his eyebrows. "That's very comforting dear. I hope that's not the only thing you would have done."

Kay touched his knee and turned to Ujima. "Caen had to seek vengeance. Toady had fallen in love with Janet. And Caen's ego couldn't take that."

"Jeez! If Kay and Thom hadn't shown up..." Alex took a ferocious bite out of a slice of pineapple. "Damn it Ujima, it did sound like you on the phone."

"You shouldn't be so gullible, and you probably need hearing aids," Ujima laughed.

"And here, take this napkin before you ruin your sweater," Kay said with a frown.

"Man, you ladies are really making me feel ancient."

"Anyway, in the end, it was Elanor who panicked and said they take the run for Canada. With even a hint of Mark's search into the company's financial records, it would be only a matter of time before the board would start an audit.

"Ah, a case of embezzlement-interruptus." Alex overrode the groans, "And whatever happened to Caen's accomplices, you know, the goons Byron and Wick saw at the beach?"

"Fortunately, the Canadian customs had enough priors on them to detain them at the border. When our police arrived there the Canadian Customs already had them talking, and to anyone else who would listen. They were adamant that no woman was involved. Obviously, Caen had never mentioned her. I think he intended to shove her out of the chopper, probably somewhere over the Straits."

Kay gasped. "That's horrible, but I wouldn't put it past him."

Ujima nodded. "Caen told his cohorts he would finish paying them off in Canada, and in American cash. It would've been a payoff all right. If things had gone as planned, we'd have never found them either."

"What about Martin," Alex asked. "What made things lethal for him?"

"Janet always confided in Martin. Unfortunately, Martin's turn-on was making Caen squirm. Janet's diary said that Martin was going to leak certain juicy items to the Spindrift. He would eventually tell all he knew if Caen didn't help him with his new business venture at the old boathouse."

"But I thought Martin had plenty of his own money," Kay blurted out.

"In my short but meaningful life on this planet, I've observed that those who already have mucho dollares want more." Ujima winked. "It's an unstoppable addiction known as galloping greed."

Alex nodded his head. "A bit of jolly blackmailing on everyone's part and that's where your jollies can get you... dead."

"No kidding," Kay agreed. "But why did Caen lean so strongly on us? It wasn't just for the right-of-way. Willie alluded to something else."

Alex raised his hand. "I found the answer to that when I opened yesterday's mail. And I discovered even more after I had a private talk with Willie this morning." He smiled smugly. "That's the surprise I hinted at earlier."

Kay turned to Alex. "My. Besides a gourmet breakfast, aren't we just stuffed with little gossipy gems." Then, ignoring Alex, she turned to Ujima. "More coffee? Say, for this very special occasion, I bought some chocolate- filled croissants at the Island Bakery. I also picked up a variety of cheese Danish- name your cholesterol."

"Yes and yes." Ujima replied. "And I'm going to be super-indulgent and to hell with our waistlines. Could we start off with a slice of your homemade, raison-cinnamon bread too? And throw in a tub of your honey butter? That would be scrumptious, girl."

"Whew, there goes the diets, but you're on." Kay shook her head and picked up the coffee tray. "I won't ask Alex if he wants anything. He's already full of food and mysterious information from Willie's breakfast, right Alex?" Not waiting for a reply she turned toward the kitchen, then said with a supercilious grin. "Oh secretive Alex, plug in the shock-monster for those who like their bread toasted."

## CHAPTER 44

# *Danish Surprise*

**Alex eyed the toaster warily.** A temperamental and ancient behemoth; Kay had rescued it from a basement cabinet. Taking the cover off, he gingerly plugged in the chord then shot a wounded look at Ujima. "Isn't anyone interested in what I have to say?"

Ujima slapped her thigh and chuckled. "Man. We knew you wouldn't be able to hold a secret. Besides, it's most likely not that important anyway."

"Not important? If Kay and I become the Spa-Gurus of Bradestone, I'll make sure we charge you triple for partaking of our healing waters. I'd say that's pretty important."

"Whatever do you mean Dear?" Kay asked flirtingly as she returned with a honey jar and bulging loaf of bread.

Alex took a slow sip of his coffee, leisurely dabbed at his lips then methodically placed four slices of bread in the toaster. Slowly and cautiously he pressed the lever down. He smiled, the slices held, no sparks flew, and he had their complete attention.

"Well, what did Willie tell you?" Ujima said in final exasperation.

Alex appeared transfixed by the workings of the toaster. When the slices popped up, he buttered each piece with exaggerated care then inserted four fresh pieces and sat down.

Kay held the coffee pot over his lap. "Don't stretch your luck. Let's hear it, and now."

"Okay. Okay! But you're not going to believe this. It begins with an old Island legend."

"You're right. We're not going to believe this."

"Very funny, anyway the story goes that an underground water source flows from the majestic glaciers of Mount Rainier, beneath the magnificent waters of Puget Sound, to the beautiful shores of Bradestone Island."

Kay rolled her eyes at Ujima. "Is it something Byron put in the coffee?"

Alex looked puzzled.

"Don't mind us." Ujima said, waving her hand. "I don't think it's catching. Continue, continue."

"Well, one legend claims there's an underground river that flows here via subsurface moraine gravels, the other claims the water gets here via an ancient lava tube." He shrugged. "Whatever the source, there's an artesian well on Bradestone Island, and it's on our property." He took a bite of his toast. "Anyway, that's according to Willie."

Alex put a finger next to his ear and twirled it. "It sounded like 'Twilight Zone'. But per Max's letter this morning and among the papers hidden in Edgar's cage are the first land surveys of this island. It appears that the artesian spring was discovered then capped, before the Petoskeys built here."

The second batch of toast popped up. Alex spread the honey-butter liberally, handed them around then turned to Ujima.

"By the way, there's an interesting sidelight to this yarn. The finder of the spring, and the original owner of our property, was a sea captain by the name of Oliver R. Reynolds."

Ujima chuckled then choked, "No way! You mean he's related to our man of the zee's Officer Reynolds?"

"Yep, Willie says he's the great-great grandson. Anyway, your man's noteworthy ancestor was pretty sharp. Not only was he a surveyor and businessman, he was familiar with the natural springs in England and European Spas and had an eye on developing a place where people would come to rest, drink healing waters and restore their health."

"I like that, especially the resting bit," Ujima said, closing her eyes.

Alex frowned. "Captain Reynolds's logging operation was right here at Cove Landing in Scoon Bay. Unfortunately, the Captain drowned when one of his lumber schooners went down in a storm off Foul Weather Bluffs."

Ujima chortled. "Sounds like he was a helluva lot more enterprising than his descendant; I can't wait till Reynolds hears this." She shook her head as she took a sip of coffee. "It might provide incentive for him to get off his butt quickly when a situation demands it, or at the very least, start acting halfway alive". Ujima paused. "How did Willie come into the possession of all those papers?"

"I asked the same questions, and he showed me."

"Showed you?"

"Yep, you remember that slant top desk, with the gallery rail at his cabin?"

"Vaguely."

"It turned out to be the business desk that belonged to our industrious Captain Reynolds. Willie discovered hidden documents and related papers when he started to restore it. Then and there he made the decision to put a false bottom in Edgar's cage, to hide the papers. Willie said there were also ancient shipping receipts and lumber contracts in the back of the other drawers."

"Where did Willie acquire this Aladdin's desk, from Toad Hall?" Kay asked.

Alex pointed to the porch ceiling. "Nope. Willie rescued it from the attic, after this house was left to the four winds. The desk is made from some kind of rare South American wood. You know Willie. He appreciates excellent craftsmanship; thought he'd better take it before some pyro burned the house down and everything with it.

Ujima nodded. "That almost happened a year ago when Caen recruited some of his thugs for a fire party."

"Lucky for Willie he moved the desk to friends, before *his* place was torched." Kay paused then asked; "How did Caen know that Willie had found those papers in the first place?"

"Willie told us he was greatly annoyed with those 'nice young men' running a land survey last year. That's when Willie said something about honoring original property deeds. He must have said something about the private water source. Of course Elanor and Caen already knew the gist of the documents and about the possible existence of an artesian well, but not that original papers were in someone's possession, nor that Willie knew the specific location of the well."

"How did they know anything about them?"

Ujima raised her hand. "It seems Caen ran across the information after he was commissioned by Templeton to research the history of this house and the adjoining acreage parcels. He found notations written on the back of some old platting papers at the county courthouse. But again, there was no specific location given. Janet knew about the well too. As Templeton's private secretary and personal confidant, nothing got past her."

"It's a long way underground from Mt. Rainier to Bradestone," Kay said shaking her head. "The whole thing sounds a bit woo-woo to me."

Ujima leaned forward. "I'm no rock-cracker either, far from it, but as Alex said this entire coast is geologically active."

Kay looked thoughtful. "Maybe a scientist could determine a relationship by chemically analyzing the water and comparing it to the runoff on Mt. Rainier." She shrugged. "But, that aside, where is the location?"

Alex smiled. "Haven't checked on it yet; however, Max said, it should be about three hundred feet down the bank from that old outbuilding." He pointed across the yard. "That one covered with blackberry vines and morning glory. Thom and Kay call it the 'Heap'."

"Why isn't the water running now?" Ujima asked.

"It is, but we don't see the outfall. Willie said the well was capped years ago, and the flow conducted underground via a wooden pipe that empties deeper into Scoon Bay. We might be able to find fresh water bubbling up, now that we have an idea of where to look."

"Nature and mankind are just full of little surprises," Kay said. "Do you remember those peculiar blue beads we picked out of the straw when we dropped Edgar's cage?" Alex and Ujima nodded. "Well, we showed them to Teri. She said they're trade beads, and might indicate an Indian burial site or remains of a summer camp somewhere on the island." Kay paused. "Blast Edgar. He had an eye for shiny things, too clever for his own good. He may only have been a crow." Her eyes moistened. "But I was really fond of him."

"Hey Kay," Ujima exclaimed. "Didn't you say there's some dee-licious cheese Danish from our local low-calorie bakery?"

Alex nodded vigorously and chimed in. "Yeah, right on, a guy could starve to death around here."

Kay sniffed loudly. "All you ever think of is your stomach, your legs aren't broken." She flounced toward the kitchen.

Alex shot Ujima an appreciative glance. "Thanks. That piece of crow-bait sure wormed his way into her heart." He shut his eyes, "One of Kay's weak spots, animals. When one of the kids' goldfish or gerbil died, they all had to have state funerals. Ancient, felt-lined watch boxes were their ready-made caskets. I don't know where Kay got them, but she had quite a collection in her upstairs closet."

Ujima laughed. "That's known as proper memorial planning."

Kay interrupted and firmly placed a tray of Danish on the table. "Here's your selection of artery blockers. Graze to your heart's content."

Ujima picked up a large cherry-filled pastry and delicately wiped her fingertips with a napkin. "I've first dibs, being a guest and all…umm, my favorite." She frowned. "And don't get any ideas about dividing it up, either. Remember, nobody, and I mean nobody, messes with the law."

Alex unsuccessfully scooped up a moist, cream-cheese filled square. Absent-mindedly he wiped at the damage with his napkin and licked his fingers. "Been thinking about Wick. He mentioned to Byron, if things turn out successfully with Martin's Will, he probably will settle here. I really like the kid. Funny thing though, he's real thorny around the edges, carries a chip." Alex looked thoughtful. "I feel he needs a little man-to- man mentorship. So I'll work with him. Shape him up, the Army way. I did a pretty good job with new recruits, when I was in the service."

Kay glanced uneasily at Ujima. "I don't think I'd rush anything. Wick has to find out what he wants to do with his life. He needs elbow room, and plenty of time."

Alex stroked his jaw. He appeared as if he hadn't heard her. "I'm still surprised he wants to stay on Bradestone. He told me that Washington State is at the ends of the earth. And this island is…"

Ujima screeched. Her coveted cherry Danish was being snatched from her plate by a flapping ball of feathers.

Kay leapt up, coffee things flew asunder. "It's Edgar!" She yelled. "It's Edgar! Alex, he's alive!"

The Amber Crow flew his prize to the roof of 'The Heap'. He ruffled his singed feathers and jeered at them loudly, his prize clutched in one balled claw.

"Cripes! The thieving magpie is back." Alex shouted.

Ujima, still a bit shaky, got up and put an arm around Kay's shoulders. "It's unbelievable, with all those burnt tail feathers; how can he fly?" She shook her fist at Edgar. "But, I don't feel a bit sorry for you. You took my favorite Danish. You damn pig!"

Kay brushed a hand across her eyes. "He's not a pig. He's a crow."

"I've heard some pigs are able to fly." Alex mumbled.

Kay cheered and put her arm around Ujima's waist; together they jumped up and down, waving enthusiastically. Alex, a wry smile on his lips, slowly joined the wave.

For a moment, Edgar gawked at the peculiar gyrations on the porch. But not one to waste time when it came to food; he made three triumphant caws and proceeded to shred the cherry Danish.

"I don't care. He can have a thousand Danish!" Kay yelled and fished a tissue from her pocket. She turned to Ujima. "You know. He saved our lives."

Alex's eyes rolled to the sky and he muttered under his breath. "With just a little help from his friends."

*Finis*

*Turn the page for a*
*Special advance preview of*
*L. C. Mcgee's next Pacific Northwest Murder Mystery*

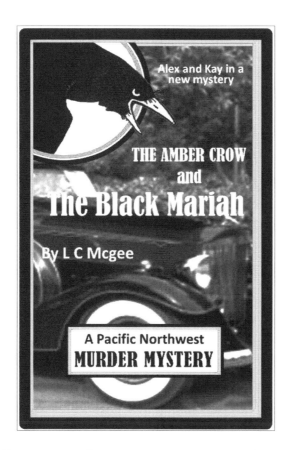

# The Amber Crow and the Black Mariah

*Available summer 2014 from TwoNewfs Publishing*

# *The Amber Crow and The Black Mariah*

## *Chapter 1*

## *Onset*

### 1972

He couldn't move, couldn't see, if only he could remember. It was the fumes, terrible fumes... overpowering, thought destroying fumes. What was it he must remember? The war...something about the war, something about...his head pounded. He forced burning eyes open. There, a blur of faded remnant in the corner of the windshield. He recognized it, the West Point sticker. Somehow he was in the old Packard.

What? How did he get...? Like the tattered wings of a dying moth, the questions fluttered desperately behind his eyes... slowly they dissolved to nothing. David stared, mouth open, and his head slumped back on the seat.

### 2000

Alex Beahzhi strode across the new roof. It was going to be an unusually warm day and the asphalt shingles heated rapidly in the late morning sun. He imagined he could feel the warmth through the soles of his boots. He paused and gazed at the beauty of Scoon Bay below. Cedar shingles was the authentic way to go for their old farmhouse, he thought, but there was the danger of fire. When Kay piped up and said she didn't want kindling for a roof and the material must be composition…well that cinched it. Luckily, on a trip to Canada, they'd found a 'screaming deal' on a rugged three-tab shingle, it was the right color, looked like cedar and fit the style of their farmhouse.

Alex grinned. Kay was great at making building decisions and handled a hammer like a pro. Together, they worked alongside Chuck McKindley, the most reliable carpenter on the island (his ad boasted); ripped off the old shingles, and nailed down sheets of plywood. The new roof was installed in less than a week; oddly for the long abandoned structure, nary a hint of dry-rot.

When they attached the last run of gutter to the back verandah, Kay shouted "Hurrah", scrambled down the ladder and returned with three cold beers to celebrate. Chuck quickly downed his and excused himself. "Another job in Manzanita," he said with a grin then nodded gratefully to Kay, gave Alex the empty, and shot down the ladder with his tool bucket. Kay waved him on his way then kissed Alex.

"I guess I'm sous-chef for lunch. You know Teri; she's extremely put upon if someone doesn't help with the cooking." Kay rolled her eyes and started down the ladder. "You guys eat like horses. Of course Byron and Wick eat more than you, but not by much."

Alex patted his stomach. "Just maintaining my girlish figure," he said then lowered his voice. "What's up with Teri and Wick? They've been a bit testy in the last few days."

Kay shrugged. "The usual guy meets girl problem. It'll work out."

"Seriously, they're a great help, but I'll be glad when Teri's in grad school and Byron's back at college," he paused, "and when Wick's legal problems are finalized he'll be busier on his boathouse theatre in

Burn." Alex sighed. "Then, maybe, hopefully, things will be a helluva lot quieter around here."

"What? You don't like my children or Wick? You've suddenly become the possessive and jealous lover?"

"You'll have to admit things get uber-lively when all are present. Not to mention the murders this spring, they were uber-deadly. And I miss my pipe and slippers...and when are we going to get an old dog to sit beside my chair? And, and, and?"

"Tsk, tsk not yet fifty and already a whiny old fussbudget." Kay shook her head. "In your condition you shouldn't be on this roof. Here, give me the empty cans and I'll assist that feeble body of yours down the ladder."

Alex leered. "You didn't mention any enfeeblement in bed this morning."

"True, true, and I think I'll keep you around for a while. You have certain plusses, skilled, handy, and carrying a full tool belt with certain admirable benefits."

Alex snorted as Kay descended the ladder. "Ah, to bed a lusty maid!" he shouted. "Was that Shakespeare? Umm, probably not, but certainly inspired by him."

Chuck's van kicked up dust clouds as it bumped down the unpaved lane from the house. Alex smiled in satisfaction. Chuck was becoming a good friend. He took his last swig of beer, stretched and reflected. The next step... spread crushed gravel on the drive. The Northwest summer was already unusually hot and dry. But when the Pacific rains come lashing in, they would be prepared. The road to the house wouldn't become a quagmire.

Chuck waved again as his van turned right onto the county road. Alex lifted his empty can in salute and walked around the railed roof top of the verandah to the front of the house.

378 | THE BLACK MARIAH

From here the view was dazzling. On the opposite shore of Scoon Bay, firs and maples carpeted the hogback ridge called Heron's Hook. The untouched green of forest continued down to a beach where a lone boy raced his dog along the ribbon of sand.

In the small bay a fitful breeze teased the main of a yellow-hulled sloop. It was Raymond Toda's boat; their athletic neighbor. He who insisted his friends call him Toady. "Lucky dude, taking the day off," Alex yelled with cupped hands. But Toady, busy setting his jib, was too far away to hear.

The breeze blew up the bank and carried the scent of fir, salt air, and the subtler odor of drying fern. Alex inhaled deeply, savoring all the complex aromas. It was a great day, they were halfway through the remodel of the 'Old Petoskey Farm'. He shook his head. The islanders had given the farmhouse that moniker in honor of the original family who built it. No doubt the name would stick for all time.

Rose Bracken, the Island Realtor who'd sold them the property, was a hoot. Rose gave everyone the impression she'd lived on the Island since the dawn of forever. But as Kay and Alex discovered, she'd arrived only a few years before they had. Along with her aura of a first woman Friday, she was an avid teller of tales. Alex liked her minute histories of island life. And like sailor's yarns, beneath Rose's colorful embellishments, there dwelt a core of truth.

Alex jettisoned his empty over the side and turned to look at the view from the back of the house. Hah, winter could come with a vengeance.

He crossed his arms and reflected on one unusually hot summer evening when Kay and Rose were settled back in the red painted wicker-chairs, each had a glass of fortified iced tea clutched in their hands. Alex sprawled on the lounge with his. They muddled the stems of fresh garden mint in their drinks and gave a collective sigh.

The ladies rested their feet on the verandah rail. All reveled in the last rays of sunlight that bounced off the treetops of Heron's Hook.

"It was that damned Sea Captain Reynolds!" Rose announced abruptly then took a loud slurp from the straw in her drink.

Kay and Alex exchanged startled glances.

Rose pointed her glass at Scoon Bay. "He was a self-proclaimed lumber baron and denuder of Heron's Hook, and the very hill this farmhouse stands on," she continued, "the Captain liked to gloat over all his logs clogging the bay so he built a one room cabin for his bride, on this very spot. Anyway, several years later, the greedy Captain Reynolds went down with one of his loaded to the gunwales lumber schooners. It happened off Foul Weather bluff." Rose placed considerable emphasis on the word 'Foul'. "Yep, couldn't have happened to a better creep."

"Er, what happened to the widow?" Kay asked.

Rose took another loud slurp. "Well, the poor girl was barely out of her teens and with two babes in arms," Rose stopped to chuckle, "but that didn't prevent her from running off with a patent medicine man from New Jersey. At that time it was the Island scandal." Rose mashed the straw in her drink. "Before she left for the mainland, she sold this acreage to a young immigrant farmer from Poland." Rose's voice softened, "his name was Ihram Petoskey. And he was the guy who tore down the shack of a cabin and built this marvelous farmhouse."

"Well I, for one, think cabins are great," Alex interjected. "I lived in one when I was a Fire-Lookout, years ago. It had a tiny kitchen, an old steel stove and one bedroom. It was neat, tidy and easy to take care of." He raised his eyebrows at Rose and to Kay's annoyance sucked loudly on the sprig of mint he'd removed from his drink. "And then there's Willie Cloudmaker's cabin." Alex waved toward the swampy end of Scoon bay. "It's better than the one that burned down, but the original was damned nice too," he snorted loudly, "and hey Rose, don't be so hard on this Captain Reynolds fellow, people have to make a living. And wasn't logging one of the ways to do it?"

Rose eyed Alex and sniffed warily, as if she smelled a potential lumber-baron-come earth-ravager, and continued. "Mr. Petoskey was a gentleman and a farmer," she said, stressing the word gentleman. "He built a milk barn, unfortunately it caught fire one hot summer, but those buildings over there are the original out-buildings," she gestured with her drink, "and on that slope he planted large vegetable gardens and plots of strawberries and raspberries. The soil is rich with manure there. And yonder, those rampant fruit trees are the sole remains of his original orchard. For years the farm was a commercial success," she said with authority. "But when the only grandson died in Vietnam, everything started to go downhill, and things got worse when Mrs. Petoskey suddenly passed away."

Kay and Alex hated to admit it, but Rose had them hooked.

"Where did you get all this, ah... esoteric information?" Kay asked with a smile.

"Well, there is the Island library and I have my personal sources. Some families still have roots here. For instance, I know that our stalwart Officer Reynolds is a direct descendant of the infamous Captain Reynolds and there still are a few people that remember the old times. Many live at the Shady Springs rest home," she smiled, "they're always ready for a good chat when I visit. I'm one of the island's history buffs, and I have one of those a personalities that engages people," Rose said smugly then winked, "coupled with an unbiased take on things and a natural curiosity, of course."

Kay bit her tongue as she recalled the 'Toady affair' and that several months ago, Rose knew little if anything about the Petoskey family and their farm. In their first dealings with her, she mentioned the place was rundown, needed beaucoup work and then tried to sell them something newer.

Alex coughed politely and said, sotto voce: "Pray continue."

The ice clinked as Rose poured more fortified tea from the crystal pitcher. "Well, Ihram did have a sister. She tried to run the place by herself. But of course it was too much for a lone woman and she died of a heart attack." Rose grimaced. "It was not a lucky family. Then nosy relatives stepped in and sold the place to a group of hippies for a commune. The Northwest is a particular magnet for them, communes that is." She continued airily. "But as those things usually go, it wasn't successful. So when the lazy louts ran out of money this beautiful place was let go for back taxes and abandoned to the elements," Rose paused, "I think the Catholic Church had it for a while, but whatever they intended to do failed and the bank took it over."

"Were there any owners after that?" Kay asked.

Rose shook her head and raised her glass. "No, just when you two came along." A sly gleam came into her eye. "You know Alex, you're right. It wouldn't take much to turn this into a spiffy Bed and Breakfast. And the Reynolds's story would be a neat draw." Her eyes became larger. "Why, maybe the ghost of old Captain Reynolds still haunts the grounds today. Possibly searching for his young bride, or..."

"Not in my life time!" Kay shot up and excused herself to refill the tea pitcher.

Rose grinned. She knew Kay was dead set against any B&B, while Alex wanted to have a go at it. Besides storytelling, Rose loved to stir the stew, as long as it was somebody else's.

As his mind came back to the present Alex shook his head. He squatted comfortably on the roof, elbows on knees. It really didn't matter if the pipe dream of his B&B ever came true. He and Kay loved Bradestone Island. Vashon, Bainbridge, Whidbey and the San Juan's had their magical charm too, but it was this island, its people and this run-down farmhouse that fits their dreams to a T.

Made in the USA
San Bernardino, CA
15 October 2014